Also by Christina Dodd

CHRISTINA DODD

In My Wildest Dreams

AVON BOOKS
An Imprint of HarperCollinsPublishers

AVON BOOKS
An Imprint of HarperCollins*Publishers*
10 East 53rd Street
New York, New York 10022-5299

To Donna Nasker,
one of the funniest, kindest women in the world
and my best wine-drinking buddy.
(I understand many of the bottles have corks now.)

And to Jerry Nasker—
may your carburetor never hang lower than your tailpipes.

Thanks, guys, we treasure your friendship.

Adorna, Lady Bucknell,
Sole Proprietress of
THE DISTINGUISHED ACADEMY OF GOVERNESSES,
Presents the story of a young girl,
the gardener's daughter,
Plagued by unrequited love
For the handsome younger brother
Of the wealthy, genteel Throckmorton family.

After an education at
THE DISTINGUISHED ACADEMY OF GOVERNESSES,
A sojourn in Paris,
And a chance to spread her wings,
The gardener's daughter returns
to the bosom of the Throckmorton family,
A beautiful, accomplished young woman—
Still in love with the younger brother,
Ready to captivate him and lead him into matrimony.

Only one man stood in her way...

BLYTHE HALL, SUFFOLK
1843

*A*dorna, Lady Bucknell, admired a man who thought honestly and spoke without artifice, but Garrick Stanley Breckinridge Throckmorton the Third gave new meaning to the term *tactless*.

"Milford," he said, "it has come to my attention that your daughter is moping."

Milford, the head gardener of Blythe Hall and a dignified East Anglian yeoman of at least fifty years, turned his hat in his work-roughened hands as he watched his employer. Apparently he was used to such direct speaking, for he neither flinched nor cowered. "Celeste is young, Mr. Throckmorton, only seventeen years. Given time and the right man, she'll settle."

Adorna pressed her fan to her lips to conceal her amusement. The sun shone into the old walled garden, displaying young Throckmorton's lack of expression.

Adorna wasn't so sure. Sometimes when she glanced

at Garrick Stanley Breckinridge Throckmorton, she suspected she saw . . . more.

"Yes." Throckmorton was seated on one of the wicker seats he had brought back from India six years ago. "Perhaps."

Of course, Throckmorton wasn't handsome like his brother, Ellery. He could never have been, for where Ellery's blond, blue-eyed allure oozed from every pore, Garrick was plain, dark and somber. Tall, but all Throckmortons were tall. Big boned and strongly muscled, betraying the common origins of the Throckmorton family. So conservative in dress and manner Adorna wished occasionally to shake him until he betrayed some real emotion. But if the birth of his younger and fatally captivating sibling had disturbed Garrick, that time had been long ago. Now the guarded gray eyes assessed events and weighed characters without revealing anything, and to Adorna such caution seemed out of place in a twenty-seven-year-old man—unless he concealed depths within his soul.

But if depths were there, he hid them well, for she had no idea what treasures they hid.

He gestured to Adorna, her arm draped across the back of the love seat in a graceful curve. "This is Lady Bucknell, the proprietress of the well-respected Distinguished Academy of Governesses in London and a dear friend of my mother's. She is visiting with her husband, and has observed your daughter. Lady Bucknell has expressed an interest in having Celeste return with her to the Distinguished Academy of Governesses in London and there be trained as an instructor."

Adorna smiled at Milford. He didn't melt, as most men did, at the application of her charm, but watched her steadily, weighing her with his gaze. The head gardener at Blythe Hall was an important personage, after all. He had to be a man of good sense.

"With all due respect, my lady—why Celeste?" he asked.

"Celeste would be an admirable governess. Children follow her, and she is endlessly patient. She's well spoken and well educated, thanks to the Throckmorton family, I believe—"

Milford nodded. "Grateful, I am."

"She seems responsible, but aimless, with no goal in sight." That was a lie. Celeste had a goal, and that goal was the love of Ellery Throckmorton. She followed Ellery about, speaking to him when she had the chance, spying on him from ill-concealed hideouts.

Indeed—Adorna's glance flicked to the wall behind Throckmorton—young Celeste seemed to have developed a penchant for spying.

Ellery never noticed Celeste was alive. Oh, he knew her name, but not that she'd grown from a knobby girl into a handsome young woman. Adorna planned to remove Celeste before Ellery did notice and thoughtlessly take what was offered.

Opening her fan, Adorna moved it slowly before her face. The branches on the willow that grew beside the wall were swaying, yet no breeze ruffled any of the other trees. Pitching her voice a little louder than her normal, husky tone, she said, "Celeste speaks French well, I believe."

Milford almost smiled. "Her mother was French."

"Our cook," Throckmorton supplied. "A master of sauces, and a way with fish that has never been matched. Even after six years, we miss her."

Milford's dignity grew to combat the dangerous weakness the mention of his wife invoked. "Aye, sir."

With a tact Adorna hadn't given him credit for, Throckmorton turned his head to inspect the hedge of roses nearby, giving Milford a chance to regain his composure. The bushes were in full bloom, a mighty explosion of pink and scent which Adorna had appreciated but which, she knew, Throckmorton had scarcely noticed. "First class work," he complimented Milford.

"Thank you, sir. The rose is called *Felicité Parmentier*, and she's a magnificent bloomer."

The two men stared at the blossoms until Adorna rescued them. "At any rate, Milford, a woman with Celeste's gifts will make an admirable addition to the Distinguished Academy of Governesses."

"She's a scatter-brain," her father said flatly.

The willow rustled violently.

Eyes narrowed, Throckmorton glanced behind him. Rising, he strolled around to lean against a low-hanging branch.

"Most girls are at seventeen." Adorna watched him while she mused that Celeste would, with a little coaching, add luster to the reputation of the Distinguished Academy of Governesses. Most of the *ton* were waiting for Adorna to fail so they might chuckle at her folly in buying such a business. Indeed, Adorna's own dear, pompous husband had been less than understanding about her desire to fill her days with something more than gossip and needlework. Her eyes narrowed as she considered the strong language Lord Bucknell had used to describe her purchase.

She would prove all of them wrong, most especially

her dear husband, and young Celeste would help her do so. "When I am done with Celeste," Adorna said, "she will be polished, independent, and a force to be reckoned with."

Milford looked to Throckmorton.

Throckmorton gave him a small nod, reassuring the anxious father.

Milford sighed heavily and displayed the wisdom that allowed him to take charge of dozens of undergardeners and acres of flowers and orchards with such success. "Very well. I'll miss her sore, but if she stays, she's going to get in trouble. So, my lady, take her."

The willow swayed.

With his eyebrows lowered in a fierce and violent fury, Throckmorton shook the tree.

The girl, Celeste, tumbled downward in a silent confusion of faded skirts and lop-sided blond braids.

Throckmorton caught at her, breaking her fall, but she landed hard in the flowerbed, mashing columbine and yellow alyssum. Her petticoats flew up to reveal black woolen stockings tied with a string around the knee. She gasped painfully as her breath left her.

Throckmorton looked thunderstruck. "Celeste!"

So he hadn't known who was up there, Adorna realized, only that someone was spying on them, and he had reacted violently. Fascinating.

Milford didn't appear surprised to see his daughter. He only shook his head mournfully. "Scatter-brain."

As soon as she caught her breath, Celeste looked up at Throckmorton and with all the passion of her youthful fury, she said, "I won't go. I won't be polished, and independent, and a force to be reckoned with. *You can't make me.*"

BLYTHE HALL, SUFFOLK
FOUR YEARS LATER

"Garrick, you must tell me—who is that beautiful lady I met at the train station?"

Lifting his attention from the row of figures, Garrick Throckmorton stared at Ellery. His younger brother stood framed in the doorway of the study, his clothing exquisitely cut, his blond hair styled perfectly, his tanned cheeks flushed with becoming color.

Throckmorton had hoped to finish writing instructions on the accounting to his secretary before putting in his first appearance at the reception, but as he studied his over-excited, excessively handsome younger brother, he realized that would not be possible. He recognized trouble when he saw it, and in this family, trouble almost always came in the shape of Ellery Throckmorton. "A beautiful lady?" Throckmorton blotted his pen. "Your fiancée, I would hope."

"No, no. *Not* Hyacinth." Ellery waved off his intended

with a sweep of his elegant hand. "Most certainly not Hyacinth."

The sound of violins, cellos and French horns drifted in from the terrace and the drawing rooms along with the babble of guests, arrived just this afternoon for five days of festivities celebrating Ellery's betrothal to Lady Hyacinth Illington. Therefore, Throckmorton realized, their own voices could be heard—not that such a paltry consideration would occur to Ellery. "Shut the door," Throckmorton instructed, and waited until Ellery had complied. "Hyacinth is quite a handsome girl."

"She's handsome enough." Ellery glanced at the cut-glass decanter of brandy on the sideboard. "But *this* was a woman, and what a woman! She—"

Determined to halt this liaison before it started, Throckmorton interrupted. "Starting an affair at your betrothal celebration is in extremely poor taste."

"An affair?" Ellery's long, elegant face grew longer. "I couldn't start an affair with that girl! She's dewy with innocence."

If Ellery didn't want an affair, what did he want? *Marriage?* To a girl whose name was unknown to him?

Oh, yes. Such a romantic flight of fancy was bound to appeal to Ellery. Handsome, frivolous, light-hearted Ellery, who wanted nothing so much as to remain an available bachelor forever.

Removing his glasses, Throckmorton rubbed the bridge of his nose. "Dewy. Hm. Yes. But, as I'd like to point out, so is Lady Hyacinth—and she's your betrothed."

In a daring rush of words, Ellery said, "My betrothed, not my wife."

Damn. Throckmorton should have known this whole

arrangement had gone too easily. He'd been waiting for the other shoe to fall, and by God, it had—not surprisingly, in the form of a woman. "You didn't object to the engagement before."

Ellery stiffened. He stalked forward. Placing his hands flat on the desk, he leaned toward Throckmorton and glared, his blue eyes narrowed. Only the length and sweep of his eyelashes detracted from the menace he projected. "Object? I most certainly did object, but you had high-handedly put the announcement in the *Times* without consulting me."

"Pah. You could have raved and shouted until I withdrew my offer on your behalf. You didn't." Throckmorton neatly corked his ink, placed his pen in his desk drawer and started to slide it closed. Something caught his eye, and he opened it again. A pen was missing. Two pens. "Have the children been playing in here again?"

"I don't know, and don't try and change the subject!" Ellery rapped his knuckles on the desk.

The governess couldn't get here too soon, Throckmorton reflected. The girls were running wild . . . or rather, Kiki was running wild and half the time dragging Penelope with her. The loss of his pens were the least of the problem.

Ellery said, "I didn't object because you never gave me a chance."

"And because Lady Hyacinth *is* a very handsome female, and an heiress, and the daughter of the Marquess of Longshaw. And because you know it's time for you to settle down." Reflecting bitterly on the fate of his pens, Throckmorton shut the drawer. "An aging roué is an ugly thing."

"I'm only twenty-six."

"I married at twenty-one." Throckmorton waved his paper briefly to dry it, then placed it in the wooden box on top of his desk. Locking the box, he dropped the key into his pocket.

Ellery observed his every movement. "Father married at forty."

"He had to make his fortune first so he could afford to buy an aristocratic bride."

"Mother would tack your ears to a slateboard if she heard you talking about her like that."

"Probably." Throckmorton pushed back his chair. The plain brown leather furniture slid on a thick Oriental rug of rich azure and peach on a background of winter white. The stripped drapes, accented with gold, echoed the azure and peach, as did the Oriental vases and the flowers they held. Each artifact, each knick-knack, each ornament was placed with taste and gave the chamber a sense of tranquility, which belied the chaos of Throckmorton's business life.

For the refined touches he could thank his mother. Lady Philberta Breckinridge-Wallingfork had been but twenty years old and the daughter of one of England's oldest earldoms when she had been forced by her family's impoverished circumstances to wed. Yet she had been a dutiful wife to Stanley Throckmorton and a good mother to the boys. Because of Lady Philberta and her family's prestige, the Throckmortons were able to circulate among the *ton*, to give parties like this one and see London's finest in their drawing rooms. The *ton* might whisper about them behind their fans, but never did those whispers reach Throckmorton's ears, as the Throckmorton males had a reputation for swift and righteous retaliation. "Lady Hyacinth will add just as much luster to the Throckmorton name as Mother did when she married Father."

Turning, Ellery leaned against the massive desk, crossed his arms, and gave his impression of an ill-used man brooding. "It doesn't hurt that Hyacinth's family owns those tea plantations in India."

Throckmorton went to the mirror and ran his fingers through his hair. "It doesn't hurt that you're handsome enough to turn any girl's head, either, but I don't throw your prettiness in your face."

Discarding the brooding like a wet cloak, Ellery turned. "Which brings us back to my mysterious lady."

"I'm glad you're not attracted to her for shallow reasons."

Throckmorton should have known it was too much to expect that Ellery would play his part in this betrothal without balking. Ellery was good at racing, whoring and drinking, but he'd been thrown from his horse too many times lately, been caught in the wrong bed too often and been unpleasantly, staggeringly drunk one too many times. It was time to get the lad married and settled down before he broke his neck—or someone shot him.

Throckmorton straightened his cravat. "Tell me about this mystery woman."

Eagerly, Ellery recited her virtues. "Her hair is light brown with streaks of gold flowing like honey. Her teeth are white and even, like a string of the most precious pearls. She's petite and curvy, like a marble Venus." With his hands, he indicated the shapeliness of the young woman in question. "Her skin is like—"

"Alabaster?"

"Yes!" Ellery smiled, his own alabaster teeth flashing.

"Of course." Throckmorton rolled down his sleeves and re-pinned his cuffs. "I suppose her nipples are like two perfect rosebuds."

Ellery's brow puckered. He seldom comprehended Throckmorton's gibes.

One didn't tease the golden boy.

"I don't know about her nipples."

With heartfelt sincerity, Throckmorton said, "Thank God for that, at least."

"Yet." Ellery's white teeth gleamed in a smile.

Perhaps Ellery did comprehend more than Throckmorton gave him credit for. But Ellery didn't comprehend how important this betrothal to Hyacinth and her Indian plantations were to the family interests—and more than family interests—or he wouldn't be babbling about some unfamiliar female guest with good teeth and rosebud nipples.

"Uh-oh." Ellery headed for the sideboard and poured himself a grand amount of brandy. "I recognize that expression. It's the I'm-the-Throckmorton-and-I-have-to-manage-everything expression."

"Strange. I was thinking how fortunate that you're seeking handsome young ladies for me."

Arrested in the act of taking a drink, Ellery said, "Don't be ridiculous. This one's mine—although it wouldn't hurt you to remarry, you know. Since Joanna's death there hasn't been a woman worthy of you, and you might not be so bloody grim if you stuck your finger in the jampot occasionally."

Throckmorton had heard it before. "I'll worry about my finger, you worry about yours."

"But you're worrying about mine, too, or you

wouldn't have arranged this damned betrothal." Ellery downed the liquor in one motion.

"You draw enough money from the company, you might as well earn your keep somehow."

"Marrying well to do my part for the company?" Ellery must have been practicing his sneer in private, for that curl of the lips looked almost sincere. "Now *there's* a role where I can at last surpass my superior older brother." Then, before Throckmorton could inquire into the nature of that remark, he asked, "So you'll find out her name for me?"

This female obviously had Ellery twisted in a knot. "Why don't you just ask her?"

Ellery turned the glass in his fingers. "She won't tell me."

Throckmorton lifted an eyebrow. "She won't tell you?"

"I met her at the train station. I was supposed to pick up Lord and Lady Featherstonebaugh—"

"What time was it?"

"Just after four."

"They came in on the two o'clock."

"That explains why they weren't there." Ellery dismissed his godparents with a shrug. "They'll forgive me."

Throckmorton agreed. They would. Everyone forgave Ellery everything.

"She was just standing there, beautiful, well formed—"

"Alabaster teeth."

"I couldn't see them at first. She got off the train and looked around, lost and alone—"

"Touching."

"But as soon as I asked her if I could assist her, she flashed the most beautiful smile in the world and said, 'Greetings, Ellery!' "

Throckmorton experienced the stirrings of real unease. "She knew you."

"She certainly did. She knows you, too. She asked about you—I told her you were dull as ever."

"Thank you."

"She laughed and said, 'Of course.' "

"And thanks to her." Always good to know one's repute. Always a relief to know the truth had not yet made its way across two continents to England.

"She asked about Mother. She asked about Tehuti, and wanted to know what kind of colts he'd sired. She asked about Gunilla, and she dabbed sparkling tears from the corners of her eyes when I told her the old dog had died." Ellery sighed deeply, his broad shoulders lifting and falling. "Her handkerchief was trimmed in lace and smelled of the most exquisite perfume." Ellery, the connoisseur of all things female, squinted and said, "Citrus, cinnamon and, I think, ylang-ylang."

"Only *you* would know that." Throckmorton shrugged into his conservatively tailored black coat. "So if she knows you, why don't you know her?"

Ellery poured the snifter full again. "I swear I don't remember that exquisite creature."

Ellery remembered every handsome female he'd ever met. "How unlike you."

"Exactly." Ellery sipped this brandy with a little more care. "And how could I forget her? She adores me."

"Find me a female who doesn't," Throckmorton said dryly.

"When I mentioned my betrothal, her big hazel eyes filled with sparkling tears again."

Whoever the woman was, she was obviously playing Ellery as if he were a fine instrument. "So you comforted her?"

Ellery put his hand to his chest. "Just a quick kiss on the cheek to bring that gorgeous smile shining through."

"Anonymous alabaster teeth."

"I depend on your good memory to serve us."

Throckmorton wanted to gnash his own straight white teeth. "Then she's here."

"I brought her at once." Placing the half-full glass on the silver tray, Ellery came to Throckmorton and tweaked his collar. "You ought to go up to your valet and allow him to tidy you."

Ellery was right, but— "No one will be looking at me anyway," Throckmorton said. "*You're* the bridegroom."

"Don't remind me." Ellery shuddered and glanced back at the brandy.

Throckmorton had no wish to remind Ellery of his dissatisfaction with the Illington match again. No, now was the time for tact and swift planning—tact being one property he labored to attain, and swift planning the attribute at which he excelled. That was how he had arrived at his present position as the head of the Throckmorton empire . . . and his current status within the English government. He would somehow head off disaster.

In a tone that heralded a significant announcement, Ellery asked, "Garrick, you wouldn't want me to be unhappy, would you?"

"I labor for your happiness," Throckmorton said.

But Ellery knew nothing of what Throckmorton did

for his family, and Throckmorton wouldn't tell him. Better his brother think him a dull blade. Throckmorton shuddered. For if Ellery, with his discerning honesty and his inability to dissemble, ever got wind of Throckmorton's true aim, he would demand his chance to help—and disaster would surely follow.

"What's wrong?" Ellery asked. "You're looking rather peaked."

"I was just wondering what you did with your mysterious beauty when you got her here?"

"Lost her! I dropped her at the door, drove the brougham to the stables—"

"You let her out of your sight?"

"The horses, man! I was driving my new matched grays to show to Lord Featherstonebaugh—you know how he is about horses!—and I didn't dare trust them to a ham-handed new groom. When I got back, she had disappeared."

"Bad luck." From start to finish, abominably bad luck.

"None of the servants knew who I was talking about, although they were all atwitter about something."

"With the guests arriving, they are atwitter about a great many things."

Ellery ignored that bit of wisdom. "Who could she have been?"

"Perhaps she wasn't a lady."

"What do you mean?"

"I mean, brother, you have a history of confusing actresses and members of the demimonde for ladies, and I end up paying them off to free you from their clutches."

Offended, Ellery snapped back, "She was dressed in the latest French fashions, she spoke with the finest of accents, and most important, she knew Blythe Hall. She knew us. She knew you. She knew *me*."

"Yes, so you told me. But she was alone. Young ladies of quality do not travel alone."

"You are an old-fashioned fusspot," Ellery pronounced.

"I suppose I am." Throckmorton had made his point, and he was content to let Ellery wrestle with it.

"Obviously she was a guest someone neglected to collect, yet when I asked she laughed with a voice like a bell—"

"Church or clock?"

"What?" Ellery's brow knitted, then cleared, and he smacked Throckmorton hard enough to bruise his arm. "Stop vexing me."

"All right." Throckmorton smacked him back hard enough to remind him who was the taller and stronger and had once, in their boyhood, force-fed him most of a bar of greasy gray soap while sitting on his chest. "I will."

Despite their differences, the brothers understood each other in a way no one else could. They grinned at each other, and Throckmorton laid his hand on Ellery's shoulder. "Come on, little brother. Let's go find your exquisite creature."

~ 2 ~

Throckmorton watched as Ellery craned his head, looking through and over the top of the swirling crowd, trying to find his beauteous maiden.

The music wafted in from the terrace on harmonious waves, the rising sounds of conversation drifting with it. The deep rumble of men's voices, made jovial with conviviality, provided a balance for the feminine cries of delight which punctuated the air as ladies found their acquaintances and renewed friendships.

Blythe Hall was made for parties. The ground floor consisted of studies and music rooms, ball rooms and the lush glassed-in conservatory. Thirty-three bedrooms and twenty lavatories lined the corridors upstairs. The large attics sheltered visiting servants, and the bottom floor housed a wine cellar and the largest kitchen in Suffolk. All this, in a limestone shell attractively built by two hundred years of wealthy owners, and set in a jewel of a park tended by the best-paid, most important landscaper north of London.

Once Throckmorton got the matter of the exquisite creature out of the way, he looked forward to the evening. Nothing matched the pleasures of making new contacts for whom he might someday do a favor or wrangle a business deal. English society was changing; no one knew it better than he, and no one used those changes as successfully. He asked, "Where is this ravishing lady?"

"I don't know." Ellery craned his neck. "I don't think she's arrived yet."

"Or she's outside on the terrace."

A man's authoritative voice announced, "There they are!"

Heads turned at the exclamation.

"Our host and the lucky man who won our sweet Hyacinth's heart." Lord Longshaw made his way through the crowd.

The crowd who moved hastily out of his way.

A thin, esthetic man, Lord Longshaw looked like a starving Cambridge professor and suffered the well-deserved reputation of a rabid wolf. Regardless of his aristocratic heritage, he had pursued business relationships and made fortunes in the name of power—power he wielded ruthlessly. Only with his wife and daughter did he soften, and when Hyacinth had expressed a wish to have Ellery for her bridegroom, Lord Longshaw had come to Throckmorton and struck a deal.

A deal, Throckmorton knew, which Ellery had better fulfill, or all the Throckmortons would be playing cricket in hell. Stepping smoothly in front of his distracted brother, Throckmorton said, "Lord Longshaw, we were just drinking a brotherly toast to your daughter's health and happiness."

"Capital. Capital!" Lord Longshaw rubbed his gloved hands together in simulated glee, but his gaze darted between the brothers. "Looking forward to your wedding night, young Ellery?"

Ellery chuckled uneasily. "Lady Hyacinth's father would be the last man I would admit that to, my lord."

"Quite right." Lord Longshaw grinned to display his gleaming, twisted teeth set beneath a dark, shaggy mustache. "Good sense, young Ellery. Glad to see you've got some." Turning to Throckmorton, he gestured through the windows to the terrace where the servants could be seen lighting torches. "Nice atmosphere. Informal."

Sensing criticism, Throckmorton assured him, "There will be balls. This betrothal will be the most celebrated of the year." As would be the wedding, even if he had to deliver the groom tied into a parcel.

"There you are, Ellery, you naughty boy. I have been looking everywhere for you!"

At the sound of a sweet, feminine voice, Throckmorton whirled in alarm, then slumped with relief when he saw the large, effusive and elderly Lady Featherstonebaugh bearing down on them. This woman most definitely wasn't the exquisite creature of the train station.

"Throckmorton. Lord Longshaw." Lady Featherstonebaugh nodded at them, the large pale-blue feather waving in her headdress. "Ellery, where were you today? We waited at that wretched train station for over an hour." She extended her hand to her godson.

With every appearance of normalcy, Ellery bent over her fingers and smiled roguishly. "I got the time wrong, ma'am. Will you forgive me?"

Lady Featherstonebaugh had once been a beauty, standing as tall as most men and looking them right in the eye. Now age had stooped her shoulders, rheumatism slowed her progress and a steadily increasing girth strained her corset strings. But she spoke with a directness that made her a cherished friend. Lady Featherstonebaugh was the original dear little old lady.

"Today is the happiest day of my life. I had quite despaired of ever seeing you betrothed, young Ellery." She rapped him on the arm with her fan and turned to Lord Longshaw. "A wild youth, my lord. Our Ellery was a wild youth, but always so handsome and kind, always dropping by for a visit when we least expected him—"

When he could charm a loan out of them, Throckmorton thought.

"—And always willing to take Lord Featherstonebaugh to the races and talk horses until I thought I would faint from boredom."

"Nonsense, ma'am, you talk horseflesh with the best of them." Ellery placed her hand on his arm.

Lady Featherstonebaugh wagged her finger at him. "Don't tell my secrets, young man. Ladies aren't supposed to care about bloodlines and racing."

Ellery smiled into her face. "In the run-of-the-mill ladies, it is most unattractive when they show such interest. Only ladies as lovely as you can get away with such impropriety."

Lady Featherstonebaugh actually blushed, her withered cheeks coloring. "Come away with me. We will find Lord Featherstonebaugh and you shall give him the details of the matched grays you just bought. He is most eager to hear about them. Gentlemen." She dismissed Lord Longshaw and Throckmorton, two of the most powerful men in the country, with a decided nod and hobbled away on Ellery's arm.

Throckmorton recognized Ellery's relief at escaping the clutches of his future father-in-law, and he hoped Ellery would stay with his godparents long enough to allow Throckmorton to escape, too. For if Ellery found his exquisite creature without Throckmorton at his side, there was no telling what folly Ellery might commit.

With a twist of the lips, Lord Longshaw stared after Ellery and Lady Featherstonebaugh. "What a handsome piece he is. Able to charm old ladies and young alike. Not worth a damn, of course, but Hyacinth—" He collected himself as he remembered to whom he spoke. "Well, they'll make pretty babies, at any rate."

Throckmorton wasn't about to address Lord Longshaw's opinion. "I shall follow and see if I can pry Ellery away from his godparents and the other well-wishers. You see if you can retrieve Hyacinth from her mother and the ladies who wish to exclaim over her ring. We'll meet in the middle and match them together." He started off and pretended not to hear Lord Longshaw's call of, "Where?"

Ellery stood conversing with his godparents, but he paid them only cursory attention. He craned his neck, tried to see around the celebratory throng in the largest drawing room, yet Lady Featherstonebaugh held him captive with his hand and Lord Featherstonebaugh spoke with such animation, Ellery couldn't slip away. And Ellery was many things, but curt to his godparents he would never be. He had a good heart, Throckmorton knew; if only he had a good head to go with it.

Ellery's distraction gave Throckmorton opportunity. He slipped through the crowd, greeting his guests, examining every face while looking for the glorious, honey-haired damsel Ellery had so aptly described.

The house party appeared to be proceeding smoothly . . . but where was the lady Ellery had described? *Who* was the lady Ellery had described? Throckmorton half-hoped she would disappear into the ether never to return. But that wouldn't do, either. Ellery would search for her until he found her. No, better that she appear and Throckmorton would neutralize her. With a hefty cash payment, most likely, to make her leave, and a hair-curling threat to make her stay away.

Finally, as he stepped onto the terrace, he saw her . . . it had to be she.

She stood at the top of the stairs that led down to the garden, her back to him, looking about as if searching for someone. Searching for Ellery.

Ellery hadn't lied about the girl's fashion sense. A plain, full bell skirt of rich velvet of the same intense azure as the blue in Throckmorton's rug swirled around her feet and rose to embrace a tiny waist. She clutched handfuls on each side, holding the hem slightly aloft, as if prepared to flee at any moment. The off-the-shoulder gown framed a narrow, elegant, exceptionally erect back and made her long, slender neck appear even longer and more slender. Tiny puff sleeves left her arms bare to the top of her long gloves, and a shawl of black Chantilly lace hung artfully draped across one shoulder. The girl sported a head of golden-brown hair, dressed in braids at the back, and it wasn't the color of honey, as Ellery had claimed. The strands resembled nothing so much as the old gold of the Spanish doubloons displayed in a locked glass case in the main foyer of Blythe Hall.

From here, she looked like Cinderella, poised at the top of the stairs and waiting for her prince to recognize and claim her.

But Throckmorton couldn't allow such romantic nonsense to lay waste to his carefully designed plans. He moved purposefully toward Miss Exquisite Creature, wanting to know her name, planning to eject her if she was, as he suspected, uninvited and undesirable.

With every intention of frightening her, he stood directly behind her and said, "I don't believe we've met, Miss . . . ?"

In a rich swish of velvet, she swung around.

He started. "Celeste!" And all became clear.

The skinny, sad-faced girl who had left Blythe Hall four years ago had returned in triumph. *She* was Ellery's exquisite creature. *She* could not be sent away. *She* was the governess Throckmorton himself had hired.

"Mr. Throckmorton!" Her generous mouth curved in a smile that told him everything. That she knew that the gardener's daughter shouldn't be present at a celebration for the *ton*. That she knew she had the grace, manners and charm to pull off such an appearance. That she waited to see how he would react. "How good to see you again."

And he didn't know how to react. This turn of events staggered him, left him unsure—he who was never unsure. "Celeste . . . I didn't realize you would arrive so soon."

"I was packed and preparing to leave Paris anyway. *Monsieur* Ambassador was transferred to a post in the East Indies. *Madame* Ambassador begged me to go with her, and the dear children, but I could not. I wanted to come back. I missed Suffolk."

"And your father?" A less-than-subtle reminder of her background.

Her smile broadened. "Definitely my father, and all the servants who helped raise me after my mother died." She gestured about her, calling his attention to the usually unnoticed staff of Blythe Hall. "Especially Esther, who always welcomed me in the kitchen regardless of how busy she was."

So Celeste acknowledged her background, but claimed the right to move between classes. Beautiful, intelligent, charming . . . dangerous. This woman was dangerous.

Stepping back, he viewed her again. The plain braided hairstyle revealed, without embellishment, the angular bones of her face. He wouldn't proclaim her exquisite, as Ellery did, but he would call her unique. Her chin was broad, her lips full, her forehead clear. Her brows gave wing over eyes that were a clear, changeable hazel, amused with him and in control of the circumstances.

Then her gaze moved beyond him, and all that control vanished. She became eager, animated, almost coltish in her excitement.

He turned to see Ellery looking tense.

"There you are!" Ellery extended his hand. "I've been looking everywhere for you."

With that generous smile that lit her face, she took his hand. "I've been waiting."

For too long, Throckmorton filled in. She wore an expression of unrequited love—long suppressed. And triumph—she had gotten Ellery's attention at last.

What a tangle, and it was up to Throckmorton to unsnarl it.

3

"Didn't I tell you, Garrick?" Ellery grasped Throckmorton's arm. "Isn't she exquisite?"

"Exquisite and more." Throckmorton looked down at Ellery's fingers. Ellery was creasing the ultrafine black cloth of Throckmorton's conservatively tailored suit, and Throckmorton allowed him the familiarity. After all, Ellery was the handsome one, Throckmorton was the sensible one, and the constant turmoil around Ellery had long ago convinced Throckmorton of the luxury of being the sensible one.

Yet he couldn't resist toying with his brother. Ellery still didn't recognize his exquisite creature for who and what she was. "Celeste was telling me that she worked for the ambassador's family in Paris."

"Ah, yes. *Worked.* Paris." Ellery's brow knit as he tried to connect "work" with his mystery lady. "Celeste . . ."

Throckmorton had begun the game, but Celeste joined

in. "Imagine that, Ellery. Paris for three whole years! The boulevards, the music, the food, the dancing . . ."

"I can't imagine." Ellery stared fixedly at her, closer to placing her but not yet able to imagine who she might be.

"You've been there, haven't you?" she asked him.

"Paris? Briefly, on my tour." His thin lips turned down. "A majestic city, if odiferous."

Paris had had nothing on Kashmir, not in majesty nor in odor, but Throckmorton never discussed his time in India. No one—certainly not Ellery—understood the fascination of the mountainous land and its mysterious people, and no one knew about the time he had spent living among the nomads, fighting their fights, trying to make a peace in a land where peace existed only as a long-ago legend.

Stanhope knew, of course. Stanhope had been there at his side the whole time. The bond between them was different from the bond between the brothers. A bond not of blood, but of shared experiences. Yet Stanhope had been restless lately, edgy in a way Throckmorton didn't understand. Perhaps his secretary needed a transfer within the organization. But not yet. Throckmorton needed him too much to transfer him yet.

In a conversational tone much at odds with his dark ruminations, Throckmorton said, "I stayed in Paris for a few months on my way back to England. I enjoyed it, but surely nothing could compare to living there."

Celeste's smile again blossomed, taking her from handsome to magnificent. "I loved it."

"You already knew the language."

"My mother taught me," she concurred.

Bewildered, Ellery asked, "Your mother was French?"

"A charming woman," Throckmorton said. "I'm surprised you don't remember, Ellery."

Celeste allowed her eyes to twinkle at Throckmorton.

The daughter had all the charisma of the mother. Mrs. Milford had had a bevy of admirers among the servants, and occasionally among the gentlemen visitors. Although she had been steadfast in her devotion to Milford, incidents had occurred . . .

Was Celeste like her mother, unwavering in her fidelity? Like her father, dedicated to her work? Or was she nothing but a giddy girl, seeking only fun and a life of leisure? Testing her, he said, "The Paris art galleries are magnificent, truly the equal of any city in Europe."

Leaning toward him, she exclaimed, "Did you go to the Louvre? Most people love the *Mona Lisa,* but I adored the Egyptian antiquities. And the Greek marbles! Did you see the statues?"

So she *had* a thought in her head. He didn't know whether to be relieved she would be a capable teacher to the children, or disappointed that she would be all the more fascinating to Ellery. "I did enjoy the statues. I suppose you escorted your charges to the museums."

"Oh, yes. And sometimes went alone."

"What charges are those?" Ellery asked.

Throckmorton ignored him. "For the most part, the work must have kept you chained to the schoolroom."

She turned to face him fully, but she retained Ellery's fingers in her own. "Not at all. The society there is much freer, less structured—a result of the revolution, no doubt. *Monsieur et Madame* Ambassador encouraged me to join their parties, and I met so many people—Eugene Delacroix, the painter. Monsieur Rendor, the Hungarian revolutionary. Monsieur Charcot, who hypnotizes people

and makes them act in amazing fashions." She smiled
fondly, enigmatically. "And dear, dear Count de Rosselin."

Like a dog snapping a dangled bone, Ellery asked,
"Who's Count de Rosebud?"

"Rosselin," she corrected placidly. "He is a gentleman of the old school, kind, generous, knowledgeable.
He taught me so much—to enjoy life, to dress well, to
cook, to laugh at myself."

"I hate him," Ellery said.

"He is eighty-six years old," she finished.

Ellery stared at her, then threw back his head and
laughed aloud, a burst of enthusiastic merriment that
drew all eyes. "You're a minx."

Time to dash some cold water on Ellery's ebullience
before they attracted too much attention. In as dry a tone
as he could manage, Throckmorton said, "Well put,
Ellery. I was thinking the same thing. Our little Miss
Milford has grown up to be a minx."

Ellery's eyes narrowed in concentration. "Miss . . .
Milford."

Celeste waited placidly for Ellery to make the connection. When he did not, she stopped the elderly footman to take a glass of champagne and a single ripe
strawberry from the bowl on his tray. "Herne, so good to
see you."

The footman reddened and shot a nervous glance at
the brothers. "Good t' see ye, Miss Celeste, lookin' so
well." Giving way to joy, he grinned. "Lookin' pleasin'!"

"I had a good visit with my father this afternoon."
She looked sideways at Ellery, then back at Herne. "I'll
be down in the kitchen first thing in the morning to see
the rest of you—Esther, and Arwydd, and Brunella . . .
is Frau Wieland still the pastry chef?"

"Indeed she is." Herne grimaced. "Bossy as ever."

"London and Paris were wonderful, but I've missed you all so much."

At last, light dawned over Ellery's perfect features.

"The gardener's daughter," Ellery exclaimed. "My God, you're Celeste Milford!"

Throckmorton had to admit Celeste handled Ellery's dismay well, sipping her champagne while waiting to hear her fate. Would she be accepted, or would she be hustled away to hide in the servants' quarters?

Surely even infatuated Ellery had to see she must go. Paris society be damned; in the English *ton,* one's only association with the gardener's daughter was to instruct her to pull a weed.

With the intention of adding to Ellery's dismay, Throckmorton drawled, "Very good, Ellery. Very democratic of you to invite the gardener's daughter to your betrothal party. If one didn't know better, one might mistake you for an American."

A tactical error, Throckmorton saw at once. Ellery must be truly infatuated—or truly rebellious, for he said, "A woman as beautiful as Celeste doesn't need the deceitful approval of the *ton.*"

Herne stood rooted in place, tray extended.

"Champagne?" Throckmorton queried his brother. "Strawberry?"

Ellery glared. "I hate champagne, and strawberries give me the mange."

"Do you still break out in those disgusting scaly patches?" Throckmorton asked. "The ones that make you itch?"

"I hardly think this is the occasion to talk about it,"

Ellery snapped. "Now, where's the brandy? Where's the cheese? Why are we serving *this?*"

"Champagne and strawberries are Lady Hyacinth's favorites." As he spoke to Ellery, Throckmorton fixed Celeste with a meaningful gaze. "You remember Lady Hyacinth. She's your betrothed."

"She should have remembered that Ellery is allergic to them. *I* did." Celeste nibbled on the ripe red fruit. "The strawberries are wonderful, Mr. Throckmorton. Did they come from my father's greenhouse?"

For all the notice Ellery took, Throckmorton might not even have mentioned Hyacinth. No, all Ellery's attention was fixed on the vision of Celeste with her rosy lips around the strawberry.

With winsome coquettishness, she finished the fruit, placed the stem on Herne's tray, and laid her hand on Ellery's arm. "You're very kind, Ellery. I've always worshipped you from afar, did you know that?"

Know that? He didn't even know you were alive. But Throckmorton had learned his lesson, and he clamped his mouth shut.

Ellery lost all the starch in his spine as he gazed at the slip of a girl beside him. "Worshipped me? That's a persuasive claim."

"From afar. I used to watch the parties from over there"—waving her tall champagne glass, she indicated a small marble alcove in the garden—"and you were always so charming, so handsome. I fell in love with you while watching you dance. The only gnat in the soup was—you weren't dancing with me."

"I can make that up to you right now. Miss Milford, will you dance with me?" Ellery extended his gloved hand.

Eager to assist her, Herne snatched away her champagne.

She thanked him with a smile. Putting her hand into Ellery's, she let him sweep her into a waltz.

"Champagne, Mr. Throckmorton?" Herne asked.

"Hm. Yes, I think that would be a good idea." He accepted a glass, then stopped Herne when he would have hurried off. "Celeste is a lovely woman."

"Yes, sir," Herne answered. "So sweet an' kind, willing t' help, an' smart! Schooled by yer own instructor, sir, an' that gennaman said he'd never seen a child as quick as her, lad or lass. We're proud of her." He bowed. "Will there be anything else, sir?"

By that little speech the footman warned him and informed him.

Throckmorton took a strawberry and waved Herne away.

Sipping his champagne, Throckmorton admired Celeste's dancing, which unfortunately was as light and skilled as any English noblewoman's.

Lady Philberta's chilly voice spoke from just behind him. "Who is she?"

"Mother." Wrapping his arm around her waist, he brought her to his side. She was a tiny woman, and growing shorter as she left sixty behind. Her shoulders were stooped beneath the weight of her silk gown and wide petticoats, and she carried a cane. She had never been a beauty—beauty might have brought her a rich *and* titled husband—but she had an aristocrat's arrogance and an Englishwoman's pride. Kissing her powdered cheek, he said loudly, "The party is wonderful, as always." He lowered his voice. "Smile, Mother, everyone will take their cue from us."

He felt the stiff indignation grip her before she let it go. Eternally pragmatic, she understood the necessity of behaving as if she enjoyed the sight of Ellery dancing with a ravishing girl who was not his fiancée.

"She is Miss Milford," Throckmorton informed her.

In an absolutely agreeable tone, Lady Philberta asked, "The gardener's daughter?"

"Exactly."

It was a measure of his mother's distress when she used his father's favorite curse. "Hell and damnation."

Herne made his stately way toward them, offering champagne and strawberries.

Lady Philberta accepted the champagne and waved off the strawberries. Like her younger son, she was allergic to them.

She waited until Herne had moved on before she continued, "You've got to get rid of her. Immediately."

"How?"

"Throw her out!"

"She is the daughter of our faithful gardener and our deceased cook. I have hired her to be the girls' governess." He paused long enough to let her ingest that impalpable truth before adding, "Besides, if I were to toss her out, Ellery would follow."

"But if Lord Longshaw sees her!"

"It's too late for that." With a tilt of his head, Throckmorton indicated the apoplectic Lord Longshaw standing in the open doorway.

"The gardener's daughter." Lady Philberta sipped the champagne and watched the dancing with fixed enjoyment. "What can Ellery be thinking?"

"The question would be—with what is Ellery thinking?" Throckmorton murmured.

Lady Philberta whipped her head around to stare at him. "What?"

"Nothing, Mother."

"You pick a poor time to show the first signs of a sense of humor."

"Yes, Mother." He supposed he had best keep his observations to himself. "It isn't as if I care whether the gardener's daughter comes to the party. I have no aristocratic pretensions. My own antecedents don't bear looking into"—he fixed her with a significant gaze—"on either side."

"You're not going to mention the highwayman again? That was a hundred years ago, and at least *he* had the advantage of being romantic."

"If you consider hanging from your neck until you are dead to be romantic."

Without drawing breath, she continued, "My ancestors aren't nearly as scandalous as your father's, with his rebellious Scottish baron and Cromwell's commander and those dreadful pirates."

It was an argument she had had often with his father. She had never won and his father was dead, but that didn't stop her from fighting.

"If anything, the family background makes this intrigue with Miss Milford all the more undesirable." Lady Philberta pointed out what Throckmorton already knew. "The *ton* could easily be made to remember how precarious the Throckmorton toehold into society truly is, especially if, in a disgraceful spectacle, Ellery rejects his betrothed—one of our own—right before our eyes."

"I realize that, Mother."

In a quiet tone that barely reached his ears, she said,

"Garrick, for the sake of Her Majesty's realm, we need the Longshaw connection."

"The capital won't hurt us, either." If his family had a motto, it might be *Money and Patriotism.* "But we must move carefully. Right now, to Ellery, Miss Milford embodies the forbidden fruit."

"I do get tired of having you be so eternally right," she murmured.

"In the future, I will try to fail you, Mother." He flashed a smile down at her. "But not this time."

"No. But what will you do?"

His smile faded. "Miss Milford's handling of Ellery has proved one thing. He *can* be handled."

All Throckmorton had to do was discover the method.

~ 4 ~

Celeste had dreamed of this moment every night of her life.

"I have dreamed of this moment," Ellery breathed in her ear.

He'd said just the right thing. They were dancing just the right dance. He was holding her in his manly arms . . .

His breath tickled her neck. "You waltz like a dream."

The music entwined them with magic. The air sparkled like the finest champagne. The stars popped out, one by one, brilliant with light, and each and every torch around the veranda burned brightly just for her. She was waltzing with Ellery. Ellery, the man she'd loved since the time . . .

"I loved you since I first saw you," he murmured.

She drew back to look up at him, and she couldn't help it. She laughed in his face. "The first time you saw me, I was probably a sniveling babe. The first time you noticed me, I was eleven years old."

"I meant . . ."

"You meant you loved me since the first time you saw me today." He looked uncomfortable, and the merriment in her crested. "You don't remember me at eleven, do you?" Dear Ellery, he had lived a life of excitement, of glamour. Of course he didn't remember. She didn't care. Nothing could ruin this perfect evening. "You tripped me."

"No!" he protested. "I could not have been so unchivalrous."

"Indeed you could." She kept her voice low pitched and soft, the way the Count de Rosselin had always instructed. "You were a boy! I was eleven and you were sixteen, and when I fell I tore my best Sunday dress."

She had Ellery Throckmorton, the most dashing rogue in England, puzzled and intrigued. She wasn't ashamed of her past; she wouldn't let him pretend she was someone she wasn't. He would accept her as the gardener's daughter, or not at all. If she'd learned one thing in Paris, it was that a beautiful young woman who held herself in high esteem could have anything she wanted—and Celeste wanted Ellery.

"I cried, and you picked me up and hugged me, and carried me to your father's study."

Their steps slowed as he listened.

"I was frightened to death of old Mr. Throckmorton, but you bravely confessed what you'd done and before Sunday next I had a new gown and my first—and only—infatuation."

He liked that; his eyes crinkled and his dimple

flashed. "You were infatuated with my father?" he teased.

"All Throckmorton men are irresistible," she answered.

"But I am the most irresistible, aren't I?"

She pretended to think.

He leaned closer. "Aren't I?"

He was almost kissing her on the dance floor, and such an action would be ruinous. She knew people were already buzzing, wondering who she was. She wouldn't give them any more ammunition than the truth. So she agreed. "You, Ellery, are by far the most irresistible."

Gathering her close once more, he whirled her in a grand circle.

Over her shoulder, she glimpsed the one Throckmorton man who was quite resistible—Garrick Throckmorton, who stood watching them, holding a strawberry and talking to Lady Philberta.

Well, every dream worth having was worth fighting a few dragons for, and Garrick Throckmorton was a very worthy dragon.

He was the one who had arranged this wretched betrothal which had almost overset Celeste's plans. Esther had confessed that Garrick Throckmorton had forced Ellery into the arms of little Lady Hyacinth, a girl whose only assets were a fortune and a title. A girl Celeste remembered as being awkward and spotted, and as infatuated with Ellery as Celeste herself.

Celeste had hated her for that.

At first Celeste had thought her dream of marrying Ellery had been crushed before it began. Then she remembered the words of the Count de Rosselin. "Celeste, a dream is worth having only if you are willing to fight for it."

So she would fight. She would use every weapon at her disposal. This time the dream would not fade. She wouldn't let it. Because of Paris, and Count de Rosselin, and the past four years of loneliness and growing up and learning how to be the most fascinating woman on the continent. No gentleman as staid and dull as Garrick Throckmorton would stand in her way.

Dancing on her toes to get closer to Ellery's ear, she murmured, "I would relish some champagne. And I would like to drink it in the grand ballroom, while the moonlight glints on the gold leaf and we dance to the distant strains of music."

Ellery drew back in amazement. "You little siren! Did you spy on me in there, too?"

For the grand ballroom, darkened on the night of the garden party, had been where Ellery took those other girls. There they had danced, and afterward he kissed them. Celeste had watched him through the window, wanting to be the girl in his arms.

"The ballroom." She slipped out of his arms at the edge of the dance floor and drifted into the house, her feet scarcely touching the ground.

Lords and ladies moved through all the lighted rooms in the house. In the drawing rooms, the corridor, the library. Dancing, gossiping, eating and drinking. They smelled of perfume and talc, dressed in taffeta and lace, and laughed and cried and bled just like her. She knew most of them, although they didn't know her. As a child, she had studied them, wanting to be like them so she could be with Ellery. Her father had said it was impossible. He said there were the aristocrats, the middle class, and the poor, and never would the lines blur. He said she created misery for herself, and it was true, she had. But in Paris she had transformed that misery into a possibility, and not even Father's disapproval could change that.

People glanced her way, discussed her behind their fans, tried to place her among their acquaintances. She didn't care. She could bear the gossip with Ellery's love to support her.

She could almost hear her practical father's voice saying, "He doesn't love ye yet."

But she had hardly begun to fight.

As she made her way and turned the corner toward the ballroom, the candelabras became few and far between. By use of illumination, the family deliberately encouraged the guests to stay near the veranda, and the dimly lit corridor wound before her.

It didn't matter. She knew her way around every bit of Blythe Hall. During her childhood, she had learned each inch of the eighteenth-century house. It came into the Throckmorton family a mere forty years ago, but for her, this had always been home.

Pausing, she looked out a window onto the veranda. Ellery stood out there, trapped in an alcove. He couldn't come to meet her, for he was cornered by Lord and Lady Longshaw, and by a girl . . . a rather handsome girl, tall and pretty, if a little awkward.

Celeste leaned her hands against the windowpanes.

Who was she? She had black hair, each strand shining in the torchlight. Her lips were shaped like a bow, waiting to be kissed. Not a spot was to be seen on her fair complexion. And her eyes . . . her eyes were violet and wide, and fixed on Ellery in slavish adoration.

Celeste snapped to attention.

It was Lady Hyacinth. Her rival. That pretty, soft,

sweet-looking female was the girl Celeste would relieve of a husband.

Pressing her hand to her chest, Celeste took a breath.

She wished she hadn't seen Hyacinth. It would have been better if she hadn't. Then she wouldn't be feeling this flood of . . . oh . . . call it what it was. Guilt. She felt guilty at the thought of hurting Hyacinth.

She didn't know why she should. The girl had everything. A title, a fortune, two parents who adored her. She never had to work, she certainly didn't have to stay up late remaking clothing she had accepted from the ambassador's wife.

But there was something about the expression on her face as she looked at Ellery . . . as if she really loved him.

Celeste glared through the window. Well, too bad. If someone had to suffer, it might as well be her. Not Celeste. Not now. Not again.

Then someone joined the little group, and Celeste glared more fiercely. Garrick Throckmorton. The architect of this whole disaster. He was the one who deserved to suffer.

Of course, if one were to be fair, one might say Celeste wouldn't be here now except for his offer of a position. But she didn't feel like being fair.

He bowed, he spoke, he observed the little group solemnly. For as long as Celeste could remember, he had been the dark, cool, remote Mr. Throckmorton, cast in the shadows by the blazingly bright Ellery. He was equitable to a fault; none of the servants would hear a cross word about him, for he pensioned their elderly, cared for their sick and treated each of them with the respect due another human being.

Indeed, Celeste well knew what she owed Mr. Throckmorton. It was Mr. Throckmorton who had declared she should go to the Distinguished Academy of Governesses to further her education and learn a trade, and Mr. Throckmorton who had paid the initial cost. She had paid him back from her earliest earnings; Celeste couldn't bear to think herself any further indebted to the Throckmorton family. So when the offer of a job as governess to Throckmorton's daughters had arrived from Blythe Hall, she had been able to decide without feeling undue pressure.

Not that there had ever been any doubt. Ellery resided at Blythe Hall.

The little group outside the window appeared to be suffering an altercation, with Lord Longshaw speaking in a heated manner to Ellery while Lady Longshaw tugged at one arm. Lady Hyacinth tugged at the other while casting anxious glances at her betrothed. Ellery looked distracted, glancing at the house as if he wished to be elsewhere—and Celeste knew where that elsewhere was. She wanted him to be there almost as much as she wanted him to end his betrothal right now . . .

And with a bustle of skirts and an entourage of three footmen carrying covered silver trays, Frau Wieland arrived.

Celeste stared. Old Mr. Throckmorton had adored pastry and desserts and had begged Frau Wieland, famous for her strudel, to come from Vienna for a good salary and the promise of the best of the servants' quarters. She had lorded it over the other servants ever since, and to a one they hated her. Now she waltzed into the middle of a *ton* party into the center of a lordly fight and demanded attention. And Mr. Garrick Throckmorton apparently thought she should have it. He gestured for quiet and indicated she should speak.

She did, so loudly that by leaning close to the window and by watching her lips, Celeste could catch a word or so.

"Magnificent new concoction . . . deserves attention . . . by invitation . . . Mr. Throckmorton said . . ."

Frustrated, Celeste put her ear right to the glass in time to hear her trumpet, "I present . . . *la crème moka gateau.*"

The footmen whisked the covers away and presented glasses filled with frothy brown, pink and white concoctions.

Mr. Throckmorton accepted the first one with an exclamation of pleasure. It appeared he had his father's weakness for desserts.

By their expressions Lady Philberta, Lord and Lady Longshaw, Hyacinth and Ellery were as befuddled as Celeste, but they all took a spoon, tasted and nodded. Hyacinth nodded with a great deal of enthusiasm, Ellery with much less.

By his gestures Throckmorton urged him to eat more. Yielding, Ellery ate as rapidly as he could. Clapping Throckmorton on the shoulder, he tried to edge away.

Throckmorton smiled the kind of smile that raised goosebumps on Celeste's arms, and glanced toward the window, his gray eyes wickedly amused.

She jumped back.

She didn't know why. He surely couldn't see her. The lights were bright outside. No candles glimmered in this part of the house. And she had no reason to hide from Mr. Throckmorton. None at all. But for some reason she didn't want Mr. Throckmorton to think she spied on them.

He smiled toward the window, then moved Hyacinth to stand beside Ellery.

Celeste fled toward the ballroom.

$\mathcal{D}$epending on her whim, the gardener's wife, Aimee, had alternately cursed and praised the size and the age of the Blythe Hall kitchen. Yet Milford had always liked the room. You couldn't call it cozy, not with the three worktables, or the huge fireplace with spit that took up one wall, or the ovens that were built into the brick. But when extra servants were brought in for a party and the place bustled with the business of cooking for a hundred guests and their servants, well, then it was a fine, loud, merry place filled with smells that reminded him of the days when his wife was in charge.

Except, of course, that above all the commotion, Esther's voice rang out. Esther, who had taken Aimee's place as head cook.

It wasn't that Milford minded having another cook take over his wife's domain. No, he was a sensible man who understood the need for food on a regular basis. It

was Esther herself who had been the thorn in Milford's
side since the day she'd arrived, hired over from the
Fairchild household, the third cook to arrive after Mrs.
Milford's death and the one who wouldn't leave, no
matter how fervently he wished it. And Scottish to
boot—that is to say, stubborn, raw boned and sharp
tongued. She had for the past eight years held the reins
in the kitchen, and during that time he'd not had one
peaceful meal. She didn't care how loud the scullery
maids got with their tales of which stable lad had asked
them to Midsummer's Night. Nor did she care if the
laughter got too raucous or the jokes too salacious. All
she cared about was whether the food got to the table
warm and on time, and despite Milford's worst expectations, that was always done. Always. No matter what
calamity befell the kitchen—and he'd never sat in a
kitchen uncursed with calamity—Esther always sailed
through with flying colors.

But none of that vexed him. No, what truly vexed
him was that she always dragged him into some spirited
discussion. Dragged him in when all he wanted was to
eat his meals in peace and quiet and then get back to his
dirt and his flowers.

Right now the kitchen staff, temporary and perma-
nent, struggled to produce the canapés that circulated
with the footmen as well as the formal dinner that would
be served at midnight. So it took the loud clang of a silver salver on the long kitchen table where Milford ate
his supper to capture anyone's attention. Herne stood
there, eyes twinkling, belly heaving, and when he had
everyone's attention, he proclaimed, "Celeste is dancing
with Mr. Ellery."

As announcements went, this one provoked the desired effect. Brunella, the senior upstairs maid, froze with her fork in the air. Elva, the newest scullery maid, stood with her scrub brush upraised. Adair, the footman who had returned to reload his tray with a variety of canapés, stared at his superior with awestruck eyes.

Esther gave a great laugh that caught like contagion among the bustling kitchen staff. "Our little Celeste has gone to the ball at last!"

Every head turned toward Milford. The bench beneath his arse grew harder, the table before him jiggled, as close by his elbow, Arwydd mashed a kettle full of potatoes, and Milford's head inched further toward his plate. Futilely, he wished he was in his greenhouse. Better to be coaxing the pinks to grow than to face this battery of interference and expectation. No one said anything for so long he had begun to hope they had given up on him.

Then Herne spoke. "Aren't ye proud, Milford?"

Lifting his gaze, Milford realized that they watched him, bright-eyed with curiosity. No matter that he'd already made his thoughts clear to Celeste. No matter that his daughter and her goings-on were none of their concern. The servants had watched her grow up, most of them. A good number of them remembered his wife with affection. So, since they figured they had the right, they would badger him until he made a statement.

So he did. "Celeste should keep in her proper place," he growled.

"But she's beautiful," Herne protested. "The lords are whisperin' an' guessin' as t' who she might be. I tell ye, she fits right in!"

Milford ignored the silly fool and went back to eating his plate of spinach dressed with vinegar and bacon.

"I vow, Milford, wearing that dour face ye're like sheep droppings floating in the eggnog." It was Esther who spoke. Of course it was Esther.

Driven to speech, he answered, "Stubborn."

"I wonder where she got that from."

"Don't know."

Alva stopped turning the coneys on the spit to ask, "Wouldn't ye like fer yer daughter to marry Mr. Ellery?"

"Men like Mr. Ellery don't marry the gardener's daughter," he answered.

"Celeste is as beautiful as any of those other, aristocratic girls," Esther said, "and more sweetly mannered and smarter, too."

He snapped, "I know my daughter's value."

"Ye've got a damned funny way of showing it."

Milford's temper seldom ignited. So seldom, in fact, he could count the times on his fingers and his toes. But something about this woman and her smug disdain and her good puddings brought a slow rise of color to his cheeks. Lifting his gaze, he stared at her levelly. "I guess that's because, unlike everyone else here, I live in a world where the sun rises in the east and sets in the west and the rich marry the rich and the only time a gentleman looks on the gardener's daughter is to give to her a bellyache that takes nine months to cure."

Esther's brown eyes flashed with yellow bits of flame. "And it's people like you who shatter dreams that should come true."

"Maybe so. Maybe so." Sopping the last of his bread in the drippings, he wiped his face with his napkin and stood up. "But I don't think it's going to be me who shatters Celeste's dreams."

* * *

Moonlight shimmered through the open windows of the ballroom, gleaming on the waxed hardwood floors in long, faint trails, setting the carved gold leaf aglow, creating the fairyland Celeste recognized from her girlhood. On summer nights when the family was away, she had come here to pretend. Pretend she was waiting for Ellery, pretend he had arrived, pretend to dance in his arms, pretend to kiss his generous lips until she was breathless and swept by desire.

But tonight, pretend would yield to reality. Ellery would escape that trap Mr. Throckmorton had sprung. He would come and make all her dreams come true. He would, because otherwise Mr. Throckmorton would have won, and Ellery was the dashing one, the handsome one, the masterful one.

Well, perhaps not masterful, but he'd never had the chance to be. Not with Mr. Throckmorton always there being tall and dark and proper. But with the right encouragement, *her* encouragement, Ellery would be masterful from now on.

Gathering her skirts, she spun in a circle, letting happiness wash over her.

Yes, Ellery was a wizard at escaping the many snares set for him; she had seen him do it. Tonight he would escape into her arms, and nothing could destroy the happiness of being young, in love, and home after four long years in exile.

Finding herself standing in one of the long trails of moonlight, she glanced toward the doors. Ellery had yet to arrive, so she gave into the memories. Backing away, she took a running start and skated along the floor, her leather-soled slippers allowing a smooth glide all the way to the window. Laughing, she flung herself around and went back, running and sliding with hoydenish pleasure.

After all, if Ellery did happen to see her, she knew well how she looked. Youthful, carefree, charming. What crime to be caught enjoying a romp? The scent of beeswax rose from the floor and the sweet scent of night-blooming nicotiana rose from the garden outside and filled the room with its fragrance.

But when a large figure appeared in the doorway, blocking the corridor's faint candlelight, she stopped in mid-glide. A glance showed him to be man-shaped, attired in a gentleman's austere suit, and of approximately Ellery's size and shape. She had imagined Ellery arriving with a laugh and a kiss. When the fellow cleared his throat, she knew it wasn't Ellery. Ellery would never clear his throat at her in that tone.

Facing the door, she peered through the darkness.

Mr. Throckmorton stepped out of the shadows and into the moonlight, holding two glasses of champagne and wearing a quizzical smile. "I used to skate along these floors just like that," he said. "Although I haven't thought about it for years."

Her sentiments warred between incredulity that Ellery had failed to appear and skepticism that Mr. Throckmorton had ever, in his whole somber life, ever slid along a beam of moonlight.

He strolled toward her and stopped at arm's length.

She stood, chin up, spine rigid with disbelief. "Where's Ellery?"

"Ellery sent me in his place." Mr. Throckmorton extended the glass. "He's battling a bit of a rash."

Uncertainly, Celeste took the champagne. "A rash?"

"Apparently he ate something that didn't agree with him."

"Something he ate?" Suspicion bloomed in her mind, and her eyes narrowed as she contemplated Mr. Throckmorton. "Ellery ate a strawberry?"

"Usually he's more careful. But tonight he seemed to be in a hurry."

In a hurry. Of course. To see her. "Was it in that—" Abruptly she remembered she shouldn't know about Frau Wieland's silly dessert, and changed the subject. "Poor Ellery! Is he going to be all right?"

"Yes." Mr. Throckmorton smiled into his glass. "Yes, I think he really is."

She took a step toward the door. "Does he need—"

Mr. Throckmorton blocked her path. "No. He doesn't need anything. Right now, he is well tended and unwilling to have anyone see him in this condition."

She wavered. She didn't know how to get around Mr. Throckmorton, and she suspected he told the truth about Ellery's reluctance to have her view him covered with unsightly blotches. And yet . . . and yet she didn't wish to be trapped in the middle of her long-cherished fantasy . . . with the wrong man.

"Ellery did tell me to dance with you in the moonlight to the distant strains of music." Taking a sip of his champagne, Mr. Throckmorton watched her closely. "Did I get that right?"

"Yes," she said, numb with frustration. "You got it right." Mr. Throckmorton had quoted her exact words back to her. Only Ellery could have told him, so Ellery had truly sent his brother in his place. She glanced around the glimmering ballroom where, only a few moments ago, dreams had been adrift. Now the music sounded off key, the gold leaf seemed dull and over-done, and the moonlight did no more than reflect the light of the sun—as Mr. Throckmorton reflected the light of Ellery.

Mr. Throckmorton took her glass and placed both his and hers on a table by the wall. Coming back to her, he extended his arms.

She didn't walk into them. It was too odd to think of dancing with, of all people, Mr. Throckmorton. He was too old, too solemn, too responsible. Everything Ellery was not.

But neither was he indecisive, for when she hesitated, he gathered her to him. His arm wrapped around her waist, his hand caught her hand, and without giving her a moment to adjust to the sensation of being in his arms, he swept her away. He shouldn't have been able to waltz. Businessmen shouldn't be able to make the music come alive with motion. But while Mr. Throckmorton danced without flourishes or extravagance, his motions were elegant, his gait smooth. He led like a man used to leading—in every situation.

She didn't know what to do with her free hand. To touch his shoulder seemed an act of insolence, almost of intimacy. But although she battled the thought and scolded herself as silly, she still couldn't bring herself to lift her palm up so far and hold him as comportment demanded he be held. Instead, she rested her hand against his upper arm . . . and discovered how his muscles flexed beneath her fingers.

"This is quite lovely." His voice sounded smooth, rich, content, when she knew he must want to be back at the party, greeting the guests, supervising the arrangements, aware that every person he made happy was one more person who might someday do business with him. "My brother will be devastated to know he missed this."

She stared fixedly over his shoulder as the walls came closer, then whirled away.

He dipped his head a bit to catch her gaze and asked in an incredulous tone, "You're not angry at me for Ellery's mishap?"

She only glanced at him. "I can't help but suspect . . ." She shouldn't say anything, but what difference did it make? Mr. Throckmorton thought her a minx. And he *had* asked. "I can't help but suspect that you managed to manipulate this convenient rash so Ellery wouldn't be able to meet me here."

Laughter rumbled through him, and she felt it everywhere they touched—in the arm he had wrapped around her waist, beneath the fingertips she rested on his arm and oddly enough, in the pit of her stomach.

"I appreciate your faith in me. But tell me, why would I disable my brother at his own betrothal party? Even if I wished to remove him from your sphere, it makes no sense to take him out of the reach of his fiancée—and he is out of reach of Lady Hyacinth. He fled to his room at the first onset of rash and is right now undoubtedly soaking in a tub of water and oatmeal."

Did he mean to give her such an unappealing vision? Dripping Ellery covered with tan lumps.

"No," Mr. Throckmorton continued, "if I wished to get rid of you, I could do so with much less finesse."

"You could, mayhap, toss me out on the street."

He appeared to give her plan due consideration. "I could. That's the ultimate in lack of finesse." He shook his head. "Ellery would tell you it's more my style to bribe you. I could offer you a thousand pounds per annum and your own house in Paris."

He was serious. She was sure he was! "A thousand pounds! You would have to wish to be rid of me very much to offer so much."

He shrugged.

The muscles rippled beneath her palm again. In an effort to distance herself from the part of him that was so mobile, she slid her hand up to his shoulder.

He seemed to take that as a signal of some kind of acquiescence and pulled her closer yet. He held her in his dominion; she couldn't break away. Not unless he allowed her, and she wasn't at all certain he would.

Their circling slowed. He looked down at her rather than where they were going, his face shadowed by night. Yet her eyes had adjusted to the dimness, the moon provided its frail illumination, and she could see his features and gain an impression of his mien—which was far more than she wanted.

Amazement etched his features. "A thousand pounds is not so much. I've paid more to Ellery's liaisons to be rid of them."

"I am not one of Ellery's liaisons." It was an insult to be described as one. "And I won't be bribed!" And she didn't like dancing so closely that his legs tangled in her skirts and his chest loomed so near to her nose she could smell the faint scent of soap, whisky and beneath it all, clean masculinity. She wondered how the scent of himself had so escaped Mr. Throckmorton's control; he didn't seem the sort of man who would allow the gardener's daughter such an intimate acquaintance.

"No, of course you're not." Mr. Throckmorton managed to sound surprised. "I wasn't offering *you* a thousand pounds per annum and a house in Paris. I was saying that my brother has cost the family a great deal over the years. That's why we had such hopes for this betrothal."

"But if he won't wed Lady Hyacinth, he won't. He's a grown man, and you can scarcely force him to the altar." So she had told herself, and her father, all through her preparations for the ball.

"Too true."

It *was* true, although the aura of power Mr. Throckmorton gave off seemed almost indomitable. Strange, she'd never thought of him like that before. She'd always known that he was the heir, of course, but she scarcely remembered when he had returned from his travels. She had been so much in love with Ellery that that man who had walked the grounds had been almost a ghost to her.

Now he was the same: quiet, observant, very much in control of himself. But different: attractive, masculine, and that control . . . it was almost a challenge. Celeste was surprised that in the impressionable years of her adolescence she had never noticed him.

"I was sorry to hear of your wife's death," she blurted, then cringed at her clumsy change of subject.

"Thank you." He didn't loosen his hold on her, or seem stricken with uncomfortable memories. "It was a tragedy."

"I imagine you miss her." Celeste didn't know why she pursued this line of conversation.

"I do. She was sensible, a good mate to me, and a wonderful mother."

The kind of praise every woman scorned! Celeste

had a vision of their marriage—arid, uninspiring, and most of all, sensible. But the vision worked well to dissipate the impression of virility which made her so uncomfortably aware of him. "How long has it been?"

"Three years. Penelope is—was—doing well."

Penelope! His daughter. Her charge. Celeste seized the topic of conversation. "I remember Penelope. She was four when I left, but even then she seemed very much your daughter."

What had made her say that?

A faint smile flirted with his lips. "Boring?"

"Not at all!" What had caused *him* to say *that?* "Only very tranquil and composed for a child so young. What has happened to cause her further grief?"

"One word. Kiki."

"Kiki? What is that?"

"Not a what. A who."

They stood in the middle of the floor now, not dancing, just swaying.

"Kiki is your other charge."

"My other charge?" Startled, she said, "I thought . . . that is, you said I would be teaching two girls, and I thought that the other child—"

"Must be mine? No, Kiki is not mine. Kiki is a force of nature, like a cyclone in the Pacific Ocean or a volcano in the East Indies. I look to you, Celeste, to tame her."

"Forces of nature are impossible to tame."

"I have great faith in you. Lady Bucknell claims you are a miracle with unruly children, and the Russian ambassador and his wife wrote glowing recommendations." Mr. Throckmorton glanced around. "The music has stopped. Shall we walk while I explain the situation?"

"Yes!" Dear heavens, yes. Walking along lighted corridors and discussing her position had to be less intimate than this darkness, this touching, this whirl of music in a chamber filled with dreams. Dreams of Ellery, she told herself, delayed only by a hapless event. Spinning out of Mr. Throckmorton's arms, she walked toward the door.

He caught her before she had taken two steps. His arm circled her waist and he used her momentum to swing her back into his embrace—closer this time than last; he pressed her chest to his. Outraged, embarrassed and uneasily aware of danger, she leaned back as far as she could. "Mr. . . . Throckmorton!"

"Do you always leave your partner on the dance floor?" He sounded stern. "Because I don't remember it being done that way in Paris, and I can assure you it isn't done at all in England."

Color rose in her face. He was right, and his rebuke had made her seem surly and ungrateful. She, who had worked so hard to vanquish all trace of rough manners from her demeanor. Yet the Count de Rosselin had made it clear that when a lady was caught in an indiscretion, her behavior did not descend into the depths, but rose to the occasion. "You're right." She could scarcely form the words, she hated them so much. "Forgive me for my lack of manners, and thank you for the waltz."

The shadows could not hide his stare, nor his grave examination. Lifting his hand to her chin, he cupped it, and he seemed to speak only to himself. "You are the most beautiful and gracious woman I have met in a very, very long time."

His voice reverberated through her, and his ardent manner made her want to flee this room. Flee Blythe

Hall. How had he turned her from resentment to . . . to this kind of appalled appreciation of him and his compliments? Why was she suddenly noticing his height, the breadth of his shoulders, the thickness of his neck and the plain strength of his face?

Then he smiled, and in a tone so light it belied his previous fervor, he said, "Thank you, Celeste. I can't remember a dance I've enjoyed more."

He released her, but she dared not turn her back on him. He had taught her a lesson: never lose sight of Mr. Throckmorton. One never knew what he might do.

He only extended his arm. She laid her hand on it, and together they strolled toward the dim corridor.

"In England, the waltz is still quite scandalous, you know," he said. "If someone other than the host—in this case Ellery or myself asks you to dance, they mean you a disrespect."

She nodded slowly. "Thank you for telling me. In France—"

He chuckled. "Yes, in France the waltz is the least of the improprieties."

She couldn't restrain her smile. It was true. In France, she had been the beautiful girl who was the ambassador's governess. In England, she was still the gardener's daughter. If not for her longing for Father, and Blythe Hall, and Ellery, she might never have returned. But she had, and she would conquer . . . everything.

But not tonight. Tonight she walked with Mr. Throckmorton to learn the details of her position.

She tried to turn toward the brighter lights and the sounds of the party.

He rather firmly directed her further into the quiet

depths of the house. "I thought you'd like to see the changes made since you left."

With another man, she might have been dismayed, but she would not be with Mr. Throckmorton. He had done nothing more alarming than waltz with her, then warn her of its ignominy. Besides, he hadn't wanted to dance; he had done so only on Ellery's request. Any misgiving she felt had been the result of the darkness, the location, and her expectations. Briskly, she ignored the squirmy sense of discomfort and the suspicions that still lingered in her mind, and in the efficient tone she found engendered trust among her employers, she said, "Tell me about Penelope and Kiki."

"Kiki is Ellery's daughter."

6

$\mathcal{S}$tunned, Celeste squeezed Mr. Throckmorton's arm.

He didn't seem to find her agitation surprising. "Ellery's daughter from a beautiful French actress who five months ago decided she no longer wishes to raise his six-year-old child."

Ellery had fathered a child? And left the child to be raised by her mother while he . . . Celeste felt rather ill.

But of course he had his reasons. He couldn't marry the woman. An actress was even less proper than . . . than the gardener's daughter. "Oh . . . dear," Celeste whispered.

"Yes. So she brought Kiki here and left her." He walked Celeste slowly through the great dining hall and stopped to point out the changes. "As you can see, Mother had the walls replastered and wallpaper put up for the feast at the end of the celebrations." Slanting a quick smile at her, he said, "But if the celebrations end in a different manner than we expected, you're not to worry. I'm sure the chamber needed renovating anyway."

She stifled a pang of guilt.

"The table is new, and I don't know if you can see"— he picked up the small candelabra on the sideboard and waved it toward the ceiling rife with cherubs and goddesses in chariots—"I had the paintings retouched. I've always been rather fond of that eighteenth century exuberance."

Pretending ease, she halted her slow perambulation and stared upward. "Exquisite exuberance." He didn't answer, and she looked down to see him observing her, specifically her throat. Unbidden, her hand rose to protect her neck, although she didn't know from what. Mr. Throckmorton wouldn't really throttle her, not even for causing such a huge disruption in his plans. Nor would he place his mouth there . . . "What happened to Kiki's mother?" she asked.

He looked faintly startled, then placed the candelabra back and led her toward the picture gallery. "The mother went off to marry, of all people, an Italian opera singer."

"Opera singers are romantic."

"If you like large men who bellow out songs while pretending to be dying." From the curl of his lip, it was clear he found nothing about the opera romantic.

"You have no *amour* in your soul."

"Not a drop."

Which she might have taken as a warning, but she still struggled with the concept of Ellery as a father.

"At any rate, Kiki was left on our doorstep, and nothing has been the same since." He pointed along the extensive length of floor toward the other door. "A new carpet from Persia. Mother assures me it is much in style."

Celeste nodded. "In Paris, also."

"If it is in style in Paris, we must of course have it."

He sounded faintly sarcastic, and Celeste recognized the sound of a man pushed beyond patience by his mother's tenacious redecorating. "The child?" she prompted.

"Oh. Kiki." He seemed more to want to take Celeste on an extended tour than to inform her of her duties. "Kiki is a hellion with no upbringing and no manners. She laughs too loudly, she sings at the table, she acts a tragedy once an hour and a comedy everyday. Nurse-maids flee in the other direction as quickly as they can."

Celeste wanted to laugh at his aggrieved tone. "She sounds charming."

"She is *very* charming. Unhappily, the child is illegitimate and foreign. To live in England, she needs to behave with the utmost propriety. She cannot continue in this fashion lest she ruin her life before it has begun."

He was right, but Celeste at once felt a camaraderie with Kiki. "She must miss her mother."

"Perhaps, but while she's making the rest of us miserable, she's also making Penelope's life miserable." In a clipped tone, he said, "I won't allow that."

"No, of course not." She hesitated, then asked delicately, "Does she find comfort with her father?"

Now Mr. Throckmorton hesitated. "Ellery laughs when she climbs on the table and jumps off the chair. He ruffles her hair when she sings. I find that his attentions make the situation worse."

Ellery *would* notice a child who was rebellious; heaven knew he hadn't noticed quiet Celeste. But in the case of his own daughter, he might realize the harm he was doing . . . and Celeste at once felt ashamed for thinking so.

As she and Mr. Throckmorton entered the foyer, they heard a rustle of silk and a man's murmur to their left. It seemed to be coming from the alcove beneath the sweeping curve of stairs, and Mr. Throckmorton indicated his wish for quiet and hurried Celeste past. When they had entered the library, he said softly, "The liaison between Mr. Monkhouse and Lady Nowell seems to be proceeding apace."

Celeste wasn't shocked; in France, affairs between married partners were treated as normal. But she glanced behind her, then at Mr. Throckmorton. "How did you know who . . . ?"

"I have excellent night vision." In a reflective tone, he said, "As does Mr. Monkhouse, I believe." He gestured around him. "Now in here, I wouldn't allow Mother to change very much. She wanted to replace the chairs with those monstrosities with claw feet and lions' head. I find the room pleasant and frequently read to Penelope here, and I refuse to have the child wake at night with nightmares of alligators and giant cats."

Celeste grinned. The man definitely disliked the disorder surrounding the renovations.

"For one thing, if Penelope has a nightmare, Kiki has one twice as dreadful and we're forced to endure days of histrionics. In French."

"In French?"

"Kiki won't speak English, although she's a bright child and I know she understands us." He grimaced. "You understand the language well, you know our home and how we expect her to behave, and I'm depending on you to return us to serenity."

If the situation was half what Mr. Throckmorton had described, she would have her work cut out for her. "I'll do my best."

"However, I don't want you to think you will be in slavery to the children. The children have a nursemaid, so your duties will be limited to the classroom. And because of Kiki's great excitement at the houseparty, I believe it would be futile to expect you to take over your duties this week—if indeed you ever have to take over those duties to which I summoned you."

"I don't want you to think I am unwilling, sir!"

"Not at all." With a gesture, he indicated she should proceed him down a short, narrow corridor with a set of double doors at the end. "I was not commenting on your eagerness, only on Ellery's good luck in having two beautiful young women competing for his attentions."

"I am not competing for his attentions," she answered with adamant indignation.

"No, one can scarcely call it a competition. As soon as his rash has disappeared, I'm sure you'll no longer have to settle for the poor substitute of his brother."

She shouldn't have made known her disappointment at Mr. Throckmorton's dancing attendance on her, nor voiced her suspicions of his motives. "I never—"

"Nonsense, of course you did. I know exactly how I measure up to Ellery." He pulled a wry face. "It's not been easy growing up with the inevitable comparisons, but I have had the compensation of my work."

She had been rude. She hadn't wanted to hurt his feelings. Indeed, she'd never supposed Mr. Throckmorton capable of feelings. "Really, Mr. Throckmorton, I never meant you to think—"

"Mr. Throckmorton?" He cocked an eyebrow at her. "You used to call me Garrick."

Oddly enough, his comment shocked her more than anything else that had happened in this very curious evening. "I . . . was a child. I didn't know how improper my behavior was."

"I liked it. You were charming, with your big solemn eyes and your diffident smile." He halted beside double doors. "You're still charming, but in such a different way. Your smile, your confidence, your gaiety, your style . . . you've grown into the kind of lady any gentleman would be proud to have on his arm."

She glanced to the side, down to the floor, abashed at having him speak to her in such a manner. In such a tone.

Leaning close, he sniffed. "Your perfume. It's wonderful—a combination of citrus, cinnamon and, I think, ylang-ylang."

She gasped. How had he known?

"I'm sorry. I've embarrassed you." He began to step back.

Impulsively, she caught his hand. She looked into his face. "No! It's not that, it's just I've never thought that you might . . . be . . ."

"Interested in women?"

He smiled, and the smile left her in no doubt that he was, in fact, very interested in women. Amazingly, interested in her. In a voice that caressed her skin like dark velvet, he said, "Dear little Celeste, when I look on you, I think of only one thing." He moved closer.

Wide-eyed, she backed to the wall.

"I think that to kiss you would be one of the delights of my life."

Realization struck her; his marriage might have been a sensible union, but he had put his wife through her paces. Celeste pressed her spine hard against the wall, but the plaster didn't yield. She didn't disappear, only watched with a mixture of consternation and heart-thumping awareness as he leaned down. His lips touched hers. Her eyes fluttered shut. Then she was involved in the stunning sensation of being kissed. By Mr. Throckmorton. And . . . and it wasn't repulsive.

Indeed, quite the contrary.

Twice before, once in England and once in France, stupid men had grabbed at her and kissed her. She had given each of them his chance, been impressed with neither, and had told herself that was because she loved Ellery. Only Ellery could give her the kiss that awakened her passion.

But Mr. Throckmorton threatened to prove that myth wrong. For he provided her with unexpected pleasure. Very . . . unexpected . . . pleasure. His breath washed over her skin, warm, scented with whisky, redolent with sensuality. His lips, smooth and firm, pressed against hers with the utmost subtlety. He adjusted their union, reacting as if her response fascinated him.

Disjointed thoughts flashed through her mind. She ought to slide down the wall and out of this kiss. He was broader than she'd realized. She was aghast at them both. She liked it when he pressed a little more firmly . . . at his gentle increase, her head fell back against the wall. *Mon Dieu,* he could read her thoughts! He knew everything—when goosebumps swept her

skin, when her breathing quickened, when the unfore-
seen rush of blood in her veins brought certain body
parts to tingling awareness.

Still her hands dangled at her side, disengaged from the
activity. The awkward freedom of her hands was the only
way she kept her sanity in this demented moment of . . .
of . . . well, not passion. It couldn't be passion between
her and the grave Mr. Throckmorton. It just couldn't.

He broke the kiss.

She thought he had set her free. And she had not been
completely swept away. Not as long as she'd kept her
head enough to not touch him as she wished.

Then he showed her the true feebleness of her pre-
text. He gripped her waist and pulled her up onto her
toes. Catching her wrists, he brought her palms up and
around to cup his neck. Now she embraced him as fully
as he embraced her, and she couldn't—didn't—remove
her hands. Instead she held him, fingers clutching the
cloth of his formal coat. Pulling her away from the wall,
he bent her over his arm. His chest crushed her breasts,
his body enveloped hers with unfamiliar heat.

He commanded, "Open your lips."

"Why?"

"Very good." His lips moved on hers as he murmured
that praise.

She could taste him. Because he . . . because he slid
his tongue inside her mouth.

He sampled her as if she were a pastry made especially for him. He acted as if she were cream and sugar,
a delectable indulgence. He breathed with her, savored
her, filled her with heat and damp and passion.

She went limp, relying on him to support her, to

guide her, to teach her. Because he did all of those things, and superbly.

Of course. This was Mr. Throckmorton, and he was well known among the servants for his preparation, his knowledge and his patience . . . but Celeste had never heard anyone mention his ardor. Maybe they didn't talk about it. Maybe they didn't know. Maybe no one knew except her, because she was the only woman to incite him.

She tried to shake her head. That way lay madness.

He stopped the movement by catching her chin. He tipped it to the side, baring her throat. His lips slid down, drinking of her skin, raising her expectations and her heart rate. He did things she didn't know she would like until he did them. He nibbled at her earlobe. He caressed the pulse in her neck. He kissed her collarbone.

She began to utter little noises. Not words; words required thought and the ability to form coherent sound. These noises were more like hums and moans—pure sensation given voice.

He rested his lips over her windpipe as if he wished to feel the vibrations, to relish every sensation.

Finally, he lifted his head.

Opening her eyes in bewilderment, she could see only him. In the dim light, his gray eyes seemed black, but large and heart-rendingly solemn. He watched her with an intensity that kept her good sense at bay, for he appeared to see in her a precious sustenance—or his dearest love. With the greatest of care, he helped her stand flat and straight. He steadied her with his elbow under her arm and when she still wobbled, he helped her rest her spine against the wall.

"All right?" he asked.

"Yes." She could barely enunciate, and cleared her throat. "Yes." That was better. Louder. More normal.

"Good. I've arranged to have you placed in this bed-chamber, but just for the first two nights. Your room near your students is not yet prepared."

He had somehow metamorphosed from the impassioned gallant back to the Mr. Throckmorton she knew, and she didn't know whether to be disappointed or relieved.

Well, relieved, of course. She had no business kissing Mr. Throckmorton. Not because he was the master and she the governess, but because she loved Ellery and always had. She was not so flighty as to think that had changed simply because she enjoyed his brother's kisses. True, it had been intimate beyond her experience, but society treated a kiss as nothing more than a greeting. So would she.

A very exhilarating, in-depth greeting.

When she said nothing, he frowned in concern. "I hope you'll forgive the oversight."

She slithered along the wall, anxious to get away before she did something stupid. "What oversight?" Kissing her was an oversight?

"That your room isn't . . ." He frowned yet more, responsible Mr. Throckmorton whose preparations had failed to materialize. "I do apologize. We didn't realize you would come so soon, and with the preparations for the betrothal party, I'm afraid your needs were delayed."

"No. I mean, that's completely acceptable." She groped for the doorknob behind her. "Understandable."

"You'll come to my office in the morning?"

"Yes, Mr. . . ."

He placed his finger over her lips and stared at her in

reproval. "Foolish, to call me Mr. Throckmorton after what we've just shared. But perhaps you didn't enjoy . . . ?"

"No! Yes! It was very nice, very . . . um . . . I did like . . ."

He smiled at her, a luxurious wash of indulgence. "Good."

"Goodnight." She turned the door handle.

"I'll meet with you in the morning."

"As you desire." In her effort not to use his name, she had said just the wrong thing. She stood immobile, stunned at her madness, staring at him as he stared at her.

All trace of his smile disappeared. A lock of dark, disheveled hair fell over his forehead. He bowed, yet never took his gaze from her.

She fled into the bedchamber before she could make yet a bigger fool of herself.

7

"Dear!" An hour later, Lady Philberta bustled into Throckmorton's study, the sounds of the still-boisterous party following her through the door. "I just heard the most amazing gossip."

Cradling a hefty shot of whisky, Garrick turned from the dark window to face his mother. "What would that be?"

"That you were seen walking arm-in-arm through the darkened corridors with a beautiful, mysterious girl."

Satisfaction soothed his stirring conscience. Mr. Monkhouse had spread the rumor with admirable speed. "How is Ellery?"

"Scratching." She looked him over, reading him as she always did. "You felled him, didn't you?"

With false innocence, he asked, "Whatever are you talking about, Mother?"

Her mind leaped to the logical conclusion. "You hid

the strawberries in that pastry. What a mean trick!"

He admitted his guilt without remorse. "But effective. Would you rather he canoodled with Miss Milford all evening long while Lady Hyacinth weeps and Lord Longshaw makes plans to break the Throckmorton family?"

"No, but—" Lady Philberta scratched her neck in unconscious empathy, then hastily lowered her hand. "You're right, of course. Better Ellery hide in his bedchamber all evening than ruin our plans." Moving to one of the straight-backed, hard-seated chairs in front of the desk, she seated herself. "If you'd pour me a ratafia, I would be grateful."

Throckmorton twisted the cork out of one of the bottles on the liquor cabinet and filled a glass. "He doesn't suspect me, and won't. My shock and disappointment in Frau Wieland, who knows better, forced me to bribe her." His lips twisted in a half-smile as he gave Lady Philberta her drink. "She had to go before she announced who ordered the strawberries in the pastries."

"But you love pastries as much as your dear father."

"Into every life a little rain must fall."

"Now what do you have planned?"

He set his chin. "I'm going to seduce the girl."

The silence that followed his pronouncement was prolonged and telling.

"Celeste," he clarified.

Slowly, Lady Philberta rose to her feet. "You?"

"Who else would you suggest?"

"Then this Miss Milford *is* nothing but a gold-digger—"

"I assure you, Mother, she is not. That would be too easy." If she was a fortune hunter, she would have seized on his attentions as an opportunity not to be missed. She would have been interested when he offered her a house in Paris and an annual income. But even when he'd reproved her for leaving him on the dance floor, she had given her apology only grudgingly. The girl was genuine. The situation couldn't be any worse.

Lady Philberta seated herself in another wooden chair, grimaced, and stood again. "Then you can't just ruin the girl."

"I will stop short of any serious seduction. I've already arranged for her tickets back to Paris and the payment at the end of our little affair. She will be grateful."

"Why is she so interested in Ellery?"

"She fancies herself in love with him."

"You can't believe that."

"Moreover, I believe this infatuation is of long standing—although I'm sure at some point she has heard it's just as easy to marry a rich man as a poor man."

Lady Philberta clutched her throat. "Marriage? She can't truly expect marriage!"

"Anything is possible to a dewy young thing like Miss Milford."

Leaning down, Lady Philberta pressed her hand onto the hard seat of the chair against the wall. "Ellery should have been thrashed when he was young."

"It's a little late to come to that realization." Although Throckmorton couldn't have agreed more. "To end this situation will require an act of—"

"Of sacrifice. On your part."

"So I fear. If we could think of anyone else to take the role . . ." He noted how easily his mother moved to sacrifice *him*. She had come to expect that he would rescue Ellery, her, the Throckmorton honor, and anything else that needed rescuing. Restlessly, he moved back to the window that looked out over the gardens. Yet the gardens were unlit, and all he could see was his own dim reflection in the darkened glass.

She settled into the chair behind his desk and leaned back experimentally. "Garrick, this is the only comfortable seat in this room!"

"Discomfort encourages productivity," he answered.

"You are a most unsociable man."

"Not unsociable, Mother—proficient. Which is why I'm too blasted old for this kind of nonsense." Muttering to himself, he said, "Seduction of a young girl."

"Too old? When were you young enough? By the time you were twelve, you had abandoned all spontaneity and made your plodding way through life."

"You forget about India."

"You never told me about India."

He flicked a glance at her. She was an indomitable woman, absolutely trustworthy, intelligent and astute. But she was his mother. She loved him; he knew that just as surely as he knew she would not enjoy a recitation of the trials he'd undergone in India. "There was war," he said curtly. "There was treachery. I killed when I had to. Is that enough?"

Her voice softened. "I suspected as much. You came back . . . changed. But we're not talking about violence here. We're talking about paying suit to a female for the good of the family."

He remembered Miss Milford's glowing face. He knew how rare that kind of joy was in this world; he mourned the crushing of that happiness, that innocence. "How indifferent you sound."

"I am sorry if Miss Milford gets hurt, but think on it, Garrick. We've another rebellion threatening in India—

will the Indians ever realize they are defeated and surrender?—and as always, the Russians do their best to encourage any conflict." Lady Philberta swallowed a good mouthful of ratafia. "Jealous bastards. They already own an empire. Why do they want ours?"

"Because ours is so very, very wealthy."

"Don't be vulgar, dear."

He corrected her. "Practical, Mother. As practical as you."

"Lord Longshaw will provide us with a base in the northern reaches of India."

Throckmorton knew the situation in India even better than his mother. He had spent his time there in exploration, in protracted diplomacy among arrogant warlords and, when all else failed, in grueling battle. Now he no longer physically labored for the good of English— and Throckmorton—interests. Instead, he directed those men and women in the field who strove to secure British dominion over the riches of Central Asia.

"We can't give up those plantations," Lady Philberta said.

"No, but I will be giving up a formidable governess." Moving to the desk, he read from the letter he had been perusing earlier.

I was a widower with two children, and I had married a widow with two children of her own. When Miss Celeste arrived, our schoolroom was in a shambles, my children were aligned against her children, my wife and I were taking sides, and we had no happy home. Then, like an English fairy, she waved her wand over our family and healed every breach. I have offered her much money if she would return with us to Russia, but she says, no, no. She wants to go back to England, and so we wave her a sad farewell and offer her to you, oh most privileged of recipients.

Throckmorton looked up at his mother.

She looked back helplessly. "She sounds perfect. To have peace reign on the third floor once again. She was a good choice, and I know how you hate it when your plans are botched. If only Celeste weren't so damnable pretty!" Her features drooped. "But she is, and we haven't mentioned the issue that is most important, for me at least. Ellery."

"What about him?"

She fixed him with the level, steady gaze. His mother's gaze, which had such power to convey reproof, anxiety, love. "We haven't talked about it, but you know what I mean. I always thought he would get himself straightened out when he got a little older, but he's worse. He's gambling as if he hasn't a care in the world. He's drinking too much. People are starting to talk. He met Lady Hyacinth. I thought he liked her more than he admitted. I thought he might straighten himself out. Now we have the glamorous, forbidden Miss Milford." Walking to him, Lady Philberta stared him right in the eyes. "Do you think you can deceive Miss Milford?"

"I've made a good start tonight."

"Ellery's rash will last only two days at most."

Taking her hand, he patted it reassuringly. "Then in two days, I will think of something else."

Ellery wove slowly through the darkened corridors, bottle clutched tightly in his fist. It was four in the morning. He couldn't sleep. He itched all over. The sounds of revelry had finally died. The last of the guests had disappeared from beneath his window and, deprived of entertainment, he went in search of someone to talk to him, to hold him, to tell him it was all right to be covered in red, scaly splotches that itched like the devil and burned when he scratched. He was sick to death of oatmeal baths; he wanted a gentle hand and a soft voice whispering in his ear.

So he sought Celeste. Sweet little Celeste, the gardener's daughter. Garrick had been sarcastic about that, about her being the gardener's daughter, but when he'd realized that Ellery really loved her, Garrick had done the right thing. Garrick could always be depended upon to do the right thing.

Made a person want to puke.

Not that Ellery didn't like Garrick. Stopping, he lifted a finger and waggled it at some invisible detractor. Good ol' Garrick was his brother, and maybe he was a dead bore and the kind of guy to whom dancing on the table was anathema, but Ellery considered Garrick one of the greatest men in the world. Why, when Ellery had broken out, Garrick had stepped right up and offered to take care of Celeste! Keeping her away from other men who would have paid court to her.

Yes, good ol' Garrick was the best brother in the world.

Celeste had grown up living beside the greenhouse in an apartment she shared with her father. Ellery knew better than to seek her there. Garrick had been anxiously waiting the arrival of this governess, and he'd prepared a suite on the third floor not far from the nursery.

But Ellery hadn't been up to the third floor since . . .

since before his daughter arrived. Grimacing, he hung on the banister and stared up the shadowed staircase.

His daughter. Kiki. He took a long drink of wine. Fiery, voluble, demanding. Just like her mother. Garrick would say—just like Ellery. Maybe so. Maybe she resembled him. He just didn't want to believe that that actress had taken seriously what he poked at her in fun. Having a child almost made him seem like . . . an adult.

Clinging to the banister, he made his cautious way up the stairs, missing only one—the top stair. He went down on his knee, right onto the hardwood. That would hurt tomorrow, but tonight he was fine. Just fine. Rising, he headed down the corridor toward the nursery and the governess's quarters.

Garrick had arranged for the governess to take care of the children, and that was as it should be. Garrick had a child. Garrick had been married. Garrick was an adult. A really, really old, wise, mature adult. But not Ellery. Ellery wasn't responsible. He couldn't get married. Asinine to think he could. And to Hyacinth, of all the women. She wasn't old enough to even know how to kiss. Once he'd pulled her behind an armoire and pressed his lips to hers, and she'd been so nervous her teeth were chattering.

He couldn't marry someone like her! She was a virgin. He might not do it right, and give her a disgust, and he'd be a worse screw-up than he was now.

No, he'd picked a bad time to think he could become responsible. Why should he ever be responsible? He didn't have anything to be responsible for. Maybe if he . . . he braced himself against the wall, tilted his head back and cackled. But no. Stupid.

A frown swiftly followed. Would he see his daughter

up here? Blearily, he looked around. The night candle barely lit the corridor. The doors were closed. Kiki would be asleep. So would Celeste, but he'd sneak into her bedchamber and make his way to the bed . . . he'd done it plenty of times before with other women.

Not that Celeste was like those other women. He truly loved her. He respected her. He wouldn't use her like some trollymog. She'd be glad to see him. She'd hold him close and tell him he looked handsome.

But he wouldn't light a light. No, indeed. Because he looked as if he'd been whipped with seaweed. Lifting his arm to his nose, he sniffed the satin brocade dressing gown. But he didn't smell like it. No. He smelled like breakfast. He thought about that for a moment, then a smile lit his face. Everyone liked breakfast.

Celeste's bedchamber was right ahead. The odor of the fresh paint and wallpaper glue was strong. Good, they must have made it beautiful for his beautiful girl.

He adjusted the lapels on his dressing gown, straightened his shoulders and swigged the last of the wine. With exaggerated care, he placed the bottle on the floor and grasped the doorknob. Opening the door, he confidently stepped inside.

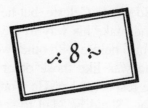

~ 8 ~

"*W*e can never do that again." Celeste spoke the words aloud. She spoke them firmly, calmly, resolutely—to the empty, echoing bedchamber. She pretended she was speaking to Mr. Throckmorton so that when she actually went to his study, she wouldn't falter. And she had to go speak to him. He had commanded it. He wanted to converse about the children . . . oh, but that wasn't why she would go to him. She would go because he had kissed her. His wickedness had her awake all night long, tossing and turning, even though the large bedchamber contained a fire and a warming pan beneath the sheets.

And how had the servants known when she would go to bed, she'd like to know? How had they known when to kindle the fire and warm the sheets?

Mr. Throckmorton must be guilty of every dreadful offense. Of giving Ellery a rash. Of carrying her off. Of kissing her until . . . until she forgot all about how he'd caused Ellery to get that rash. For he surely had. In the bright light of morning, she was sure that rash could not have been so convenient.

Peering into the small mirror, she checked her appearance. She looked tidy, clothed in a gown of serviceable serge. But the gown was the same color as leaves in spring. She knotted a generous length of pale gold ribbon around her waist, tied at the front with its ends trailing down into the folds of her skirt, and threaded a narrow band of the same ribbon through her long braided upswept hair. She wore a gold tiered collar with a scalloped edge to dress up the neckline, and her long sleeves accentuated her slender arms. During her sojourn in Paris, she had learned a great many feminine tricks, not the least of which was to accentuate her features attractively and economically.

Yet the reflection that peered back at her was one of a sensible woman. She had taught four children, lived abroad, visited Italy and Spain, spent summers in Russia at the ambassador's country home. In the process, she had transformed herself from a drab, shy, silly girl to a woman. Nothing should be able to shake her composure . . . and yet dull Mr. Throckmorton had unsettled her on the very first night.

Well, she'd tell him it couldn't happen again. Nothing would ever happen between them again, because she loved Ellery.

She marched out into the dim corridor. She muttered the words while she walked through the library—*We can never do that again*—and reassured herself she sounded both resolute and mature.

Yet her feet dragged as she approached his office through the sunny antechamber. This chamber had been designed for ease, with bookshelves and tall windows and comfortable chairs that welcomed anyone who waited to speak to Mr. Throckmorton. Tiptoeing to the open inner door, she listened but heard no sound. Oh, why did she remember so clearly what had happened last night in the silence of that corridor? When she thought of seeing Mr. Throckmorton, she remembered the taste of him. Other women, women not nearly as sophisticated as she, kissed the occasional gentlemen without succumbing to chagrin. Other women didn't seem to find the act as intimate as she did, but perhaps that was her lack of practice, or perhaps—arrested, she stood with one foot in the air—perhaps Ellery would prove to be a better kisser than his brother. Ellery's kiss would erase the sensation of Mr. Throckmorton's lips on hers.

So she needed to just stride right in there and say, *We can never do that again.*

Instead she knocked on the door frame. "Mr. Throckmorton?" she called. No answer.

Stepping inside, she stood in the middle of the empty office and looked about her. It had been redecorated. Each piece of furniture had been bought with forethought and exquisite good taste, and showed not a bit of Mr. Throckmorton's personality—whatever that might be.

She frowned. Not that she understood Mr. Throckmorton's character. She knew the Garrick of her childhood; the man she met last night didn't seem to be the same man. Mr. Throckmorton had always intimidated her, but after last night she was not intimidated, she was . . . she didn't know what she was. Determined not to be kissed, that was for sure.

Seating herself in the upright wooden chair in front
of the big, shiny desk, she decided that her curiosity
about Mr. Throckmorton was only natural. In Paris, she
had discovered herself to be a friendly woman with a
great deal of vivacity. An absorbing character such as
Mr. Throckmorton would certainly incite her interest.

She found the chair was hard, and placed so that her
back was to the door. She moved to another chair, one
against the side wall, and wondered if she should sojourn to the kitchen for breakfast. Yet she so wanted to
get that conversation out of the way, the one where she
told Mr. Throckmorton . . .

Out in the antechamber, a brief, hushed flurry of
speech caught her attention. Someone, a female, was
upset, almost gasping with dismay and haste. Someone
else, a man, answered. With a start, Celeste realized
they both spoke in Russian, which she understood.

"The Englishman was betrayed. The police picked
him up at the meeting place. They took him away, and
he hasn't been heard from since." The woman spoke in
lower class Russian, just as the ambassador's servants
had.

Shocked, Celeste drew back against the wall. What
had happened? What was the Russian woman talking
about? What was she doing in England?

"Are you sure? You saw this with your own eyes?"
The man used the more aristocratic intonation, but his
Russian was rough and irregular.

"All of it. I, too, might have been caught, but my cab
lost a wheel and I was late."

"A lucky circumstance." The man didn't sound as if
he thought it a lucky circumstance.

"Someone revealed the location," the woman said urgently, gutturally. "That's the only explanation. Stanhope, you must tell the master."

Stanhope! Celeste remembered Stanhope. He had been Mr. Throckmorton's secretary, his companion from his years in India, and as she recalled, they had been very close. Tall, urbane, Mr. Stanhope had combined the reckless air of the adventurer with a British nobleman's self-satisfaction. His brown hair was perfectly cut. His freckles danced across his pale snub nose. His smile charmed men and women alike. He wore clothes well, blending in with the lords of high society and the soberly clad London businessmen who visited so frequently.

"I understand, Ludmilla," Stanhope answered. "I will tell the master. Now you must go rest. You've come a long way, and you must leave as soon as possible."

"I'll see the master before I go?" the woman asked. "So you can tell him exactly what I say?"

Stanhope had not blended with the servants. The kitchen servants all mocked him for his airs and his orders, and more important, her father hadn't liked him. He'd called Stanhope an interfering, high-in-the-instep fool. Celeste had learned to respect her father's judgments.

Right now she didn't like the tone Stanhope used to speak to the poor, shaken woman.

"I don't know if the master has time to see you," he snapped. "He's busy, and no one must know."

"I realize, but—"

"You didn't withhold information, did you?" Stanhope sounded stern.

"No, but I wish—"

"Then you have nothing to fear. I'll speak to him. I'll

tell him everything you said, and all will be well."

The voices were fading, but Celeste clearly heard the woman's anguish. "But so much has been bad, I fear for my life."

"I will handle everything . . ."

They were gone. Celeste sat pressing the back of her head against the wall, trying to comprehend the meaning of the overheard conversation. The master? Mr. Throckmorton? Why should he receive information about an Englishman and his arrest? Why was the woman worried about her life? Why . . . ?

She heard two men walk into the antechamber. The door shut behind them, and Celeste uncomfortably wondered if she should make her presence known.

Stanhope said, "She didn't want to see you. She wanted to go back at once. You know how shy she is."

"I still would see her." Mr. Throckmorton. Of course. "This is serious." It sounded serious. *He* sounded serious.

They must be speaking of the Russian woman.

"She is already gone. She assured me it was a coincidence that our man was taken. That he was simply in the wrong place at the wrong time."

Celeste wondered how much of the conversation between Stanhope and the woman she had missed. Or perhaps . . . Stanhope's Russian was cultured, but not fluent. Perhaps he hadn't understood the nuances. The antechamber door opened.

"Send someone after her," Mr. Throckmorton instructed, his tone imperative. "See if you can stop her. I want to speak to her."

"Yes, sir." There was a slight tap, as if Stanhope had clicked his heels.

The door shut. Celeste hated this, knowing she had to face Mr. Throckmorton and knowing how it looked that she had hidden inside his office and overheard so much. But this reminded her of the intrigues which lurked around every corner in the Russian ambassador's mansion, and there she had learned to face any situation immediately and without embarrassment.

So she stepped out from around the door and, with all the dignity of a woman who knows herself in a difficult position, said, "Mr. Throckmorton? Sir?"

He was walking toward the office, and he didn't pause, didn't start. It was almost as if he had known she was there. He looked straight at her. "Garrick."

She should have known he wouldn't forget. "To speak so informally isn't proper when—"

He stopped right in front of her, his toes touching her hem. "When we're working? When it's daytime?" He leaned closer, his mouth unsmiling but very memorable. "When we haven't kissed?"

When had he learned to be so disconcerting? "Working. Daytime. No kissing. We can never do that again."

He straightened away from her. "Call me Throckmorton."

"Throckmorton."

"Only my mother feels comfortable enough with me to call me Garrick. I was a fool to think you might be"— he sighed—"different."

She didn't think he'd originally planned to say *different*, but she scarcely dared consider other options, such as brave or even compassionate . . . Mr. Throckmorton was a wealthy, busy man. He couldn't be lonely.

Deliberately she turned away from the idea, and the stirring of tenderness it evoked. "Mr. Stanhope didn't understand the woman correctly." Then she realized how very blunt she sounded, and tried to rephrase. "What I mean is, I was sitting in here waiting for you and I heard Mr. Stanhope talking to Ludmilla—"

Mr. Throckmorton strode past her, took his seat behind the desk, and folded his hands. The sun shone through the window behind him, the contrast of light and shadow making him nothing but a dark, still shape. In a tone as chill as the Russian steppes, he said, "Stanhope spoke to Ludmilla last night."

"Oh." Celeste floundered. "I guess . . . I assumed you were speaking of the Russian woman who was just here."

A long pause followed. "Just now, you heard Stanhope speaking to a Russian woman?"

"Just a few moments ago. Out there." She gestured.

Mr. Throckmorton paused again. He stared at her, his gaze so intense it seemed to strip the skin from her flesh. "What did the Russian woman say?"

"That the Englishman had been betrayed and arrested. She had almost been involved, too, but an accident put her there too late. She wanted to speak to you—that is, she wanted to see the master, and I assumed that was you, but Stanhope said no, you were too busy. He sent her somewhere to rest."

"Do you realize what you're accusing Stanhope of?" He shot the question at her.

"Of being unable to comprehend Russian?"

He rose from behind his desk, blotting out the sunshine with the breadth of his shoulders. "Yet if you are right . . ."

"It is a very difficult language." She excused Stanhope. "I went to Russia with the ambassador and his wife. They refused to speak any other language in front of me so I could learn to speak correctly. If not for their insistence, I would probably not understand it at all, for they are fluent in French and English."

He walked to the door. "Wait here."

From the tone in his voice, she knew it was an order.

Throckmorton strode along the corridor toward his mother's bedroom suite, his analytical mind putting together the facts.

FACT:　For the past year, there had been too many missteps in his intelligence organization.

FACT:　The Russians wanted dominion over Central Asia, and for much the same reasons the British did—the wealth of India and the lands beyond was unimaginable.

FACT:　He had to rely on an interpreter, for he couldn't speak Russian.

He gritted his teeth on facing *that* fact. He could solve the most difficult mathematical problem. He understood the nuances of diplomacy. He could outfit an expedition and lead it through the passes of the Himalayas. He could arrange a party, dance a waltz, and kiss Celeste into submission. But he could not speak more than a few words in any language other than his own, and he understood even less. It was his failing. He hated to fail, and he hated even more the position of dependency in which his shortcoming placed him.

Which led him to the next fact: he depended on Stanhope to interpret the messages that came to him in those other languages. Stanhope spoke Russian and German,

French and Italian, Urdu and Hindi. His secretary had the talent for languages which Throckmorton did not. It was that which first attracted Throckmorton to him.

FACT: Celeste had worked for the Russian ambassador for three years.

Celeste could be a spy.

He rapped firmly on Lady Philberta's door. His mother's maid, Dafty, opened the door, prepared to yell at the interruption, but paused when she saw him. Dafty was not in his service. She worked solely for his mother as her lady's maid. She ran errands and performed missions most women would have shuddered to imagine. Dafty shuddered about nothing; the elderly Englishwoman showed a constant and invaluable steadiness of nerves.

She curtsied. "Sir?"

"I must speak to your mistress at once."

She disappeared into the depths of the suite. He heard her speak, then almost at once she returned. "She's finishing her toilette, sir, but she says ye can go in."

He followed Dafty into the dressing room, and there saw his mother clad in her dressing gown, her face bare of cosmetics, her hair straggling around her shoulders. Now, at this moment, she looked every day of her age, and she reminded him of a sailing vessel stripped of its sails, awkwardly bobbing at anchor.

"What problem is so important it can't wait?" She sounded calmly interested.

"The problem is Celeste."

Her eyebrows shot up. "You can't handle her?"

"It's not that. She says Stanhope lied about a message given me today."

"She said that?"

Dafty patted a powder puff over Lady Philberta's
cheeks.

As the talc flew, Lady Philberta sneezed.

"Not exactly. She said Stanhope didn't understand
Russian well."

"Of course, she would speak it." Lady Philberta nodded. "How does she know . . . ?"

"She was in my office." He explained the situation as
Dafty finished Lady Philberta's coiffure. When he had
finished speaking, she took the rouge pot away from
Dafty and said to her, "Dear, would you run and see if
you can find Ludmilla within the house? We badly need
to speak to her."

Dafty curtsied.

"Make haste," Lady Philberta added. "And don't let
Stanhope see you."

With a quiet competence that lent weight to Lady
Philberta's faith in her, Dafty left the room.

"The Russians have found you out. Well, you've co-
ordinated the matter of Central Asia for four years.
That's as long as anyone can expect to go undetected,"
Lady Philberta said philosophically.

"It happens to us all, so they tell me." Annoyed with
the timing, but knowing no time would have been a
good time, he held himself very still and thought. "We'll
have to increase the guards around the estate."

"The children." Lady Philberta rested her hand over
her heart. "Given a chance, the Russians will not hesitate to take Penelope or Kiki and use them to extract
sensitive information from you."

He'd already thought of it, and an unfamiliar fear roiled in his belly. "The children will have a bodyguard at all times, not just when they're outside." No precaution was good enough, but he had picked his men with care. He would speak to them, ascertain that their loyalties had not wavered as he feared Stanhope's had done. "If Dafty finds Ludmilla, how will we speak to her? We'll have to send for a translator. You have no gift for languages, either."

"Yes, and I'm sorry I passed that trait on to you." She placed a beauty mark near her mouth. "If we find her, I fear we must agree Stanhope has lied to us."

"Why? Why would he lie to us? Why would he . . . betray everything we have worked for, everything we hold sacred?"

"Money." She waggled her head. "Dear, I know he is your friend, but consider. When you secured him a place at university, he didn't have the patience to finish the course to become a barrister. When you handed him the stewardship of the estates, he proved incompetent to deal with the accounts. And his romantic misadventures rival Ellery's."

"Yet he's been with me for years, a faithful and indispensable servant to me and the British Empire. He traveled with me to the most horrendous outposts in the most primitive of lands. He proved utterly reliable during negotiations with rajahs and hostile officials."

Leaning toward the mirror, she dabbed rouge on her cheekbones and smoothed it with her fingertips. "Yes, but I've known other men who were grand adventurers, but were never able to settle down to the reality of everyday living. Stanhope is getting older, and despite a promising start, he's nothing more than your secretary."

"We climbed the Rohtang Pass. We survived an avalanche." Throckmorton raked his fingers through his well-ordered hair. "We drank curdled yak milk together."

She sighed impatiently.

His friend's betrayal tore at Throckmorton's guts. "Mother, he saved my life."

Her fingers hesitated over the charcoal pencil. "Did he?"

"In an ambush. He took a knife meant for me."

"How many years ago?" she asked with pointed significance.

He turned to the window to wrestle with his doubts.

"His father was a baron. His mother was an earl's daughter and one of the coldest women I ever met. He was raised among the *ton*, and expected to take his place with the finest when his father lost it all in a single game of whist and shot himself." Lady Philberta sounded completely analytical as she stepped into her dressing room and called, "You're respected. You're wealthy. And you have a family, albeit a difficult one."

"Parts of it." He heard the rustle of silk.

"You appear to have everything. He resents you."

"Yes, but what appears on the surface to be perfect, is not, and he knows my secrets. He knows the hours I work. On my instructions, he's gone to pay off Ellery's lovers." Throckmorton offered up Celeste as a sacrifice. "Celeste could resent the family's success, also. The gardener's daughter could be the Russian spy."

"She could be."

He found little comfort in the lush, civilized prospect below him. "But you don't believe it's likely?"

"No, but I've been in this business for forty-seven

years." Lady Philberta walked back into the room. "Nothing is impossible."

Throckmorton pinched the bridge of his nose. That was not the answer he'd been looking for. He'd wanted assurances, but his mother, former operative for the British network, could scarcely give him that.

"We should not underestimate the Russians' acumen. Wiser men than you have fallen for a pretty face. They could hope to trap you."

He faced his mother. "But to send Celeste, when her activities these past four years were so well known! It doesn't make sense. It doesn't make sense that she would return to disgrace her father. It doesn't make sense that she would make a play for Ellery when I'm the great prize."

Lady Philberta's silver georgette tea gown billowed behind her. Her white hair was gathered at her neck, and wings swooped down to cover her ears. She now moved like a graceful ship at full sail.

As always, he marveled at the transformation.

Pausing by the chair, she gathered a cashmere shawl and draped it around her shoulders. "Where is she now?"

"In my office, awaiting my pleasure." He winced. A bad choice of words.

Lady Philberta kindly ignored it. "One must always consider that she may have manipulated the situation to get to you. She *is* in *your* office."

"The Russians would be fools to depend on her beauty to cloud my judgment."

She laughed at him in open amusement. "You're insulted that they might think you could be susceptible."

The day had started badly and was disintegrating rapidly, and he thought he knew who he could blame for his vexation. "Ever since she appeared yesterday . . ."

With difficulty, Lady Philberta sobered. "You can't blame it all on Miss Milford."

"That's true. I can blame Ellery, too."

In her most severe tone, she said, "I would say you'll suffer no complications from Ellery today."

"Come, Mother, you can't imagine I could foresee that disaster in the bedchamber!"

"I think you foresee more than you say."

"He wasn't hurt."

"Seriously." She held up a hand to halt any further protestations. "No matter, dear. It's done. As long as you've got Ellery handled, we can concentrate on this Stanhope predicament." She walked to the door.

"Ellery is handled," he said. Celeste waited in his office, a woman who, if she was not the seducer, would be seduced.

9

Celeste was nodding over a book that she'd pulled from Mr. Throckmorton's bookshelf when she'd heard his footsteps. She scrubbed at her cheeks to clear away that drowsy sensation, then rose and faced the open door.

"Celeste!" He moved toward her with a smooth, flowing gait.

He no longer looked grim, and although he wasn't Ellery—she'd never seen a man as handsome as Ellery—he conveyed strength and confidence with every motion. Her comments about Mr. Stanhope's linguistic skills had caused greater unrest than she'd realized, but she felt sure Mr. Throckmorton would handle the situation. He was the kind of man who handled every situation.

Indicating the book in her hand, he said, *"Oliver Twist.* What do you think?"

"I don't like it."

A slow smile blossomed on his face. "Really? Why?"

"It's overwritten and slow, and Oliver is such a little martyr it's hard to care whether he survives or not." Remembering that the volume was his, and probably a favorite, she added, "But I'm sure it will get better as I read."

"Don't bother." He plucked it from her grasp. "I had earlier judged you a woman of uncommon sense. It's good to have my opinion confirmed."

His frankness and lack of tact made her want to laugh out loud, but somehow, in the light of day, shared laughter seemed more dangerous than a shared kiss. So she watched him gravely. "What about the woman? Did you find her?"

He sealed her lips with his finger. "Forget about her. The matter is taken care of. In fact I would prefer that you not mention her again. Not to anyone. Promise me."

She nodded, but her mind raced. How intriguing. Mr. Throckmorton apparently thought Stanhope had deliberately misinterpreted the woman's words, but why?

"Stop thinking about that," Mr. Throckmorton insisted. He pressed his finger more firmly against her lips—he seemed to like touching her lips—then lifted it away. "It's not important. Let's talk about . . ."

"That we can never do *that* again." He hadn't responded last time she'd said it, so she faced him with her chin raised. "It wasn't right. I realize it was only a spontaneous response to the dim light and the music, and nothing to cudgel ourselves over, but I feel I must make my position clear."

His eyebrows lifted during her speech, and remained at a questioning high. "Pardon me, my dear, but—your position on what?"

"That kissing!"

The eyebrows descended. They were rather nice eyebrows, bushy and dark over gray eyes rimmed with dark eyelashes, but Celeste found herself disconcerted by the fact he could transmit opinions through their use. Right now he was diverted, and she waited for the rather condescending comment about how she made too much of a simple salutation.

But he didn't say that. He said, "*I* was hoping to discuss Ellery."

"Ellery?"

"You remember Ellery. My brother? Tall"—he measured a height just below his own—"handsome, light on his feet?"

Throckmorton suffered a rather nasty tendency toward sarcasm. "Yes, *I* was hoping to see Ellery today."

Throckmorton's expression never changed. "As you wish, but he won't like it."

"I don't mind viewing a few blotches."

"It's more than a few blotches, now." Throckmorton cleared his throat. "Ellery suffered a bit of a catastrophe last night. I think every one of the servants on the upper floor heard it."

She caught her breath in dismay. "What kind of catastrophe? Is he . . . ?"

"He wasn't badly hurt." Throckmorton seemed to be having difficulty maintaining his gravity. "In the dark, he wandered into the wrong bedchamber. He crashed into a mélange of paste and old paint, and brought down a ladder and newly hung drapes. Scared the good sense out of the housekeeper, and the nursery maids screamed so loud they woke the children."

"He was in the nursery?"

"A bedchamber beside the nursery. Now, in addition

to taking oatmeal baths, his valet is having to cut bits of wallpaper out of his hair, he's wearing a sling and he's limping. Luckily, the paint came off straight away, but it has made patches of his skin turn blue."

"Blue?"

Throckmorton gestured, helpless to describe the color. "That blue one gets when the laundry accidentally puts blue stockings in with the white linens."

Sadly, Celeste struggled against the appalling urge to laugh, too. "Oh, dear." In dismay, she cleared her throat. Laughing! About Ellery! With Mr. Throckmorton! This would never do. "I wish to make myself very clear." She tilted her chin at him and braced herself. "I plan to marry Ellery."

He blinked as if her vehemence astonished him. "Well . . . yes. I thought that's what all the fuss was about. Which reminds me, I want you to come to the garden tea today."

"Don't change the subject. I can make Ellery love me, and . . ." His meaning struck her. "Tea? In the gardens?" Teas were a Throckmorton tradition every day the family was in residence, and in the summer the garden teas served both the famous and the infamous in government and society. Lady Philberta was justly celebrated for their elegance, their variety, and the liveliness of the company. Her father was justly celebrated for the beauty of the setting. Certainly never before had the gardener's daughter been invited to do more than serve. "Why . . . was this Ellery's idea?"

With a stern quirk of his brow, Throckmorton said, "I control shipping and interests around the world. I'm in charge of plantations in the East and the Americas. Do you think me unable to plot the simple coup of positioning you to take the *ton* by storm?"

She wet her lips. "I didn't realize—"

"That I managed so many interests?"

"That you were positioning me to take the *ton* by storm."

"Something must be done. Ellery charged me to take care of you. I've considered every course, and I believe you would be more comfortable meeting everyone at tea than at a formal supper." He took her hand and patted it. "You must do as you like, of course, but if I could presume to advise you?"

She nodded, her thoughts racing to her bedchamber where her wardrobe waited. What did she have that was appropriate for an English garden tea?

He continued, "I wouldn't immediately mention my relationship to Milford."

Her mind returned to this room as she considered whether to take offense. "Mr. Throckmorton, he's my father and the best gardener in England. I'm proud to be his daughter."

"As he's proud of you. I'm simply suggesting that once the *ton* has taken you to their bosom—and with your style and wit, they will—they will be hard pressed to deny you for any reason. It's for Ellery's sake I propose this. He would not like to be shunned."

Throckmorton presented her with a potent blend of flattery, reality, and dream come true, and Celeste found herself both excited and frightened. "Thank you for your guidance. I will try to do as you suggest."

"But?"

"But if I'm asked I will acknowledge my background."

"Of course. Never lie. It makes it too difficult to re-member to whom you told what. Now come." He tossed the book aside. "I'll take you to Ellery's chamber."

He turned her hand in his, holding it as a lover might, and tugged her along. Her palm tingled where his palm rested, and her fingers twitched as if nerves jumped be-neath her skin. She pulled back a little, wanting to take a stand against this intimacy, but before she could object, he placed her hand on his arm.

The walk through the house was fraught with imped-iments, most in the form of the few guests who had risen before noon to wander the corridors in search of break-fast. Each person stopped to greet Throckmorton and be introduced to Celeste. He did so with grace and ease. When the guest would have probed into her back-ground, Throckmorton excused them by saying they had promised to visit poor Ellery.

Celeste didn't know how she and Throckmorton looked together; she only knew how the guests gazed at them. Speculatively. Surely they didn't think . . . but it didn't matter what they thought. They would discover the truth soon enough. In the meantime she would see Ellery.

Ellery, whom she really truly loved. Ellery, who she had declared she would marry. And Throckmorton's re-action had been . . . underwhelming. She'd been braced for a fight, and he had just shrugged and agreed. She should be experiencing jubilation. Instead, she felt wary. Uncertain. A bit deflated.

Throckmorton had taken the news so well, and she couldn't help but wonder . . . why?

They traversed the passageways, climbed the stairs,

and came at last to the door at the end of a broad corridor.

Throckmorton nodded to her.

She knocked and called, "Ellery, it's me, Celeste!"

At first she heard nothing. Then the knob slowly turned, and the door creaked open no more than two inches.

"Celeste?" Ellery's voice sounded earnest, manly. "Darling, is that you?"

She pressed her hands to the wood. "Ellery, I came to see you."

"Not while I look like this."

For some reason, she glanced at Throckmorton. He stood still and quiet, his face totally without expression. But his eyebrows must have been expressing an opinion again, for she sensed censure. Very well; Ellery was vain. But at least he had something to be vain about. She spoke to the door. "I don't care what you look like."

"The splotches are getting better. Soon I'll be able to see you again." He hesitated. "My hair may be cut in a new and original coiffure . . ."

"I don't mind." She didn't mention that Throckmorton had told her why.

"And I've developed a limp."

"I just want to see you." She dared not admit it aloud, but she wanted rescue from the constantly hovering presence of Ellery's brother.

"Throckmorton, are you there?" Ellery asked.

"I'm here." Throckmorton sounded reassuring.

"You're taking care of Celeste as you promised?"

"I am."

"There you go, Celeste," Ellery crooned. "Throckmorton has promised to care for you as you deserve, and Throckmorton always keeps his promises. You do what he tells you and go where he says. I vow you'll be safe with him."

Throckmorton touched her arm and indicated they should leave.

She pressed her hands harder on the door, feeling the weight of Ellery against the paneling, wanting to feel the reality of Ellery beneath her palms. "I wish . . ."

"I wish, too, darling," Ellery said. "Go with Throckmorton, and I'll see you tomorrow."

Throckmorton put his arm around her waist and drew her away.

She wanted to refuse to go, but how foolish. To demand to be allowed to stay and talk to a door. To insist that Ellery, obviously unwilling, continue to communicate with her when he would rather soak in an oatmeal bath or sit with his injured leg up.

"Farewell." Her voice failed in a most distressing manner.

"Farewell, my darling. Have a care for yourself." Ellery sounded warm and sincere, but the door clicked firmly and he was gone.

She stumbled on the carpet runner in the corridor.

Throckmorton supported her with his hand under her arm. "You heard Ellery. You must have a care for yourself. It wouldn't do to get hurt."

"No." She felt cross and out of place. Nothing was going as it should. She felt at odds with herself, not sure if she belonged in the garden, the drawing room or the schoolroom. She knew where her father would say she belonged. She knew where she insisted she belonged.

She glanced sideways at the man who held her arm.

But what would Throckmorton say? He was a mystery to her; apparently an ally, yet . . . yet he wasn't the man she remembered. The man she remembered had used the force of his personality to make her attend the Governess School. He had insisted she would adjust, that the experience would be good for her, and assured her if she didn't like it after the training was done, he would personally come to escort her back to Blythe Hall.

Of course, he'd been right. She had loved London, loved being part of a crowd of girls just like herself, and loved adventure.

But now . . . well, now she was home and feeling out of place.

What should she do? How could she find herself?

They neared the landing where the grand stairway descended and the smaller stairway rose toward the third floor. It was there she discovered her answer. She announced, "It's time for me to meet the children."

This time Throckmorton stumbled. "The children?"

"My charges. That *is* why I came to visit you this morning."

"So it is." He hesitated. "Yet I wish you to prepare for the garden tea."

"The garden tea isn't for another four hours."

Taking her arm, he guided her toward the ground floor. "Listening to you talk to Ellery, it reminded me again of the importance of a good impression at the garden tea. Take whatever maids you wish to help you ready yourself."

She looked back at the staircase. "But the children!"

"It would be better if we don't introduce you just yet. Not until we discover what your true role will be."

"But—"

"I can't lie to you. The tea today may be difficult, filled with the pitfalls society creates to distinguish those who belong with those who don't. When you appear today, I want you to be rested, freshened, bathed and fed." At the corridor leading to her bedchamber, he bowed. "Your beauty, of course, accompanies you everywhere."

He left her standing there, staring after him, unhappy and confused.

What oddness had gotten into usually urbane Mr. Throckmorton? Why didn't he let her meet the children?

"Father, do you think Throckmorton is deranged?"

Milford looked up from his planting to see his daughter, the light of his life, standing beside him with a fancy tray and an anxious expression.

So. It had started already.

"I brought you your dinner," she added.

"Thank ye, daughter." He placed the trowel to the right of the azalea—he always placed it there, for trowels had a way of disappearing—stripped his gloves from his hands, then stood and stretched the kinks out of his back. He was probably too old to be doing the shovel and weed work, but he liked to get his hands in the Suffolk rich peat. He knew Celeste understood.

Ah, she understood a lot of things about him. How he'd mourned her mother. How he worried about her. What she didn't understand was herself and her place in the world, and his heart ached when he thought of how hard she would fall when all was said and done. But no one knew better than him that a young person had to learn their lessons on their own.

"Deranged, is it?" He accepted the tray. "Throckmorton, is it?"

"He told me to call him that," she said defensively.

"No, I mean . . . thought you'd be talking about Mr. Ellery."

"Oh." Celeste twitched at her skirts. "Mr. Ellery has a rash from strawberries."

"Does he?" Seating himself on the stone bench under the willow tree's drooping branches, Milford looked at the tray in his hands. Esther had sent him a round of bread, slices of Stilton cheese, dried apples baked in a pie, a crock of ale. Apparently the cook hadn't had time to send out her usual elaborately arranged supper, with its sliced bread and carved furbelows of cheese. Maybe the job was getting to be too much for her. "A silly sort of complaint."

"He's itching!"

"Bet he won't let anyone see him, hm?" Milford nodded at her betraying huff. "Got a bit of conceit, does our Mr. Ellery."

"With reason."

The sunshine flickered through the leaves and onto Celeste as she stood there looking so much like her mother Milford cleared a catch in his throat. "Sit with me. Share my tray."

She sat with a flounce of her skirts.

Aye, she acted like her mother, too. All female and indignation while a man had no idea what he'd done. Tearing off a chunk of bread, he offered it to her.

Taking it, she nibbled on the end. "I thought you'd be

helping arrange the garden." She gestured across the lawn and toward the knoll where dozens of maids and footmen could be seen scrambling to prepare for the tea.

"Done my part. Flowers are in full glory." He didn't have to look to see the zigzag of hedges, walks and walls that led up to the top of the hill. There, sometime in the last century, some fool with too much time and money had built a castle. Oh, not a real castle. Not even a useable building. It had been constructed to look like a ruin. The rich folks called that kind of castle a gothic trifle, and just thinking about it made Milford want to snort.

But seeing that it served as the centerpiece of the garden, he did what he could with it. Ivy grew over the stones. Here and there he'd planted a few wild roses to climb and provide color in spring, and yellow honeysuckle to give off a sweet scent. The rich folks liked it, climbing the steps and sitting on the benches to take in the prospect of the gardens all about and the countryside beyond.

It was the gardens below that made Milford's heart swell with sinful pride. Each little walled garden bloomed with a profusion of scents and colors. Each walk was a pleasure, with oaks to provide shade and plants to please the eye and nose. And in the large central garden where even now the workers set up tables . . . why, there his gift for placing the flowers where they could reach for the sun or snuggle into the earth truly shone. Aye, the rich folks would be all over his garden today, the men stomping about with their big cloddish feet, the women shredding the blossoms with swipes of their wide skirts. They would exclaim at the splendor, and that was what he lived for.

He took a bite and admitted it was as excellent as ever. Esther fixed a fine loaf, dark and dense, just the way he liked it. She knew it, too. That was the problem with that woman. She knew her worth all too well. No need for a man to praise a woman like that. Not with her always praising herself.

There was some who would say she was a fine figure of a woman: about his age, tall, raw-boned, with a generous flesh spread about in pleasing proportions. Her hair was red peppered with gray, and her hands showed the results of years of labor in a kitchen. She wasn't pretty; no, he'd have to argue with anyone who said she was. But when she smiled, she could make a man forget those features and want to bask in her gladness. Too bad she smiled so seldom at him.

He chewed slowly, swallowed, and decided he didn't care. Celeste's hand sneaked across to take a slice of cheese, and his mind returned to her opening question. "I think Mr. Throckmorton's as sharp a man as they come. What makes ye think him deranged?"

"Lots of things." Her fingers threaded together. "He danced with me last night."

Milford looked at her sideways. "Ye're a pretty girl."

"Does he usually dance with pretty girls?"

"Usually talks business night and day."

She nodded. "There you have it. He spoke to me of dancing and Paris. He took me on a tour of the house."

"Wanted ye away from that party and Mr. Ellery."

"No, he did it because of the rash, and because Ellery asked him to."

Milford nodded again. "That's what I said."

"So you think he somehow gave Ellery that rash? That's what I thought, too." She swallowed.

He wanted to comfort her, but he didn't know how. He'd already told her what he thought of this plan to catch Mr. Ellery. She'd heard him. She wouldn't want to hear it again, but he supposed that was why she was here now. To hear more sense from him. Different sense.

"I was supposed to meet the children this morning," she said.

"Ye are the governess."

"Instead, Throckmorton decided I should spend the time getting ready for the garden tea."

Good ale. Esther couldn't lay claim to making the ale, and he'd wager that got her goat. "Ah, what are ye doing for the garden tea?"

"Oh." Celeste arranged her skirts again. "He invited me."

Milford stopped eating. "He? Mr. Throckmorton? He invited ye?"

"So you see, Papa, it's not so unlikely as you think, that I should dance and eat and be with Ellery." She smiled at him saucily.

But he saw the uncertainty beneath her smile. "Mr. Ellery going to be there?"

Her face drooped.

Milford ate a bite of the pie. Apparently the rush in the kitchen hadn't disturbed Esther's hand with the crust. He hated to admit it, but she made the flakiest he'd ever eaten. Too bad her tongue was so sharp, and she was always honing it on him.

Celeste gazed out over the gardens. "Throckmorton seems much more pleasant than I remember."

Milford paused, his hand halfway to his mouth. "Mr. Throckmorton?"

"He seems lonely, too, and rather wistful."

"The elder brother?" Milford clarified.

"The only reason I can propose that he didn't want to introduce me to the children this morning is just what he said—that he is so concerned that I make a good impression at the tea, he wants me to take my time getting ready."

Milford tried to interrupt, and never had his slow speech served him so poorly.

In full flight, she continued. "It's rather delightful, when you think about it, although not a bit flattering. I'm able to get ready in less than an hour. All I have to do is change gowns. In the meantime, I shall go meet the children on my own. He shall see what an efficient woman can accomplish."

By the time Milford managed to form a protest, Celeste had kissed him on the cheek and hurried toward the house.

Shaking his head, he wished he could bear the pain he saw looming in her future. But there was no cure for it. She had hard truths to learn, and he couldn't learn them for her.

10

"By George, Throckmorton, there's that comely young woman with whom you've taken to traversing the corridors, and she's holding two moppets by the hand."

Colonel Halton's comment pulled Throckmorton out of his enthusiastic discussion of the potential for aluminum in paint and jewelry—he owned part of the refinery—and right back to the garden where his mother's tea was taking place. The gravel on the walk crunched beneath his feet as he turned to see Celeste, framed in the arbor flagrant with white climbing roses—and as far away from him as it was possible to be in the sprawling main garden.

She held Penelope and Kiki by their hands.

By Jove. Not four hours before, he'd given instructions . . .

"The children are . . . yours?" Lord Ruskin asked.

Throckmorton ignored the implied query. He had instructed the servants that Miss Celeste was to get ready for the tea. Nothing else, he'd said. The garden tea must take priority. The servants had glowed when he'd given his commands, imagining that he supported Celeste's foolish scheme to marry Ellery. He'd even felt guilt about raising himself in their eyes when he meant to trip her up.

But those servants believed Celeste could do no wrong. None of them would think anything of her taking the children to the garden tea.

Well. She'd done the children no harm, so perhaps she wasn't a spy.

Instead, she had brought Ellery's illegitimate child to the garden tea to parade before the *ton* in an obvious attempt to ruin his betrothal.

Throckmorton would not allow that to happen.

Turning back to the gentlemen, he smiled the kind of smile that frightened his servants. "Excuse me." Although it gave him a chill to do it, he clapped his hovering secretary on the shoulder. "Stanhope can fill you in on the other wonders of aluminum, and my ideas to expand the plant."

Stanhope bowed to the assembled gentlemen. He handled situations like this with aplomb, blending in with the lords of high society as well as the London businessmen with whom Throckmorton dealt. A great many people—oh, admit the truth—all people enjoyed Stanhope's company more than Throckmorton's.

People were a lot of silly cows.

Looking at that familiar, friendly face, Throckmorton could scarcely believe Stanhope was capable of any misdeed, much less . . . no, it didn't seem possible. "Stanhope is my right hand. Ask him anything you wish." Sketching the briefest of bows, Throckmorton threaded his way along the paths and through the chatting guests toward Celeste. He really must turn her back before too many people saw the children.

Too late. The youthful Viscount Blackthorne stepped into Celeste's path. Celeste dimpled and curtsied. She leaned down and spoke to the children.

They curtsied obediently, Kiki with a flourish that showed off her beruffled purple gown, Penelope neatly and efficiently.

The arrival of an illegitimate child did not require an announcement, so most of the guests must wonder about Kiki's identity. What was Celeste saying about the child?

He glanced toward Lord and Lady Longshaw and Hyacinth. They stood staring at Celeste and the children. Now was no time for them to discover Kiki's existence, not when they were feeling uncertain about Ellery's affections.

Unfortunately, everyone would speculate about both the children and the reason for their appearance. Children did not come to the garden tea. Tea was an adult activity, filled with adult conversation and adult cuisine.

He glanced toward his mother for help, but she sat in the midst of her cronies with her back to him.

Celeste and the children took a few steps, Lord Blackthorne speaking animatedly to them.

The twice-widowed Earl of Arrowood leaped like a gazelle across a low hedge to place himself in Celeste's path. The appropriate courtesies were exchanged. Kiki did a little dance of impatience, tugging at Celeste's hand. Penelope stood quietly, her practical dark blue gown and plain pinafore a reproach to all the gauze and lace of the assemblage.

The little group moved forward, Lord Arrowood now also trailing in Celeste's wake. With Celeste's beauty, her accent, her open smile, of course she would attract the gentlemen, especially in such an informal setting where they could take the liberty of introducing themselves.

Throckmorton, who traveled a path parallel to Celeste's yet had no intention of leaping hedges from one path to another, didn't stand a chance of catching Celeste and the children before they swept right through the middle of the party. But he had to reach them soon, before disaster struck. *What explanation was she giving for Kiki?*

Celeste wore a vibrant rose-colored gown which brought the glow of sunrise to her complexion. A broad, old-fashioned lace collar swooped around her neckline and equally broad cuffs encircled her tiny wrists. The width of the skirt emphasized her trim waist, and the fit of the bodice emphasized her firm bosom . . .

Throckmorton broke off his thoughts. He should not be noticing Celeste's complexion, her waist or her bosom. He should be concentrating on what to do at this unusual turn of events, and he should be noting the obvious—that Celeste owned beautiful, expensive gowns far beyond the reach of a governess's wages. Surely that was a sign of complicity with the Russians.

"Mister . . . Throckmorton?"

He ignored the uncertain call from behind him, concentrating all his attention on Celeste and her ever-greater retinue.

Fingers tugged at his elbow. "Or . . . um . . . Garrick?"

"What?" he snapped impatiently as he swung around—and found himself facing Hyacinth.

She leaped back at his tone, her eyes the same bruised violet color of a hyacinth blossom.

"Oh. Lady Hyacinth." *Too fragile,* he thought. *Too easily hurt. I'm going to kill my brother.* "I'm sorry. I had something on my mind."

"Yes, you were following that girl," Hyacinth said in a rush. "I thought maybe I could come with you."

Another complication in an already complicated state of affairs. "Why?"

She looked taken aback. "Well, I thought I could join the other young people rather than stay with my parents."

"Yes!" He didn't have time to talk her out of it. "Jolly good idea." And she probably needed distraction from her worry over her betrothal. "Take my arm!"

With a shy smile, she did. "Thank you. I love my parents, but sometimes they are rather dull. But they trust me with you, because you are—" She stopped, her eyes wide and horrified.

He marched her forward at a great rate. "Almost as dull as they are," he finished for her. For some reason, her assessment annoyed him, although why it should he didn't know. He prided himself on being pragmatic. He couldn't complain because a foolish young woman perceived him as tedious.

Ahead of them, Lord Featherstonebaugh tottered right in front of Celeste. Ellery's godfather fancied himself an elder roué, irresistible to girls, and the girls thought him harmless and even encouraged him while Lady Featherstonebaugh rolled her eyes and made comments about old fools.

Celeste listened while he spoke, then gestured to the children and gave some kind of explanation.

Lord Featherstonebaugh stepped back with a bow, a

rueful smile playing across his wrinkled lips.

Celeste had charmed another one even as she dismissed him.

"Stupid old gaffer," Throckmorton muttered.

Hyacinth ignored him, her gaze fixed on Celeste. "She's so pretty. Who is she?"

"She is Miss Celeste Milford. She has but recently returned from Paris."

"Of course. That explains her stylish air." Hyacinth's voice was rife with admiration. "Her clothes are not quite the thing for England, but she sports an élan I've not seen in the other girls." She hesitated. "If I could be so bold, brother . . . I heard that she has your favor."

He almost sagged with relief. So he had done one thing right. Hyacinth did indeed believe that he, not Ellery, was involved with Celeste. "As you said, she is very pretty," he said in a neutral tone.

They turned a corner so that at last they were following Celeste, but Throckmorton couldn't see her through the throng. They were headed up toward the knoll, toward the silly, tumbled-down castle which crowned his land. This was not the way he had planned Celeste's debut. This wasn't the way he'd intended it should proceed. He'd imagined she could stay by his side, cling to his arm, silent and uncertain in the new environment. Instead, with all the attention she attracted, she might have been a visiting dignitary. The tea might have been in celebration of her, a possible spy and certain seductress, rather than of poor little Hyacinth.

He glanced down at the girl on his arm. "Are you enjoying the party?"

"Well, I . . . it's lovely, of course, everything as it should be, except Ellery . . ."

Dear Lord, her lower lip was quivering!

"Yes. Dreadful shame about the strawberries and the other accident." He heard her gasp. No wonder her father was so protective. She was so open, so honest, so vulnerable. If she was going to survive in the cutthroat world of high society, she should learn to guard herself and her reactions.

"What other accident?"

His shoulders clenched, and he fumbled for his handkerchief just in case she took to sobbing. "He took a bit of a tumble, that's all."

"Oh, dear." She glanced backward. "I should go to him."

"He won't talk to you. Only through the door. But . . . yes, later, you should go talk to him." He didn't know what to do with a girl who loved Ellery and wanted to marry him. Well, he did, but he couldn't romance *Hyacinth*. "The dear boy's feeling neglected." In fact, Throckmorton relished the thought of his brother dealing with a tearful girl. Let Ellery handle a little of his own mess.

She lowered her voice to a whisper. "He won't . . . he won't see me?"

"But he'll talk to you."

"Then I will go to him," she said, her voice alive with resolution.

"But after the tea," Throckmorton said. "This is, after all, in honor of you."

As they climbed, he lost sight of the little group surrounding Celeste. Turning a corner, he saw the path was clear, but off to the side he heard a squeal of glee.

"A swing!" Hyacinth sounded as excited as Kiki. "I love swings."

She hadn't yet journeyed too far from childhood, Throckmorton realized. Detaching herself from him, she hurried forward.

Placed on a flat spot between two jumbles of rock, hung from the sturdy frame painted white, and overhung with trees, the board and rope swing was every child's dream. Throckmorton remembered it well from his youth. Now Kiki had already commandeered it. Kiki with her blonde curls and her big blue eyes, her olive skin and her flashing smile. *What explanation had Celeste given for her?*

His eyes narrowed at the sight of Penelope standing off to the side, her hands folded before her, patiently waiting her turn. With her straight brown hair and her direct gaze from brown eyes, Penelope looked like him. But she looked like her mother, too, with her pale, creamy skin and slender grace. Joanna's death had shaken the foundation of their little family; Penelope had been lost and forlorn, and he'd worked to give her a sense of security. She had been growing up into a child poised beyond her years, and he rejoiced in her maturity.

Now Kiki had come, and their serenity had been shattered. Penelope was given to outbursts of unruly activity and mischief.

His gaze shifted to Celeste. She had seemed so perfectly suited to the task of restoring peace to the house. He hated to lose this opportunity; he hated to have his plans laid waste. But if she wasn't a spy, she was still a siren.

More young men and women appeared, brushing past him on their way to the heart of the celebration. Toward Celeste.

Celeste stepped behind Kiki and gave her a push. Kiki screamed with joy as she rose into the air, her skirts fluttering around her knees.

"That will never do," Celeste announced, and stopped the girl. She tucked the material tight around Kiki. Hyacinth hurried to help, and Throckmorton saw Celeste say something to Hyacinth, and saw Hyacinth laugh. Celeste had charmed another unsuspecting soul. But not Hyacinth. This would never do. What was she telling Hyacinth about Kiki?

He started toward the swing.

Hyacinth gave Kiki a push. Ellery's daughter shrieked again.

Celeste watched for a moment, then took Penelope by the hand, and walked . . . toward him. Her eyes met his. She smiled.

But he hadn't realized Celeste knew he was anywhere near. He was dressed like the other men in a dark jacket and trousers. He had followed far behind the throng. And she had never seemed to see him. Now she acted as if she had known all along.

Celeste noted everything that went on around her, either through a natural, bright awareness, or through training by a master of intelligence, or both. If she weren't already working for the Russians, he would like to hire her himself.

He would like to do a lot of things to her himself.

"Papa!" Penelope smiled with pleasure at the sight of him and caught his hand.

His interrogation of Celeste could wait a few moments. He smiled back at his daughter and squeezed her fingers. "Child." Looking at her was like looking into a mirror.

In a bright, cheery tone, meant to head off his wrath,

Celeste said, "You mean to scold me, I suppose, for meeting the children when you had instructed I should not. I slipped away from the other servants. They didn't even know what I was doing, so you'll confine your reprimand to me." She beamed at him, dimples flashing, as she acknowledged her duplicity.

She would indeed make a fine spy, for it would be a cold-hearted hangman who placed the rope around her neck.

As luck would have it, he had many times been described as cold-hearted. "Why did you bring Kiki?" he demanded.

"I couldn't bring Penelope without Kiki."

Prevarication. He narrowed his gaze at Celeste. "Why did you bring Penelope?"

"That's a long story." She slid a caressing finger along Penelope's cheek. "It seems I got to the nursery in the nick of time. I'm afraid, Mr. Throckmorton, you're going to have to hire a new nursemaid."

He stared at Celeste. She didn't *look* like a spy and a wrecker of betrothals. He glanced down at his daughter. She stood quietly, composed, waiting for her story to be heard. "A new . . . nursemaid," he said.

"When I got to the nursery, she was tied to her chair while the girls skipped rope in the corners."

"Tied to her chair." He feared his secretary was a traitor, his brother wanted to break his engagement, and his daughter tied her nursemaid to a chair. And Celeste . . . Celeste was too beautiful, too well dressed, and too smart. "Penelope, you let Kiki tie your nursemaid to her chair?"

"Actually, it was my idea," she confessed without shame. "Kiki is useless with knots."

Looking down at her, Throckmorton saw a flash of something . . . what was it his mother used to say? "If you're looking for a rogue, it's Ellery. If you want mischief done right, it's Garrick every time."

But Penelope had never been like that before. Tugging at his trousers, he knelt beside his daughter. "Penelope Ann, you must never tie up your nursemaids ever again."

"But, Papa, she wouldn't let us go outside because she said we'd be in the way of the tea preparations, and she wouldn't let us jump inside because she said we gave her a headache." Penelope seemed to believe herself to be the voice of logic. "You must admit, those are poor reasons for not allowing us to skip rope."

He held up his hand. "Tying up anyone because they don't let you play as you wish is not a good enough reason."

She put her hands on her hips. "Then why did you teach me how to do it?"

He heard a muffled laugh from Celeste, but he kept his attention on his daughter. "In case bad people come and try to take you away. But only then, Penelope." Standing, he nodded to Celeste. "There. That should take care of matters."

Celeste looked at Penelope. Then she looked at him. "You taught your daughter to tie people up?"

"I don't know how to teach embroidery," he answered, deadpan. "Didn't your father teach you how to tie people up?"

"No, he taught me how to tie roses to an espalier."

"Hm. Odd." He squinted at the swing. "Isn't it someone else's turn?"

"Come on, Penelope." Celeste hurried toward the swing. "You're next."

Throckmorton braced himself for an explosion of wrath from Kiki, but Celeste spoke to her, and without incident, she slid off the swing. Penelope jumped up and Hyacinth gave her a push.

Then Celeste brought Kiki back to him.

The child was babbling in French, as always, and as always she ignored his English greeting. If she would just reply once . . . but he had to be patient. She had lost her mother, just as Penelope had. She responded by refusing to face the facts of her new life. He could understand, but he couldn't countenance her making his child miserable, or teaching her sedition—or ignoring him so steadfastly.

Kiki bobbed about, waved her hands expressively, and babbled in French.

"Tell her she is not to tie anyone else up," he instructed Celeste.

"I did."

"Does she understand?"

"She does." Celeste didn't have to say it—*but she doesn't care.* "She wants you to teach her to tie up people, too." Celeste seemed to be having difficulty retaining her gravity.

His gaze narrowed on her.

"Apparently she was very impressed with Penelope's efficiency," Celeste said brightly.

He wavered. He wanted to snap that no, he most definitely would not teach Kiki to tie knots. But this was such a good opportunity . . . "I don't teach knots in French." He was watching the child; he saw the flash of understanding. She comprehended him perfectly, and he and Celeste waited while she struggled between her desires and her rebellion.

In the end, her rebellion won. *"Je ne parle pas l'anglais,"* she said to Celeste.

Celeste turned to him. "She says she doesn't speak English."

"Well, I don't speak French."

Kiki stomped her foot. *"Trés stupide."*

"She understood that fast enough," Throckmorton observed.

"No one here is quite as ignorant as they pretend." Celeste dropped a little curtsy toward him, then toward the glowering Kiki.

Nothing about his interrogation had gone as it should. He caught Celeste's arm and pulled her away from Kiki. "What are you saying about this child?"

"About Kiki?" She had the gall to look surprised. "To whom?"

He gestured about him. "To anyone."

"Nothing."

"What do you mean, nothing?" he snapped. "You have to have told them something about the child!"

She understood him now, for she sobered. "I have given no explanation about Kiki. She could be a friend of Penelope's, come to visit for the day. She could be the child of one of your guests. She could be a cousin—your father's side of the family is an enigma to the *ton*. Your guests don't care who she is, Mr. Throckmorton. Only you know there is a mystery."

She managed to do something only a few had ever managed to do. She made him feel foolish.

"I assure you, Mr. Throckmorton, I wouldn't use a child as a weapon."

He now felt defamatory and suspicious. "I appreciate the assurance," he said stiffly. Then he realized—he still had a seduction to perform, and now Celeste eyed him with considerably less partiality than she had last night. So he added, "I apologize for my unwarranted misgivings."

She accepted his apology with grave appreciation. "Thank you. Now is as good a time to tell you as any— I'm going to spend the evening in the nursery, and sleep there, too."

He hadn't planned it that way, and he was tired of being thwarted. "You will attend the dinner tonight."

"Such an imperious pronouncement! Tea today is sufficient for my first outing." She gave him the impression she had handled everything with deliberation, bringing the children as a diversion, creating a youthful, informal atmosphere that discouraged in-depth conversation.

She irked him. This was her first official social event here at Blythe Hall; she shouldn't be so poised. She shouldn't tell him what to do. She shouldn't make the plans.

"I'll choose some women from among the servants to be with the girls until I've found *two* new, experienced nursemaids."

"Certainly, but I think the new nursemaids will want some kind of guarantee of safety. I can safely promise them Penelope and Kiki will be better supervised by me." Kiki starting babbling, pointing toward the swing. "You have to share," Celeste answered. Then, to

Throckmorton, "Why don't you just build two swings?"

Throckmorton's jaw dropped. "Two?" He'd never thought of such a thing.

"No one should have to share a swing," Celeste said seriously. "It colors the whole experience, gives a sour taste to the joy, to know your pleasure is finite and controlled by someone else."

He stared at her. She stood, framed by willow branches, a rose-clad, practical dreamer. Her hair, braided and upswept, bared her neck where little tendrils dusted the skin. Her hazel eyes slanted up, dressed with lavish lashes that flirted without design. Her ears were tiny and delicate, her nose a tilted button, her lips . . . he'd kissed her last night. He'd done a good job of it, just as he did a good job of every task he performed. But he hadn't admitted to himself how much he enjoyed it.

For a seductress, she kissed with a remarkable lack of skill. She'd sagged against the wall, and her hands had dangled by her side as if she didn't know what to do with them. She kissed with her lips closed and when he'd used his tongue she'd jumped—and moaned. He'd kissed her neck, mostly to see if he could startle more of the little sounds out of her. He had. Untutored sounds of pleasure, most flattering to a man. And while most beautiful women tasted like caked powder and acrid perfume, she tasted like sweet clean flesh and a lover's dreams. For a moment, just a moment, he'd wanted to take further liberties, kiss the curve of her breast, slide down her arm to press his lips against the pulse of her wrist.

But good sense intervened. With Garrick Stanley Breckinridge Throckmorton the Third, good sense always intervened.

He must have been staring at her for too long, for Celeste glanced away, then glanced back, and a color that matched the rose of her gown glowed in her cheeks. "Is there something . . . wrong?" She sounded quite faint, as if she knew exactly what was wrong but didn't want to contemplate the truth.

Because, of course, she loved Ellery. The knowledge left a nasty taste in his mouth, and he realized this was the perfect moment to pursue his plan. "Not at all." He bowed. "I was simply contemplating your beauty and feeling quite . . ." He trailed off as if unable to frame the words.

Celeste blushed harder and looked everywhere but at him.

He would have said more, but Kiki interrupted with a fierce barrage of French.

Celeste's relief matched his irritation.

Celeste answered her in French, then translated to English. "It is time for Penelope to get off, but it's also time for other people to take their turn."

"*Qui est-ce?*" the child asked.

Celeste glanced at him and took revenge for his suspicions. "Mr. Throckmorton, for example."

Throckmorton stiffened and glared.

Kiki didn't even have the delicacy to cover her mouth before she laughed.

"I have swung on a swing in my day," he said stiffly.

"I'm sure you have, Mr. Throckmorton." But Celeste's eyes were dancing, too. "Why don't you take a turn?"

He straightened his shoulders, donned his dignity like a barrister's black robe, and answered, "All right. I will."

Throckmorton strode toward the swing. The crowd opened before him. Behind him, he could hear Kiki prattling in French. He could hear the rustle of Celeste's skirt as she hurried to keep up with him. He heard a cough. A snort. A gasp. The movement of many shuffling feet. He could almost savor the crowd's astonishment lapping at his back.

At the swing, he observed Hyacinth, smiling at Lord Townshend, who pushed Penelope. He saw Penelope, swinging with the blissful smile he saw too seldom. He hesitated; it seemed a shame to interrupt her pleasure. But if not him, it would be someone else, and he would show Celeste . . . he shouldn't want to show her anything, yet somehow her amusement, her conviction that he would never relax his dignity enough to take a turn on the swing . . . well, she irritated him.

At the side of the swing, he grasped one of the upright

poles and waited, as any youth does, for his turn. Hyacinth noticed. Lord Townshend was clearly nonplussed.

Penelope dragged her toe in the gravel. She didn't seem at all surprised to see him standing there. "Did you want a turn, Papa?"

"I want a turn," he affirmed.

Penelope hopped off and patted the seat. He smiled at her, then at Hyacinth who, to his approval, seemed quite able to contain her amazement. Indeed, she even smiled back.

He turned a chilly eye on the immobile Lord Townshend, "I won't need your assistance."

Townshend backed off so quickly he tripped over one of the braces for the swing.

Throckmorton looked out of the crowd. He'd never seen so many mouths hanging open at one time. Even little Kiki, blond, blue-eyed, beruffled, looked as if a support had been knocked out from under her. He'd show them all he wasn't the predictable, stuffy fellow they thought him.

He sat down and pushed off.

He noted that Celeste didn't look dumbfounded. She watched him . . . no, she observed him. If she was a spy, she was a very good one. She manipulated him into doing what he hadn't even realized he wanted to do.

He hadn't remembered how it felt to swing. He hadn't thought of it in years. The smooth backward glide skimmed him back among the branches. The thrilling drop, then the upward swing that, if he strained hard enough, revealed a brief glimpse over the edge of the ridge to the plain and the winding river far below. Then another stomach-clenching backward drop before the rope and board caught him and carried him back among the branches again.

He *would* order another swing built right beside this one.

He swung up and back, lying back far enough to have the branches catch at his hair, to see the sky through the leaves.

Celeste was right, no one should have to share a swing. And something she hadn't thought of; it was more fun to swing when there was two. He could almost imagine her laughter and the flutter of her skirts beside him as she rose and fell with the rhythm of the swing.

Like a wave on the sea, like a bird on the breeze, he soared and descended. He kicked his feet out and back. He felt the rush of hair on his face and heard the murmur of voices as if from a distance. This was freedom—from business, from family, from duty. He never wanted to stop.

No, no one should ever have to share a swing.

As he sailed forward once more, he glanced out at the crowd. And saw, near the edge, one of his soberly clad gentlemen.

Pleasure dissipated as if it had never been.

Duty called.

It wasn't her.

"Where is she?" Ellery asked in loud, slurred indignation.

"Sh." Throckmorton adjusted the weight of Ellery's arm across his shoulders. "You'll wake the guests."

It wasn't Celeste who was the spy, but Stanhope, the man Throckmorton deemed his friend. Stanhope had sold information about English troop movements on the

Indian subcontinent. Stanhope had killed English sol-
diers as surely as if he'd used the knife himself.

"Where is my sweet little Celeste?" Ellery stopped
his trek back down the long, dim, downstairs corridor.
Taking Throckmorton's shoulders in his hands, he
stared at his brother in bleary disbelief. "The servants
said her bedchamber was here. So where is she?"

The scent of brandy on Ellery's breath almost
knocked Throckmorton off his feet, and he thanked his
lucky stars he'd been working in his office and heard his
intoxicated brother calling Celeste's name. "Celeste is
sleeping in the nursery tonight to look after the children."

Through Stanhope, Throckmorton had to correct the
damage done—as soon as possible.

Which left him with one obvious plan.

"I haven't got to see her in days and days." Ellery
frowned with the excessive anguish of a man who had
tippled too deep. "My sweet little petunia."

"Only one full day," Throckmorton pointed out. "And
you're the one who won't come out of his room."

"I'm ugly."

"You're handsome, as you very well know."

"I'm blue."

Throckmorton steered Ellery toward one of the night
candles and squinted at him. "The color appears to be
fading." Which in its way was too bad. "In fact, you're
rather rosy."

"Washed." Ellery took a quavering breath. "A lot."

"Cleanliness is next to godliness, old chap." Throckmorton hoisted his brother's arm back around his shoulders. "If you'd come out, you could see whoever you
wish. Preferably your betrothed."

Not Celeste. Celeste, to whom Throckmorton would provide false intelligence about the English plans. Then he would foster the impression he was truly in love with Celeste. Indulging in pillow talk. Being indiscreet. Stanhope would seek her out, and in his charming, ruthless way, he'd pump Celeste for the information. Celeste would tell him all, and the Russians would be misled.

"She came to visit me today."

Throckmorton steered Ellery toward the stairs. "Your sweet little petunia?"

"No." Ellery sounded surly. "Hyacinth."

"She would be your sweet, tall climbing rose."

Ellery was too far gone to comprehend even so simple a jest. "She's not, either." Then, thoughtfully, "Although she does smell nice. I like a woman who smells nice, don't you?"

If they could just keep the conversation on Hyacinth, perhaps Ellery would be reminded of his duty. And perhaps Throckmorton could forget his. "Lady Hyacinth smells very nice."

Back to surly again. "Have you been smelling my betrothed? Because you're supposed to be smelling my sweet little begonia." Lifting his head, he caroled, "Celeste! Where are you?"

"Sh!" Throckmorton jabbed his elbow into Ellery's sore ribs.

Ellery flinched away and bumped into the banister. "Why? I want to speak with her. My pretty little carnation."

"If you try to talk to her at this hour of the night alone in her bedchamber, her father will scoop your heart out with a trowel and bury you beneath the honeysuckle."

If Milford knew that Throckmorton planned to use

Celeste, he'd do the same to Throckmorton—and Throckmorton would deserve it. He'd used innocents such as Celeste before. He didn't like it. He never liked it. But he told himself the end justified the means, that the future of the British Empire was at stake, that innocent lives depended on such subterfuge.

Yet the thought of leaving Celeste alone with Stanhope, a traitor and a murderer, made his skin crawl.

Which was why Ellery could never see her at night. A guard stood outside her bedchamber—a bedchamber that would change as Throckmorton decreed—and would until she returned to Paris. That would be when the party was over. When she had been shown she could never have Ellery or Throckmorton. When she had served her purpose for British espionage.

"Do you really think it would matter if I married the gardener's daughter?"

"Are you going to marry her?"

"Thinkin' about it."

"Because she smells nice?"

"Because she's . . . pretty and she smiles . . . a lot."

Throckmorton wanted to push his stupid brother back down the stairs. A hank of hair and a couple of dimples, that's all Ellery saw when he looked at Celeste? "*Lady Hyacinth* is pretty," Throckmorton said between gritted teeth. "*Lady Hyacinth* smiles a lot."

"But Celeste doesn't . . . expect anything out of me." Ellery belched loud enough to raise a ghoul.

Throckmorton hoped he hadn't raised Hyacinth's father. "What does Lady Hyacinth expect?"

A shiver quivered through Ellery's frame. "She says I'm a good man. She says I'm smart and I work hard and I know what to do all the time. She says she respects

me, 'cause I'm going to be the head of our household
and be a good father to our children. Can you believe it?
She told me all that!"

Throckmorton wanted to drop his forehead onto
Ellery's shoulder. The foolish girl had scythed the deal
by, in essence, telling Ellery it was time to grow up.

Just two hours ago, Throckmorton had listened to a
half-drowned woman babble in a different language
while she coughed up the water she'd inhaled from the
river. He'd seen the finger marks on her neck—the marks
Stanhope had put there. He had had to face the betrayal
of his friend. He now planned to use an innocent maiden
as an instrument to correct a great injustice.

And Ellery was frightened by the face of maturity.

The ridiculous, fatuous fribble.

Ellery gave a hiccup. "I don't even know what to do
with the tyke I have now."

"Just pay her some attention," Throckmorton
snapped. "That's all Kiki wants."

Ellery brightened. "Celeste knows what to do with
my kid."

"Leave her in the nursery to do it, then." Irritation
made him move Ellery along with considerable more
briskness.

"Hey!" Ellery said in exaggerated torment. When
Throckmorton didn't respond, Ellery showed some
remnant of wit. "What'sa matter, you ol' brother, you?
You tired? You ought t' go t' bed."

"After I get you to your room. Come on." Throckmorton marched him along. "So Lady Hyacinth came to
visit you today?"

"She loves me," Ellery said in a most self-pitying
tone of voice.

They had reached Ellery's bedchamber. "You encouraged her."

"Thought I was going t' marry her. Because she's really a nice woman, you know? She's smart and she's funny when you get t' know her and she's really young but she's going t' be one of those fascinating women I could listen t' forever. Today"—he staggered sideways, pulling Throckmorton with him—"today she said so many great *bon mots*. She made me laugh. I even let her see me. She made me feel . . . like I could conquer the world. Then"—his voice lowered to a whine—"she told me she thought I could. Me! She's got the wrong brother." Ellery poked at Throckmorton's chest. "You should marry Hyacinth."

Throckmorton lost his patience. Shoving Ellery against the wall, he leaned his face close. "Now, you listen to me, little brother. You look handsome. Your haircut will start a fashion. And our guests are wondering where you are. There's a hunt tomorrow. You will come out of hiding. You will be pleasant to everyone, *especially* Lady Hyacinth *and* her parents. You will let *me* handle the matter of Celeste."

Ellery nodded. "You and Celeste."

Throckmorton grabbed him by the arm before he tottered into his room. "Most of all, you will not drink yourself into oblivion."

Ellery hesitated.

"You will lose all if you do."

"Garrick, I don't want to do that." Ellery's voice sounded husky, almost as if he struggled with tears. Maybe somewhere inside that pitiful conscience of his, he comprehended the consequences of his deeds.

And who was Throckmorton to judge Ellery and his

conscience? He had Celeste and her well-being on his.

Giving him a quick hug, Throckmorton pushed him inside where his sensible valet waited up. Poor man. Like everyone else, he worshipped Ellery, but Throckmorton couldn't imagine when he got to sleep.

Throckmorton strode to the stairs and paused, then gave in to impulse. He allowed his steps to carry him upward, toward the nursery. He told himself that as long as he was awake, he might as well look in on Penelope. He told himself that his excessive worry was normal for a man involved in this desperate international game of conspiracy and counterconspiracy.

Yet he knew it was Celeste who drew him. She had shown him how well she worked with the children, and shown him, too, her determination to do the task for which she had been hired.

Yes, as soon as the house party was over, Celeste would be sent back to Paris, Stanhope arrested, and of course, because the Throckmortons were fair and wonderful people, they would settle a large sum on Celeste for her trouble and help.

Throckmorton's mouth twisted cynically, then smoothed.

He identified himself to the bodyguard as he approached the nursery. Through hard experience he had found such caution saved him a brutal blow to the head.

Mr. Kinman—large, quiet, innocuous—opened the door. "Sir."

Throckmorton slipped inside. The playroom glowed in the light of a single candle. The children and Celeste slept in the bedchamber just off the playroom. He stepped gingerly, taking care to avoid the wooden train strewn in pieces across the nursery room floor, the skip-ping rope snaking over the smooth boards.

He'd learned to move without noise while in India; it had proved to be an asset in his line of work, and he blessed that ability now. Lifting the candle, he carried it into the bedchamber and over to Penelope.

She slept restlessly, her braids tangled about her, her blankets twisted and thrown back, her nightgown-clad body curled into a tiny, shivering ball. He covered her. Smoothing the hair from her face, he experienced that tug of emotion only a father can understand as he looked on his sleeping child. He wanted to protect Pene-lope from all hurt. He wanted only good things for her. He wanted her to be happy.

She relaxed into the warmth of the blankets. That was all he could do tonight.

He moved to Kiki's bed. The rambunctious child slept peacefully, as if in sleep she found the contentment she fought so defiantly during the day. Poor girl. When he saw her like this, he wished he could give her what she sought. But she didn't seek it from him; she wanted affection and approval from her father, and Ellery was too selfish to know how to give. So the turmoil contin-ued, unless . . .

Drawn by a need he couldn't explain, he went to the third bed. To Celeste.

She slept with her hand under her cheek, a frown on her face, as if during sleep she fought the demons he would loose on her unsuspecting head.

It wouldn't be so bad. She'd be safer here than any-where in England or on the Continent, and she'd be helping her country.

Odd to see her without the animation of conscious-ness. She was so alive, so keen to the enjoyment of life, he could almost catch her youthful fever to know, to be, to go, to experience all that youth had to offer. She would have been a fit mate for Ellery; the two of them would have been a living proclamation for spirit and verve.

But even if she came out of this yarborough without harm, she would be hurt if she discovered that he had romanced her to detach her from Ellery.

Sighing, she flung out an arm. Her hand rested palm up on the blankets, her fingers slightly curled. The frown smoothed from her face, leaving only the content-ment of slumber. His hand rose and hovered over her forehead. He wanted to stroke the hair back from her forehead as he had done for Penelope. Yet the tender-ness he felt for Celeste contained nothing of fatherly af-fection. Rather, this need to touch Celeste had its roots in want and seduction. He had to wonder at himself; could it be he was stalking the girl? Was he motivated less by duty than by attraction?

He stared as her chest lifted and fell. She wore a plain white cotton gown with a modest neck. The sheet cov-ered her, too. Yet without seeing—without ever having seen and never allowing himself to see—he knew what her breasts looked like. Smooth, creamy young skin lift-ing above her ribcage in two perfect curves, topped by round blossoms of color so soft they could scarcely be called rose. He didn't have to close his eyes to see the stretch of flesh above and below; his imagination took the delicacy of her features and the hint of skin showing above her neckline and filled in every detail. She was like a portrait and he the artist—and he had even less talent at painting than he did at languages.

Except with Celeste.

What was happening to him? *Ellery* lusted. *Ellery* romanced. *Ellery* seduced. Not Throckmorton. Not after two days. Not without a foundation of common beliefs and interests. Not madly. Not passionately.

Not ever.

Yet . . . yet . . . what harm would he do? He could look and not touch.

Leaning over, he smoothed a lock of hair off her cheek.

He could want but not take. He would have to, for if he sent her away, he had no way to trap Stanhope, and as long as she stayed at Blythe Hall, Ellery would be in pursuit. So Throckmorton had to make the effort to keep her out of Ellery's grasp. If Throckmorton suffered the occasional odd flashes of conscience, as well as this ridiculous surge of tenderness and the inconvenient heat of desire—well, it was probably no more than he deserved.

A whisk of wind lifted the tendrils of hair off Celeste's forehead. The cloudy afternoon smelled like rain. Targets stood in a row on the far back lawn.

"I'll wager you twenty pounds she strikes dead center."

"Nice try, chap, but you're not the only one who's been watching her shoot all afternoon."

Celeste overheard Colonel Halton and Lord Arrowood's exchange behind her with a mixture of satisfaction and triumph. Throckmorton had suggested that she find a way to keep her identity secret and so allow Ellery his position in society. She had done so, and the hunters had straggled in from the marsh to find a most unusual contest proceeding.

Celeste lifted the rifle to her shoulder and shot once more.

The bullet struck the bull's-eye.

Lord Townshend, her last competitor, dropped his own rifle in defeat.

A burst of applause followed, with a few hurrahs from the younger gentlemen who cared nothing for her prowess with a rifle and everything for her air of mystery and her physical attributes. That was fine. Count de Rosselin had told her to enjoy the blindness her beauty afforded, but to depend on her wits. She thought she had done so very well when she suggested a shooting competition.

Lady Philberta's eyebrows had raised. "Among whom, Miss Milford?"

"The gentlemen who don't care to hunt," Celeste began.

"Capital!" Colonel Halton said.

"And those ladies who can shoot," Celeste finished.

"Unfeminine," Lord Arrowood had snorted.

She had unmanned him with a touch on his sleeve and a low-voiced plea for tolerance of youthful spirits. "Besides," she had told him, "no lady has a chance of winning against an expert such as yourself."

He'd imagined she spoke true.

To Lady Philberta's obvious gratification, Celeste eliminated him in the first round, then fluttered her eyelashes so winningly he'd actually laughed at himself, settled back to watch the fun, and collected a rather large bank of winnings from the weary hunters who returned in groups of two and three.

Now Celeste dimpled and dropped a curtsy first to her able opponent, then to the cheering crowd. They were really very nice people when you got to know them. She was an unknown, the underdog, and she had won, so they took her to their hearts.

"*Brava!*" Hyacinth called to Celeste.

Celeste forgot herself enough to smile at the girl. Their brief acquaintance of the previous day had been unsettling for Celeste. She'd rather liked Hyacinth, when before she'd cherished a conjectural dislike to the girl. That was the trouble with getting to know people. The truth did not always support one's aversions.

Still clapping, Lady Philberta came to Celeste's side. "An amazing performance, Miss Milford. Tell us where you learned to shoot like that."

"In Russia." Celeste accepted Lady Philberta's embrace, and wondered at her easy acceptance of Celeste's intrusion. Celeste wouldn't have thought the aristocratic Lady Philberta would care to have the gardener's daughter pursuing her son, but she had been genial. Perhaps Celeste had braced for obstacles that never had been there. Projecting her voice to be heard all over the lawn, Celeste said, "When I traveled there in the company of the Russian ambassador and his wife, I discovered the country rife with wolves and other, more human, threats." With a smile that downplayed the threats of highwaymen, of murderers, and of the occasional revolutionary whose eyes glowed with the strength of his convictions, she glanced about her.

A movement off to the side caught her attention. Newly returned from hunting, Throckmorton subjected her to a thorough scrutiny. Mud spattered him from boot to thigh. His damp, black hair stood at attention over his forehead. Tiredness ringed his eyes, and grimness bracketed his mouth.

She lifted her eyebrows at him, wondering what she had done to cause such intensive observation. She wanted to go to him, to ask what she'd done wrong, to assure him she'd been all that was discreet. "Russia is a country of madmen," she added.

Another man stepped out of the crowd. "Hear, hear!" he called. "Well said, Miss Milford, and well shot."

It was, she realized with a shock, Ellery.

Ellery, whose blond hair was cut in a shorter style, but who appeared breathtakingly handsome next to his weary, dirty, older brother.

"You're . . . well!" she exclaimed.

"Limping a bit." He directed at her a smile so bright each one of his teeth might have been a lit candle. Lifting his sling, he added, "And I wrenched my arm, but they're remodeling a bedchamber up by the nursery. One of the maids was up on the ladder hanging wallpaper, and I heard her scream, and . . . well . . . she would have been badly hurt if she'd fallen."

The younger guests had swarmed around him, so no one noticed Celeste's start of skepticism.

"You rescued a maid?" Hyacinth asked, stars in her eyes.

He barely glanced at her. "Someone had to."

"But you were hurt doing it," one of the other debutantes exclaimed.

He lavished a smile on her, too. "Just a bit. One doesn't think in a situation like that, one just gallops to the rescue." Turning toward the house, he walked, and such was his power everyone walked with him. "But enough about me. What excitement has been happening since I went into seclusion?"

Hyacinth trotted alongside him. "Nothing, Ellery. Without you, there was no excitement at all."

* * *

"You look tired, sir." Stanhope came to stand beside Throckmorton as he watched Celeste walk away with Ellery.

Throckmorton took three long breaths before he answered. "Absolutely. I was up half the night."

Perking up like a setter going on point, Stanhope said, "Not because of your *special* business, I hope." Glancing around, he ascertained that no one stood near, then in a lowered voice said, "You could have woken me at any time."

Throckmorton turned to his secretary, his friend—his betrayer. Stanhope wore the marsh's mud like a badge of honor. The brown wool hunter's hat proclaimed him to be an English gentleman, and its rakish angle proclaimed him an adventurer. He had shot the most birds, and his back probably ached from the constant slap of congratulations from his fellow hunters. Complacency clung to him even more deeply than the mud.

But soon, Throckmorton would strip everything from him. Everything but the mud. "I don't think you could help me with this. I was with Miss Milford."

There was nothing simulated about Stanhope's astonishment. "Sir?"

"She and I have discovered we have . . . a great deal in common." Throckmorton had never before noticed how deliberately Stanhope cultivated the combination of polish and a hail-fellow-well-met manner. Stanhope had been riding on his reputation of a dashing explorer since they'd arrived back in England.

"In common? You and the gardener's daughter?" A nobleman's scorn filled Stanhope's voice.

It was time for Stanhope to grow beyond his youthful

exploits, and take responsibility for his activities. Throckmorton would make personally sure of that. "Come, Stanhope," Throckmorton said, "you wouldn't be a man if you hadn't noticed that she's changed since she returned."

"Damme, yes." Stanhope took the opportunity to leer at Celeste's slender back.

Throckmorton wanted to smash his smug face into the grass.

Then Stanhope dismissed her with an aristocrat's sniff. "But she's still the gardener's daughter."

"She'll always be that." *And better than you.*

Colonel Halton strode past. "Capital entertainment, Throckmorton! That girl'll be the talk of London."

"Thank you. Yes, won't she?" Throckmorton called after him. Almost every guest had passed, so he started toward the house. He wished for no one to hear this conversation, and he dawdled convincingly.

Stanhope looked ahead where Ellery and Celeste climbed the stairs to the veranda. "From the looks of it, she's still in love with Mr. Ellery."

"Not at all." Too emphatic, and sounding rather as if he doubted her fidelity. Throckmorton tried a friendly smile. "She came back for Mr. Ellery, and of course he's always ready to indulge in a little light flirtation."

Although Ellery's head might have been stuck in that angle of looking toward Celeste, and his fatuous smirk never faltered.

Throckmorton lifted one shoulder in a shrug. "What can I tell you, Stanhope? You came from a noble background. I did not. It's only lucre that defines the difference between your station and mine."

"Yes." Stanhope thought himself so secure in his circumstances and his treachery he allowed bitterness to bleed into his tone. "I don't have any."

Throckmorton kept his voice genial. "I pay you a fair salary, I would say."

"Of course, sir. I meant no criticism."

"Of course not." Throckmorton rubbed at the mud on his jacket.

Apparently, Stanhope read something in Throckmorton's manner that warned him to return to the original subject. "You were telling me about Miss Milford."

"Oh." Throckmorton allowed a smile to cross his face. "My mother, of course, is from a great family, but my father's common as dirt, so there's no great difference between Miss Milford and me."

"I would disagree, sir. She hasn't a ha'penny."

Aristocrats arranged their marriages for monetary increase. Sometimes Throckmorton was proud to be common. "She has beauty beyond price. She is kind, good with the children, and she kisses . . . pardon me. You don't want to hear this." Throckmorton let Stanhope wrestle with the tidings before saying reflectively, "Although I'm surprised you haven't heard the gossip."

"Why . . . no, sir, I haven't heard a word."

Lying, Throckmorton diagnosed, or distracted. Too enthralled in the dangerous game he played to pay attention to the rumors swirling around him. After Throckmorton's confession, he would seek out the scandal, and there existed just enough to convince him.

"It's sheer nonsense, of course," Throckmorton said. "I would have swung on that swing even if she hadn't urged me."

"Excuse me, sir." Stanhope stumbled on the first step up to the house. "You swung on a . . . swing? As in—" Stanhope made a pendulant motion with his hand. A ruby set in gold glinted on that hand; a gift from Throckmorton for years of faithful service.

"Yes. What's so odd about that?" Throckmorton wrinkled his brow as though puzzled. Actually, he *was* puzzled. His mother had accosted him with his "bizarre behavior," as she called it. Surely she realized he could kick over the traces occasionally. Although if he doubted she would call his early morning visit to the nursery "kicking over the traces." More like—madness.

"And you kissed the gardener's daughter?" Stanhope clarified.

"There was a great deal more than . . ." Throckmorton caught himself again, smiled like a man with a secret, and climbed the stairs. "Beg pardon. I just haven't felt this way for years. Maybe ever." That was true, at least. He had never felt like he wanted to throttle his secretary before.

Stanhope didn't bother to hide his astonishment.

"Your disbelief fails to flatter," Throckmorton said dryly.

"Not at all, sir, but compared to . . ." Stanhope gestured feebly at Ellery as he walked ahead of them with Celeste.

"You're referring to the fact I'm not nearly as handsome as Mr. Ellery." It had never mattered before. Throckmorton didn't know why it should now, but in fact he was getting dreadfully tired of having Ellery's comeliness thrown in his face. "But I freely admit it. I'm infatuated with Miss Milford, and I'm as ruthless in my courting as I am in my . . . business."

Celeste, for no reason Throckmorton could see, curtsied to excuse herself from Ellery and his group, and hurried away.

Ellery watched her, but when she turned the corner he rejoined the merry group.

Throckmorton glanced toward Hyacinth. The poor girl stumbled along, trailing ever farther behind the pack of fashionable youths and mincing debutantes. Her stricken gaze never left Ellery.

Throckmorton would have to fix that situation. He had to fix every situation, and exhaustion tugged at him.

"I see," Stanhope said.

"I gave Miss Milford strict instructions she was not to linger for fear we would betray ourselves."

Clearly unconvinced, Stanhope protested, "But Miss Milford doesn't seem your . . . she seems so . . ."

"Young? Exquisite?"

"Improper. I haven't understood why you allow her to mingle among the guests. That is to say—I understand you have needs, just like the rest of us, but it surprises me that you'll indulge yourself with the gardener's daughter. I know how well you think of Milford and how considerate you've been of him all these years. To dally with his daughter seems—"

"You misunderstand, Stanhope!" Throckmorton was almost having fun, dragging Stanhope along the conversational path he'd designed. "I do not dally with innocent young ladies. I am quite serious about Miss Milford."

"Serious? As in . . . marriage?"

"She is mine." Throckmorton experienced a wave of intense satisfaction as he laid his claim.

This playacting was sweeping him away. He *had* to cease.

With a touch on the arm and jerk of the head, he indicated Stanhope should follow him to the office. In there, drama had no place. The serious business of espionage reigned within, and in less than a week, Throckmorton would destroy Stanhope. Without preamble, he shut the door and said, "I'm in trouble."

Stanhope fixed a polite expression on his face. "What kind of trouble, sir?"

"There have been problems. Problems for our men in the field." In a voice weighty with trouble, Throckmorton said, "It would seem that someone among us is selling information to the Russians."

Stanhope took a deep breath. "No!"

"Yes, and I'm the prime suspect." Without waiting to see Stanhope's expression of disbelief or relief, Throckmorton walked to his desk and drummed his fingers on the dark, shining surface. "I don't have to tell you that's not true."

"Of course not, sir!"

"But I don't know who is guilty."

"You have your suspicions, though." Stanhope's voice warmed to oily invitation.

"Indeed I do." Flattening his hands, Throckmorton leaned on them and stared at Stanhope so fixedly Stanhope's hands bunched into fists. Then Throckmorton declared, "It is Winston."

"Winston?" Stanhope's fingers sprang open and his forehead knit with incredulity. "Why Winston?"

"We started having little slips about a year ago. About the time he joined the team." Throckmorton seated himself on one of the uncomfortable chairs before his own desk. "I know you like him, but he has betrayed us."

"It doesn't seem possible."

"It could be someone else. I'm open to any suggestions."

"But of course you must be right."

You would say so.

"The betrayals did start when he joined our organization—or at least, if that's the truth, it must be him."

"Exactly." The chair really was as uncomfortable as everyone said. But Throckmorton didn't want to sit behind his desk. He wanted Stanhope to see him stripped of confidence, of dignity, of the badges of his office. "The bad news is . . . although I will continue to receive dispatches about the plans for the newest troop movements in India, the home office in London demands that I keep those plans secret."

Stanhope paused in the act of seating himself on the chair opposite. "I thought you said you were a suspect."

A misstep. "Not necessarily me. But one of my men, and that makes me an incompetent, doesn't it?" Throckmorton smiled with cold brilliance. Indeed, even though Throckmorton knew every director lost men to perfidy, Stanhope's betrayal stabbed at the heart of his pride.

"You'll need help proving Winston's guilt."

"Didn't you listen? London made it very clear my organization contains the prime suspect. They'd never allow me to provide proof. They have sent their own men to follow him and, I'm sure, to watch me. You'll see them on the grounds." And indeed they were there, pretending to follow Winston while in truth watching Stanhope, trying to see who his accomplices might be, and guarding the children. "So until we have proved Winston's culpability, I have no use for you as a secretary. I do beg your pardon for this breakdown in trust, and beg that you weather the storm at my side."

"Of course. Whatever you wish, but . . ." Stanhope traced the swirl of wood on the arm of his chair. "It seems to me that someone needs to, um, write up the answers to London and such. You can't be expected to do that on your own."

"I'm not," Throckmorton said briskly. "Dear Celeste will help me."

Stanhope's eyes bulged. "Celeste? That little . . . girl?"

"Exactly! A female with no more knowledge of the Great Game we play in Central Asia than that of an English setter puppy, but who speaks French and Russian. I tell you, Stanhope, she's a gift from heaven, and good on the eyes, too." Throckmorton chuckled. "I probably wouldn't have thought of it, but last night I slipped with a bit of information about the impending invasion. She didn't understand me at all."

"The impending invasion?"

Throckmorton put his finger to his lips.

"Of course, sir. Yes, sir, but"—Stanhope shifted in the hard, misshapen chair—"can you be sure Celeste is trustworthy?"

"You mean she might be a spy sent to distract me?" Throckmorton chuckled indulgently. "Really, man, who would ever have dared to think a man in my position would fall in love with a lovely young birdbrain?"

~: 13 :~

"If you follow the arc of the Big Dipper's handle, you'll find the bright star named Arcturus." Celeste steadied the telescope for Penelope. "Arc to Arcturus. That's how you remember its name."

Kiki imitated Celeste's gesture toward Arcturus. "*Oui, mademoiselle.* Arcturus."

"Arcturus is the brightest star in the summer sky, part of the constellation Boötes." Kiki didn't repeat that, so Celeste added, "Boötes is from the Greek word meaning 'plowman.' "

"Boötes," Kiki said.

Penelope kept her eye to the eyepiece as she asked, "Why do you talk to her at all? She doesn't speak English."

"Yes, she does. She would have to be a very stupid girl not to, and she's a very intelligent girl."

The stars glittered in the clear summer sky, moonrise

was a premonition on the eastern horizon, and the garden wall sheltered them from most of the glow from the house windows, but Celeste could almost see the glance Penelope shot at Kiki, and the grimace Kiki sent back. Celeste smiled. The girls struggled toward a kind of accord, and if she stayed on as their governess or . . . or as someone's mother, she would like to guide them. "Can you see the rings on Saturn?" she asked Penelope.

"They're turned sideways, and they're different colors. What makes them different colors?"

"No one knows."

"When I grow up, I'm going to find out," Penelope stated.

Hearing the gritty determination that sounded so much like her father's, Celeste didn't doubt she would try. Yet experience compelled Celeste to warn, "The learned astronomers would not welcome a female colleague."

Indignation sounded loud in Penelope's voice. "They shouldn't care if I find out things better than they do."

"They will care even more if you find out things better than they do."

With insouciant confidence, Penelope said, "Then they're stupid."

Celeste wondered if she should, as Penelope's governess, urge her to be less judgmental and to employ more tact, especially when dealing with the masculine gender. But there was time enough for that later, so she said, "Yes."

"Who taught you about the stars, Miss Milford?" Penelope asked.

"My father," Celeste answered, a wealth of affection in her voice.

"Oh, I like him!" Penelope poked her head out from around the telescope. "He showed me how to plant basil seeds in the kitchen garden, and they grew!"

Kiki tugged at Celeste's skirt. *"Ou est-elle, l'Étoile du nord?"*

"You already know where the North Star is," Penelope said scornfully.

Of course Kiki did know that, but she wanted attention, so Celeste knelt beside her. "We find the North Star by using the two pointer stars on the Big Dipper. The five constellations that circle the North Star are . . . ?"

"Cassiopeia, Draco, Ursa Minor, Ursa Major, Cepheus," Kiki answered.

Celeste looked at her, saw the faint breeze ruffle the blond curls, and wondered when she would admit at last that she was destined to stay in England. It was as if the child believed denying the facts of her life would change them. Celeste's own heart ached to see her seeking contentment in so very much the wrong direction. If only Ellery . . . but he didn't know what to do. His new wife would have to teach him how to be a father to this unhappy waif.

Penelope stepped away from the telescope. *"I* learned the names of all the summer constellations."

"Tell us," Celeste invited.

Kiki jumped up and down on the gravel path. *"Moi aussi!"*

"It's Penelope's turn," Celeste said.

"Non!" Kiki tore herself away from Celeste's restraining hand, ran a few steps up the path, and shouted, "Libra, Pegasus, Andromeda—"

"See, she does understand English. The little prat."

Penelope stood straight as a ramrod, arms crossed over her chest, staring at the capering Kiki.

Oh, dear. Cast in the shade by her younger, prettier cousin, Penelope had good reason for such sentiment. At the same time she had so much more than Kiki—the security of her father and her home.

"I just hate her. I'm good and no one ever notices me," Penelope continued. "She's naughty and she gets all the attention."

Celeste wrapped an arm around the stiff little figure. "Not tonight. Let's lie on the rug." When they'd arrived at this high, secluded spot in the garden, it had been dusk, and Herne had set up the telescope and spread a large blanket over the grass. Now she and Penelope sprawled on the blanket. As they lay on their backs, their skirts billowed with each passing breeze, but who cared? There was no one to see. This night, as music floated faintly from the house and all the proper, wealthy, patrician adults attended yet another party, Celeste and the children learned a lesson in astronomy, and another in sharing. Looking up into the firmament, Celeste asked, "Isn't it beautiful?"

"Capricornus, Aquila, Cygnus—" Kiki yelled.

Shoulder to shoulder with Celeste, Penelope stared upward, rigid with tension. "Aren't you mad at me for saying I hate her?"

"She's your cousin, and you live together like sisters. Everyone hates their cousins occasionally, and even more people hate their sisters." Celeste shrugged, and she knew Penelope felt the gesture. "The trick is not to allow your hate to make you unhappy."

Penelope began to relax. "Papa said that when he was young sometimes he hated Uncle Ellery."

Celeste didn't want to hear that. In only a day, she had observed the children's similarities to their fathers. Penelope, so much like solemn, responsible Throckmorton. Kiki, so much like the carefree, impish Ellery. And both of them capable of so much more. "Does your papa hate him now?"

"Well, I don't know, but I heard him say he's just impatient with Uncle Ellery for being so worthless."

Ellery is not worthless. The words sprang to Celeste's lips. But she didn't utter them, for she feared that the analytical Penelope would enumerate exactly how worthless Ellery was.

"So when I am old like you and Papa, will I hate Kiki less?"

With artless candor, Penelope grouped Celeste and Throckmorton together as adults, and Celeste, who had so long considered Throckmorton her elder, found herself disconcerted and distracted. How had this happened? When had she become Throckmorton's contemporary? "I . . . yes. Yes, you'll even love Kiki most of the time."

"That's what Papa says," Penelope said with satisfaction.

Kiki called, "—*et* . . . Orion . . ."

"Kiki, that's a winter constellation," Celeste said with just the right amount of indifference. "Now look up, Penelope. All the stars move, and the planets move, and the earth moves around the sun. When you lie here very still, you can almost see the universe sweep past before your eyes. Do you see what I mean?"

"Yes." Penelope's voice contained awe. "I can feel the earth move beneath me."

With a loud, exasperated sigh at their indifference, Kiki flopped down on the other side of Celeste.

"Remember, Penelope, there's more to astronomy than knowledge and a telescope," Celeste said. "Never lose your wonderment at the universe God has created for us."

"C'est grande," Kiki said.

"Oui, c'est très grande," Penelope answered.

Celeste wrapped her arms around the girls and hugged them both against her. It was good to be home.

"Attention!" Kiki pointed at the three-quarter moon hefting itself over the horizon.

As if propelled by a spring, Penelope sat up. "Can we see that through the telescope?"

"It's too bright," Celeste said. So bright, in fact, the dark blobs of trees, bushes and walls began to assume dimensions and recognizable shapes. "It's better to view the moon when it's less than half-full."

One of those recognizable shapes standing by the gate looked very much like a man. She hadn't noticed his approach, but the back of her neck prickled. She strained her eyes, trying to identify that still form.

"We'll come out when it's half-full?" Penelope asked with obvious anticipation.

"Yes." But Celeste wasn't really paying attention. Moving with innate caution, she sat up, still watching and not liking the unease that swept her. Then he—whoever he was—shifted, and she jumped like a startled deer. Celeste's heart pounded as she stared, then—

"Papa!" Penelope leaped up and ran to him as Throckmorton stepped into the moonlight.

Celeste put her hand to her chest to still the thumping of her heart. She didn't know why he had frightened her so, only that he had. Even now she sensed a tautness in him as if he were primed to fight or . . . or perhaps when she saw Throckmorton in this perfumed dark, she remembered that kiss in the dim corridor and how well he performed it.

She wanted to leave, now, before she also remembered how thoroughly she had responded.

"Did you come to look through the telescope?" Penelope asked.

"No." If he suffered uneasiness akin to Celeste's, he hid it with an air of congeniality. "I came because Mrs. Brown said it was time for you and Kiki to go to bed."

The girls groaned in unison.

Celeste had recommended Throckmorton hire Mrs. Brown as their nursemaid; the widow from the village had raised nineteen children of her own, needed the salary, and Celeste thought that nothing Penelope and Kiki could do would take Mrs. Brown by surprise. Rising from the blanket, Celeste brushed at her skirts to avoid looking at him. "I'll take them up at once."

"No need." Throckmorton gestured toward the shadows.

One of the largest, darkest, stillest shapes moved.

Kiki gave a small shriek.

Penelope jumped.

Celeste stepped forward, fists clenched.

"You're all very nervous. It's just Mr. Kinman, a friend of mine," Throckmorton said in a soothing tone. Raising his voice, he called, "Out for a smoke, Kinman?"

"Yes, Throckmorton." Mr. Kinman shambled up.

The moonlight struck his flat face. Celeste couldn't recall previously seeing that battered nose or beetled brow among the guests, but he wore a black suit and a dark cravat, so she supposed he must be a gentleman. Probably he had just arrived. Possibly she should trust Throckmorton to invite only proper guests. Yet she found her eyes narrowing as she considered him.

Still, he bowed elegantly, and how gentle he looked! As he surveyed the girls, his gruff voice softened. "Just came away from the party to indulge in a cigar. I stayed out for a few moments, enjoying the night, as did these young ladies. Did you girls learn a lot about the stars?"

"Yes, sir." Penelope stepped forward, so sure of herself her voice was firm and confident. "I'm going to become an astronomer."

"Oui, Monsieur, moi, aussi," Kiki said.

Kinman squatted so that his face was at their level. "You two will keep those astronomers on their toes." Straightening, he smiled down at them. "Remind me of my little sisters, you girls do. I miss their liveliness."

Celeste's discomfort eased. Mr. Kinman obviously liked children.

Throckmorton moved to Celeste's side, but he watched Mr. Kinman as if some grand communication was passing between them. "Mr. Kinman can take the girls up to the nursery."

"No, Mr. Throckmorton. That's not necessary. I can take the children myself." Celeste didn't enjoy being excluded like a child to be protected or a silly woman to be seduced. Moreover, she really didn't like not knowing in which category these gentlemen placed her. "I'm sure Mr. Kinman would rather rejoin the party."

The rising moon sculpted half Throckmorton's face with harsh strokes. The white light created an aggressive thrust to his chin, a blunt avowal of cheek and nose, and a dark socket lit by the faintest glint of his eye. The other half remained in brooding darkness. "Celeste, I wish to speak to you." Beneath the mildness lurked the tone of a man who expected to be obeyed.

She would obey him . . . but not about this. "I will return and find you as soon as I've taken the children upstairs."

The dark, menacing, overgrown bully beside her placed a hand on her arm. He exerted no pressure, but clearly he would if she tried to move. "I will speak to you now."

"I don't mind, miss," Mr. Kinman said in a placating tone. "I was going that way, anyway."

He held out his hands to the girls. Penelope walked over to him, and Kiki skipped after them.

Hands on her hips, Celeste watched them walk toward the house, and she refused to erase the note of disapproval in her voice. "You shouldn't allow the girls to trust a stranger so unquestioningly."

"Penelope knows to trust those I tell her to trust."

"Mr. Kinman said he came out for a smoke, but I don't believe him."

She thought Throckmorton inspected her critically, but when he spoke he sounded mildly surprised. "Not smoke? Why do you say that?"

"I didn't spot the glow of his cigar, and he didn't smell like smoke. I don't know why he was out here, but I don't trust a man who lies."

At first, she thought Throckmorton didn't believe her. Then he looked down and scraped his boot against the gravel path. "You've found him out. He's shy, hates parties, slips away every opportunity he gets. Look around anytime, and chances are you'll see him standing just on the outskirts of any celebration."

"Oh." She thought about Mr. Kinman's face, unrefined and plain.

"He really is a good man. I would put my life in his hands." He smiled without humor. "Indeed, I've done more than that. I've put my daughter's life in his hands."

"Very well." She should, perhaps, allow Mr. Kinman his bashfulness. "When next I see him, I'll try to draw him out of his shell."

Throckmorton coughed, then in a rasping voice, said, "That would be kind of you."

He was laughing, and she didn't know why. Probably she'd said something an English lady wouldn't say. Perhaps she had presumed where she shouldn't. She didn't like having Throckmorton laugh at her.

He didn't realize it, or else he thought he could jolly her out of her chagrin, for in a jesting tone he asked, "Why are *you* so suspicious, Celeste? Do kidnappers and murderers lurk on every corner in Paris?"

"In *Russia*." She considered. "Sometimes in Paris, too."

"You must tell me about your travels. I begin to suspect you've had some fascinating adventures." Taking her around the waist, he sank down on the blanket and took her with him.

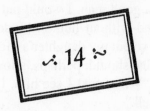

~ 14 ~

"Mr. Throckmorton! A gentleman would never use his strength against a lady." Celeste wanted to kick him in his soft parts, but as a girl she'd been taught to hold him in respect. And she was off-balance, fighting to keep her petticoats from flying up around her knees.

"I thought we would rest on the grass as you were doing with the children. Rest, look up at the stars, and you could tell me about Russia."

He sounded benign, but if it had been any other man than stodgy old Mr. Throckmorton who had tumbled her onto the ground in the night, used his voice like dark velvet close to her ear, and spoken of looking at the stars—well, with any other man, she'd have been up and running.

Even with Throckmorton, she was rightfully alarmed. Two nights ago he had kissed her, and although she had warned him further attentions were not welcome and although he had thus far listened, she realized a hitherto unintelligible fact—Throckmorton was not merely a money-making engine driven by power and omnipotence. He was also a male, sharing traits with all other males, both animal and human.

But it wouldn't do to show her wariness, so she pulled herself up to lean on her elbows. Looking down at him, she established her poise by chuckling. "Throckmorton, I never suspected you of being a *bon vivant.*"

He undermined her aplomb with a long moment of silence. Then, in a thoughtful tone, he said, "Nor I. It must be you who has brought out the vivacity in me."

Vivacity seemed a strong term, but then, if three days ago someone had told her Throckmorton would be next to her on a blanket in the night, flat on his back, relaxing . . . vivacity was perhaps an apt description, after all.

Or craft. Father said Throckmorton never did anything without purpose. What could Throckmorton's purpose be now?

Tilting her head, she looked up. The stars were there. She knew they were. But she couldn't concentrate on them *and* on conversation, for she'd kissed this very man only two nights ago. So the capacity to observe the stars—indeed, to observe anything—had to be sacrificed to the effort of discourse.

"I was wondering," he said, "why you aren't inside dancing with Ellery."

"Oh." Unerringly, he put his finger on a source of uneasiness.

"He did invite you to the party, did he not?"

"Of course! After the shooting contest today, he told me I must come." Which she had intended to do.

"I hesitate to broach a subject of some delicacy, but perhaps you are in need of a ball gown . . ."

"No!" Throckmorton's almost-offer horrified her. "Not at all."

"On a governess's salary . . ."

Was Throckmorton suspicious of her honesty? She tilted her head further, knowing that the moon shone off her right shoulder, and she presented Throckmorton with the silhouette of her throat's slender length. This time her chuckle was genuine and amused. "The ambassador's wife was most generous with her cast-offs."

"Ahh." He accepted that with a hint of relief. "Then why are you not at the party?"

All her life, she had imagined herself flirting with Ellery. Smiling at Ellery. Dancing with Ellery. That was what she'd wanted, what she dreamed of. Yet today, every time she'd dreamed that dream, a tall, thin, female figure had hovered on the fringes of her conscience— Ellery's fiancée, Lady Hyacinth.

"I thought I should get to know the children," Celeste said. As the moon rose higher, the sweet scent of night-blooming nicotiana grew stronger, carried by the gentle breeze.

"You shouldn't teach them yet. Not until we know what your role will be in their lives." He sounded sincerely disapproving.

Not that she relished being disapproved of, but she rather welcomed a gentleman who involved himself with his child's welfare. She looked down at him again. "I told them we hadn't decided if I should remain as their governess. I assured them that this week would be the proving ground. I told them tonight was only for fun. I believe they enjoyed it."

"Celeste, I suspect you feel derelict because you are not working."

She started. Only the faintest shadow of guilt that had haunted her since she set foot into Blythe Hall—the guilt of a working woman taking unearned leisure. She had scarcely noticed it. How had he? "I assure you, sir, I did no harm."

"I have the solution to your guilt." He tucked his arms under his head and gazed up at her with earnest candor. "I would like you to translate messages for me."

First she thought, *But I don't like Mr. Stanhope.* Then she realized, *But I would be spending yet more time with you.* And that increasingly had become a dangerous prospect. "Mr. Stanhope has always been your translator."

"You proved to me he isn't quite as competent as I had hoped."

"What about the children?"

"You aren't acting as their governess yet."

"The guests would wonder what I was doing."

"We shan't tell them."

"They'll notice."

"Dear Celeste." He drawled with all the bored assurance of a dandy. "The last place party guests wander into is a chamber where work takes place."

She scrabbled for an excuse and produced one strong enough for any misogynist. "Women cannot be secretaries."

"You, Celeste, will be whatever you put your mind toward being."

She could see the glint of his teeth. Throckmorton was smiling. He continued, "You needn't worry Stanhope will be unhappy with you for supplanting him. I told him he'd been working too hard and since you were here he was to take this week as a rest."

"Generous of you." *To give him leisure and take mine away, and make us both happier.* Irked and afraid she would show it, she stared up at the stars once more, but this time she didn't care if Throckmorton noticed the curve of her throat.

"Of course, Stanhope will want to know what's going on in the office. I hope you don't mind speaking to him occasionally."

Actually, she *did* mind speaking to him. When she was in Throckmorton's presence, she never remembered that his education far exceeded hers, that his acumen made him the awe of the business community, and that his foreign experiences gave him a shrewd edge.

With Mr. Stanhope, she never forgot that she was the gardener's daughter and he the aristocratic explorer.

What could she say, but, "Of course, Throckmorton, I'd be delighted to work for you as your secretary and report to Mr. Stanhope as he wishes."

"Good. Thank you."

She waited, but he said nothing else.

She'd been posing for him. Posing, suffering a kink in her neck from some bizarre feminine desire to show off her handsome figure and carefree attitude, when she didn't care whether Throckmorton noticed her at all. Probably he hadn't, anyway. The man's veins ran with ice water. Not champagne, like Ellery's. Ice water. With a silent huff, she flounced backward—and when she laid her head back, it landed on something. Something warm, something firm . . . how had he managed to get his arm out from under his head and under hers? He might have ice water in his veins, but he also had excellent reflexes.

She would have sat back up, but Throckmorton utilized that dark velvet voice again. "I've never been to Russia," he said. "Tell me about Russia."

Unwillingly, she relaxed. If it wasn't Throckmorton beside her, she'd have called that a "seduce-you" voice. But Throckmorton was too sensible to think a starlit sky and an interest in her journeys would bring her to his bed. Not when he'd just been so dreadfully manipulative.

"Russia. Very, very far away. Immense. Overwhelming." She didn't like to talk about that trip. The experience had been too colossal for mere words to encompass, and when she tried people got bored, or they just couldn't comprehend the vast horizons, the contrasts of heat and cold, poor and rich, and her own sense of alienation from everything familiar. "We left Paris in March to spend the summer on an estate in the Ukraine. The travel took weeks by rail, by ship, by carriage."

"To a land where everything is strange and new."

With a jolt, she recalled that Throckmorton had been to the Americas, to India and to places beyond. "The food, even the food I liked, tasted different," she said.

"The clothes are wild brilliant weaves, or primitive skins, or so dirty one can't tell the original color."

"Everything smelled like smoke or sweat or horses—"

"Or something so exotic you couldn't even guess at its origin."

"Yes!" He did understand! She turned her head—to find him so close they were nose to nose. He reclined on his side, facing her. Their lips almost met. His breath whispered warm across her cheeks.

She stopped breathing, stopped moving, and just stared. In the darkness, she could see only the outline of him, but she had observed him far too closely these last few days not to know his expression held that grave intensity he wore when he wished to kiss her. When he would kiss her.

Her eyes fluttered shut, a tacit consent.

The arm beneath her head wrapped her closer. His other arm embraced her, pulling her close against his warmth, his strength. His mouth touched hers . . . and it was the same as it was before. Better, because she knew what to expect. The warm, firm pressure, the gentle urging. She opened her lips to him, allowed him access, curled her tongue around his in the intricate, ancient dance of desire. Pleasure spiraled deep in her belly and everything she felt and knew and was—was Throckmorton.

As she yielded, his tempered passion changed. He tasted her more greedily. He held her more tightly. The grass, crushed and rich with summer, gave off its growing scent and mixed with the scent of him—the scent of citrus soap, of starch, of leather and of masculine warmth, faint but enveloping. She would recognize his scent anywhere, for it made her mouth water and her body yearn.

Finally, he lifted his mouth with an impatient grunt. Rolling her onto her back, he rose above her, dominating her with his height, his breadth, his scent and strength.

Her eyes opened, seeing him as a silhouette against the stars. The stars that were still there, but no longer familiar. Brighter, cleaner, and changed somehow. Instead of the constellations that had illuminated the night sky from time immemorial, they had shifted to form different shapes—flowers blossoming in the eternal night, lacy gowns of white, lovers wrapped in each other's arms.

Then he leaned over her, blotting them out. He kissed her lips urgently. He tasted of velvet night sky, of darkness that went on forever. He tasted of stars burning far away, of grandeur barely glimpsed, of worlds lost in the ether where exotic emotions held sway and he could command her body and all its responses. Each stroke of his tongue took her farther away from this place, this world, and she went willingly, not knowing where she wandered or why.

He kissed her cheeks, tilted her head aside, kissed her neck. Her throat. His mouth traveled, open and damp, up to her ear. His weight pressed her into the blanket. He wanted. She surrendered. But she wasn't afraid. Instead she wrapped her arms around his waist and whispered his name. "Garrick. Garrick."

Without warning, he hurled himself off of her and flung himself to his feet.

Lifting herself onto her elbows, she pushed her hair from her eyes. "Garrick?"

He stood with his back to her, hands on his hips.

"Throckmorton, what's wrong?"

"Go dress in your finest gown." The velvet voice was gone, replaced by the guttural tone of a beast who had barely mastered the power of speech. "Dance with Ellery. Flirt with Ellery. Let me see you with Ellery, or you will find out just how little I care that you love Ellery."

* * *

Seated at his desk, Throckmorton tapped his pen incessantly on the smooth, polished wood and stared at the blasted girl, head bent over the letter she was translating. Outdoors, rain dripped off the eaves and sluiced down the gutters, making the morning dark and drear. Candles flickered in candelabras set on either side of the desk to light the work so necessary to the perpetuity of the British Empire. And each little bead of light danced in the blonde strands that mixed with the honey brown of Celeste's hair and lent a creamy patina to the smooth curve of her neck. She was beautiful, she was efficient, and the previous night, she had dared to do just as he told her to do. She had put on a ball gown of white, silken beauty and proceeded to flirt and dance with Ellery.

Throckmorton tapped the pen more quickly.

That hadn't been how he'd planned it. Oh, he'd commanded her, but he hadn't meant it. He'd wanted her to hide in her bedchamber, the bedchamber between deaf Lady Francis and hard-of-hearing Mrs. Landor, the bedchamber he thought an advantage should Ellery come to pound on Celeste's door. Last night he had realized that bedchamber would be an advantage to him, Throckmorton, too. If he were to slip inside, the old ladies on either side would never know of his presence as he schooled Celeste in the luxury of love.

He had better move her into the now finished bedchamber beside the nursery, for thoughts like that could prove dangerous for his sanity . . . and for Celeste's chastity.

How could she have gone to the ball? Throckmorton had wanted Celeste to dream of him and his kisses. Kisses he had found disturbing, intimate . . . almost uncontrollable.

His only objective, of course, was to save Ellery from her clutches, *of course,* and to preserve the very profitable union between Lord Longshaw and the Throckmortons.

"Throckmorton?" Celeste gazed directly at him through those hazel eyes. "The spelling on this document is rather erratic. I need to concentrate. Would you please stop tapping?"

"What?" He looked down at his constantly moving hand. "Oh. Yes." He stopped.

She had the nerve to calmly go back to work.

Didn't she comprehend how irked he was? Entire countries trembled at his command. She seemed not to care that she distracted him from his work, nor did she note how desperately he wished to rise, circle the desk, tilt her chin back and kiss her until she no longer remembered any other man's name.

Kiss her.

He laughed harshly.

She paused in her writing and looked at him with the faintly alarmed expression of a woman confronted with a lunatic.

Which, perhaps, he had become. For when had he ever hungered for a woman like this? He currently had no mistress, and no taste for finding one when the only thought on his mind was Celeste, and Celeste, and Celeste.

The truth was, he wanted to do more than kiss her. He wanted to unfasten her bodice, the bodice which laced up from her tiny waist, over the curve of her breasts and just to the narrow V of her collar. That lacing challenged any man worth his salt, leading him into the kind of temptation forbidden in every precept of proper and Christian society.

Yet Throckmorton did not give in to temptation. He wasn't that kind of man.

No, but he did imagine things. Things like loosening the tie on her lace chemise to view her breasts, with their silken textured skin and their pale, soft nipples. He dreamed of how they would taste, how they would pucker when he suckled on them.

If he were not the man he was, if he were irresponsible and lacked discipline, he would show her that his kisses were but a prelude to other delights which he alone could teach her. When he ran his hands up the silk-stockinged avenue of her legs, he would note each soft secret curve of flesh. At the top, he would open the slit in her pantaloons. At first he would touch her delicately, giving her time to get used to his fingers brushing the tight curls which hid her inner sanctum.

But when she looked up at him with those beautiful, changeable eyes and begged him for more . . . ah, then he would open the folds and find that most precious nub of feminine sensuality. And when he had caressed her until she was sighing and twisting, her marvelous sweet voice begging him for release then, and only then, would he enter her with his finger.

That, too, would be a prelude. He would linger over her like a musician over a fine instrument, and he would prove his competence extended beyond business and espionage. If he allowed himself the pleasure of pleasuring her, he would wipe her mind clear of any name but his. His was the name she would call in her ecstasy. He would teach her that. He would teach her everything.

If he allowed himself.

Which he would not.

He had to remember who he was. He had to remember who she was. He had to remember that her father was his faithful gardener, that he planned to send her back to Paris, that she was a virgin and he would never, ever dishonor a virtuous girl. Not even a girl whose smile brought him a pleasure he hadn't experienced for too many long, lonely years.

"Mr. Throckmorton, please!" Celeste was glaring at him.

Had she read his thoughts?

No. She was glowering at the pen in his hand, which tapped and tapped and tapped.

"I cannot work any more quickly, and you are distracting me." She sighed in aggravation. "Why don't you walk out and consult with Esther on what she's making for tonight's entertainment? I understand it's a musical evening, and I'm sure you'll enjoy hearing the ladies display their gifts."

His gaze dropped to her bosom, but he knew she didn't mean those gifts.

Unaware, she continued, "When you get back, I promise I'll be done."

Carefully, he placed the pen on the desk. "I'll stay."

Because under no circumstances would he stand and display himself in this aching, aroused, desperate condition.

A burst of laughter from the conservatory stopped Celeste in her tracks. The rainy morning had turned into a rainy afternoon, and the youthful group who surrounded Ellery had taken up residence among the marble columns, the half dozen soft sofas, and the blaze of Milford's cherished flowers.

Ellery's smooth, practiced voice said, "You're witty as well as handsome, Lady Napier."

Lady Napier. Celeste allowed herself a private sneer. That smiling, flirtatious, covetous beauty. Last night she had dared raise questions about Celeste's sudden appearance and mysterious antecedents.

If Celeste was still the Celeste who had arrived from Paris, she would march right into the conservatory and snatch Ellery out from underneath Lady Napier's thin, aristocratic nose. But that Celeste had danced until three in the morning, eaten too much rich food, drunk too much champagne. Some intermediate Celeste had spent the morning translating documents from unintelligible Russian into pristine English for an ominous, snarling Throckmorton. Now the Celeste who stood here found retrieving Ellery to be too much of an effort.

So when he shouted, "Let's go gamble away our ill-gotten inheritances," Celeste pressed herself against the wall behind a miniature potted orange tree and watched as the whole, silly bunch of them fluttered and stomped out on their way toward another afternoon spent doing . . . nothing.

The scent of citrus faintly wafted from the white blossoms. A few fledgling green oranges hung with the promise of fruit. Celeste stared at the waxy, emerald-veined leaves and pressed her fingertips to her forehead. She really had to get over this onslaught of fastidiousness. She had wanted Ellery forever, and she didn't understand her own confusion, her appalled attraction to stodgy old Garrick.

And when had she begun to think of him as Garrick?

She didn't think him more attractive than Ellery, so she hadn't gone completely mad. But Garrick interested her; he was an enigma, a puzzle of darkling glares, fascinating insights and bone-melting kisses.

His kisses had driven her to the ball last night. She had needed the music, the dancing, the sight of Ellery to drive the sound, the feel, the sight of Garrick from her senses.

She had succeeded. If only she had not agreed to work with Garrick . . . not that he'd given her a choice.

She peered around the orange tree. Ellery and his crowd had rounded the corner. When the noise had died and she was sure the corridor was empty, she stepped

out and prepared to go in the opposite direction—when
the stifled sound of a sob within the conservatory
stopped her. Somehow she knew she shouldn't go to see
who was crying. Some higher power warned her she
would be sorry.

But whoever it was followed the first sob with a second, and a third, and the most long, pathetic sniff Celeste had ever heard. So with no more intention than to
offer her handkerchief, she stepped into the conservatory.

Windows covered the outer wall and looked out onto
the garden and the circle drive where carriages assembled to discharge their passengers. Potted blue clematis
climbed up trellises between the windows. In the winter
when the winds blew cold, and during the hottest days
of summer, the velvet drapes of royal blue could be
drawn, but even then the conservatory exuded the
warmth of a much-loved chamber. Huge blue vases of
yellow roses stood on tables and in corners, and in the
center of the long room, two orange trees grew in huge
pots, scenting the air with their delicate, spicy fragrance. The slender branches met overhead to form a
dense green tangle, and like a flood of gold, alyssum
frothed from the base of the trunks and down the sides
of the pots.

The rustle of her skirts must have given her away, for
the sobbing came to an abrupt halt and someone—a
woman, Celeste deduced from the soft patter of leather
slippers and the rustle of petticoats—hid herself.

Celeste wanted to bang her head on the white marble
column beside her. Only one of the refined thorough-
breds at this house party was so unsure of herself that
she would hide to cry, and she was the one girl Celeste

should leave utterly to her own devices. Instead, she found herself calling softly, "Lady Hyacinth? Is that you?"

"Y . . . yes." The girl sounded soggy and pathetic.

"What's wrong?"

"N . . . nothing."

Celeste looked down at the floor, decided to believe her and escape while she could. "All right. If you're sure."

"Y . . . yes. I'm . . . I'm fine." The last, blatantly obvious lie was followed by a burst of crying desperate enough to melt even Throckmorton's heart.

"Oh, my dear." Celeste went to the column where Hyacinth was hiding and wrapped the humiliated girl in an embrace. An awkward embrace, for Hyacinth towered a good six inches over her, but Celeste cradled her as she would any wounded creature. "What's wrong?"

Hyacinth didn't flatten Celeste with a box to the ears. A good sign, considering that last night Celeste had spent from eleven to three making Ellery laugh and say things like, *You're witty as well as handsome, Miss Milford.*

Ellery really ought to come up with some different way to reprise that old chorus.

"It's . . . Ellery," Hyacinth said.

Of *course* it was Ellery. Celeste had first heard him spout the "witty/handsome" chestnut to Lady Agatha Bilicliffe outside the walled garden. Celeste had been fourteen. Ellery had been sent down from Eton. And Celeste had dreamed of the day Ellery would compliment her with such splendid eloquence.

Hyacinth stared into space and twisted her damp handkerchief. "He isn't paying attention to me."

None of Celeste's dreams were turning out as splendidly as she had hoped. Certainly she had never imagined she would be caught giving comfort to Ellery's fiancée. "Why do you say that?"

"You saw him. He hasn't spoken to me in two days. He ignores me as if he can't bear the sight of me. Today, he didn't notice I remained behind." Hyacinth turned tear-filled eyes toward Celeste. "Why, last night, he even flirted with you!"

"Well. Yes, he did." Abashed, Celeste looked everywhere but at Hyacinth. "He flirts as easily as he breathes. It doesn't mean anything." Except it did mean something when he flirted with her. It *did.*

"But he's not doing it with *me.*" Hyacinth started to cry again, and this time she bawled like a baby, without control, wheezing with great, gasping sobs.

Wishing she were anywhere but here, Celeste led Hyacinth to the sofa.

"Big . . . tall . . . gangly," Hyacinth sobbed.

Celeste inferred Hyacinth was talking about herself. Going to an exotic teak chest, she opened it and removed one of the woven blankets from its interior.

"Clumsy . . . couldn't learn to dance . . ."

Returning to Hyacinth, Celeste wrapped the throw around the girl's shoulders.

Hyacinth huddled and shivered. "Never learned conversation . . . embarrassed . . . spots on my face . . . dreadful."

Alarmed at the blue tinge to Hyacinth's complexion, Celeste instructed, "Take a breath."

Hyacinth obeyed with a long, quivering gasp, and managed to articulate, "Father bought me the most handsome man in England, and I love Ellery *desper-*

ately, and I can't . . . make him . . . interested." The last word came out on a wail.

Stuffing her handkerchief into Hyacinth's hand, Celeste said, "I'm sure that's not true."

"You know very well it is." Hyacinth mopped her eyes. "Look at me. Overgrown. All arms and legs. Ellery probably wonders if I can beat him in a fair fight."

"Well, of course you can, given a good rifle and a chance to aim." Celeste essayed a smile at the startled Hyacinth.

"That's another thing! You can shoot, and everyone thinks you're still ladylike, but if I try to talk about my Greek studies, they all act as if I've developed a dread disease." Hyacinth viewed Celeste with damp resentment. "Why can you evade censure, and I can't?"

"Because most men believe in their secret heart of hearts that, if necessary, I would falter if required to use a gun in defense or attack." Celeste invited Hyacinth to share her grin. "They have a bit more trouble believing themselves the better of a woman whose mind is equal or, heaven forbid, superior to theirs."

"Oh." Hyacinth returned the grin, but with a pained edge. "But I do get tired of pretending to be stupid. Will I never again be able to discuss the Greek classics in Greek?"

"You can with me, but I'm afraid you'll be amused by my accent and bored by my opinions, for I was instructed with the other serv—" Celeste caught herself. She had almost said too much. She had almost revealed her background, and last night she'd trod her way through the interrogation too successfully to give up her secrets now. "I doubt my education was the equal of yours."

"But that's wonderful!" Hyacinth's eyes glowed with pleasure. "I think we will be wonderful friends, if not sisters."

Celeste jerked back.

Eyes wide, Hyacinth covered her mouth with her hand. "I'm sorry. That was premature and tactless. Only I saw Throckmorton watching you last night, and I could tell he . . . admires you greatly."

Throckmorton had been watching her this morning, too, and hid his admiration behind a scowl and a constantly tapping pen. "I should leave now—"

"Wait!"

The panic in Hyacinth's voice stopped Celeste as she tried to retreat.

Hyacinth's head was bent. She picked at the stitching on the handkerchief. The rain sluiced across the large south-facing windows, and the room was drear and dim and silent.

Celeste prayed for rescue.

Instead, Hyacinth said in the rapid tone of someone who anticipates rejection, "Please. Everyone admires you. Ellery admires you. Won't you teach me how to win him back?"

Celeste's father would say she had found herself with her rump in a vise, and inform her she deserved it, too. As it was, she could only stare at the red-eyed, swollen-faced, miserable Hyacinth and stammer, "I just . . . I don't know . . ."

"Yes. Yes, you do!" Hyacinth took Celeste's hands. "You are from Paris. You have an air about you. Everyone admires you or envies you, especially that snake Lady Napier. What can I do to be like you?"

"Um, well . . . you have to act happy."

"Act happy." Hyacinth started patting at the cushions on the oversized sofa as if she were looking for something.

"What are you doing?" Celeste asked.

"I'm looking for my pocketbook. I have paper in there and I can take notes—"

Celeste put her hands over Hyacinth's. "You don't need to take notes. You can remember this. Smile."

"I don't really feel like—"

"It doesn't matter. Smile."

Hyacinth stretched her lips over her teeth.

"That's right. A false smile is better than a real scowl. If you smile, everyone will want to be with you because you're happy, and then you really are happy because you have friends who feel good when they're around you."

"It's so insincere."

"And society is not?"

Hyacinth laughed and for the first time since Celeste had entered, she relaxed. "That's your secret?"

"Think about it. Have I done anything else to make myself attractive?"

Hyacinth's smile disappeared. "But you are attractive."

"So are you." Once again, Celeste tried to stand. "Now, go back to the party—"

"Wait." Hyacinth caught Celeste's hand and Celeste sank back down. "There must be more you can tell me. Tell me how to make him notice me *today*."

Details. Hyacinth wanted details. Very well. Celeste would give her details. "You smile at him and turn away. You watch him through your lashes. You move with womanly grace, then trip and let him catch you. You accidentally brush his arm with your breast."

"That's devious. That's"—Hyacinth took a shaking breath—"genius."

Celeste was unwillingly flattered. "If you are going to keep a man like Ellery interested, you have to play the game better than he does." Celeste gave a Gallic shrug. "Count de Rosselin said a woman can keep a man in thrall forever if she knows when to tease and when to be generous."

"Did the count say how to know that?"

"Listen to your instincts. Practice in the mirror. And make Ellery work to win your love."

"But I . . . I already love him." Hyacinth's eyes swam with tears.

Celeste hated to see the young girl so stricken. With a comforting hug, she said, "But he doesn't have to know that."

"I've told him."

"You are so very young, you could fall out of love with Ellery and into love with that handsome Lord Townshend without pause."

"But I'm not so fickle!"

Celeste smiled. "Ellery doesn't have to know that."

"Oh." Hyacinth's brow wrinkled as she reflected.

"Tonight, arrange your dance card so that you dance with Ellery, then with Lord Townshend. When Ellery relinquishes you to Lord Townshend, turn to the lord, smile and say, 'Where have you been all my life?' Not too loudly, just so that Ellery can hear."

"What will Lord Townshend think of me?"

"He'll think you're flirting, and he is used to that. All men with a fortune and their own teeth are used to being courted."

Hyacinth nodded. "He helped me push the swing."

"So he likes you. Ellery will watch you then, and you can smile up at Lord Townshend as if he were the brightest star in the sky."

"I don't know how."

"Of course you do," Celeste said. "That's the way you smile at Ellery. That's why he thinks he has you wrapped around his little finger."

Hyacinth lowered her head and glared narrowly at Celeste. "He does think that, doesn't he?"

"Indeed he does. Now, dance a little too close to Lord Townshend and ask him about his dogs."

"His dogs?"

"He breeds hunting spaniels. As long as he's talking about them you won't lack for conversation and he won't wonder what you're up to. When he returns you to Ellery, let your hand linger on Lord Townshend's arm for a moment too long."

"What if Ellery doesn't notice?"

"He will, and I promise he'll draw the correct—or in this case, incorrect—conclusions."

"And he'll love me again?"

"Yes . . . yes, he will." The folly of what she was doing struck Celeste. Why was she telling her rival how to keep Ellery when *she* wanted him? She hadn't shared a few words of advice, as she'd originally intended. She had forgotten the contest and told everything she knew.

But surely it didn't matter. Telling Hyacinth what to do and having Hyacinth do it correctly were two different things. Hyacinth had had no practice in the feminine arts; she couldn't be good at it, even with the incentive of wanting Ellery as she did. And Ellery . . . Ellery wanted *her,* Celeste. He wouldn't be swayed by Hyacinth's bids for attention. Just as she wouldn't be swayed by Throckmorton. By his conversation. His interest. His kisses.

She had only kissed Throckmorton because she had thought . . . that is, it had seemed . . . well, the kisses didn't matter. Just a meeting of lips, the scent of his breath, wetness and warmth . . . she shook herself. "Now I must go . . ."

"There's one other thing," Hyacinth said quickly, so quickly the words tumbled over each other and embarrassment etched each syllable. "I can't ask anyone else. I just can't."

Desperately, Celeste wished she had made her exit the first time she'd tried. Or the second. Or the third.

"Mama keeps hinting about my duty to my husband, and I don't know what she's talking about and she won't tell me." Hyacinth stared earnestly into Celeste's eyes. "Please, *please* won't you tell me what she's hinting at?"

Not sure whether she had been insulted by a master or by an idiot, Celeste jerked her hand away. "I don't know what she means. I've never known a man!"

"Known a man," Hyacinth said in surprise. "As in the Biblical sense?"

"Exactly as in the Biblical sense."

"Oh, dear, dear Celeste, I didn't mean . . . well, I didn't even realize that was what Mama meant. I know you have never been married, only I thought that everyone who went to Paris discovered all about the world, and you are older and so much more polished than I, the little country bumpkin." Again Hyacinth took Celeste's hand, and Celeste let her have it. "I am so sorry if I offended you. It's just Ellery is slipping away from me, and there's no one who I can talk to. No one who will listen to me!"

Celeste sighed. It was true. Hyacinth was young, ardent, obvious, like a large, clumsy puppy trying to impress her new master. Celeste had dismissed her as a rival. Everyone within the two families assumed Hyacinth would do as she was told without demur. Even the servants—loyal to Celeste—ignored Hyacinth when she spoke. Without a doubt, the girl needed assistance if she were to be Ellery's wife—or anyone's wife. And unfortunately, she reminded Celeste of herself in the early throes of her crush on Ellery. Surely a little moral support would not come amiss, nor would it spoil Celeste's own chances with Ellery.

"All right, I will tell you about what will happen on your wedding night," Celeste said. "But you must promise not to scream or cry."

Hyacinth's hand squeezed Celeste's. "It's worse than I feared." She straightened her shoulders. "Very well, I will be brave."

"Between a man and a woman, there is much"— Celeste paused, but could think of no delicate word to describe the condition—"nudity."

Obviously shaken, Hyacinth asked, "Whose?"

"Both."

Eyes large, Hyacinth swallowed.

"Your husband will touch you in . . . places."

Hyacinth gasped and shuddered. "He won't want *me* to touch *him,* will he?"

Celeste considered the information she had been given. "I don't know. I never heard about that, but I know men always like women to serve them in every way."

"Yes. Yes, you're right. Papa likes it when Mama . . ." Hyacinth paled. "Oh, I don't want to think about that!"

Remembering the sharp-eyed Lord Longshaw and the plump Lady Longshaw, Celeste said, "But your parents are so old!"

"In their forties." Hyacinth nodded solemnly. "I fear for their health, if what you tell me is true."

"You haven't heard the worst of it yet." Celeste lowered her voice. "Your husband will want to service you, as a stallion does a mare."

The news clearly shook Hyacinth. "You mean climb on me and—oh!" She clapped her hand over her mouth.

"Yes." Celeste nodded.

"Put his . . . into my . . ."

"As I understand it."

"But that's horrible!"

Celeste chewed her lip indecisively. Truth to tell, she thought it sounded horrible, too, but the facts didn't seem to bear that out. "That's the amazing part. Madame Ambassador always seemed rather giddy when Monsieur paid her attentions, and in the morning they both seemed very blissful! Also, Count de Rosselin told me that it is up to the man to make the woman happy, or he is no man at all."

"Then Ellery must be a wonderful . . . wonderful . . ."

"Lover."

"Yes! Lover!" An almost audible breaking of maidenly bonds accompanied Hyacinth's use of the word. "Ellery must be a wonderful lover, for that's the problem. All the women smile at him. All the women whisper to him." She smacked her fist onto the arm of the sofa. "I am sick of it!"

Carried away by her enthusiasm, Celeste shook Hyacinth's shoulder. "Then you must be better than they are. You can do it!"

"I'm off!" Hyacinth leaped to her feet, tossing the blanket aside like Boadicea throwing off Roman shackles. "I will do just as you advised me, Miss Milford, and thank you so much. You are a good, good person!"

No, I'm not. "Don't forget. When Ellery realizes you are falling in love with Lord Townshend, he'll try to win you back with charm and compliments. You will not be swayed."

"I won't?"

"No. It takes more than a few false smiles and easy compliments to buy your affections. You will be indifferent. He will be puzzled and intrigued."

"And while I'm pretending I don't care, I brush his arm with my breast. Yes, I understand it all." With a rustle of skirts, Hyacinth was gone.

Celeste collapsed back onto the sofa cushions, amazed at her own, and Hyacinth's, bravado.

But Celeste started when Throckmorton's drawl interrupted her thoughts. "I would say she doesn't quite understand it all."

~ 16 ~

Throckmorton stepped out from behind a fluted marble column. Walking to the doors, he shut them. They clicked closed with the finality of a prison cell. Returning, he observed Celeste in a way that made her want to check her laces to see if they were open. "I'd have to say I don't understand, either. Was Lady Hyacinth too easy a rival before? You advised her because you wished for stronger competition?"

"I just thought that she . . . she deserves something more than . . . a lifetime with an indifferent husband." Courageously, Celeste tacked on, "Whoever he might be."

Throckmorton took no notice of her defiance. He just watched her, his freshly shaved cheek creased in a crooked smile that projected no warmth. "You know an awful lot about what goes on between a man and a woman."

She caught her breath. Of course. He'd heard . . .
How much . . . ?

But it didn't matter how much he'd heard. No matter
what, she'd embarrassed herself, and a blush exploded
onto her cheeks, heating them like fire.

"I heard enough to make me think you are a very astute young woman." Walking toward her, he offered his
hand.

She took it, because he was Garrick Throckmorton
and always in control of himself and his reactions.

As he drew her up, she realized her mistake. He
didn't step back to allow her room. He simply pulled her
into himself. Releasing her hand, he caught her waist in
his arms and, while she was off-balance, he swung her
around to lean against the column.

"A move smooth enough to remind you of Ellery."
He sounded sarcastic, indignant, even angry, not at all
the determinedly even-tempered man she had come to
know.

"Yes. Yes, of course, it does." She lifted her chin and
stared him in the eyes. "But if it were Ellery, it would
have been accompanied by a laugh."

"Try this instead." Angling his face, he kissed her.

The catch of breath, the press of lips, that was the
same as before. But that was all. The gentleman Throckmorton had vanished. He left behind his well-considered
kisses that had showcased his skills. He no longer displayed consideration for her lack of experience. No, this
time he ravaged her mouth, opening her to his tongue
without finesse or courtesy.

She responded because she didn't know how not to.

He pressed her against the column. Her starched petticoats crackled in protest. His weight seemed more

than it had on that blanket beneath the stars, for he hadn't a care for her comfort. His male scent filled her mind like a heady incense. His taste . . . ah, it wasn't urbane passion, nor was it starlight and velvet. Those impressions had been cloaks he had donned to hide the truth about him. No, now he tasted of dark passion and of hidden, fevered tempests of the soul.

Frightened by his ardor, by his strength, by her own response to the darkness within him, she whimpered and struggled.

Catching her wrists, he raised them over his head, lifting her onto her toes, holding her against him. He wore his jacket, his waistcoat, his shirt and cravat and trousers, but he might as well have been nude. The layers of clothing couldn't hide the firmness of his muscles, the superiority of his strength. If he meant to make her feel helpless, to know how little she could do to save herself, he had succeeded admirably.

Lifting his head, he glared at her, his dark brown eyes fierce. "Unless I allow it, you will never be free."

A threat. A threat that meant more than just the words could convey. She stared back at him. "Mr. Throckmorton, you're being a dolt, and I do not kiss dolts."

"Does that stare and that tone of voice usually work for you?" He sounded interested and worse, intrigued.

She tried again. "You're acting like an impertinent school lad."

"Very frightening. Do the lesser men wither and run away?"

They did. When faced with her governess stringency, lesser men always ran away.

She was a fool to think Throckmorton was a lesser man. "I don't know why you're upset, but really, it is time to loose your grip before my arms snap off."

Very slowly, he lowered her arms, allowing her to once again lean against the pillar. For a brief and marvelous moment, she was free of the potent authority of his torso against hers. Then he leaned forward, pressing his lower body into the full bell of her petticoats, holding her again with his body and his hands, showing her in no uncertain terms that she was helpless in his grasp. She swallowed and her gaze clung to his face, seeking tolerance, humor, even the intelligence she knew formed Mr. Throckmorton. But the dark shadow of his beard, the flare of his nostrils, the smile that looked so much like a snarl: all betrayed the primal savage that lurked in wait . . . for her.

In the brusque tone of the beast, he said, "I don't know if Hyacinth really believes you are a virgin, you who know so much—"

"Hearsay!"

"—But I do believe. If you were an experienced woman, you would know better than to wear your bodice laced up the front."

Confused, she glanced down. She was decent, more than decent, with her pale green dimity gown and its dark green ribbons tied almost at her neck. "What do you mean?"

"No Englishwoman wears her bodice laced up the front. Doing so makes a man think of unlacing it."

"Buttons up the back—"

"Aren't nearly so enticing." With her wrists held in one hand, his other dropped to the lacing he taunted her about.

He touched right in the cleft between her breasts. She drew a quick, indrawn breath. Valiantly, she tried to protest, but her voice failed her at the last syllable. "This is preposterous."

"A woman's back can be a marvel of physical pulchritude, but nothing compares to a woman's breasts—"

"Mr. Throckmorton!" Weak. Weak response, but she was truly shocked. He had not only touched her, but he had used that word. *Breasts*. No one, not even in Paris, ever spoke so bluntly about the feminine form. Such language was taboo. It was vulgar. It was familiar. And because he spoke of her breasts as if he held every right over her body, her heart thumped in an uncomfortable, irregular beat. It was almost as if she'd been running from him, and he'd caught her, and would do with her as he pleased.

But she hadn't been running from him.

Had she?

And he certainly hadn't been giving chase.

Had he?

Without a shred of shame or decency, he untied the ribbon of her bodice. She had double knotted it, but he proved dexterous and speedy.

Celeste shuffled her feet to the side, trying madly to sneak away.

Slowly, as if he were unwrapping a long anticipated package, he pulled the lacing loose, one ribbon at a time.

She twisted, trying to liberate herself before he—

He tugged at her shift, baring her breasts. And he looked.

The cool air touched her bare skin, bringing her nipples to a tight pucker.

A smile tugged at the edge of his mouth. "See." He smoothed a single finger over her. "You show your desire."

"It's not desire." She hated the smug comprehension lurking on his features. "I'm cold!"

His eyelids drooped over his brooding gaze. "I can warm you."

A blush began at her waist—or maybe lower. Lower certainly felt odd, with a twisting in her belly, a fullness and moisture in her womb. "No. Just cover me." She glanced toward the door. It remained thankfully shut, but she whispered furiously, "Please, Mr. Throckmorton!"

"You needn't speak so quietly or worry so much." His own voice was deep and husky, rich with pleasure and, she feared, expectancy. "No one's going to look in on us. There's a party going on. No one cares where we are."

"I do!" In a burst of inspired defiance, she added, "And . . . and Ellery does!"

At the mention of his brother's name, Throckmorton pounced on her. Pounced, kissed . . . she might have been a mouse in the grip of a lion, he held her so competently and kissed her so thoroughly. When she tried to struggle, he just . . . held her. Leaned against her, crushing her bare breasts to his waistcoat, holding her chin in his fingers. He moved his hips against hers in a leisurely, painstaking roll.

When she realized he'd released her hands, she grabbed his hair in a ferocious grip and tugged him away—and thought better of it when he lifted his head.

Who was this man? She'd thought him civilized; overcivilized, even. But his pupils had widened so his brown eyes looked black and demonic. He grinned, his teeth white in his tanned face. Leaning down, he took her lower lip between his teeth. He didn't bite down; the friction might even be called erotic. But it was a threat, and this time when he lifted his head, he did it on his own accord.

She couldn't take her gaze from his. "I'm afraid of you."

"No, you're not." He slid his hand onto her breastbone. "It's not fear that makes your heart pound. It's this." He cupped her breast, then pinched her nipple. Almost. Like the bite on her lip, it wasn't painful, but . . .

Her knees knocked together in fear and . . . oh, what was this mixture of embarrassment and excitement? He'd given her a taste of it before, but this was different. This time there was no tenderness, there was no control. There was only a madman who wore a familiar face. "Why are you threatening me?" she asked.

"Better to ask, what am I threatening you with?" He laughed, a gravelly sound that sent a chill up her spine. "You think you know, but you don't."

"Know what?" she demanded. He was speaking in riddles and she hated everything about this. His attentions, her discomfort . . . her unwanted, illicit anticipation.

"I'm going to show you why the ambassador's wife was giddy when her husband paid her attentions."

"You can't!" His threat—for such it was, for all his denials—sent her grappling toward freedom. "It's not fitting."

"I'm weary of always doing what's right, and I promise you when I'm done, you'll be happy." Through gritted teeth he added, "And I won't."

He let her go, then used her escape momentum to whirl her around and tumble her onto the sofa and onto her back.

"Why are you angry at me?" She struggled to sit up.

He pushed her back down. "You let me think you were just the gardener's daughter. Just another girl who was in love with Ellery." He wasn't rough, but he didn't permit rebellion. "You lied."

"What's wrong with you? I am who I said. I never lied."

"I'm not lying about this." He sat on Celeste, trapped her between his thighs. "I'm going to take my revenge."

"How dare you presume to pass judgment on me? I didn't perform any misdeed!" She twisted sideways. "I simply talked to Lady Hyacinth. I gave her sound advice."

"I don't care about Lady Hyacinth. You're generous. You're sweet. You're kind, even to a rival. You're the most dangerous kind of woman there is. It's you who has laid my plans to ruin." With scrupulous care, he tore her chemise from top to bottom.

The sound of ripping material shocked her. This was Mr. Throckmorton, the most normal, restrained, disciplined man of her acquaintance, and in a considered move, he had torn her chemise. The world had gone mad. *He* had gone mad.

Leaning down toward her breasts, he brushed one with his cheek. "I promised you a lesson. I will give it, Celeste."

"This isn't a lesson you have the right to give."

"Now, today, I take whatever right I choose." His breath was a brush of air against her skin. "I choose to teach. Lesson one—your breasts are more than enticing, pale and capped with rose. They are also sensitive to touch." His tongue encircled her nipple.

Gooseflesh rose. The blood rushed through her veins.

"Point proven." His voice had thickened. "And for further proof . . ." His mouth clamped down and suckled.

She shoved at his shoulders, tugged at his hair. How could he do this? How could he make her burn with . . . with embarrassment and . . . and desire at the same time? The damp of his mouth, the roughness of his tongue, the sensation of suction on her nipple brought her arching into his arms. She didn't want to want this, and at the same time a passionate folly, quite outside her control, ruled her body.

Lifting his head, he demanded, "Look at me."

She did. She recognized him . . . yet she didn't. The ruffled hair, the burning gaze, the menace, the boldness . . . How could this man with his driving sexual demands be Garrick Throckmorton?

His knee pressed between her legs, opening them. "I'm not going to hurt you. I'm not going to take you. Believe me."

"If you think that's reassurance, think again." She slapped at his head.

He trapped her arms, held them close to her side. "But I want to see you when I take you beyond pleasure. I'll never have more than that, but that memory I will have." It sounded like a vow. Sliding his lower body off of the sofa, he knelt on the floor beside her. He lifted her skirt, slipping his hand up her calf.

She twisted against him. "This isn't right!"

"That's one true thing you've said tonight. It isn't right, but you deserve the lesson. Of touch on silk"—his fingers skimmed along her stocking, then past her garter—"and touch on bare skin. Of pleasures muted and pleasures bold."

His caress on her thigh gave her a sense of his implacability, but he sounded almost poetic. What moved a man like this to poetry?

Only this, she supposed. Only the physical. Trapped, rigid with resistance, she said, "I still don't understand why."

"You need to understand the embers you've brought to flame."

She tried to kick out.

He used her action to part her drawers. His fingers brushed between her legs.

The action, that fragile encounter inundated her in sensation. The power of speech fled; her vision blurred.

"So sensitive," he said. "I'm learning, too. You're so sensitive to the slightest touch. You'll burn for me today. And I swear I will burn for you forever."

"I don't want that," she moaned. But she did. All the conflicting emotions of the last few days rose and battled within her. Mr. Throckmorton was a figure of authority and austerity. Garrick was a man of passion and warmth. She couldn't reconcile the two images, but the power of Mr. Throckmorton only added to the attraction she felt for Garrick, and she wanted them both.

How could he have made her hunger for him like this?

His arm now blocked her, holding her thighs apart, opening her to his exploration.

"A clumsy man would sweep in boldly." He used his most intimate, deep midnight voice.

His thumb parted her feminine folds and slid upward, opening her to his artistry. Did he seek to plunge into her? The isolation of her virginity had never been so breached. She braced herself to reject him.

"You need time to adjust. You're shy, unused to a man's touch, unaccustomed to the feast of the senses." He continued on, searching . . .

She perceived what he would do, and foreboding twisted in her gut. How did he know? How had he learned of that one place where the brush of a washcloth brought delight? Her heart rolled and rumbled. She couldn't catch her breath, and everything he touched felt swollen, almost painful, fully stimulated.

This was she, Celeste. Her body, herself. This was private, and with his skill he undermined her innocence and taught her, instead, the lore of desire.

She'd given up arguing; when? She should be defying him. Instead she waited in agonizing anticipation for his touch on that one, sensitive place . . .

She shuddered when his thumb lightly brushed her.

He chuckled, an unsteady sound that lacked mirth, and leaning forward, he kissed her eyelids. "Close your eyes," he whispered. "Feel this. Just . . . feel."

She didn't want to do anything he commanded, but if she didn't have to see him, surely it would be better. Surely she couldn't feel *more*.

Above her, Garrick breathed heavily, a rasp of ardor unfulfilled. His thumb brushed her again, and again, increasing the pressure with each pass. Passion seared her veins, coiled in her belly, rode between her legs. He released her arms; she didn't fight, but grabbed at him, at the pillows, at anything which could connect her with the real world while this torturous pleasure built and built until she thought she would cleave from the force of her rapture.

She heard herself whimper. Clamped her lips shut in self-consciousness. Whimpered again.

"Let me hear you." He was the bringer of the whirlwind, the center of the passion. "I want to know everything."

She shook her head, trying to deny him one triumph,
at least.

"Don't tell me *no*. Not when I can't . . . won't . . ."

With force and precision, his finger swept inside her.
He rode easily on the dampness he had called forth; he
turned the heel of his hand to press against her. The surprise, the motion, the rightness brought her to sudden
and shocking climax. She convulsed, her voice the high,
incoherent cry of a girl turned woman.

Garrick Throckmorton led her all the way through.
He held her in his embrace as she recovered. And when
she dared open her eyes, and she saw his face, taut and
still with craving, he said, "Don't forget this. And don't
ever forget me."

Stanhope drew back, bumping into the pot that held the
ridiculous little orange tree, knocking a few of the tiny
green fruit to the floor. He ground them into the carpet
in his hurry to conceal himself, but he needn't have
bothered. The gardener's daughter ran past him, clutching her open bodice in her hands, blind with embarrassment and residual passion.

He feared Throckmorton would surely catch him
lurking. He debated between running after Celeste and
hoping he wasn't recognized, or standing here and acting as if he'd observed nothing, when in fact he'd seen
Throckmorton giving the girl the kind of good time a
man gives only to a girl he wants to impress.

Well, someone had been impressed, and that someone had been Stanhope. He hadn't believed Throckmor-

ton's story yesterday. When he'd had time to think about it, he had decided it had all sounded likely—all except the part where Throckmorton, the inimitable spy master and ever-proper autocrat, trifling with the gardener's daughter. And if he didn't believe that, the whole story stank, and maybe it was time for him to get his savings from under the floorboards of his room and make run for it.

But that scene in the conservatory . . . that was confirmation that he could stay and make just a little more cash.

How could he use this to his advantage?

Stepping to the middle of the hall, he pretended he had been strolling past for no good reason, and waited to bump into Throckmorton as he left. But Throckmorton didn't leave, and Stanhope glanced into the conservatory.

Throckmorton sat on the sofa, head on his hands.

Stanhope didn't understand why Throckmorton held his head. He'd be willing to bet it wasn't his head that ached.

Continuing on his way, Stanhope grinned. Now he had best find young Celeste, charm her and pry every last secret out of her empty little head.

Lady Hyacinth how to entice Ellery." He stared at Lady Philberta as if expecting outrage.

He got confusion. "Why would she do that? She says she wants Ellery."

Leaping to his feet, he paced across to the desk. "Because she's a virgin, that's why."

She was asking questions. He was answering. But somehow the questions and the answers didn't match. "Garrick, have you been drinking?"

"Not yet." He shook his finger at her. "It's a conspiracy of virgins."

Puzzlement battled with exasperation. "I suppose it's possible she's a virgin, I'll even admit it's probable, but—"

"Oh, she's a virgin, all right." Picking up her inkwell, he held the bottle up to his eye and squinted at the liquid as if he were a jeweler and the ink a diamond. "No doubt about that. I just proved *that* to my satisfaction."

Lady Philberta almost choked with horror. God help them, they were going to lose their head gardener.

Not only that—Garrick had lost his mind. "You just proved that . . . Garrick, did you take her?"

"No, I didn't take her!" He slammed the ink down hard enough she feared for the bottle. "What kind of man do you think I am? Do you think I'm as careless and unthinking as Ellery?"

"No, but—"

"I would hope not. *I'm* the responsible brother and I wouldn't despoil Milford's daughter, virgin or no virgin, although what I did do was . . . but she provoked me."

Lady Philberta lifted her painted-on eyebrows almost to her hairline. "What did you do to her?"

"I just . . . she just . . . she also told Lady Hyacinth

"Mother, this is not going to work!"

Startled, Lady Philberta looked up from her writing to see her elder son storm into her sitting room.

"What won't work?"

"I can't continue this." Garrick ran his fingers through his hair, ruffling the already ruffled strands into a telling whirlwind of madness. "She has got to go."

"Who?"

"Celeste, I tell you!" His cravat dangled half-off, he'd torn the fastening on his collar and he sported a small, still-bleeding scratch above his eye. "She's got to go back to Paris, Ellery or no Ellery, spies or no spies."

"Damn, son, lower your voice." Lady Philberta stood and hurriedly shut the door. "Now sit down and tell me what's happened."

He sank down in the chair she indicated. "She told

what to expect on her wedding night." He snatched up her best quill pen and waved it wildly about. "What do you think about that?"

"I think somebody needs to tell these girls what's about to happen."

"You would think that." He glared at her fiercely. "Some mother you are. If she hadn't been wearing that bodice. And she was nice to Lady Hyacinth. Nice. Genuinely . . . that girl . . . she's a scheming harlot trying to break up the suitable alliance I worked so hard to bring about. You should have seen how easily it opened."

"The alliance?" Lady Philberta questioned carefully.

"The bodice!"

She was starting to find logic in this lunacy, and she didn't know what to think. Garrick, her Garrick, her shrewd, rational, bloodless son, had been carried away on a wave of passion for a girl ten years his junior and miles below his station. Because she'd been *nice?* "Celeste's kindness to Lady Hyacinth offended you?"

"I like my people to stay true to type." He pointed his finger at her. "First there's Stanhope, spying for the Russians, then Penelope is tying up her nursemaid, and now Celeste is being pleasant . . . have you noticed this whole thing started when she arrived?"

"Penelope tied up her nursemaid?" Lady Philberta grinned. She had always thought her granddaughter was too solemn for a child of such tender years. "Good for her."

"That's proof, I say! We'll have Lady Hyacinth flirting with other men and brushing her breasts against Ellery—"

"I don't understand this at all."

"The thing is, Mother, I had my hand up her skirt."

Lady Philberta was beginning to master this free-wheeling conversation. "You had your hand up *Celeste's* skirt?"

"All the way. And she . . . she was so shocked, but at the same time, she"—his eyes had gone unfocused, and he brushed the pen's feather across his cheek—"she was sweet and passionate, and she's just as beautiful as I imagined. I would have . . . she made me so angry." His attention snapped back to his mother. "Why the hell can't people act as they're supposed to act?"

"Because they act like themselves." Her imperturbable son had actually sworn and raised his voice, all in the space of a few minutes. If it wouldn't have hurt her lumbago, Lady Philberta would have jumped for joy.

"Why don't I always know what that is?" Anguish sounded in his voice.

"Sometimes we don't read them correctly. That is an occupational hazard." Something had gone very wrong in Garrick's youth. Looking back, she couldn't put her finger on the moment when he began to conceal parts of his personality. She knew when, at the age of three, he gave up that battered stuffed cat, his father had been pleased. When Garrick was eight and learned to control his rages, she had praised him. And when he came back from India at the age of twenty, she'd been proud of the logical, calm, controlled gentleman he had become.

Only recently had she realized that Garrick's discipline kept him apart from human emotions. Where did Garrick hide the passion, the temper, the emotion that had made him so alive as a child?

"We can't use Celeste. I'm going to have an escort take her to the train station and all the way to Paris. She's not going to ruin Ellery's marriage, and she's not going to stay here making me do things that . . . I like women, Mother."

"That gives an old woman comfort." This whole scene was giving this old woman comfort. She had feared Garrick would never scale the heights of passion, but it appeared little Celeste had dragged him up there by her bodice strings.

"But I don't let women make me feel like I can't control . . ." He sank back down in the chair and put his head in his hands. "She's leaving *tomorrow*."

The gardener's daughter wasn't the mate Lady Philberta would have chosen for either of her sons. The girl was beautiful and accomplished, true, but common. And what kind of ceremony would it be with the servants on one side of the church and the ton on the other? Lady Philberta's head ached at the thought.

She took a deep breath. Garrick's impeccable reputation would survive the scandal, and if Celeste shook that formidable discipline on which he prided himself, then Lady Philberta herself would deliver the chit to his bedchamber tied in a ribbon. "Dear, I know how you feel"—because she had fought her way to passion with her much older, unrespectable husband—"but you must think of our mission. Stanhope has done much damage, we can't tell how much yet."

"Celeste has got to go."

"Celeste is our only chance to rectify the damage."

"Tomorrow." His voice was muffled by his downturned head. "As far away as possible."

"We don't even know who Stanhope's accomplices are yet. Come, Garrick, we only have two days of the house party left. You can fight this thing for two more days." With a little push from Lady Philberta, neither

Garrick nor Celeste stood a chance. He was shaking his head, so she played the guilt card, the one reserved for mothers. "Dear, until I handed this position over to you, nothing like this scandal with Stanhope had ever happened." That she would admit to him. "I really think you should have seen the signs in your secretary. This is ultimately your fault."

Slowly, he lifted his head from his hands and glared at her. "Mother, we will find some other way."

A firm knock sounded on the door, and Dafty stuck her head in. "Lady Philberta. Mr. Throckmorton. I hate to interrupt you, but there's a messenger here, and it's serious. There's been an explosion."

Throckmorton opened the door to the nursery, and breathed in the scent of camphor and chamomile, rocking horses and childhood memories. He'd always loved the nursery. His childhood had been of the best kind, with parents who adored him, a tutor who rose to the challenge of an inquiring boy, and a pest of a little brother who always tagged after him.

He didn't fool himself. Today's events had fractured the foundation of his assurance. He'd lost control in the most elemental fashion. He'd done things with—to!— Celeste, things he'd only imagined in his most secret carnal dreams. And just when he'd resolved to do the right thing, to save her, and himself, from this madness which possessed him, the news of the blast had arrived. Two Englishmen, one his agent, one a possible traitor, had been in the Crimea when a bomb had gone off.

Coincidence? Of course not. Now one man was buried on foreign soil. Another hung onto life while rocking in a scrubby transport back to England. If MacLean lived . . . well, if he lived, it would be a miracle.

So Celeste would stay and, all unknowing, perform her duty to her country, and Throckmorton would have to dredge his soul for the discipline he usually commanded so effortlessly.

Now he'd come seeking comfort from the old familiar nursery things. The expanse of wood floor, gleaming in the late afternoon sunshine. The red and blue curtains, boldly patterned and thick, designed to keep out drafts. The shelf of books, some worn, some new.

His daughter.

Her face lit up, as it always did when she saw him, and some of his baffled misery faded.

The rocking chair creaked as Mrs. Brown knitted an unending brown scarf. An ample woman in clean, simple garb, she glanced up and saw him, and nodded pleasantly. Penelope sat curled into the corner of the shabby stuffed chair, reading his old copy of *Robinson Crusoe*.

Just last week, before the houseparty had begun and all hell had broken loose, he'd been reading it aloud to both the little girls. *Both* little girls.

A curl of alarm rose in him as his gaze searched the nursery. "Where's Kiki?" he asked Mrs. Brown.

"I don't know. She's hidin', and she's a good little hider." Mrs. Brown winked and nodded toward the big toy closet with its louvered doors.

There his old toy soldiers marched beside Penelope's dolls and Kiki's soft stuffed animals. A good place to hide—he'd hidden there many a time himself. He relaxed. He wished the children didn't have to have a guard standing outside their nursery, but most of all, he was glad he'd discovered Stanhope's treachery and took measures to protect his own. As danger crept ever closer he worried about the girls, helpless and innocent. The men he opposed in this game of espionage had no ethics, no principles. Now that they had discovered his identity, they would not shy from taking the children and using them to manipulate him into doing their bidding. He loved Penelope with a father's unwavering devotion, and in the last few days of disillusion and confusion, he'd discovered how thoroughly Kiki had worked her way into his affections.

She might exasperate him, but she was his niece. In a deliberately loud voice, he asked Mrs. Brown, "Have you searched for her?"

"Ever so much, but she's just too clever for me," Mrs. Brown said comfortably.

They heard a tiny giggle from the closet.

"Then we'll have to wait until she comes out," he announced. Truth to tell, he was glad to have time alone with his own little daughter. Walking toward Penelope, he asked, "How are you, sweeting?"

Flinging the book aside, she ran to him. "Papa!"

Big girl that she was, he swung her into his arms and hugged her.

"I've missed you." She kissed his cheek, then drew back. "But I didn't expect to have time with you until this dratted house party had ceased."

He grinned to hear her sound so much like him. "No one cares whether I go down to gamble and dance. Your Uncle Ellery owns all the charm, and besides, he's going to be the bridegroom."

"I like you best," she said stoutly.

"No. Do you?" He pulled an amazed face.

She cradled his cheeks between her thin hands. "Of course, you're my papa."

He'd dreamed of filling the nursery with his own children, but he had only Penelope. And Kiki was in residence, too, of course . . .

"Would you like me to read to you?" he asked.

"Robinson Crusoe!" she answered.

"But you're reading it by yourself." He carried her to the chair and settled in it, her in his lap.

"I don't know all the words." She folded her hands and turned her dark, serious eyes on him. "I need to start taking lessons from Miss Milford, Papa. I know she would help me to read."

He did *not* want to talk about Miss Milford. "You do wonderfully well." She did. He thought her unusually bright for a child her age, and he wasn't at all prejudiced. "But I'll start where I left off." He was conscious of Kiki, hiding in the closet. Kiki, who pretended not to understand the words but always managed to hang about when he read. Opening the green, worn leather binding, he found his place and began, loud and clear, to tell the tale of the lonely castaway.

In the closet, Kiki peered through the louvers and snuffled softly.

Her father didn't read to her. Her father couldn't bear to look at her. Her father didn't tell her she did wonderfully well. He didn't even speak to her. He just laughed when she jumped around and patted her on the head before he walked away from her.

Kiki blinked and swallowed the big lump in her throat. That man who worked in Uncle Garrick's office had told her all that, and it was true. That man said no one cared for her here in England. He said she ought to go back to where she'd come from.

Back to France, where she understood everybody. Where the sun shone all the time. Where it was always warm.

Where *Maman* was.

But *Maman* wasn't there anymore. No one was there, and before *Maman* left her in this horrible England she told Kiki she couldn't stay in Paris because there was nowhere to sleep except in the streets.

Kiki looked through the louvers again. That ugly, selfish, *lucky* Penelope sat snuggled on her papa's lap, her head on his chest, his arm around her. He read slowly and loudly. He acted as if he wanted to be around his daughter. Something in Kiki's chest swelled until it hurt.

Lots of children slept in the streets of Paris, and they were strong and brave, and they would like her. So she resolved then and there she *would* go back to France. Back to her home.

Pressing her tattered rag doll to her lips, she stifled her sobs.

"Celeste!"

Celeste wanted to just keep walking through the music room, through the long gallery, down the stairs and to the kitchen, there to eat her breakfast. This morning, she didn't want to talk to anyone noble or pretentious, only to people whom she understood—and who understood her. Most especially, she didn't want to talk to Mr. Stanhope, secretary to the powerful bully, Mr. Garrick Throckmorton.

More insistently, Mr. Stanhope called again, "Celeste!"

She lurched to a stop and wheeled to face him.

His tanned face beamed in a convivial smile. "So good to see you this beautiful morning."

Suspicious, for she had never viewed his conviviality up close—a glance outside told her it was still raining— she took a step backward.

"I haven't had a chance to welcome you back since your return."

Why was he being so charming? "Thank you." *I think.*

"It's been quite the triumphant return for you."

She didn't like his height, his open, affable manner, his overripe conceit. Stanhope was completely different from Throckmorton, and although that should have worked in his favor, it did not. "Yes, sir."

"Come, you're no longer a schoolgirl. You can call me Mr. Stanhope."

"Thank you . . . Mr. Stanhope." *And you can call me Miss Milford.* As Throckmorton did when he was displeased.

"You're on your way to . . . ?"

"The kitchen," she said flatly.

"Ah." Obviously, Stanhope didn't like being reminded of her background.

She found she liked reminding him. Maybe if she reminded Throckmorton . . . but no, he spoke easily with his servants, especially with her father, according him a respect he showed few aristocrats. No, she couldn't avoid Throckmorton in that manner.

"I'll walk with you," Stanhope said.

As Throckmorton had predicted, Stanhope was interested in the information she'd learned from her translation. She considered just blurting it out, but somehow that seemed too easy, and Mr. Stanhope had always had everything too easy—or so her father had said. Actually, Celeste had heard Mr. Stanhope talk about how he'd soldiered in India, adventured through the towering mountains, fought for his life among treacherous natives. Such hardship wasn't so easy, but she understood what her father meant.

Mr. Stanhope was an aristocrat who had been given an education, a blueblood background, contacts among the finest people, and now, at Blythe Hall, Throckmorton had made him a trusted companion, ignoring his friend's idleness and incompetence because of some wayfaring brotherhood.

Which was odd, because she'd never thought of Throckmorton as a wayfarer or an adventurer, but he must have been, as much as Mr. Stanhope. Until two nights ago when Throckmorton had kissed her under the stars, she'd never thought of him as a traveler, but he had seen more of the world than she had.

And yesterday in the conservatory, he had proved he'd learned the art of pleasing a woman, even an unwilling one. Oh, she would never forgive him. *Never.*

Obviously irked by her lack of response, Stanhope said, "I thought we could take the chance to catch up."

"We haven't spoken before." She stopped at the window overlooking the Roman fountain. Rain still fell in gray sheets, but off to the east the early morning sun lightened the hovering clouds. "How can we catch up?"

"Believe me, if not for my wretched ethics, we would have done more than spoken. From the first time I saw you, I recognized your beauty." Turning, he leaned against the sill and looked earnestly at her. "But you were so young. It wouldn't have been fair to either of us to embroil you in . . . conversation."

Like Throckmorton, Stanhope thought well of the effects of himself and his . . . conversation. She glanced at him sideways. She could assure him his . . . conversation . . . lacked even those skills Throckmorton sported.

"Obviously, Paris agreed with you," Stanhope went on.

His gaze swept her, and she found he was one of those rare men who managed to compliment with a glance.

Mr. Throckmorton wasn't like that. When he looked at a woman, his dark gaze scorched each curve until she wanted to cover herself with her hands so he couldn't see those places meant to be hidden . . .

"You speak French very well, Throckmorton says. And Russian . . . do you have any other talents hidden beneath that comely veneer?" Stanhope charmed with a smile; he behaved as if he were impressed by her.

She'd met men like him on the Continent. They were patently insincere, but in most ways that made this encounter easier. "My talents wouldn't be hidden if I told you."

He chuckled. "Very true, very true." He glanced down at his feet, managing to appear manly and at the same time modest. "I imagine Throckmorton told you why you were doing his translations and I was not."

"Yes."

For a brief moment, his real annoyance peeked through his affable mask. "*What* did he tell you?"

She toyed with the thought of revealing the truth, that his incompetence had been found out, but that would be disloyal to Throckmorton, and besides . . . she didn't want to make Throckmorton angry again. Who knew what kind of outrage he would perpetrate if she provoked him on purpose? "Mr. Throckmorton said you'd been working too much and would take the week to recover."

"You make it sound as if I'm an old man."

She widened her eyes with false innocence. "Oh, not *so* old."

She glimpsed the whip of his annoyance when he

snapped, "Of course I *am* much older than you. Almost ten years. Almost as old as Throckmorton, yet you seem to find him young enough for—"

She straightened. Stanhope had been gossiping about her? He had been listening to, encouraging the sniggering such gossip would invite? She wouldn't stand here and be insulted by this ingratiating, conceited lout. In her sharpest tone, she asked, "For what, Mr. Stanhope?"

But Stanhope realized his misstep, for he said hastily, "I'm grateful to Throckmorton for the furlough, and intend to take full advantage of my leisure, but I find myself curious about the business. You could keep me abreast of the news."

"As you wish." She watched him without smiling. She wouldn't soon forget his insolence. If Throckmorton knew, he would have him horsewhipped. Except . . . well, perhaps not, for Throckmorton had always supported Mr. Stanhope in every enterprise, and Throckmorton couldn't have made his contempt for her more clear.

Mon Dieu, she wanted to press her hands to her eyes until she blotted out the memories.

"Have you translated any new letters?" Mr. Stanhope asked.

"Just the one that said there would be a big meeting south of Kabul."

"Kabul." His eyes narrowed.

"It's in Afghanistan," she said helpfully.

"I know where it is." He took a breath, then shrugged with studied, carefree modesty. "I've visited Kabul."

"In Mr. Throckmorton's company?"

Mr. Stanhope smiled tightly. "Some would say he was in my company."

Quite deliberately, she had annoyed him, and she enjoyed it more than was becoming. But she wanted to go to the kitchen, to be with Papa and Esther and the others who loved her. So she broke off the diverting activity and said, "A battalion of merchants will be assessing Kabul for investment opportunities. I suppose that many Englishmen will make a huge impact on the local economy." She had her own opinion about the meaning of the letter and, after speaking with Mr. Stanhope, was beginning to suspect her role in this triangle of letter, Stanhope and herself.

Throckmorton had come up with the scheme. If she dared consider him, she might wonder what role Throckmorton played in the greater world beyond Blythe Hall.

But she wouldn't think of him, and besides, the scent of bacon seeped up from the kitchen and her stomach rumbled.

"A huge impact. Yes." Stanhope had already forgotten her, focused on the task ahead. Turning, he hurried away. But something reminded him of her—the need to pump her again for information, she supposed—and he tossed over his shoulder a preoccupied thanks.

Relieved to be rid of him, she proceeded briskly in the direction of the kitchen, hoping that the appearance of being on a mission would protect her from further interruptions.

Futile hope!

Ellery leaped out from the cubbyhole beneath the stairs and snagged her hand. "Celeste!"

She jumped and half-screamed.

He laughed and tugged her into the dim hiding place. "Darling." Wrapping his arms around her waist, he smiled down into her face. "I've been hoping you'd pass by."

He smelled strongly of ale. He sported scratches on his face. He had bags under his eyes and his nose was red. He was still more handsome than Throckmorton.

Yet she found herself wanting to back away, to ask why Ellery hid away so as not to be seen with her, to demand that he unhand her. But Ellery wasn't the problem; Throckmorton was. So instead she settled for a patently false smile, one like she'd advised Hyacinth to utilize, and a strained, "Ellery, you frightened me."

"Do I frighten you with my ardor?" He leered outrageously.

Against her better judgment, she laughed and relaxed. This was Ellery, the Ellery she'd fallen in love with, the Ellery of charm and sophistication. She couldn't love Throckmorton with his solemn demeanor and unexpected depths. "What are you even doing up, Ellery? It's barely morning."

And she'd thought she would be left alone with her morose thoughts. Foolish optimism.

"I haven't been to bed."

"Of course not." She touched the scratches. "What have you been doing to earn this?"

"You weren't at the musical evening last night, so I went looking for you and I . . . tangled with one of your father's rose bushes."

"Pardon me, but I don't understand." She had lain awake last night, listening to her neighbors, elderly ladies both, snore with all the finesse of steam locomotives, and wished she had Throckmorton there so she could tie him to the bedposts and torment him as he had tormented her.

Sadly, then her fantasies had taken a wrong turn. Last night, she had outraged even herself.

Oh, everything that was wrong was Throckmorton's fault!

"I had heard you were staying in your father's cottage."

A vision of her home filled her mind, a stone cottage connected to the greenhouse covered with climbing roses, with rose hedges, with miniature roses bordering the walks and large bushes lifting toward the sky.

"I went there," he said, "it was dark. I thought I remembered your bedchamber being in the loft."

"Papa's bedchamber now," she said faintly.

"I threw rocks at the window to wake you—"

She couldn't help it. She giggled, and when she saw his expression of chagrin, she leaned her head against his chest and giggled harder.

Not surprisingly, he released her and moved away to lean against an occasional table. "This is incredibly unflattering."

She laughed, hiccuped, laughed again.

"I devote my evening to discovering where my love has vanished, and all she can do is snicker."

But he sounded wry and self-deprecating, and when she looked at him she saw the puckered mouth and twinkling eyes. If Throckmorton had found himself in such a dilemma, he would never have laughed at himself. No, Ellery was most definitely not deep and complex with dark patches on his soul, and for that she was profoundly appreciative. Carried on a wave of thankfulness, she said, "You are really a dear man."

"A dear man." Where her laughter had not offended Ellery, her comment obviously did. "I'm a roué, a so-

phisticate, a gallant . . . Garrick is a dear man, not me."
You don't know him at all. But she didn't say that. "I
must away, I haven't had breakfast."

Ellery thrust his hands into his pockets. "Apparently
I'm not a very successful gallant."

"What do you mean?" She edged out of the cubbyhole. "I adore you, Lady Hyacinth adores you, all the
ladies adore you."

"I have you trapped under the stairway, it's dark, we're
alone, and *you're* in a hurry to leave. Hyacinth is drooling
all over that tub Townshend. Even Lady Featherstonebaugh would rather hide in corners with a valet than
talk to me."

"Lady Hyacinth danced with Lord Townshend?"

He eyed her with blatant suspicion. "Yes, how did
you know?"

"I just assumed when you said she was drooling on
him that probably she'd done it in the dance."

"Smiled at him, acted like a little fool over him when
everyone knows all he wants to breed is his dogs."

"Ellery!" She pretended to be shocked, but in reality
she wanted to give a little cheer for Hyacinth. Smart
girl, she had done just what she was told, and successfully, too.

"But it's no matter, if she's in love with that fop
Townshend, that leaves the way clear for *us.*"

"Us?" With a shock, she realized she wasn't supposed to want Hyacinth to succeed with Ellery. *Celeste*
wanted Ellery . . . but yesterday, in the conservatory,
she'd done an impressive imitation of a woman who
wanted Throckmorton.

Confusion pressed her from all sides. She just
wanted to go to the kitchen, to be with her friends. "We

can talk about us later." She backed into the foyer while Ellery watched her with an expression her father would call mopey. "I simply must eat. I'm almost faint with hunger."

"I suffer from the opinion you're avoiding me, too." Now Ellery was definitely accusatory.

"Not at all."

"Aren't I handsome enough for you? Rich enough? Powerful enough?"

She knew that Ellery had been drinking, but now she realized he was still drunk, and angry with it. "It's not that at all . . ."

"Maybe it's not playacting after all. Maybe you really would rather have Garrick. I've always gotten all the girls, but everything else is slipping away. Maybe along with all my brother's other talents, he's better with women than I am."

Morose, angry, and lashing out at her. She hated scenes, hated this scene more than any other, for Ellery's accusations held more than a germ of truth and the guilt she suffered added an edge of desperation to her denials. "I don't want Mr. Throckmorton, I just want . . ."

"Me?" He snorted at her expression, and in a sarcastic drawl, said, "You want me. Then tell me, my little Cinderella, where is your bedchamber? Could it be, perhaps, close to Garrick's?"

She jerked back in shock. "It is not!"

"Then where is it? I've been searching for it for nights on end, and if you really loved me—"

The jackass! Oh, she knew he'd been seeking her bedchamber. But to demand the information crudely . . . Coolly, she told him, "It's in the North Tower. Third door from the right. You can't miss it." Whirling, she stalked away, leaving Ellery wordless at last.

This time she made it almost to the stairway leading down to the kitchen before she heard a masculine voice call, "Miss Milford!"

She staggered in a circle, leaned her hand against the wall, and stared with an accusing gaze at Mr. Kinman. "Yes, sir?"

He smiled amiably. "I just saw Throckmorton."

Slowly she straightened her sagging shoulders. All of her other attempts to avoid conversation had been practice for this. This was the message she had dreaded.

"He wants you to come to his office." Mr. Kinman scratched the back of his head as if puzzled. "Something about translating a letter."

For one wild moment, she thought of saying *no*. No excuse, no pleasantries, just no. But good sense prevailed—she would, after all, have to see Throckmorton again someday, probably today, and undoubtedly accompanied by humiliating embarrassment. Just . . . not until she'd had her breakfast. Not until she'd been fortified by the support of her friends. "Mr. Kinman, are you going to see Mr. Throckmorton again?"

"I suspect I can."

"Tell him I will come to his office after—no." She had a better idea, one that would not only delay the inevitable but also put Throckmorton in his place. "Tell him to send the letter to my bedchamber, and I'll translate it there."

The big man looked taken aback. "I don't think that's exactly the answer he'll be looking for."

"That's all the answer he's getting." Once more, she turned toward the kitchen.

In a tone quite at odds with his previous lack of confidence, Mr. Kinman said, "Miss Milford, surely it isn't *comme il faut* to refuse your employer when he calls."

Coldly furious, she swung back on Mr. Kinman. "May I say that you seem to know more than you should. Has Mr. Throckmorton been confiding in you?"

He ducked his head. "No, miss, I've just been observing the situation."

She remembered how many times she'd seen him lingering about in the past few days. He *had* been observing the situation, and now she wondered why. Because he was infatuated with her? He didn't appear to be the type. Nosy? Perhaps. For some more sinister reason . . . ?

And had Throckmorton brought her to such a pass she now questioned every sentence spoken, every gesture made?

"Just tell Mr. Throckmorton what I said." She didn't look back as she ran down the stairs and pushed open the door to the kitchen.

A cry of greeting went up when Celeste stepped inside the kitchen.

"Look oo's 'ere!" Brunella had been the senior upstairs maid ever since Celeste could remember. "Our Frenchie girl, all dressed up glorious."

Celeste's simmering indignation began a slow fade, bathed in this uncritical balm of admiration and affection.

She loved the kitchen. She'd grown up here under her mother's skirts, and after her mother's death Esther had encouraged her to continue as the beloved child. Celeste knew every scullery maid, had teased every footman, and here she could gossip and question without worry of censure. Here it didn't matter that she moved in circles above her station and that Mr. Throckmorton had involved her in some global scam of Mr. Stanhope's. Here it didn't matter that her life was a confusion of cherished love for one man and indecorous desire for another. Here she could be herself. Here, she even knew who that was.

At a gesture from Brunella, she turned in a circle, lifting the black velveteen shawl away from her shoulders to show off her full-skirted gown of blue and white plaid madras.

"Ooh la la." Brunella's gruff, Suffolk-accented voice made a hash of the French expression. "Very nice." With barely a pause, she handed a tray to a gentleman's valet and sent him on his way upstairs.

Esther, the cook, dropped her spoon and hustled forward to hug Celeste. So did two of the older kitchen maids and Arwydd, the stillroom maid, who had made preserves and liquors for as long as Celeste could remember. They exclaimed over her and reminisced with her until Esther sent the kitchen maids back to work, told Arwydd she needed the raspberry jam for the afternoon's trifle, and gestured toward the long table that stood groaning under the weight of the servants' breakfast. "Celeste, sit ye down now and we'll give ye some real food," she invited. "Nothing with snails in this kitchen!"

Celeste didn't mention that she'd actually consumed *escargots*, or that she had quite enjoyed them. Instead she said, "Thank you. Breakfast smells wonderful."

Large mackerel pies dotted the boards. Bowls of oatmeal cast curls of steam into the air. Pale cream sat in colored pottery pitchers. Triangles of crusty brown scones were piled high on a platter while pats of butter melted on them, dribbling down to form a golden pool. And like a scarlet blot of disgrace, a large bowl of sliced strawberries sat right in the center, waiting to be spooned over the scones or the oatmeal.

Celeste averted her eyes. Out of loyalty to poor dear

Ellery, she shouldn't want any . . . but she did.

Mr. Throckmorton didn't get hives because of strawberries. Mr. Throckmorton was so tough, he probably didn't get a sting from a nettle.

All of the outdoor crew sat on benches at one of the laden tables—the stablehands and the under-gardeners, and at one end the head hostler and at the other Celeste's father, face damp from a scrubbing and hair slicked back with water. In the last four years, he'd lost a little more hair and what hair he had was a little grayer, but for the most part his long drooping features and rough frame looked much as they had for as long as she could remember. Yet he talked more slowly and less; Celeste thought he had been lonely in her absence, and her gaze roamed the kitchen while she tried to pick out one woman who had the good sense to want him and the ability to trap him.

Her gaze settled on Esther. Esther, who boxed the scullion's ear for turning the roast too slowly and punched down the rising bread dough at the same time. Esther should be the one, but would the memories of Celeste's mother ruling the kitchen get in the way?

"Good morning, Father." Coming to his side, Celeste kissed his cheek.

"G'mornin', daughter." Hand on her arm, he held her close for one moment. "I'm glad to have ye back."

She kissed him again, then thanked the fellows as they shifted down to allow her a place by her father.

Seating herself, she watched the bustling kitchen with nostalgic appreciation. The Blythe Hall servants struggled to prepare trays for the aristocrats and feed the army of ladies' maids and valets who had arrived to serve them. At the same time, Esther still had to supervise a breakfast for every Blythe Hall servant and plan for the coming meals throughout the day.

" 'Ere, Celeste, 'ave a scone." Toothless old Travis, though he had been on the estate fifty years, hailed from the streets of London, held the plate below her nose.

Smiling at him, she took one. Then all the men passed Celeste dishes and, depending on their age, watched with affection or infatuation as she filled her bowl with oatmeal and cut strawberries over the top. When she had more than she could possibly eat, they pressed her with questions about her life.

"Is Paris as frolicsome as they say, Celeste?"

"Did ye dance every night, Celeste?"

"Tell us about those fereigners, Celeste. Did ye like them better than us?"

Holding her spoon above her oatmeal, Celeste smiled. "Yes, yes, and no."

"Let the girl eat," her father commanded. "She's too thin already."

"But so comely," one of the gardening lads breathed.

Celeste grinned at him.

Digging into her oatmeal with an appetite she never dared expose above stairs, she satisfied the worst of her hunger and looked up to find Esther watching with her hands placed on her broad hips.

"Nothing like good cookin', is there?" the cook said, her Scottish burr warm and friendly.

"The best I've had in years," Celeste answered.

Herne, an inveterate gossip and a nosy parker, or so Milford called him, shifted from foot to foot. "If ye're done eating, Celeste, tell us how's it going with Mr. Ellery."

Celeste flinched, and hoped her father hadn't noticed.

"He's better. His rash is gone and the bruises are mostly healed."

"Last night he tangled with a rose bush, and he's sporting some new scratches." Milford took a drink of ale.

Celeste avoided her father's calm gaze.

"But you didn't go to the musical evening last night." Herne obviously took this as an offense. "Did he make improper advances?"

Esther landed another punch into the rising bread dough. "He's a dear boy, but if he has, I'll put castor oil in his whisky bottle."

"No, no!" Celeste scrambled to correct matters before they got out of hand. Ellery was a favorite of all the servants, especially the female servants and most especially of Brunella, whom he often charmed out of a fresh baked loaf or a midnight feast. "Mr. Ellery's been all that's kind." Except today, when he'd been drinking and making accusations about her and Mr. Throckmorton.

Mr. Throckmorton, who had sent for her. Mr. Throckmorton, whom she had defied. Mr. Throckmorton, whom she would not think about.

But considering the tangle she was caught up in, Ellery's petty insinuations had meant nothing. "I didn't go to the musical evening because I'm trying to . . . to be with the children, and . . . and you know I can't sing or play the harp, at least, not well."

Neville, who polished silver and acted as an extra footman during dinner parties, said, "I heard from Hod, who heard from Rawdon, who heard from Dinah who was dustin' Mr. Garrick's office, that ye was supposed to be workin' for Mr. Garrick, doin' some o' his papers."

"Really? What's wrong wi' Mr. Stanhope?" Arwydd had crept back out of the stillroom.

"Got a cob stuck sideways," Herne said.

Brunella waited until the general snickers had died down before she asked, "So, Celeste, how ye like workin' fer Mr. Garrick?"

"Fine." Celeste no longer wanted to be here in the kitchen. That sensation of being home had vanished as soon as the servants had started gossiping about Garrick. Yet she'd never cared before; for her as the gardener's daughter, for all the servants, the goings-on of the folks above stairs had been fair fodder. Now she felt torn in her loyalties, unsure how to answer, and she didn't want to think about him anyway.

In a speculative tone, Esther said, "Mr. Garrick's even richer than Mr. Ellery."

"For God's sake, ye're not going to bring that up again!" Milford objected.

"Remember, Celeste, I've told ye many a time, it's just as easy to marry a rich man as a poor one." Esther patted Celeste on the arm and glared at Milford, who resolutely stared back.

They glowered at each other so fiercely Celeste released all thought of uniting them. "I'm not given to mad fancies, Papa, and I understand the difficulties better now, Esther. But—"

"But I don't understand." One of the village girls who had been brought in to help during the party stood listening, a frown on her broad face. "Are ye interested in Mr. Ellery, or Mr. Garrick?"

"Mr. Ellery," Celeste answered promptly.

The girl continued as if Celeste had not spoken. "Because it seems t' me either one o' them would be a fair catch fer th' gardener's daughter—an' th' match as un-likely as th' sea marryin' th' shore."

Hot with embarrassment, Celeste retorted, "I am not interested in marrying Mr. Throckmorton. There isn't enough gold in his coffers to make me want a man as cold and passionless as he is."

She finished her fervid declaration. No one an-swered. Except for the rhythmic turning of the spit and the hiss of the fat as it struck the coals, silence struck deep. Esther's eyes were wide and warning, and she watched Celeste as she bent her head toward the open door.

With a sense of impending doom, Celeste looked to-ward the tall, dark, still figure who stood in the entrance.

Garrick. His broad shoulders filled her vision, his hands flexed into fists, his feet were braced like a sailor on rough seas.

He had come for her. Of course. He would never ac-cept a message such as she had sent to him. His gaze swept the kitchen, brisk as the slap of a winter wind.

The men sitting at the benches stood. The other ser-vants looked away, or fidgeted. Herne coughed and tried to sidle back into the crowd.

Then Garrick looked at Celeste, and in a voice so even the servants around him relaxed, he said, "Miss Milford, if you would attend me please?"

But in his gaze she glimpsed a now-familiar fury . . . hot and filled with that passion she had denied he pos-sessed.

As if no force could rouse her, she clutched the bench below her until her knuckles turned white.

When she didn't rise, Garrick added, "Attend me *at once.*"

Esther nodded to her and smiled encouragingly.

Her father touched her shoulder. "Go on, then, girl."

How could she refuse? She could tell no one here about that scene in the conservatory.

Uncurling her fingers, she let go of the bench. Sliding out, she stood. In the slow progress of a criminal facing execution, she trudged toward Garrick, face burning, looking not at him, but just past him.

He stepped to the side to allow her room to pass.

She walked through.

Shutting the door behind him, he grasped her arm just above the elbow as a governess would a recalcitrant child.

Celeste tried to jerk it out of his grip. "Would you please let go of my arm?"

"No." He shoved her up the stairs ahead of him. "A man as cold and passionless as me is not given to kindness toward my gardener's daughter, especially when she scorns my proposal of marriage."

"You haven't proposed marriage."

"Yes." He managed to sound both astonished and sarcastic. "I seem to remember that now."

At the top of the stairs, Celeste wrestled herself free and turned on the mocking, rude, detestable lecher. "You dare to act indignant because I did not claim to worship at your shrine? After the way you treated me?" The man she viewed was the Mr. Throckmorton she had always known, but beneath the veneer of gentility she recognized the same savage who yesterday had claimed so large a part of her innocence in the conservatory.

Brutish, conquering swine.

She stalked down the empty corridor.

He followed close on her heels. "You were gossiping about me to the servants."

"I was not. *They* were gossiping. *I* was retorting. Infernally uncomfortable it made me, too." Uncomfortable was the least of it. Tears sprang to her eyes. *"I'm* caught between two worlds, and all *you're* interested in is your precious sublime character."

Derision still reigned in him when he asked, "When you decided you would have Ellery by any means possible, did it not occur to you you would have to decide whether you would be upstairs or down, in the garden or in the house?"

Of course it hadn't. In her dream, she moved smoothly between the *ton* and the servants. Being brought forcibly face-to-face with reality did not endear Garrick to her. "When I decided I would have Ellery, I didn't think I would have his brother humiliating me in the conservatory."

"There's the crux of the matter. You're angry because I . . . humiliated you." He pushed her, resisting, backward into the same alcove she'd so recently occupied with Ellery.

She shoved at Garrick's chest, a foolish gesture for one who knew so well the steadfastness of the man, as well as the strength of his frame. "Let me go. I am not doing this again with you."

Paying no heed to her resistance, he placed his hands on the wall behind her. "Is that all it was? A humiliation?"

She wanted to stare sternly up at him. Instead she remembered her own discovery of ecstasy, and looked everywhere but at him. "You know what it was. It was a deliberate act of . . . you pleasured me with the sole intention of proving your command over me."

"I admit that." But he didn't *like* admitting it.

"And don't you dare tell me I incited you. *Nothing* that happened in the conservatory was my fault."

"I take total responsibility."

He didn't like that, either. And it didn't make her feel better.

"Why? I want to know why."

"I lost my temper. It was a new experience for me. I didn't handle it well. I beg your pardon for any distress I may have caused you." He shot short, blunt sentences at her, using the right words of repentance, but a tone of such intense annoyance she might have been holding a gun to his head.

She did not appreciate the sentiment. "Temper is no excuse."

"I know that! Do you think I don't know that? I have never allowed anyone who works for me such a feeble defense. I would discharge any man who tried to excuse himself in such a manner." He paced away from her, allowing her a brief breathing space. Then he paced right back to steal her air. "But I cannot discharge myself, I can only offer my sincerest apologies for any distress I may have caused you, and beg that you forgive me."

Infuriated by that mockery of a repentance, she shook her finger at him. "That is not an apology, that is a command."

Dull red climbed into his cheeks. "I am not in the habit of apologizing. I apologize if my apology was unrefined."

"Oh, I feel so much better now." She dipped every word in the acid of sarcasm. "I don't understand you. I don't understand how you could carry out such a cold seduction."

"Cold?" Fire leaped to life in his gaze. "You call that cold?"

"Yes, I do!" Now color rose in her cheeks as she remembered how she'd moaned and writhed under his masterful touch. *"You* were never affected."

Leaning his face so close she saw every frown line and furious grimace, he asked, "Was I not, my dear Miss Milford? Then tell me why I spent the night—"

A door slammed upstairs. Voices called.

Garrick lowered his voice. "—Pacing the corridors, holding my—"

"Mind your language, Mr. Throckmorton!" But she was glad to hear he'd been awake and in agony.

"I'll do as I please, Miss Milford." Leaning over, he kissed her. "And as you please," he muttered.

Gripping his cravat between her hands, she wished first to strangle him. He acted as if he could do anything he desired with her, as if an apology grudgingly given could soothe her vexation. She wanted to cherish her rancor, not be beguiled so easily he would think himself exceptionally gifted in seduction.

But he kissed like a man in the throes of desperation. He held her as if she were his last hope of happiness. He took her breath as if it were life to him. Each thrust of his tongue was slow and sweet, and yes, she should hold him off, but the steamy warmth built and her blood heated, she yielded, melted, wished she was back in the conservatory, gasping beneath him.

More voices called above, but she barely heard them. Instead, she thrust her hands into his hair, holding him prisoner to her desire.

When they broke apart, gasping for breath, she managed a reproach rendered ineffective by her pliant body against his. "You ought to be ashamed for deliberately mortifying me."

"I've suffered," he assured her feverishly.

Feet stampeded across the wooden floors above.

Taking her hand, he guided it to the front of his trousers.

Of course she knew how a man was built, for she had visited Rome, awash with decadent statues. Of course she understood the rudiments of mating, for she'd lived in the country for her first eighteen years. But to actually touch a man, to discover what desire could induce . . . she didn't know if she should remain to explore or run shrieking to safety.

Exploration beckoned. She wrapped her fingers around his manhood, slid her palm up and down the length. And the length was so great . . . shrieking and running seemed like a good idea, too.

She verified her misgiving with another sweep of her hand, not believing he actually contained within him so much desire which he wished her to take into her self. Looking into his gaze, she whispered, "It's impossible."

"It's not the span of the wand, it's the magic contained within," he whispered back.

"It would have to be magic."

"I promise enchantment." Closing his eyes, he pressed her hand hard against him.

"You promised you wouldn't."

"You can't hold me to that. You can't." Pain or passion etched his features, made austere with an ardor she didn't yet completely understand. "But you're right. I will not . . . I shouldn't . . . but we've got this." Placing both her hands around his neck, he kissed her again. His hips rolled against her.

Footsteps ran down the stairs.

How did he do this? How could one kiss from this man induce anger, euphoria, and above all, desire? It wasn't fair that when he pressed his lips to hers, she forgot his sins and remembered only the gratification of being held in his arms, titillated and cared for and taught. She wanted to be incensed. Instead she was desperate to lie down with him and discover the magic he promised.

A large woman ran past, calling in frantic tones, "Mr. Throckmorton. Where are ye, Mr. Throckmorton!"

All of him, all of his desire and his determination had been focused on Celeste.

Now his formidable attention snapped away from her. Without a gesture or a sign of regret, he stepped out of the alcove. "Mrs. Brown! What's wrong?"

The plain, unshakable nursemaid sounded sick with anxiety. "Have ye seen th' two little girls?"

Guilt and apprehension crowded out Celeste's frustration. Joining Garrick, she demanded, *"Why?"*

"They're gone." Mrs. Brown held up a piece of crumpled paper with smooth, block lettering. "Miss Penelope left a note. She said Miss Kiki had run away, and she was going after her."

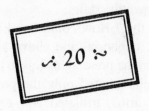

~ 20 ~

"*I* told you not to come. Why did you come?"

Penelope slogged along after Kiki, answering her in English because while Kiki insisted on speaking in French, Penelope could be stubborn, too. "Because every time you get in trouble, you get all the attention, and I'm tired of it." Which was true, Penelope told herself stoutly, except right now she was suffering a twinge, just the smallest twinge, of worry about Kiki.

She didn't know why she should. For the past year, Kiki had made Penelope's life miserable. She had come in all pretty and Frenchified, dancing and singing like a street performer, prancing about making trouble and in general being a tagalong pest. But something about this petulant, head-tossing, foot-stomping tantrum seemed different.

Probably that Kiki had done all her head tossing and foot stomping after Penelope had caught up with her, and without the benefit of any other audience. "Where do you think you're going to go?" Penelope asked.

Kiki stomped her foot in a puddle and tossed her head. *"Chez moi."*

"Home's back there." Penelope pointed back at Blythe Hall. They were skirting the grove of oaks and poplars on the west lawn, heading at an angle toward the river. The rain had stopped, but water dropped in large blips off the branches and splashed on the girls, and from the approaching growl of thunder, Penelope thought it was likely that the heavens were going to open again, and soon.

"C'est chez toi—"

"It's your house, too."

"—Avec ton père et ta nursery et ta bonne d'enfant—"

"She's not my nursemaid, she just came this week."

"—Et tes livres et ton père . . ." Kiki's voice had thickened.

"You can read the books and your papa is at Blythe Hall, too." Penelope wasn't sure, but she thought Kiki's arm came up to swipe at her nose. "Didn't you bring a handkerchief?"

"Non! I am not so English and *distinguée* as you. Everyone makes sure I know this."

Penelope was really tired of hearing only French from Kiki. "I thought everyone made sure I knew I wasn't as pretty as you."

"Tu n'es pas aussi jolie que moi!"

"I am too as pretty!" Penelope shoved Kiki right in the middle of the back.

Kiki stumbled forward, then turned like the savage she was and shoved back. She was shorter and more slender than Penelope, but she packed a good wallop and Penelope found herself flailing backward. She would have gone down, but she smacked into a tree trunk.

"Crétin!"

"Noodle!" All the disgruntlements of the past year rose in Penelope, and she would have tackled Kiki and knocked her to the ground and made her go back to the house where they belonged and they'd be safe.

But Kiki gave up the fight, turned and ran. Ran like the wind, sobbing loudly all the way.

Penelope hesitated. She didn't know how Kiki had sneaked past the poor man who guarded the nursery room door, but Penelope had had to pretend to be playing hide-and-seek, and the man had trusted her. She ought to go back and tell Papa, but by then Kiki would be gone. And telling seemed sneaky. Besides, Kiki was acting oddly, crying so her nose ran and she looked ugly, then fleeing instead of fighting. The decision wasn't easy, but Penelope raced after her cousin.

The rain started falling again, falling faster and harder than before. Lightning flashed and thunder growled, and Penelope kept wiping the water out of her eyes and hoping Kiki tripped and landed flat on her face so she'd give up.

Kiki never did what Penelope hoped. She headed for the river, and Penelope ran as fast as she could until she caught her. Grabbing her by the arm, Penelope shouted, "Let's go up there." She pointed at the castle ruins set up on the wooded hill.

For the first time on this wretched morning, Kiki acted like Kiki. Her eyes lit up as lightning jagged behind the castle ruins, giving it a desolate, melodramatic appearance. *"Oui."* She put the back of her hand on her forehead and said in French, "I can die there in peace."

"I just want to get out of the storm."

"You have no *théâtre* in your soul."

"I know a farce when I see one."

Kiki jerked herself free and stalked up the hill. Stalked until the lightning struck again, so close the thunder clapped around their ears. Then she screamed and ran up the path.

Penelope beat her to the castle. Penelope had longer legs, and Penelope had never liked thunder.

The two girls crowded into a cramped cave formed by a big vertical rock, a stone wall, and the wooden roof Mr. Milford had built so the honeysuckle would have somewhere to grow. On a normal summer day, Penelope would never have entered for fear of the bees which buzzed around the scented yellow blossoms, but today all the bees showed more sense than the girls—they stayed home.

Penelope shuddered with cold as she crouched beside Kiki, not touching her, just peering out at the lightning that struck all around them like fingers of an angry god—a thought which made Penelope shift her feet guiltily. "Do you think God is angry at us?"

Kiki stared at Penelope as if she'd lost her mind. *"Non, le bon Dieu nous aime."*

"But we've been bad."

"Je ne suis pas méchante. Je vais chez moi. Toi, tu es méchante."

"I am not bad! *You* are. And you can't go home. Don't you understand, you silly goose? There's no one for you anywhere but here."

Kiki's face worked, and her voice quavered as she answered in French, "No one is here. I miss *ma mère*.

Miss Milford likes you better. Your *père* loves you and reads to you. *Mon père* doesn't love me. No one likes me here." She ended in a cry that sounded like that of a starving baby cat.

"Do you know how stupid you are?" Penelope wanted to slap Kiki. "I'm here and I'm wet and I'm cold and I'm scared, just so you won't be alone. Of course I like you. You're stupid."

Kiki didn't say anything for a very long moment. Then, *"Vraiment?"*

"Yes, you're really stupid."

"Really you like me?" Kiki asked in French.

"When you're not stupid."

"Oh, Penelope!" Kiki threw herself at Penelope so hard she knocked Penelope onto her bottom. *"Je t'aime bien aussi. Et tu es stupide."*

"I must be." Penelope accepted Kiki's embrace, then cuddled into it. Kiki wore a wool cape that had expelled some of the rain, and here she was almost warm.

Kiki draped the corner of the cloak over Penelope and in French, asked, "Why did you run away wearing no coat?"

"I was afraid I would lose you."

"We are sisters, now, *oui*? We love each other, we share everything, we—"

Penelope slapped her hand across Kiki's mouth.

Kiki pushed it away. "You can't take it back!"

"Sh." Penelope strained to hear through the rain. The whistle of the wind faded again, and again she heard a man's shout.

"Our papas! *Ils doivent nous sauver.*" Kiki began to crawl out of the cave.

Penelope grabbed her ankle. "Stop. Maybe it's not

our papas." She spoke softly. "Papa said I must always make sure it is him."

Something of Penelope's alarm must have captured Kiki's attention, for as rapidly as she'd gone forward, she crawled backward. *"Pourquoi?"*

"Because there are bad men who would like to take me—and you—away." Had someone seen them leave the house? And if they had, why hadn't they been rescued sooner? Everything about this troubled Penelope, and Papa had said to trust her instincts.

"Les vilains!" Kiki skittered toward the small opening at the back of the cave. *"Qu'est-ce que nous faisons?"*

"He's coming closer." Penelope strained to recognize the voice, but she didn't. What was a stranger doing poking around the grounds, especially up here? "We'll go back through that hole. As soon as you get out, crawl around and run for home. I'll follow." The voice moved closer yet. Too close. In a whisper, she commanded, "Hurry. Stay low. If I can't get out, tell Papa right away."

"Penelope!" Kiki's eyes grew big and scared.

But not as scared as Penelope. It took all her courage to shove Kiki toward the hole. "I'm behind you." She made sure Kiki had squeezed through, then she turned and faced out, taking care to hide the outlines of the opening.

"Miss Penelope," the voice called. He was friendly. Too friendly. "I know you're around here. Your father sent me."

Penelope didn't recognize his voice.

"I'm Uncle Bumly," he called. "Just tell me where you are, and I'll save you from the storm."

Uncle Bumly? She didn't know any Bumly, and he

certainly wasn't an uncle. Her heart began to beat so hard she could scarcely breathe, and she started to ease back as quietly as she could.

Then— "There you are, sweetheart," Bumly shouted. "I'll get you!"

Bumly had spotted Kiki. Penelope knew she couldn't let him get Kiki. So she screamed like a silly girl, screamed until a long arm reached into the cave and dragged her out. Screamed when Bumly said, "This is the right one."

Screamed until he hit her across the face and told her to shut up.

Then she did as her Papa had instructed, and waited for him to rescue her.

The rain fell. The old bloodhound sniffed and ran. Throckmorton held one leash on the dog, and one— barely—on his temper. The children had disappeared. The timing was suspicious.

Someone lured the girls away. Whoever he was, he would pay.

Kinman organized the men to search the grounds. The servants poked into the house's every nook and cranny.

Throckmorton ran behind the dog, rain soaking his greatcoat and mud caking his boots. He ran and prayed. Prayed the rain wouldn't wash away the girls' scent. Not yet. Not yet.

Celeste had wanted to accompany him, but he had ordered she remain behind to see if she could find any trace of the girls. In this crisis he didn't want to be responsible for Celeste's safety, also.

He and the dog turned toward the river, then veered

back, toward the hill in the middle of the estate. Toward
that silly castle ruin. Straining his eyes, he watched the
woods and brush for movement. Nothing. He couldn't
see anything through this rain.

Penelope knew he always set a man to watch over the
children; he had explained the reason as best he could
without frightening her. Yet Kiki had gone, and Penelope had lied to escape.

Fury and fear burned in Throckmorton. Yes, someone
had lured the girls away.

The dog took the path toward the top. The wet gravel
slipped beneath Throckmorton's feet. The dog strained at
the leash, woofed once—and from off the path, from the
slop above, a small missile almost knocked him down.

He grabbed for the child.

Kiki. He recognized her by her size, by her frantic
grip . . . by her French.

*"Je vous en prie. Vous devez venir avec moi tout de
suite. Il l'a kidnappè! Il tient Penelope!"*

Never had his linguistic inabilities frustrated him so
much. He held Kiki's shoulders, shook her. "What?
What?"

*"Un homme! En haut. En haut, de la cave avec la
chèvrefeuille!"* She was pointing up, but he still didn't
understand, and with a huff of frustration, she shouted
in English, "A man captured Penelope! Up by the honeysuckle cave. Save her!"

"Yes." Kiki had given in. She'd spoken English.

He'd feel triumph later. Now he hugged her hard. Giving her a push down the hill, he commanded, "Go back
to the house. Tell the men to come with guns. Hurry!"

"You hurry," she retorted, and sprang like a young
goat down the hill.

Just as he'd feared. A man, a stranger, held Penelope. Threatened Penelope.

Whoever he was, Throckmorton would kill him. Interrogate him if he could, but mostly kill him.

He touched the pocket of his waistcoat. Still dry above the loaded pistol he carried.

Wrapping the leash around his wrist, he allowed the dog his head.

Stupid, to carry a loaded pistol so close to his body when it could accidentally discharge at any moment, but he might have need of it.

The dog began barking steadily, deep, gruff woofs that sounded more threatening than a bloodhound had any right to be. Master and dog raced up the path, united in pursuit. They reached the top.

No one was there.

Throckmorton observed the area while the dog sniffed in circles, finding only a muddle of scents to confuse his refined nose. Then— "There." Off the path, into the trees. Broken branches. Grass muddied beneath large, careless feet.

A red hair ribbon, dropped for Throckmorton's keen eyes to see.

Penelope. His darling daughter.

"Here, boy." Throckmorton led the dog to the spot, lifted the ribbon for him to sniff.

The dog plunged off the path. They dashed downhill, raced toward the river. Throckmorton's feet slipped out from under him. He barely slowed as he tumbled head over heels, then rose again and ran.

The bloodhound tugged. His bark grew more frantic. They were nearing their prey.

"Papa, Papa!"

Penelope. She was alive, and shrill with terror. Throckmorton and the dog raced along. They skidded to a stop as they cleared the woods. On the plain that led to the river, a man sprinted, holding Throckmorton's struggling daughter.

Throckmorton would see him dead.

He let the dog go. The bloodhound bounded after his prey. Drawing his pistol, Throckmorton shouted, "Halt!"

The man did halt. Turning, he faced Throckmorton, holding Penelope as a shield in front of him.

Throckmorton's eyes narrowed. Vaguely he recognized the man. A servant. He must have come with one of the guests.

Seizing Penelope's slender neck in one large, brutish hand, the beastly fellow twisted it and yelled, "Call off your dog, or I'll kill her!"

He would break Penelope's spine.

Throckmorton called the dog back.

Penelope's voice was high-pitched with panic, but she called, "Shoot him, Papa!"

Brutally, the servant tightened his grip on the child. "You'll kill her if you do. Or I will."

Throckmorton feared it was true. He was a good shot, but pistols couldn't be trusted. Not at this distance. Not with his daughter's life on the wager.

He began to lower the gun.

Reaching up behind her, Penelope grabbed blindly. She caught the fellow's ear, his hair, and yanked.

He doubled over, dropping her. Before he came up again the wet child slipped out of his grip. Desperately he lunged for her.

She rolled away.

Throckmorton pulled the trigger.

The bullet slammed into the blackguard's chest. He staggered back and fell.

Throckmorton experienced one moment of frightful, savage joy, the elation of a primitive who has rescued his progeny from danger.

Then, from out of the trees, a female form ran toward Penelope.

Throckmorton flung the useless gun aside. Swept along by dread, he lunged for Penelope, too. Then he realized . . . it was Celeste. Against all orders, Celeste had come after them. He was glad. She would care for his child. Gathering Penelope into her arms, Celeste held Penelope as she sobbed.

Throckmorton changed courses for the unmoving body in the mud. The bastard rested, face up, quite dead.

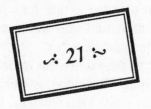

"Mam'selle Milford, you should have seen my cousin."
Kiki sat beside Penelope on her bed in the nursery, hug-
ging her closely, speaking in faintly accented English.
"She so bravely sent me on ahead and stayed to face that
canard who tried to take her from us."

"So I understand." Celeste lit a match from the fireplace and touched it to each of the candles. Both girls had
been steeped in hot baths until their shivering stopped.
Both girls were swathed in their voluminous white night-
gowns. Both girls had had their supper. And hours after
returning to the house, both still had the wide, amazed
eyes of children who had faced an adventure and survived.

Garrick had carried Penelope all the way back to the
house, her head buried in his shoulder. Through the afternoon and evening, Celeste had cuddled the child every
chance she got. Mrs. Brown would stay on a cot in the

nursery tonight in case of nightmares. But when Penelope calmed down, she seemed merely thoughtful. When her father took her to task for slipping away, she gazed at him calmly and said she had no choice. She had to go after her cousin.

Kiki reacted to the excitement in her own way—by chattering nonstop. "Penelope screamed to attract *le gredin's* attention while I ran down the hill."

"Penelope is very brave," Celeste answered.

"I found Uncle Garrick and told him what had happened, but he did not understand me! He does not speak French, so I told him in English, and you should have seen his awe!" Kiki giggled and laid her head on Penelope's shoulder. "He looked so funny with his eyebrows waggling and his mouth open."

Massively patient, Penelope sighed. Already today, she'd heard the story at least a dozen times. But she allowed Kiki to tell it once again, saying only, "You should have told him in English to start with."

"I forgot about the English," Kiki admitted.

"I suppose I'll never be so lucky again," Penelope said mournfully.

Celeste hid a smile.

Kiki cocked her head. "I do not understand."

Penelope put her arm around Kiki. "I mean I'll always get to hear you talk . . . and talk . . . because you're not going to run away again."

"Non." Kiki shook her head so hard her blond braids flew. "Never again. I will stay with you always, *ma cherè cousine.*"

"Very touching." Mrs. Brown bustled in with the heating pans for the beds. "But ye've both had a lot of excitement today and it's time for sleep. Come on, now, let's tuck ye in so Miss Celeste can go downstairs and join the party. 'Tis the final evening, ye know, and she'll want to dance all night long."

Kiki allowed Penelope to escape after one big kiss on the cheek. Kiki hopped across the cold nursery floor and between her newly warmed sheets.

Celeste leaned over for a goodnight kiss.

Kiki snuggled beneath the covers. "Are you going to marry my papa?"

Celeste shouldn't have been startled, but she was. Of course the children had watched the adults and listened to the servants' gossip. Of course they must be wondering at the week's events and how it would affect their lives.

But Kiki's ingenuous question made Celeste face a hard fact—a fact she had known almost from the moment she had returned but had refused to acknowledge.

She didn't love Ellery.

She had loved the bright, superficial image he cast across her life. She loved the idea of living with him, being the envy of other women, listening to him laugh, knowing her life would be a constant whirl of frivolity and pleasure.

But Ellery was not the man the Count de Rosselin counseled she seek. The count had told her to settle for nothing less than her soulmate, the other half of herself. Ellery was not that.

Smiling at Kiki, Celeste shook her head. "Your papa is betrothed to Lady Hyacinth. I think he will marry her—if she'll have him."

For in the excitement of the kidnapping, the truth about Kiki's parentage had been revealed to everyone. Celeste well remembered the expression on Hyacinth's face. The girl had had reservations about Ellery before; now she must be thinking hard about her future with him.

Penelope was already snuggled beneath the covers, and when Celeste leaned over to smooth her hair, Penelope looked up and asked, "Are you going to marry *my* papa?"

Frozen in place, Celeste stared into Penelope's dark eyes.

Marry? Garrick Throckmorton? She'd rejected the idea just that morning in the kitchen. Heaped it with the scorn it deserved. She had never really considered such a thing. But now . . .

Today he had been everything she dreamed of. He had rescued his child, he had vanquished evil, he had been honorable, strong and worthy of love.

"He likes you." Penelope watched her, her gaze discerningly like Garrick's. "Better than anybody else. I can tell. I think you like him, too."

Celeste swallowed. She did like Garrick. More than that, he was the man the count had urged her to seek. He was the man of her dreams.

"You should think about marrying my father. He'd like that." Then in a discerning flip from old woman-wisdom to childish complaint, she whispered, "Do I *have* to be nice to Kiki all the time now?"

Penelope had shaken Celeste to her core. So Celeste experienced a little ignoble satisfaction when she whispered back, "Yes."

Leaving Mrs. Brown in charge, she retreated to her bedchamber, the new one next to the nursery. A fire whispered in the fireplace, candles flickered in the sconces, and water steamed in a bath.

Going to the window, Celeste stared out at the night sky. The storm had blown away leaving the blackness of night and the stars which, two nights ago, had witnessed so many brilliant kisses between her and Garrick.

She loved Garrick Throckmorton. She *loved* Garrick Throckmorton. The very thought was alien to her, yet it nestled inside her like a babe. This explained the animosity and confusion of the last few days. She had come back from Paris confident in herself, comfortable with who she was, certain she could make the life she wanted for herself.

Instead she had been waylaid by Garrick, and what she wanted had changed. When Garrick had shown her that the dream of Ellery she'd cherished for so many years was nothing but a chimera, she had been left rudderless, tossing in an ocean of uncertainty.

Now she knew herself, and she knew the truth. She loved Garrick Throckmorton.

She couldn't fool herself. Probably he didn't return her love. He had made it clear that the lust he felt for her was uninvited and unwelcome. Yet that knowledge didn't change *her* feelings.

How could she respond to this love? What should she do to show Garrick?

She knew without a doubt. Walking to the cupboard, she pulled out her loveliest ball gown, a rich gold velvet which brought out the honey highlights in her hair, turned her hazel eyes to green—and sported a low-cut bodice with large, easily opened buttons up the front.

Just how Celeste found him in the dark conservatory, Throckmorton would never know. He wouldn't have thought she'd come for him. Not when the musicians played a waltz in the ballroom and Ellery performed his usual charming patter. But she had; Garrick heard her skirt rustle as she strolled in.

He sat, cup of coffee in hand, on the sofa where he had performed that intemperate seduction. Staring out of the windows and into the night, he pretended not to hear her. It seemed safer.

She carried a candlestick which she placed on a table against the wall, bringing light, although it wasn't enough to illuminate the large room, thank heavens. He didn't want to see her, beautiful and unattainable. So he didn't move, didn't speak, until she stopped right beside his shoulder.

"What do you want, Celeste?"

She gasped a little, as if the sound of his voice surprised her.

Her own voice sounded warm, rich, with that faintest of French accents she developed in emotional circumstances. "How did you know it was me?"

"The noise your heels make on the floor. Your perfume. The way I . . ." He hesitated.

She filled in. "The way your body reacts when I'm near?"

He glanced up at her. Her hair was dressed loosely atop her head. A few tendrils already straggled down. Instead of looking untidy, Celeste looked enticing, like a woman about to prepare for bed. "You have lived in romantic Paris too long."

"I'm sorry if I'm wrong, but I thought that might be it." She slipped onto the sofa beside him, bringing a hint of her perfume. "Because my body reacts to you."

Citrus, cinnamon and ylang-ylang. He recalled the ingredients in her scent, but had forgotten all propriety.

"Let's not talk about that." He laughed, a brief bark of bitter amusement. "You love Ellery, remember."

"Well." Turning toward him, she relaxed, placing one gloved arm in a graceful arch over the back of the sofa. "I fear I've had a revelation today."

"A revelation." He took a sip of his steaming drink and tried not to notice her dress. "Sounds dangerous."

"It was. I try to avoid them when possible, but today I fear the naked truth slapped me in the face."

"Uncomfortable."

"Very."

The gown was yellowish. The material shimmered in the faint light of the candle. The smallest of satin straps served as sleeves, leaving her shoulders bare . . . not to mention her bosoms, which, when she adjusted her skirt, moved with a gentle, mind-boggling quiver.

He tore his gaze away from her and looked back out the window. The reflection of the candle formed the single bright spot on the night-glazed glass. He could see himself. Today he had shot a stranger. He'd rescued his daughter. To no avail, he'd interrogated guests and servants as to the kidnapper's identity. And he'd explained to Hyacinth's satisfaction (he hoped) how Ellery came to have a child whom no one had yet mentioned. But in the glass Garrick appeared to be a man of no particular distinction, a man dressed formally except for his rumpled cravat hanging loose around his neck, a man quietly thinking his own thoughts. Not a man who drew beautiful young women to sit at his side when the last, the greatest ball of this fabulous house party went on nearby.

Yet Celeste was here, and no matter how he tried not to, he could still see her profile. She seemed pleased with something, for the dimples in her cheek appeared and disappeared for no discernible reason. Her little shell of an ear peeked out from one of those loose tendrils like some mischievous body part playing hide-and-seek—with him. Her neck rose in an elegant arch, and her lips, so full and red, puckered as if blowing him a kiss.

Obviously, libidinous frustration had destroyed what little intelligence he had left after this lousy week, this horrible day. More than ever, he wished to find relief and release with this woman. This woman only.

Turning her head suddenly, she looked into the window and caught him staring. She smiled; all the enchantment and allure she had first bent on Ellery, she now lavished on him.

He might wonder what game she was playing at, but this week had convinced him Celeste was one of those rarest of creatures—an honest and genuine person. So why was she smiling at him? The possibilities made him want to seize and possess. Curse her; she bombarded the impregnable structure of his discipline until the very foundations shook. "Aren't you supposed to be at the ball?" he snapped.

"Aren't *you?*"

"It's the last ball. You had better attend."

"If you will."

She kept watching him in the window, her gaze steady and pleased. Her smile didn't fade, but bathed him in a continuous warmth.

This afternoon, they had been caught up in a maelstrom of terror and pursuit. This morning they had shared moments of debate and passion. And yesterday he had pleasured her quite against her will. She should *not* look as if the sight of him gratified her.

"I'm avoiding the receiving line, and the official announcement of Ellery's betrothal. I suspect Lady Hyacinth might object."

"I would think you'd want to be there to handle the situation."

"Mother can handle it. If Lord Longshaw takes a swing, let Ellery take the blow. It's time."

"More than time."

She startled him with her cool verdict. So the bloom was truly off Ellery's rose. Throckmorton straightened, and with military resolution, said, "You failed to comply with my orders this afternoon."

"What orders were those?"

"You were not supposed to follow me when I went after Penelope."

"I thought you might need help."

"As you saw, I had the situation well in hand."

She smiled and folded a tuck into her skirt. "I thought you were very glad to see me."

He hated to admit it, but it was true. Out there in the rain and the mud, he'd felt inadequate to handle Penelope's distress. His pragmatic daughter had sobbed and sobbed. He had petted her hair, but she'd clung to Celeste. He'd suffered a mixture of hurt because she'd turned to another in her misery, and relief that he didn't have to handle it alone. A man who took care always to maintain control scarcely knew how to handle an outpouring of emotion. "She had never seen a man shot before," he said.

"I would hope not."

"Did you tuck her . . . the children into bed?"

Now her lovely smile failed, and she glanced down at her lap. "I did, and I wanted to talk to you about them."

Dear God. He straightened, the coffee sloshing in his mug. "They are here? They are well?"

"Very well." She placed her gloved hand on his sleeve. "I'm sorry, I didn't mean to frighten you. After this day's harrowing ordeal, you must be all in a twitter."

Irritated beyond all belief, he said, "My dear Miss Milford, I am never all in a twitter."

"Of course not." She lowered her gaze, her long lashes sweeping downward. "I forgot that you are always unaffected."

He felt it only fair to warn her. "I am one of the most unfeeling men in all of England."

Her lashes rose. Her gaze peeked forth. Her dimples quivered. "I understand."

He put ice into his tone. "I don't think you do."

"In truth, I feel responsible about what happened to the children today."

Astonished, he looked directly at her. "You do?"

"I'm their governess. If I'd taken care of them as I should, Kiki wouldn't have run away, and Penelope would have come to me instead of going after her."

He flattered himself he understood human nature. Everyone, *everyone,* ducked when blame was apportioned. But once again Celeste had amazed him. She not only accepted responsibility, she *took* responsibility. A man scarcely knew what to do with a woman like her— or rather he did, but such madness was not acceptable.

"You were commanded by me to attend this week of festivities celebrating Ellery's betrothal," he said. "There can be no dispute."

"I know what's right." Her chin jutted out. "I know what's best. In the future, I'll spend less time on frivolity and more time in the performance of my duty."

"Everything that happens on my estate is *my* responsibility."

She slid toward him. Her fingers trailed along his cheek. The silk of her gloves caught on the burr of his whiskers. "You have too much responsibility." Her voice sounded husky and far, far too warm. "You should let me ease your . . . disquiet."

Her big eyes spoke just as eloquently as her voice. For some reason which he could not discern, she wanted him.

But he was who he was, and so he bluntly declared, "I'm not the man for a girl like you."

Her finger wandered over his lips, and lingered. "Really? Yet a girl like me recognizes a master of seduction."

"Oh, that." He tried to look bored, a difficult matter when the tent peg in his trousers was strong enough to support a royal pavilion. "Think nothing of it. I seduce so many woman that I—"

She laughed, a ripple of allure. "You seduce no one, Garrick. Except me. I well remember your habits, and if I did not, I have friends among the servants. They gossip, you know."

He glared at her.

Her white lace gloves reached above her elbow, giving the illusion of modesty, but only the illusion; and when she unbuttoned her gloves, he found the presentation of the pale, delicate flesh of her inner elbow to be insupportably erotic.

She dropped one glove over the back of the sofa, the

other over the front. Her arms were bare, her fingers slender and capable.

"Only this morning you took my hand and pressed it here." Sliding her palm down his chest, she brought it to rest over his cock. "You promised me enchantment. I've come to collect."

Somehow, he retained the sense to say, "You don't know what you're doing."

For a long moment, she stared at him in silence. "Do you mean I was wrong when I told Lady Hyacinth about the act being similar to horses mating?"

He couldn't help it. He sputtered with laughter even as his groin ached with need. "No, you have that . . . that is correct. But you don't realize the ramifications of relations between us."

"It's very simple, really." She was smiling again, relaxed. "You're Garrick Throckmorton. I'm the gardener's daughter. I'm not expecting marriage, and I don't plan to be your mistress. But I know that you know how to pleasure a woman, and I want my first time to be with you."

"After what happened in here last time, why would you even want to come near me?"

She blessed him with her dimpled, full-of-joy smile. "Because I love you, Garrick Throckmorton."

He jumped away from her, backing into the corner of the couch like some imperiled maiden. "I think not!" She couldn't mean that. She didn't know what she was saying.

"You can think as you like, but you don't know my mind." She leaned toward him, presenting a cleavage that fixed his attention. "You see, I've been familiar with you all my life, so you can't say I'm deluded as to your character."

"You are." Of its own accord, his hand lifted and smoothed the surface of her breasts right along the neckline.

"Why?"

Her flesh was softer than that velvet of her gown, and it glowed with the radiance of the sun. Yet he retained enough sense to reply, "I can't tell you."

She took a breath that lifted her chest into his hand. "Then if I am, I have no one but myself to blame."

Blast the woman. *Love.* How dare she announce her love for him? She had loved Ellery only a few days ago . . . but he believed that to be nothing more than infatuation. His belief had been how he had justified his decision to change her mind. Now it appeared he had succeeded only too well. She said she loved him. Such a statement from this woman at this time worked on him as a powerful seduction.

He had to make his current quandary more comprehensible. "If you don't leave now, I will have to take you."

She stared back at him, her eyes wide and clear.

"Do you understand?" he asked. "Probably, after the way I've treated you I deserve to be teased to the point of agony. But the chaotic events of the day ruined whatever small modicum of discipline I have left."

She kicked off her shoes.

Intent as a wolf scrutinizing a tasty dove, Garrick watched each of them fly across the conservatory. If she wished to undermine his discipline, she was doing an excellent job.

Love. Dear heavens. She was beautiful, innocent, and ten years younger. Just because they shared experiences such as foreign travel, not to mention the common background of Blythe Hall, and just because she seemed mature—except for loving Ellery, a matter of rampant immaturity—and just because she had observed him in the past and claimed to know what she was getting into . . . none of those were reasons to suppose she actually understood the ramifications of declaring love to a man such as he.

He had to make himself more clear. "In an effort to bolster my prudence, I've eaten fortifying foods. I've been drinking coffee rather than liquor. But the food and the drink isn't strengthening my resolution. So unless you want me to take your virginity, you should get up and walk to that door and leave me alone."

She stood.

She comprehended. She took him at his word.

Disappointment ripped through him. Yet he had no right to feel regrets. He ought to be glad she had the good sense to run.

On bare feet, she padded to the door.

He ought to be glad she recognized him for what he was. Realized the irrevocability of a union with him. Saved him from the worse sin of all—the despoiling of an innocent, the daughter of his gardener, a woman of high morals and distant dreams.

The door clicked shut. The handle rattled.

Leaning his head against the back of the sofa, he closed his eyes and fought for mastery of himself. He'd always known he had a prodigious and passionate appetite. But he'd also assumed his will was greater than that appetite. Now he wanted nothing so much as to follow Celeste. To pick her up and carry her back here. To make her his own in the most direct and primitive way he could devise.

And she didn't want that. She deserved better.

Silk rustled behind him. Every muscle in his body tensed. A scent tickled his nose. Citrus, cinnamon, and ylang-ylang. Vaguely he wondered if abstinence caused hallucinations or worse, madness.

Then Celeste's hands settled on his shoulders. "Lie down with me."

Celeste massaged the tense shoulders beneath her hands. She watched Garrick's reflection in the window as he opened his eyes. He looked right at her; his mouth was set in a straight line, his eyebrows dipped low. As he stared at her in the glass, his chest rose and fell in harsh breaths; she could almost see his struggle between the enlightened gentleman and the primal male.

But he'd admitted he was tired, and that his resistance was low. She could have him, and with the skillful application of feminine wiles, she would. Smiling, she said, "I admit, I have never done this before, but I suspect most men don't look so grim when presented with a chance to fornicate."

A shudder ran through his frame, and he shut his eyes again.

But just for a moment. When he opened them, the severity had vanished. His hands covered hers. He lifted first one, then the other, to his lips, and pressed a kiss on each palm. "I'm a grim man."

But he smiled at her with such sensual intent she tried to take a startled step backward. She hadn't expected that, that he would transform from the weary, wary gentleman to the purposeful amorist in the blink of an eye.

"Did you lock the door?" he asked.

"I did."

"Good." Retaining her hands, he stood and crossed her arms as he faced her. "You are my opposite. Darkness and light. Harshness and joy." Crossing around the sofa, he stood so his gaze could sweep her from toe to crown. "Have you come to save me, Celeste? Will you drag and coerce me out of this sterility and forward into bliss?"

When he was at his severest, he exuded a dark sensuality. When he was inviting, his allure colored the light, scented the air, flavored her passions, and wrapped her in the earthy joy of being in his company. And when he was touching her . . . lifting their entwined hands . . . she curled their fingers together, taking pleasure in each sensuous stroke of fingertip and pad. "Is that what you feel when you look on me?" She placed his hands on her shoulders, then boldly walked her fingers up his chest and down his waistcoat. As each button slipped through its buttonhole, she smiled with the voluptuousness of the task. "Bliss, Garrick? Do you feel bliss?"

He looked down at his own white shirt, now visible after her ministrations, and when he spoke, she surmised his teeth were firmly clenched together. "Before you take such liberties, please remember who you are."

Her fingers halted on the button of his trousers. "The gardener's daughter?"

He caught her chin between his fingers and held it so firmly she couldn't look away. "Don't ever suggest I am such a snob again. To me you're not the gardener's daughter or the governess. There isn't a label or a title large enough to embody your being." Angry, stern, he spoke in his Mr. Throckmorton voice that demanded she listen and understand. "To me, you are Celeste. You are joy personified."

"Oh." She clenched the waistband of his trousers, warmed by the heat he radiated, warmed by his words.

"And I was warning you to be careful with your liberties, for while you are all those things, you are also the virgin who I want to gently initiate into the mysteries of physical love."

"Ohh."

His chest rose and fell like stiff bellows that worked with great difficulty. One hand clenched her shoulder, the other her chin, and both trembled with strain. And his trousers . . . with a lightning-quick touch, she slid her hand down over the front.

His member was there again, just as it had been earlier in the stairwell, and she couldn't repress a smile—and a tremor. "That is so flattering," she said, "and so fearsome."

"I'm going to pull the curtains now." He wheeled away.

She smiled at his retreating figure. Her quivering awareness battled with her fear of intimacy, of nudity, of unknown moves and painful invasion. But on the balance, it was good to know that, in his turn, Garrick struggled to contain his desire. That desperation made him more human; more like her.

He pulled the long, heavy, indigo drapes, shutting

them into a den bound by velvet and scented with flowers. Going to the sofas, he pulled the cushions off and onto the carpet between the two orange trees. He tossed pillows about with abandon, draped the whole area with wraps and blankets from the trunk, pulled one sofa close. With a grand gesture, he indicated their nest.

Filled with the courage of recklessness, she stalked toward him. He drew her into his arms. He was so much taller than she was; the top of her head came to his chin, and she could rest her cheek on his chest—and did. For a long moment, he held her cradled against him. Her hand stroked his collarbone. His fingers threaded into her hair, and his breath whispered against her forehead. They were two people, brought together by long acquaintance, by unexpected circumstance, by love, and before they took the final, irrevocable, ardent step, they shared the warmth of belonging.

Unhurriedly, she straightened. "I didn't get to finish undressing you."

"But I want to undress you."

She shook her head. "This time, it's my turn."

He cupped her cheeks in his hands and looked into her eyes. "You are going to make me pay for what I did here yesterday, aren't you?"

"Oh, yes. I want my revenge."

Stroking her cheeks with his thumbs, he stared into her face as if absorbing the sight. "Very well." Stepping back, he flung his arms wide. "Do your worst."

Exultation and fright fought for supremacy within her; how could she feel like this and not burst from the joy, or make a fool of herself? But better a fool who embraced one perfect moment than one who longed eternally and never dared take what she wanted.

Sliding her hands beneath his jacket, she slipped it off his shoulders and allowed it to drop onto the marble floor. His shirt was easy; she tugged it loose from his trousers and pulled it over his head.

His bare chest startled in its perfection. Clothed, Garrick gave the appearance of bulk and strength, but exposed to the light, he proved to be a mass of large, smooth muscles beneath olive skin, and dark, curling hair that stretched from shoulder to shoulder and down his flat stomach. She'd never seen anything so alive, and she touched him in curious amazement, stroking her hands first down his arms, then down his sides. "You're beautiful," she whispered.

"Men aren't beautiful."

"You are." She circled him, dragging a finger around his abdomen and around to his back.

His back showed the same sturdy build. "You're not constructed like an aristocrat," she said. "More like a farmer or a laborer."

"My father *was* a laborer." Garrick paused while she ran her hands up the indent of his spine. "He thought a man should know how to lift and toil, and I spent some time working on the docks. And in India—" He froze when she pressed herself against his back and tried to span his neck with her fingers. When she stepped back, he said in a conversational tone, "Your breasts scorched my flesh where they touched."

She chuckled and stroked the long muscles that extended from his shoulders to his spine. "I see no signs of burn."

He turned on her and seized her wrists. "Celeste . . ."

Giving him her sauciest smile, she reminded him, "You were telling me about how you labored in India."

For a moment, he looked bewildered as if he didn't know what she was talking about.

She freed her hands, then lightly slid them up his arms. Standing on tiptoe, she whispered in his ear, "You were telling me how you developed such a marvelous brawniness, and I really, really want to hear."

In a gritty voice, he said, "I will make you pay for this."

"I'm depending on it." Her discovery of love for him hadn't blinded her to the advantages of being initiated by Garrick. He was a perfectionist, the exact man to instruct her. He would insist on nothing less than pleasure for them both. For her. It was that confidence that gave her the audacity to tease him when his hands bunched into fists and he lusted after her with his gaze.

"India," she urged.

"I spent a few months in a nomad's camp, herding yaks."

"What's a yak?"

"It's a furry beast of burden that gives milk."

"Why would a businessman herd—"

"Because I was traveling with the nomads!" He sounded exasperated.

She leaned her head against his shoulder and hid a smile. "What else?"

"I spent more than a few months a captive in Kabul, sweating blood in the rajah's quarry."

"You've had adventures."

"At the time, they felt like punishments."

"You'll tell me sometime?"

"Not now."

"Not now," she agreed. Searching through his chest hair, she found his male nipples and circled them with her fingertips. "Different, yet the same. When I touch you, does it feel the same?"

"As when I touch you?" At her nod, he lifted one shoulder. "I can't say, but I like it. I like it very much."

She pinched gently, as he had, and when he groaned she said, "Yes. I think it feels much the same for both of us." Satisfied she had achieved a small measure of revenge—and knowledge—she once more slid her palm over the bulge in his trousers. It hadn't diminished; if anything, it had grown.

She swallowed and fumbled a little as she unbuttoned him.

He took her shoulders as she did, whether to support her or himself, she didn't know. "I promise you—" he began.

She interrupted. "I know." Untying the string of his drawers, she slid her hands along the side of his hips and down his thighs, following his clothing toward the floor. Kneeling, she was saying, "We just need to get you out of these trousers . . ." when she noticed . . .

All right, she'd known his penis was there. Curiosity had suggested this method for a closer look. But it was so close and so . . . well . . . big. Gorgeous, but big. Especially at eye level. Especially . . . leaning back, she viewed his whole figure.

The hair on his chest extended over his furrowed abdomen to join the quantity of dark hair at the junction of his legs. His hips weren't slim, made for slipping between a woman's legs, but solid, heavy-boned, with a strength that would weight on a woman and imprint her with his claim. And likewise his member, a sweep of smooth, olive skin, dark veins and subtle graduations, would dominate a woman. "Dear heavens." In amazement, she glanced up at his face.

He stared down at her, his gray eyes intense, his lids heavy. "Well, Celeste? What do you think?"

"I think I want to touch you."

His member twitched.

She scarcely heard him say, "You haven't asked permission before."

Extending one finger, she touched him. Just the tip.

His breath hissed out.

Glancing up, she saw the way he watched her—as if she were the torturer stretching him on the rack. But she couldn't be hurting him, so this must be like what he'd done to her, a pleasure so great as to be pain.

Gently, she wrapped her hand around the shaft.

Odd, to think that pleasure could be almost unbearable. Odd, also, to find that arousing him could arouse her, but it did. As she held him cupped in her palm, as she rubbed her fingers over the cap, the ridges, as she found the strength of the base and heard the faint, deep groans her exploration invoked: she discovered her cheeks flushed, her breasts ached with need, and a damp warmth grew between her legs.

She wanted.

Grasping his thighs, she rubbed her cheek against the rough hair and marveled. Sturdy, solid, like every part of Garrick. Each large muscle delineated, masculine, evocative of the strength of the man.

His breath rasped above her. He touched her hair, a light caress.

Because it seemed right, because it seemed daring,

she leaned forward and kissed his member, and ran her tongue up its length.

Suddenly he waited no longer. Pulling her to her feet, he unbuttoned her in a fury of movement.

"Garrick?" Her voice squeaked a little.

He didn't seem even to have heard her. He concentrated on disrobing her to the exclusion of all else, concentrated so hard her heart began the slow, deep thump of terror and exhilaration.

"Garrick." She half-laughed as he pushed her hands away from him so he could remove her gown. "What's the hurry?"

He didn't answer, didn't slow as he stripped the dress away, turned her around, untied her petticoats. They dropped to the floor, rustling as they landed in the starched heap. Wrapping his arms around her, he picked her up and out of her clothing, kicking everything aside in his quest to reach the cushions on the floor.

As their bodies met, they both froze.

He wore nothing but a pair of boots.

She wore nothing but a thin, white, lacy chemise and silk stockings.

There might have been nothing between their heated bodies. Her puckered nipples pressed into his chest. His penis prodded her belly.

He stared at her, face to face. "Corset?" he asked.

"None."

His eyes dilated until the pupil swallowed the gray iris. "Pantalettes?"

She shook her head. "I was coming to you."

The world dropped away as he fell backward, landing on the cushions so she could land on him. She didn't even catch her breath before he rolled until he was above her. She cried out, not from fear exactly, but from surprise and bewilderment as he pulled her chemise out from under her and up to her waist. Opening her legs with the thrust of his knee, he placed himself between them, his hips pressing her hips, his chest against hers. The onslaught, the rush, his seizing of domination brought a tardy brush of prudence.

She tried to push against him.

He paused to catch her hands and wrap them around his shoulders. "Hold on." Sliding his hand beneath her neck, he lifted her face for a brief kiss. "Just hold on."

His hand disappeared. He touched her . . . below. A brief touch at first, nothing more than a brush of fingers. Reconnaissance, it would seem, for next he moved to open her to his touch.

She squeezed his shoulders, his arms. Caution clogged her throat and brought heat to her skin. Caution was natural the first time a woman—any woman—was with a man—any man. And the first time altogether . . .

How could a man in such a blazing hurry handle her with such delicacy? His thumb grazed her lightly, but with such precision she cried out again. But this time there was nothing of protest, and everything of delight. Her legs . . . she didn't know what to do with her legs. Her feet moved restlessly on the floor . . . she and Garrick had fallen only partially on the cushions . . .

He found the entrance to her body, circled it lightly with his finger, then entered. Not much, just far enough to make her bear down with her feet and lift her hips.

"That's it." He pulled away.

"Don't go." Now she clutched at him.

"It's far too late for that." He shifted position, put his hands beneath her hips, lifted her and touched her again.

She smiled. "Better."

Then the pressure grew. His weight bore down on her.

Oh, God. He was on her. He was *in* her.

It burned. She struggled. He paused, but didn't retreat. Shiny, black and straight, his hair fell about his forehead. His cheeks were concave with strain. One drop of sweat trickled down his temple, and his chest rose and fell with harsh breaths.

How dared he look as if he were suffering? She wanted to smack him. "You promised me enchantment," she said, indignation smoldering in her tone.

"Soon." He smiled at her, a slash of villainy.

"You lied." He had. He knew he had, too.

"I just . . . didn't tell you . . . all the truth." Lifting her hips, he adjusted their bodies, sliding a little away, giving her ease.

But before she could sigh with relief, he drove forward and the pressure started again.

He had the audacity to say, "Patience."

Worse this time. The stinging was worse, with an inner resistance that brought tears to her eyes.

Grabbing his hair, she tugged.

Intent on his task, he paid no attention.

So she distracted him, pulling him to her for a kiss, nipping his lip as he had done to her, thrusting her tongue in his mouth. Angling his head, he kissed her back, fighting her for command.

Deep within her, her maidenhead yielded, but she did not. The kiss deepened, flared into fire, damped down and flared again.

And all the time he forged on.

She didn't know when he started thrusting in and out,

she only knew when she drew back from the kiss and gasped for air, the pain had faded to discomfort. Everything about this was alien, yet . . . her body knew how to respond. He made it easy; he moved unhurriedly, sliding in all the way, pressing his pelvis to hers, putting himself right where she felt him the most. Then he moved back, a deliberate sweep that compelled her to acknowledge every inch of him. Back he came in purposeful cadence, deep inside her, then back. In and out . . . in and out . . .

She found herself waiting on his advance, taking pleasure in his advance yet desperate for that moment when he was all the way inside, his member touching her womb, his body against hers, as close to her as he could be. Then when he pulled away, the pleasure changed, became impatience rendered bearable by the promise of more to come.

She watched him, memorizing his determination, his vehemence. He was hot, like a stove, and as he thrust his heat entered her, stretching her. Her legs shifted around him, lifting to clutch his hips, her feet sliding on the back of his thighs. Her hands grasped at him, roaming his neck, his shoulders, his arms. Her hips rocked and her back arched.

And all the while he kept up that slow, measured, calculated rhythm, each thrust a little more intense, each moment bringing her a little closer to climax. In and out . . .

He was relentless. When the pleasure got too powerful, she began to shy away. The blood throbbed in her veins. She found it an effort to keep her eyes open, and each time they fluttered closed she could hear her body that much more clearly. She panted, and someone—oh, it was she!—moaned with the advance of sharp, desperate desire. She wanted to move more quickly, to finish this her own way, but he controlled her; his hands beneath her buttocks rocked her toward him. He forced her to maintain his pace, his fingers clasping and releasing in a pulse that echoed the one inside.

He adjusted his weight, leaning his chest against hers, forcing her down further into the cushion. Close against her ear, he spoke in that slow, inexorable, dark velvet voice. "Celeste. Let me see you. Let me hear you. Show me your joy."

She didn't know where she found the strength to defy him, or even why, but she did. "No." She could scarcely whisper.

Deep inside, the pressure grew, yet she fought to hold together, to keep from letting Garrick see her, exposed and desperate and wanting.

"This is pure pleasure." He thrust a little more slowly. "Can you feel how much I love being inside you?"

"Yes." She tossed her head back and forth on the pillows.

"How each inch glides in?"

Her back arched as, in her mind's eye, she saw their joining. "Yes."

"You're dark and warm inside. So tight." He drew the words out, making each one a counterpoint to the advance on her body and on her emotions, making her more aware of the motion, the heat, the pure sexuality of their union.

She whimpered.

"Hold me deep inside you." He caressed her with his

language. He overwhelmed her with his body. "Hold me."

She tried. She tightened her muscles on him—and climax struck her like a tidal wave, roaring along her nerves, lifting her hard against him. She convulsed, drowning in pleasure, mindless with the agony and the rapture. She cried out. She hung onto Garrick with her nails and her love. She forgot him in her ecstasy and memorized him in her heart.

And when she was done, when the wave rolled and she was left panting and exhausted, she opened her eyes to see him, watching her, holding her . . . moving on her.

"I love watching you," he whispered. "Show me again."

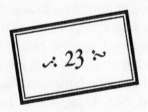

∼ 23 ∼

*M*ost men would not feel so grim when they woke in the morning to find a beautiful, nude woman kissing their way down their chests. Most men would not be suffering from guilt after having spent a night of bliss in Celeste's arms. Most men would count themselves lucky to find themselves in such a fix.

But Garrick Stanley Breckinridge Throckmorton the Third was not most men.

Keeping his eyes firmly shut, he lay among the cushions in the conservatory, suffered the sensation of her mouth on his skin, and considered his dilemma.

There was nothing about the evening before of which he could be proud. Equally, there was nothing about the evening before that he regretted.

And he should. Blast it, he should. He had, in sound mind and in total sobriety, taken the virtue of a young lady, a sweet woman, the daughter of one of his employees, and exulted in the process.

Of course, she had claimed to know her mind. She had claimed to love him.

He swallowed.

Sadly, he wanted it to be true. She was the gardener's daughter, yes, but as he'd told her the night before, he considered the difference in their stations immaterial, a product of the aristocrats' need to set themselves above everyone else for no reason other than their heritage. He judged people by their characters, and Celeste was everything he wanted in a woman: clever, beautiful, witty, open.

His.

No other man had had her, and the sentiment wasn't pretty and it wasn't respectable, but pride and possessiveness held him in twin grips.

Celeste stroked her palms along his ribcage, following the grooves toward his back. She moved lower, pressing her fist hard against his abdomen, seemingly fascinated by its unyielding quality.

What kind of man was he? Not the man he'd believed himself to be. He had thought himself a responsible businessman of dignity and good sense. Instead, he'd proved that dignity and good sense didn't stand a chance against temptation, true temptation. Temptation with the name of Celeste.

She ran her hands down the tops of his thighs, then down the outsides, then in a slow, strong glide, she traveled up the insides, and finally she rested her cheek against one.

For some reason, she seemed obsessed with his thighs.

For some reason, pride made him flex his thighs.

Vanity, he supposed.

He hadn't ever thought about his body. He was big, and for that he was thankful for his size gave him an advantage in a fight. He rode, he fenced, he practiced boxing with a retired boxer; all requisites for a man who lived with the threat of danger. But those activities had honed his muscles, and right now, as Celeste examined him, he was glad, for like a child with a new toy, she inspected everything. She rubbed his calves, lightly touched each toe, glided all the way back up his leg . . . he tensed, waiting, hoping . . .

Temptation had kept him awake half the night, tormenting him with the need to take her again. He imagined sliding into her from behind as she slept, wakening her with his gentle thrust. He imagined kissing her lips, fondling her breast, waking her with arousal, facing her and taking her. Mostly he had imagined spreading her legs, entering her from above, and coercing her, once more, to acknowledge him as her master.

Celeste's fingers glided over his hip bones and down into the sculpted concave of his belly.

He wanted to dominate this woman, engrave her with his possession, make sure she never doubted that her place was by his side. There was nothing to admire about such an archaic instinct; nevertheless the need burned in his gut.

This morning he needed to stop imagining and show some bloody wisdom. He firmly believed if a man made a mistake, he should accept the consequences and do everything to set the matter straight. He, Garrick, had to face the fact he'd gone wild for Celeste, breaking all the rules of society and civilized behavior, and reparations must be made. He knew what those reparations must be; he would face what must be done and do it like a man.

As he made his resolution, Celeste stroked his dia- bolical cock. His erection stood at stiff attention, just as if he hadn't blasted his seed into her last night like some youth with his first woman.

In his adolescence, he would never have been able to hold back as he had, for like all youths he had thought what worked for him would work for her. He knew dif- ferently now, and last night, once he had surrendered to his baser needs, he had been determined to show Ce- leste all the pleasure a woman could find. After all, what was the use of giving into temptation unless he em- braced it wholeheartedly?

Of course, when she had approached climax, she'd tried to evade it, and him.

That hadn't surprised him. Before, in this very con- servatory, he'd forced her to climax. It had been a lesson for him in his own beastly nature, and a lesson for her, too. She hadn't easily accepted that her body could turn traitor to her good sense. Moreover, he had not joined her in ecstasy, but compelled her to experience it alone.

So for all her openness and pledges of love, she had been wary, and was still. Instinctively she knew that, for her, surrender was not the giving of her body, but the ac- ceptance of pleasure, the yielding of the self.

She explored him with a light touch, weighing his testicles in her palms, discovering the shapes within with a succinct, "Gracious!"

Today in the light, her curiosity led her, but she didn't understand. She thought maybe last night had been a fluke, or that she hadn't really cried out and convulsed in his arms, or that now she could control herself.

He knew better. She *would* yield again, and each time she'd come closer to knowing that he wouldn't harm her, or ever betray her. He'd teach her to trust him, one climax at a time.

A difficult task, but one to which he would willingly— no, eagerly—apply himself.

She licked his nipple, once, twice, then stopped. He peeked beneath his lashes to see her, nose wrinkled, taking one of his curling chest hairs off her tongue.

He wanted to laugh. Blast her! He had been gravely considering how he should make amends, then she made him forget both restraint and the momentous topic at hand. She had made him want to laugh.

Glancing up, she caught him watching her. Dropping the hair off the cushion, she asked in the most prosaic tone possible, "How do you avoid this?"

Sunlight leaked through the curtains, showing him a rumpled Celeste: hair tangled, lips swollen, and proudly naked. She sat on her heels, her skin glowing brighter than the golden roses that bloomed in their pots. "It's a constant hazard," he admitted.

"Only for me," she said grumpily.

Now he did laugh. Bless her for an innocent! "For me, too."

"Why? I don't have hair on my chest."

"No." He tucked his hands beneath his head. "Not on your *chest.*"

"Well, where else would you . . . oh!" She clapped her hands over her mouth and stared at him with huge, appalled eyes.

He smiled at her with wicked delight—and that was another change she'd made in him. He'd never been any kind of wicked before.

Worse, he liked it.

She realized he liked it, too, for she straightened her slim shoulders and folded her hands primly in her lap. In a lofty tone, she announced, "You can't be serious."

He sat up, a slow flexing of muscles, a purposeful message of intent. He was bigger than she, stronger than she, more experienced than she.

She didn't stand a chance.

Which she realized at once. "No," she said.

He reached for her.

She didn't waste any time. She scrambled backward. "No." She sounded a little more desperate.

He caught her around the waist. He picked her up—she weighed no more than a feather—and carried her to the sofa.

"No, no, no!"

But she wasn't really fighting. She struggled more from a combination of shock and the maidenly embarrassment that made her insist, "No!" as he sat her on the sofa.

He sank to his knees before her. Holding one ankle, he straightened her leg, lifted it to his mouth and kissed her toes.

She caught her breath. "No." But she lost her tone of unequivocal denial.

He slid his lips along her arch, up her heel, up her calf.

"Garrick, no." Her voice had lowered to that husky, knowing-woman tone.

He lingered at the soft skin of her inner knee, kissing it, wetting it with his tongue.

She put her other foot on his shoulder and pushed, but not hard enough to shift him.

He kissed his way up her inner thigh.

Her head fell back on the cushion. She breathed his name.

Placing her leg over his shoulder, he carefully, tenderly, parted the lips to reveal her sweet, inner core.

Her eyes closed. Her breath came quickly.

"Beautiful." Last night, he had bathed her with his handkerchief and water from the pitcher, pressing the cool cloth against her to ease the ache. But in the dim light, he'd not been able to see. Now he could, and he smiled. How pretty she was, pink and fragile, everything shyly hidden, the feminine opposite of his bold genitals. Unable to resist, he stroked each place where he had been last night, where he would go today.

Cheeks aflame, she moved restlessly. He enticed her, yes, but he embarrassed her, too. How peculiar women were, that they would allow the deepest intimacy yet be uncomfortable to show themselves! Women were inscrutable creatures, never revealing all of their hearts, their minds. He could be with Celeste for years and never discover all her secrets.

But he would reveal at least one now. With delicate precision, he placed his mouth against her. She tasted like woman. His woman. With slow, sweet, hot caresses, he found each sensitive spot. He entered her with his tongue again and again, imitating his kiss, imitating coitus.

Her hips surged beneath him. The foot braced against his shoulder trembled.

He wanted her. He wanted to be inside her.

Yet there was another place, one he'd already proved to be responsive. Moving up the scant inch to her feminine nub, he coaxed it into his mouth and traced its outline.

She made a sound; perhaps a protest, perhaps involuntary encouragement.

Meticulously, he suckled.

"Garrick." She bucked beneath him. "Garrick!"

She was on the verge when he pulled back.

She cursed him.

"No, love. I've got to be inside you. I've got to feel each tremor and ripple."

On the edge of climax himself, he awkwardly stood and pulled her to her feet.

She blinked, swayed unsteadily, unsure what he expected.

"For you." His voice was hoarse, probably because all his body fluids were elsewhere. Sinking down on her seat, he added, "It's your turn."

She still didn't understand; probably she'd had too many surprises to comprehend, but he pulled her down on his lap, her delightful bottom right on his bare thighs. "Face me," he instructed, and noticed with a distant amusement that she could still look shocked.

Shocked, but not confused. She comprehended now, and with wary curiosity she slid around to look toward him. Her thighs opened and embraced his.

Hands on her hips, he urged her up on her knees. "Take me," he said.

She looked down at his cock. She looked up at his face, and in the tone of an interested pupil, asked, "Does anyone else know about this position?"

He couldn't laugh now. It was impossible when his cock was only inches from paradise. But he did, a laugh that cracked in the middle. "It is perhaps not as common as the other, but I didn't invent it."

Reaching between her legs, she took his cock and

guided it to the entrance to her body. "Where did you learn it?"

How could she talk now? She couldn't be impervious to this fever. Not when he'd prepared her so well.

Not when he was so desperate.

She paused, holding him, taunting him. *"Where?"*

Her voice slurred a little, he noted. Her lids drooped, her cheeks flushed. She did want, but he had given her power and she was going to exercise it. That was what he'd wanted, for her to know the freedom of coupling; but did she have to take advantage *now?*

Of course she did. She was a woman. Goaded into speech, he said, "India."

"Ah." She lowered her weight on him.

His balls ached with need. He wanted to thrust his way inside her body, take her quickly, spend himself violently.

But she'd been a virgin. Last night he'd proceeded deftly; he had still hurt her.

So now he allowed her to move about, pressing on the head of his penis, learning how to accept him into herself. He'd aroused her with his mouth; she was damp and ready. Nevertheless, the penetration proceeded inch by wary inch. Only her expressions of caution, then pleased surprise made the torment bearable. When finally, *finally* she slid all the way onto him, her look of triumph warmed him . . . when he was already about to go up in flames.

Tentatively, gingerly, she lifted herself, sliding up his shaft almost to the tip. With a little more confidence, she slid back down. The measured pace quickened. It was almost worth the agony of waiting to see her alive with delight.

He loved that about her, that she showed her emotions rather than conceal them. She was totally open, totally the opposite of him. She smiled, her lovely, carnal mouth alive with wonder. She held his shoulders for balance, leaned back and leaned forward, experimenting with the stroke. Her breasts, small and firm and round, swayed in unconscious licentiousness, and inside she wrapped him in the warm, rough silk of her body. He no longer remembered his other liaisons, but he knew he'd never craved any woman like this before.

Catching her around the waist, he lifted her long enough to catch her breast in his mouth. She gasped, paused, suspended and scandalized. He drew strongly, suckling for his pleasure and hers. Her nipples tightened. Her breath grew harsh, and she moved now with insistent urgency.

He kissed her shoulder. She arched her neck and he kissed that, sliding up to her ear, her cheek, giving her a brief buss on the lips. His heartbeat thundered as they moved toward completion. He fought the urge to grasp her hips and overrule her pace. Instead he moved as she commanded, so taut with pleasure he groaned with each stroke. She was going to kill him. She was going to kill him with sex.

At last, she cried out, her entire body convulsing as with earthy exhilaration she gave herself over to orgasm.

And he, fool that he was, held off and savored the sight and the sensation of her sheath constricting on his cock. Not until she collapsed on his chest did he allow himself to plunge, and plunge, and fill her with his seed.

For moments after, he could think of nothing. Nothing but the sweet, damp body in his arms, nothing but his absolute satisfaction.

Then, oh most horrible notion, he began to plot how to do it again.

This wasn't him. He couldn't be like this, lured by Celeste and her marvelous body—he smoothed his hand down her supple spine—to abandon discipline for the pleasures of fornication. He had his duty . . .

His duty.

"Celeste." Her head rested on his shoulder. He whispered in her ear. "Celeste, listen to me."

Slowly she turned to face him. She smiled, that trusting, open smile that flattered and charmed, warmed his loins and notified him he had better do his duty now, or he would never remember to do it at all.

From the first, he hadn't enjoyed involving Celeste in the business of espionage, but he had always ruthlessly used the tools at hand. With her knowledge of Russian, she had been a very useful tool indeed. Later, he'd realized how dangerous she was to his control, and he had wished to be rid of her regardless of her value. Now conscience spoke. A man didn't exploit the woman with whom he made love.

Darting a kiss to his cheek, she asked, "What, darling?"

"We have to get dressed." Throckmorton didn't have a choice. He had to employ her. Stanhope had already taken the first message to London and given it over to another man, an English merchant of good standing who had left the country at once. Stanhope had returned, had enlarged the stash under his bedchamber floorboards, and no doubt eager to hear the contents of another letter. He would return to Celeste for those contents. "We must leave here."

She groaned like a child deprived of a treat. "Must we?"

He kissed her as reward, a kiss that started as nothing more than a peck and ended with a long, slow, deep provocation, the kind that made his cock, which should have known better, twitch and try to rise. But no. He subdued it sternly.

Stroking Celeste's hair, he said, "The morning is advanced. We'll be lucky if we are not met and conclusions drawn."

She showed none of the appropriate dismay. "The right conclusions?"

"No doubt the right conclusions. We both missed the closing ball. I fear we are already the objects of speculation."

She groaned again, but this time she gradually sat up in his lap.

Surely it wasn't so bad, to utilize her knowing this was the last time, that after this, communication would be routed through another agent and deciphered, and the messages which would come to Stanhope would lead the Russians into disaster. She was a reasonable girl. Probably, if she knew her role, she would agree to it avidly. "I beg your forgiveness for abandoning you after such a night, but I have to ride out." He was trifling with the truth, but he needed to be away from the house while Stanhope interrogated her. "I received letters yesterday—"

"That's right, I forgot." After all their activities of the night before, she looked guilty over a task left undone. "Do you want me to translate them now? Or rather, after I've bathed and changed into a morning gown?"

"No need. They came from London already partially translated, and by comparing them to your previous work, I managed a fair approximation of the contents."

A fair approximation? He glanced at her sideways. He knew exactly what the letters said. He'd written them in English and sent them to London to be translated into Russian, then received them back. Only she had refused to come to his office, and then all hell had broken loose.

"See?" she said encouragingly. "Translation isn't so difficult. It's just a matter of applying what you know and interpreting the rest."

If it were only that simple. He eased out of her, carried her to the cushions, and laid her down. Standing, he stared down at her and thought himself a dunce. A wise man would stand her up and shake her until his seed spilled from her. Throckmorton wanted Celeste on her back, his seed safe within her womb. He was far gone; a man who had lost all judgment. Only professional ethics remained to him, and by this afternoon he would have satisfied those ethics. Then he would set matters right with Celeste, and all would be well.

Having formulated an acceptable plan, he nodded and loosened her stockings from atop a rose bush.

Still lounging on the cushions, she giggled like a girl as he dropped them atop her. "You look even more complacent than normal."

He had leaned down to gather her petticoats off the floor, but he halted as he straightened. "What do you mean, *more* complacent than normal?"

"You always look as if you know exactly the right thing to do, and are doing it." Kicking up her feet, she pulled on the stockings and eased herself to her feet. "For those of us who aren't quite so certain, it can be an intense source of irritation."

"You're not certain of yourself?"

"Not always. Sometimes I do the wrong thing." She

saw the expression on his face, and stepping close, she stroked his cheek. "Oh, I didn't mean last night. That is the one action I've taken since my return of which I am absolutely confident."

Catching her hand, he kissed her palm.

Digging her chemise out from among the covers, she donned it. "Mostly you irritate Ellery."

"Ellery?" He didn't want to talk about Ellery *now.* With *Celeste.* "What has he got to be irritated about?"

"He's not as perfect as you are."

"Perfectly handsome," Throckmorton said in exasperation. "What else could he want?"

"I don't know. I think he's restless." Taking the petticoats from Throckmorton, she pulled them on.

"Restless? He could try reporting for work."

"Be realistic. He'll never work in an office. I think he needs adventure as you had in India." Her gown lay in a wad on the floor. She shook it out and said sadly, "These wrinkles aren't going to come out."

He didn't appreciate her advice; he didn't appreciate it at all. "He's going to get married. That should be adventure enough for him."

She wrestled the gown over her head and while she was hidden, she said, "He should be a spy or something." Her arms reached into the sleeves. Her head appeared.

She didn't look any different, but she should have. She had just reawakened every one of Throckmorton's suspicions. What did she *know?* "A spy." He tried to sound neutral. He succeeded in sounding guarded.

"Or something like that." Blithely, she fastened her buttons, shutting herself away from his touch, changing herself from his lover to ... who? "You never answered. Do you want me to check your translations?"

She couldn't know anything. She couldn't. She was artless, generous, kind. She had given him her virginity. Her comment about a spy had to be merely coincidental. And if it weren't—well, she had been well-guarded during her time here. He would ensure she would continue to be watched. "The translations . . . yes. I would have asked Stanhope to help me, but he was busy charming the ladies."

Without expression, she said, "He does that very well."

Throckmorton didn't like that. "Has he been flirting with you?"

"Stanhope would flirt with a swine if he thought he could get any use from the bacon," she said acidly.

Jolted by her uncanny reading of Stanhope's character, Throckmorton gathered his own clothing. Celeste really was too clever by half. But it didn't matter; even if she were a spy, even if she had turned to the enemy, he would not allow her to be imprisoned and hung. No, no matter that he believed in justice for all, he couldn't bear for that justice to overtake Celeste. He would hide her duplicity from his associates, make sure she never again had an opportunity to operate, and never, ever let her out of his sight.

She misread his silence. "I'm sorry. He's your friend. You're fond of him. I had no right—"

Having made his decision, he felt well enough to say, "No, don't apologize. I fear you're right." In India, he had learned to dress quickly if the occasion warranted, and he believed this occasion did. His drawers, his trousers, his shirt went on without hindrance. "Nevertheless, I find I can't easily dismiss him or the service he has rendered. I know it's asking a great deal, but should you see him, could you convey the contents of the latest letter?"

"Why don't *you* tell him?"

"Male pride forbids that he ask me. I'm going to ride out. I . . . well, I would rather you read the letters and confirmed my opinion of their contents."

"Ah." She donned her gown.

She seemed to have nothing more to say, and that made him uncomfortable. It was almost as if she realized his deception and judged him by its villainy. But she couldn't have; probably the enormity of her own actions last night had just begun to weigh on her. Or she was somehow in league with the Russians.

Impossible. "The letters are in my bottom left desk drawer. It's locked. Here's the key."

She took the key he provided and looked at it, then gravely up at him. "After I have bathed and dressed."

"Yes, of course." Sitting on the couch, he began the difficult process of pulling on his boots. "I think they speak of a meeting in the Crimea between the French, the Turks and the English." Let the Russians worry about a threat to their precious Crimea while the English troops in Afghanistan moved where they would.

"I'll look at the letters and tell Stanhope when he asks." Searching, she found her slippers and donned them, then went to the drapes that covered the windows. She took hold of the edges.

He half-rose from his seat. "What are you . . . ?"

"After so many rainy days, Papa would want sunshine on the plants."

"Wait!" But it was too late.

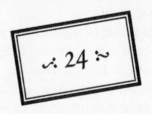

~∴ 24 ∾~

"Thank you, Celeste." Stanhope lounged behind Garrick's desk, fitting perfectly in the elegance of his surroundings, yet a usurper on the king's throne. "You've made my task ever so much easier."

He had discarded the winning ways with which he earlier treated her. Now he grinned, a coxcomb grin that made Celeste want to slap it off his face. She thought she knew what his attitude meant; she would convey her conviction to Garrick as soon as possible. Meanwhile, she stood before the desk and presented Stanhope with a cool smile. "I'm always happy to help you and Mr. Throckmorton."

Stanhope laughed, a whoop of condescending amusement. "Yes, you've got your uses. To me, and to Throckmorton."

To him? Yes, she now thoroughly understood her role in this play. She listened when Garrick told her what was in the letters, she checked the contents of the letters, she presented the contents to Stanhope. Very clean, very easy, and not worth angst even when Stanhope rifled through Garrick's unlocked drawers like some petty thief. She could have given him the key to that one locked drawer; she held it fast within her pocket.

But her uses to Throckmorton? She didn't make the mistake of thinking Stanhope was talking about her position as governess. Not after that dreadful moment when she'd opened the drapes of the conservatory and saw old Lord and Lady Featherstonebaugh waiting while the servants loaded the baggage onto the Featherstonebaugh carriage—and all of them saw her, clad in her ball gown, and Garrick pulling on his boots.

Celeste and Garrick had broken the first rule of the English affair—discretion above all else. Nothing happened unless you were caught.

They had been caught. And she was not going to listen to any smarmy remarks about their affair from Stanhope. She gave the briefest of polite curtsies. "I must attend the children. If you'll excuse me—"

"Don't worry," Stanhope announced, "you've got Throckmorton by the short hairs."

She stood stock still, stunned by his impudence. "You . . . vulgarian!"

"He is enamored with you."

Her fickle, foolish heart gave a musical little trill. "He . . . who . . . Throckmorton told you that?"

Stanhope actually put one of his boots on the shiny surface of Throckmorton's immaculately carved desk. "Oh, yes. But he thinks you're stupid."

"He doesn't think I'm stupid," she flashed.

"A birdbrain." Stanhope apparently relished the

phrase. "If he respected you, he wouldn't have treated you as he did in the conservatory."

She blushed a mortifying crimson. So Stanhope *had* surmised what they were doing last night. She shouldn't have opened those drapes, but as she had told Throckmorton, who would have thought any English aristocrat would be awake and ready to leave at the unprecedented hour of eight o'the clock?

Throckmorton had looked grave, but told her not to worry. He would fix things, he said, as soon as he got back from his ride.

Stanhope suffered no compunction about humiliating her. "Throckmorton stuck his hand under your skirts. He trained you to lust, softening you up for the kill. Men have been doing that with their governesses for eons, Miss Milford."

The color died from her cheeks. It wasn't last night Stanhope spoke of; he knew about that mortifying scene two days ago. Not about the night of passion, but that afternoon in the conservatory when Garrick Throckmorton had proved how well and easily he could manipulate her.

No one knew. "How . . . how did you discover that?"

Stanhope cocked a jaunty eyebrow. "Men talk, Miss Milford."

Her stomach tightened. Garrick had told Stanhope . . . but no. Stanhope was a liar and a traitor, and Garrick would never be so crass as to gossip. Not about her. Not about that. "I don't believe you."

"Believe what you like." Standing, Stanhope strolled toward her. "But I *do* know about that, and I predict the next thing that will happen is he'll put his prick where his hand was."

She hated Stanhope. How dared he speak to her in such a manner?

How dared he be right?

"If you were part of the *ton*, he would have never treated you with such familiarity. If you were part of the ton, your father would kill him. But your father is the gardener, and he can't do anything for his daughter's honor or he'll lose his position."

"I don't need to listen to this." She turned to walk away.

Stanhope grabbed her arm in a cruel grasp. "Don't you walk away from me, you little . . . peasant. You're not worthy to lick my boots."

She tried to tug free, but his fingers bit into her, bruising her. "Let go," she said softly, "or I will tell Garrick what you're doing."

"Garrick?" Like a bulldog, Stanhope held on and shook her arm as if it were a hunk of meat. "You call him *Garrick*? The nerve of you. You're the gardener's daughter. He's descended from a line of peers that goes back to William the Conqueror."

His contempt slapped her in the face. She had been living in a dream world, cushioned by Ellery's infatuation, her experiences in Paris, and Garrick's tolerance. Stanhope's was the attitude her father had warned her about. Birth mattered in England; nothing else could compensate for an aristocratic pedigree. She looked down at Stanhope's hand. "Mr. Throckmorton's father was a commoner."

Stanhope's eyes blazed with a nobleman's disdain; the disdain that would greet her at every turn of society should she dare to raise herself above her station. "Diluting a fine old bloodline once was more than enough."

He didn't so much release her arm as toss it from him. "But he has no real plans to wed you, of course. He's already got your return tickets purchased."

She found herself taking careful, shallow breaths. "My return tickets to where?"

"To Paris." He smiled, a slight, gracious curve of the lips. Going to Garrick's desk, Stanhope fumbled in the top drawer and drew out a red velvet drawstring purse. Opening it, he dumped the contents onto the desk. "Look. He purchased them the day after you arrived."

Her fingertips grew cold, and colored specks dotted her vision. She sat down hard in one of Garrick's uncomfortable chairs. "I don't believe you."

Holding up a sheaf of papers, he itemized them. "Train ticket to London. Ticket on the packet across the Channel. Train ticket to Paris. Throckmorton has incredible contacts to get these so quickly." He held up a key. "A house in Paris." He shook out a letter and extended it so she could see the heading. "A note authorizing a bank draft for the amount of one thousand pounds per annum."

On the first night she had returned, Garrick had mentioned a bribe. A house in Paris and a thousand pounds per annum. Now she realized he hadn't been offering that bribe; he had been telling her what she would have. A red mist passed before her eyes and she couldn't get enough air into her lungs.

"Throckmorton's paid more to get rid of Ellery's liaisons. You shouldn't sell yourself so cheaply." Stanhope's voice changed from slyly malicious to sharply uneasy. "You're not going to faint, are you? For God's sake, you didn't really think you could reel in Ellery, did you?"

"No. No. I never really thought I could reel in Ellery." The dream was truly dead.

"And you couldn't have imagined Garrick would have you."

She flinched.

"You can't *love* him." Stanhope observed her expression. "You *do*."

Her soul shriveled at his amusement, horror and pity.

"Look, girl, Throckmorton's an unconventional man in a lot of ways, but his family comes first. There's enough doubt in the *ton* about the Throckmorton heritage without bringing *you* into the line."

She wanted to vomit. She wanted to call Stanhope a traitor. She wanted to reveal what she knew, but not even for that satisfaction would she betray her country . . . or Garrick.

God save her from principles, but she wouldn't sink to Garrick's level.

Shaking off her queasiness, she lifted her chin. "I'm a governess—and you're just a secretary. You work for a living, too."

His pity evaporated under the heat of her derision. "You don't have to worry about sullying yourself with this irresponsible, churlish adventurer again. I'm shaking the Blythe Hall dust off my boots for good. I've always known it was possible to have too much of a good thing, and that it would all have to end someday." He strode to the door, then turned. "It's a lesson you should learn, too. Save you from embarrassing yourself again."

Light-headed with shock, she stared at the empty door, then leaned forward and put her head on her knees.

*   *   *

Celeste sat, her feet placed side by side, her knees pressed together, her hands folded in her lap. Her back did not rest on the back of the chair, but remained stiffly upright, and she found when she remained in this position, the discomfort of her body negated the discomfort of Throckmorton's chair. Her bottom hurt from the hard seat, yes, but worse was the ache within her loins, the stretched feeling in her thighs, the sensitivity of her breasts.

The bruising of her heart.

Her teeth did not chatter from the shock, but remained clenched tightly together. She heard the guests leaving, but couldn't decipher their words. She stared ahead with a direct gaze, but didn't really see.

She couldn't bear to. If she did; if she looked around, saw Blythe Hall, this home, this place from which she would be exiled in the most dire and humiliating of circumstances . . . if she really saw what she would miss, she'd be forced to pick up those antique Ming Chinese vases that decorated Garrick's office, and throw them until they were all shattered into tiny, expensive, worthless shards.

"Celeste!"

She flinched. It was him. Garrick. That Man.

She had waited here for hours, anticipating this confrontation, but now that it was upon her, her fingernails bit into her palms and her mouth dried. Well enough to cherish rage, but this was Garrick, the man she thought epitomized honor. The man who manipulated, organized, directed lives from the loftiness of his tower of superiority. And she loved him.

"Celeste, darling, I must talk to you."

Her neck, held stiffly erect for uncounted minutes, creaked as she turned it to see him stride in, clad in riding gear, disheveled, solemn, grim again although what he had to be grim about, she did not know. He had, after all, achieved his every goal—even her ultimate betrayal. Especially her ultimate betrayal.

Standing over her, he asked, "Did you . . . speak to Stanhope?"

"Yes."

"Good."

"Yes, that's one task out of the way," she said.

He paused in the act of sitting in a chair opposite her, and eyed her oddly. "Are you . . . well?"

"Perfectly."

He must have been willing to take her at her word, for he seated himself and leaned forward, elbows on his knees, hands clasped together in some dreadful parody of supplication. "This morning, we never settled anything."

She found it was possible to speak when her lips would scarcely move. "Everything is settled."

"No. No, it isn't, for I've been thinking about the night and what occurred and . . ." Color rose in his cheeks. It was obvious just which part of the night he was remembering; even more obvious when he leaned back and stretched out one leg to ease the pressure.

She stared at him, not helping, just staring. She hoped he was suffering. If she could have moved from this frozen, painful position, she would have made him hurt more.

"Ever since we parted, I've been thinking about my role in this. My responsibilities." As if he were a real human rather than a machine of smooth, cold, steel parts, a lock of dark hair fell over his forehead. "I admit I'm at fault here."

He was handsome. Why hadn't she seen it right from the start? How could she have been so blind to the satin of his lips, the width of his brow and the boxy strength of his jaw? She had compared him to Ellery and dismissed him. Foolish, foolish Celeste. As bright and charming as Ellery was, so Garrick was dark and dangerous, a man to whom it was wise to give wide berth. Instead she had imagined the light would overcome the night. Now she sat here in toe-curling agony and waited to be sent away.

"Events such as we experienced last night cannot be allowed to occur without amends."

A ticket to Paris. An annual income. "I'm sure you're experienced in this."

His smooth lips curved down into a severe line. "I do not seduce young women who are in my employ."

Bastard. "Apparently you do."

"No, never before."

"So my mistake was taking the position you offered." She winced. After a night such as they'd shared, one had to be more careful than normal about one's terms. "Of governess," she clarified. "Then you wouldn't be facing a challenge to your mores."

He cocked his head and studied her. In an excessively patient tone, he said, "You are perhaps worried about my habits—"

"No!"

"As you have every right to be."

"I don't."

"But I assure you, I have kept my indulgences far

away from my home. Therefore I believe—"

"You did not seduce me. I am not so craven as to allow myself to be debauched." Self-loathing filled her tone. "I remember very well that I asked for your expertise."

Bafflement and then indignation knit his brow. "Your tone puzzles me. Did you find me repugnant?"

"No."

"Inept? Uncaring of your gratification?"

"No. No."

Leaning back, he twitched the crease of his trousers and smiled that loathsome, complacent smile. "Of course not. I quite satisfied you. I didn't allow you to hide your joy—even though you tried."

Color flooded her face. She hated this scene. She hated herself. Most of all, she hated him, with his relaxed form and his smug mouth and his tranquil perfection. And she loved him because . . . because . . . right now she couldn't remember why she loved him. She only knew love mixed with the humiliation, the disappointment, the hatred to create a formidable brew of anguish and fury.

"I've been thinking about your future."

"You have it all settled," she muttered. *A ticket to Paris. An annual income.*

But he surprised her.

Kneeling at her feet, he captured her hand.

She twisted her fingers, trying to free them. She had achieved calm. His touch could destroy that. *Why was he kneeling? What did he think he was doing?*

He tightened his grip, not cruelly, but enough that if she fought, she would hurt herself, and in a pompous, know-it-all, typically Mr. Throckmorton tone, he said,

"I know you must wish that I would go to the devil. I'm not Ellery. I'm not dashing, or carefree, but as you rightly pointed out, I didn't seduce you."

"Get up."

He ignored her. He even looked puzzled as he continued, "You participated fully, even eagerly."

She didn't care if she hurt herself. She wrenched her fingers away, then cradled them against her bosom. "Don't remind me."

"But I must, for we have only one possible remedy."

She began to understand; this was even worse than being sent away. "We don't need a remedy. No one's sick."

"Celeste, I am older and wiser in the ways of the world. You must trust me to know our best course."

Oh, he sounded good. Sincere, intense, dedicated to her best interests. Another woman might have been duped, but just this morning he'd held Celeste in his arms and suggested she pass Stanhope a message. She'd seen Garrick's hesitation; he had known the unseemliness of putting the woman he had just debauched into danger.

He'd done it anyway, and now he was trying to pretend it hadn't happened.

She reminded him. "Did Stanhope pass the message?"

Garrick shook his head like a wolf who'd been struck with a cudgel. "What?"

"Did Stanhope pass the message to his contact, thus betraying his country and making your use of my unwitting assistance worthwhile?" She experienced the satisfaction of seeing Garrick's tanned skin pale.

"How did you know that?"

"Let me see." She enumerated the reasons on her fingers. "First, I hear a Russian lady, who badly wants to see *you*, talking about how an Englishman is betrayed, arrested and never heard from again. Why? I wonder. Why should she wish to see you? Then Stanhope lies to you about the message. You're clearly suspicious about him and about me, but I must have passed the test because suddenly Stanhope is no longer acting as your translator, I am. But I am to pass any messages I interpret onto him if he desires, which he does, even enough to be courteous to me when he asks. The passing of messages becomes so important that, this morning, you manage to remember to give me a message even before the sweat had dried from our bodies." She wanted to smile scornfully, but she found her lips would not work in that manner. "Let me reassure you again. The message is passed. Your duty to England is done, or rather, that particular duty is done."

He had risen to his feet. "What do you mean?"

"I know who you are, Garrick Throckmorton." She stared up at that unyielding, staunch, mountain of a man. "You direct all of England's spy operations."

He hesitated, then confessed, "Not all. My specialty is India and beyond."

"The Great Game," she said, giving name to that struggle between England and Russia for Central Asia.

He paced away, then turned to survey her.

She knew what he saw; a petite, attractive blonde who scarcely appeared clever enough to dress herself. Most men saw her that way. Such an appearance of helplessness was both a blessing and a curse, for while being underestimated worked in her favor, at the same time it could be a source of incredible irritation.

Right now, she was irritated.

"You discerned all that on your own?" he asked.

She managed both the smile and the scorn. "All with my own puny, feeble, feminine brain."

"I have never thought you feeble, and you've just proved you're almost too intelligent." Leaning over her, he put his hands on the arms of her chair and thrust his harsh face into hers. "It's imperative that you tell me the truth. How did you know this?"

"I worked for the Russian ambassador. The Russians eat, breathe and live espionage. How could I not recognize the ambassador's counterpart in England?" She knew so much about how the Great Game worked, how the spies thought, she even knew that Garrick must now suspect her. "Do I know too much?" She mocked him. "Will you have to send me to prison—or worse?"

"Have you told anyone?" He took her shoulders. "Did you tell Stanhope?"

"As much as I would like to teach you the pitfalls of exploiting your lover's talents, I'll have to admit I don't consider you or I or our affair so important when weighed against the good of my country." She enunciated clearly, "Will you let go of my shoulders now?"

He did, and she hated that she missed his touch. He stood, fingers stroking his chin, watching her, weighing what she knew against her antagonism, trying to decide how best to turn the situation to his advantage. She could almost see the wheels turning in his head, and thought how pleased she should be that the end of the scene was in sight.

In an absent tone of voice, he said, "The duration of a director of operations is brief, for sooner or later his identity is always discovered. Obviously my identity is no longer a secret. Considering Stanhope's treachery, my family is in danger. I've handed the job onto the next chap. The London Office will put someone else in charge of Central Asia. I won't know who."

She might have cynically wondered if he told her because he still harbored fears about her loyalty, but she chose to take the report at face value. "For the children's sake, I am relieved."

"But I'm at a loss. If you knew about my business and understood your part of it, and still came to me last night . . . why are you so unhappy with me? I want to marry you!"

He seemed to think she would jump at the chance . . . to wake in his arms every morning, to talk with him in the day, to cradle his children in her arms.

Furious with her own weakness, she shook off temptation. "No!" She stood, a laborious act as she forced her limbs to move at last. "I'm not refusing you because of your occupation. I'm refusing you because you, Garrick Throckmorton, are a liar."

"If I have to be," he admitted readily, "but I can't think when I've lied to you."

Once again, she found herself light-headed, and she clutched the chair for support. "A liar of the most loathsome sort. I understand why you lied to me about Stanhope. You plotted to advance our country and defeat our enemies. But you plotted against me, too."

Becoming cool, distant, wary, he said, *"Plotted* seems an immoderate term."

"Tickets to Paris. An annual income." She observed him closely.

For a brief moment, his eyebrows shot up. Then he smoothed all trace of emotion from his face. He became a machine who thought.

She didn't want to marry a machine. "I'm the gardener's daughter," she said. "I'm the governess. When I stepped on your plan for Ellery's marriage, you could have sent me back to the Governess School. You could have refused me the run of the house. You could have done anything rather than attempt my seduction."

In an excessively reasonable tone, he said, "I would have lost my gardener. Ellery would have been distracted."

"And *I* would have been heartwhole and virtuous. Ah, but I forget—I'm not as important as the state of the Throckmortons' gardens or the well-being of their younger son." Her feet and hands tingled as blood rushed in and brought them to painful life. She feared seeing Garrick and talking to him was having the same effect on her feelings.

"It was not well done. I admit that. But it wasn't a lie, not technically. I'm offering reparation."

"No." She looked down at her hands as she flexed them. "You're offering marriage."

"What other reparation would you have me offer?"

"Hm." Going to his desk, she opened the drawer and pulled out the red velvet drawstring purse. She looked at it, considered the contents, knew she would need the tickets and the bankdraft to return to Paris. But when she had a job, she would pay him back, every cent. "It would be met if you . . . jumped off the highest tottering tower of your gothic trifle and smashed yourself onto the stones of the courtyard below. Perhaps you would be lucky. Perhaps you would land on your heart, and rise uninjured."

"But you have to marry me. I've never had such pleasure with a woman." As soon as the words were out of his mouth, Throckmorton wanted to kick himself.

Celeste stood very still beside the chair, gripping the ladder back with white knuckles. She held her shoulders too wide. Her complexion flushed and paled with disproportionate intensity. Her erotic, joyful mouth smiled not at all, and she mocked him with word and tone. "That would, of course, be the defining reason to give up any hope of happiness."

He seldom said the wrong thing, but this time his blunder stunk like carrion. Rattled, he compounded his mistake. "You would be happy. I would make sure of it."

"This morning has almost killed me." She turned toward the door, moving as stiffly as his mother when the wind was in the north. "I don't think I can bear much more of your kind of happiness."

In an unusual turn of events, Garrick Stanley Breckinridge Throckmorton didn't know what to do. Forcibly sit Celeste down and enumerate the advantages of
marriage to him? Let her go and assume she would get
over this little upset—which in truth he didn't quite
comprehend—and return to him on her own accord?
Take her in his arms and kiss her until she softened and
clung? Somehow none of the choices seemed the right
way to handle her. There had to be a better way, one
he'd overlooked.

An idea flashed into his mind. "You have to marry
me," he tossed out. "We've been compromised!"

She favored him with a withering glance, the kind
that made him feel insignificant and inept.

He didn't like that, and took a stride toward her—
when with a rustle of skirts and a pounding of boots,
Hyacinth and Ellery rushed into the office.

"She's the one." White-faced, Hyacinth pointed a
shaking finger at Celeste and said to Throckmorton,
"She's the reason Ellery's been neglecting me." Turning
on Celeste, she yelled, "You're the one Ellery fancies
himself in love with!"

What an unfortunate time Ellery chose to be honest
with his betrothed! Now not only did Throckmorton
have to manage the problem with his own courtship, he
had to handle Ellery's, too. He glanced at Ellery, who
didn't take his gaze off Hyacinth.

She did seem rather more animated than previously,
and she was in the same room with Ellery and not hanging on his every word. That had to be good. Lacking
even a jot of finesse, Throckmorton said, "Lady Hyacinth, I'm sure you and Ellery would prefer privacy."
He wanted to be alone with Celeste to settle the matter

of their marriage. If he just said the right thing, she would surely see reason—if he could just calculate the right thing to say.

Hyacinth ignored and avoided him, moving toward Celeste instead. "I admired you. I trusted you, and you lied to me."

"I did not!" Celeste answered.

Hyacinth pointed at Celeste, a sweeping gesture quite unlike her previous, timid motions. "You did so, in the conservatory! I poured out my heart to you about Ellery, and you never said *you* were the reason he was neglecting me."

Celeste stalked over to Hyacinth, a miniature virago facing an Amazon. "That isn't a lie. I just didn't have the heart to tell you."

Throckmorton couldn't resist. "Exactly," he said.

Celeste whirled to face him. "You keep out of this!"

Throckmorton subsided, satisfied he had made his point.

"I'm sorry," Celeste said to Hyacinth. "I should have never tried to steal your fiancé, but if it makes you feel any better, I've been thoroughly punished."

"No punishment could be payment enough for such a betrayal," Hyacinth shouted.

Oh, no. Throckmorton didn't want the argument to proceed in that vein, so in his most soothing tone, he said, "You needn't ever have worried, Lady Hyacinth. I took measures to keep Celeste otherwise occupied."

"Yes, Lady Hyacinth. Calm yourself. Mr. Throckmorton took measures to keep Ellery and me apart." Celeste batted her eyelashes at Ellery in mock adoration. Her voice rose. "But I don't want Ellery." She turned on Throckmorton in a rage. "I wouldn't have either one of

these treacherous, lying, cheating Throckmorton swine
if they were roasted with an apple stuck in their mouths
and served on a silver platter."

"Neither would I!" Hyacinth declared.

"Now, wait—" Throckmorton began.

The women paid him no heed. In a rustle of starch
and cotton, they rushed to the door, each racing to reach
the exit first. Hyacinth won by virtue of her height, but
she stumbled when Celeste hurried close on her heels
and stepped on her skirt.

Unsure exactly what had happened, Throckmorton
stared at the empty doorway.

"That went well," Ellery drawled. He leaned against
the liquor cabinet, legs crossed, arms crossed, examining Throckmorton as if he were a writhing asp and
Ellery a boy with a rock.

Throckmorton didn't enjoy having his hell-bent
younger brother view him in such a manner.

Ellery added, "When you're done with the spy game,
perhaps you could go into diplomacy."

Throckmorton's composure collapsed. Did *everyone*
know? "What do you mean, spy game?"

Seemingly unimpressed by Throckmorton's ire,
Ellery asked, "What do *you* mean, you took measures to
keep Celeste from me?"

"Answer me," Throckmorton snapped. He couldn't
be distracted. After all, what was more important here?

"Because I trusted you. You're my brother. You said
you'd help me with Celeste, and now I find out you took
her for your own."

Throckmorton could be distracted after all. "Where
did you hear that?"

"Every one of the departing guests were gossiping

about how Lord and Lady Featherstonebaugh saw you with Celeste this morning. She was rumpled and still in her ballgown. You were putting on your boots." Ellery pushed away from the cabinet. Looking as murderous as ever the easygoing Ellery had looked, he stalked toward Throckmorton.

Hands up, Throckmorton backed toward his desk. Ellery had reason to be upset, but Throckmorton didn't want a fight.

"My own honorable, upright, morally superior brother seduced the gardener's daughter."

"I've offered to marry her!"

"So that makes it all right?" Ellery roared. "You jack-ass! That beautiful, laughing girl is unhappy, and it's your fault!"

"Lady Hyacinth's unhappy, too, and it's your fault." He was trying to shift the blame, Throckmorton realized. It was one of Ellery's favorite tricks. Now Throckmorton utilized it in the desperate hope Ellery wouldn't realize the full depths of his iniquity.

As a ruse, it failed miserably. "You let me handle Hyacinth. It's Celeste we're talking about now."

"You think you can handle Lady Hyacinth?"

"As well as you handled Celeste."

"I thought Lady Hyacinth was going to be angry about Kiki."

"She was." Ellery made a right turn to the liquor cabinet and poured himself a glass full of whisky.

Throckmorton wanted to curse. Ellery was drinking again. Still. "You don't need that. If Lady Hyacinth won't marry you, you've got nothing to drink about."

"But now I want to marry Hyacinth. I always wanted to, she just scared me with her expectations and her worship. I knew I'd fail her sooner or later." Ellery took a healthy swallow of the amber liquid, then chuckled as if amused at himself. "Guess it came sooner. So"—he straightened his shoulders—"if I can't marry Hyacinth, I want to be in espionage, just like the rest of my family."

With a jolt, Throckmorton remembered. Ellery *knew*. Throckmorton played for time. "In . . . espionage?"

"Yes, in espionage," Ellery mocked. "Men riding in and out at all hours of the night, guards around Blythe Hall, women babbling in foreign languages . . . no one pays any attention to me, but that doesn't mean I don't pay attention to you."

Throckmorton had always thought he was the epitome of wiliness. Now in the space of an hour, two different people had proved him wrong. "Does everyone in England know?"

"You mean did I tell?" Ellery took another long drink, then lifted the glass in toast. "Not even when I was foxed, dear brother."

"I mean—have I been so obvious?"

"No. Most people see what they want to see, and a good part of the goings-on can be explained by the business. But I live here, Garrick, how did you expect to keep me in the dark?"

Throckmorton didn't have an answer.

"All my life, I've been waiting for someone to ask me to join in. First Father and Mother played the game, and then you. No one ever invited me in, even when I hinted. All you could say was, 'Come into the business, Ellery.' Well, I'm not good at business, but I'd be good at spying."

"You don't know what you're talking about."

"Garrick, I speak four languages and could easily learn more. More important, I'm a worthless libertine. Do you know how much people say in front of me?"

"I hadn't thought—"

"Just because they think I'm too stupid to comprehend. Why, in the past year, I'd wager I've heard Stanhope pass half-a-dozen messages to that slick valet of his."

Throckmorton's jaw dropped. "You . . . heard Stanhope . . . pass messages—"

"You're stammering, Garrick. You did know about Stanhope, didn't you?"

"Found out this week!"

Ellery poured another glass full and offered it to Throckmorton. "Drink?"

Throckmorton took it.

"I thought you must be using Stanhope as a double-agent, so I kept my mouth shut."

Throckmorton tried to remember Stanhope's valet. A quiet, efficient man of medium height and build, with medium brown hair and medium blue eyes. He looked no different than half of England, and right beneath Throckmorton's nose he had been passing messages to the Russians and paying Stanhope for the information.

Ellery grabbed Throckmorton's arm and shook it, sloshing whisky all over the oriental rug. "If I'd been in the know, this would have been nipped in the bud."

"You should have come to me."

"No. You should have come to me." Ellery pointed to his chest. "Take me in, Garrick. I want to work for you."

Throckmorton looked at Ellery. Blond, handsome, debonair. Throckmorton couldn't bear to think of him at risk, shot or blown to bits. And if the Russians took him and held him for ransom . . . Throckmorton didn't want his patriotism put to that kind of a test. "I can't," he said. "As of today, I'm out."

"Then put me in touch with someone who's in charge," Ellery demanded.

Throckmorton shook his head. "I want you safe. Mother wants you safe. Don't ask this of me."

Ellery jerked back as if Throckmorton had hit him. He smiled, a bitter parody of his usually cheerful insouciance. Picking up the bottle, he hugged it to his chest. "Then I'll go to hell in my own fashion."

The family was going to hell.

Lady Philberta's cane crunched in the gravel as she hobbled along the garden path. Ellery was drinking. Hyacinth was livid. Throckmorton had seduced the girl he was supposed to be ousting. And Celeste . . . well, Lady Philberta needed to talk to Celeste, to find out why Throckmorton was in his office, alternating shouting about Stanhope's valet, who had managed to slip away, and staring into space.

Lady Philberta had heard something about Celeste not accepting his offer of matrimony. Lady Philberta grinned. She'd also heard something about stodgy Garrick and radiant Celeste in the conservatory in full view of Lord and Lady Featherstonebaugh. On hearing the report, Lady Philberta wanted to laugh and dance. Instead she wandered the garden, following the leads given by the under-gardeners. She found Celeste and Milford in the walled kitchen garden, both down on their hands and knees, weeding the herbs.

Poor Celeste. She glanced at Lady Philberta, and when she realized who had limped into her domain, she put her head down and weeded faster.

Lady Philberta didn't blame her. "What a healthful activity!" Lady Philberta said. "Back when I could, before I suffered with this lumbago, I used to love to pull weeds in the kitchen garden. Do you remember, Milford?"

Milford got to his feet. "Yes, ma'am, I remember."

"The scents of the herbs clear the mind and the exercise strengthens the body. Don't you find it so, Celeste?"

Milford nudged his daughter with his foot. Celeste slowly stood and wiped the dirt from her hands. "Yes, ma'am."

"Milford, may I borrow your daughter for a time?"

Milford considered Lady Philberta. They had known each other a very long time, and she clearly read his warning. *Don't hurt my daughter more.*

She nodded at him, an unspoken promise that she would care for Celeste.

"Go on, then, girl. I'll finish up here." He gave Celeste a gentle push in the back.

Celeste stumbled forward resentfully, then recovered to walk at Lady Philberta's side.

It was a lovely late afternoon, the kind only Suffolk could produce in the summer after a rain. The gravel paths had dried in the sunshine, the trees wafted in the lightest of breezes, and the flowers bloomed in exuberant celebration.

"That rain made my lumbago act up, so we'll walk toward the house," Lady Philberta announced.

In sullen compliance, Celeste said, "As you wish, my lady."

Lady Philberta wanted to laugh. Young people were so dramatic, so sure each twinge of love would result in disaster. Wait until the girl had been married for a time. Then she'd find out the true depths and heights of being married to that most difficult of creatures—man.

They turned onto the broad straight path, lined with oaks, that led to Blythe Hall. "I simply want to tell you how grateful I am, Celeste. You care for my grand-daughters. You weed my garden . . ." She waited until Celeste had cautiously turned to look at her before she added, "You are so industrious. You even sleep with my son."

Celeste blushed furiously. "My lady . . ." she faltered.

"I can't tell you how happy I will be to have you join the family." Lady Philberta folded Celeste into her arms. "We need some fresh ideas to liven us up."

Celeste didn't jerk herself away—she'd been taught respect for the aristocratic and the elderly, and Lady Philberta wryly knew herself to be both—but she held herself perfectly rigid. "My lady, I am not going to marry your son." She thought for a moment. "Either of them."

"Well, not Ellery. He's taken. But Garrick, I think."

Shock or dismay confined Celeste's answer to a brief, "No."

Lady Philberta gestured toward the house, visible through the overhanging branches. "It's a beautiful home, and I'll hate to leave it, but of course you'll wish to run it as you see fit."

"I'm not going to marry your son." Celeste was thinking again, Lady Philberta could see, uncertain of Lady Philberta's plan, suspicious of her motives. "Al-though I appreciate the generosity of your welcome," Celeste added at last.

There were damn few times when Lady Philberta relished being aristocratic and being elderly, but this was one of them, for she was able to say with devastating bluntness, "Why won't you marry my son? Garrick, I mean, not Ellery."

"Thank you. You're very kind." Celeste was gaining confidence in Lady Philberta's intentions. "With all due respect, my lady, Garrick is a manipulative liar."

"A liar? Really?" That surprised Lady Philberta. "What did he lie about?"

"It was a lie of action. He made me think he liked and respected me when all the while he was maneuvering to send me back to Paris."

Lady Philberta wisely kept quiet.

Celeste tossed her head. "I'm going."

Surprised, Lady Philberta exclaimed, "Back to Paris? Now? After last night?"

Celeste looked away and swallowed. "What happened last night is of no concern to anyone."

"It seems to be of great concern to Garrick. He's been sulking in his office all day. And it's of great concern to me if it should result in a babe."

Celeste tripped and almost fell.

Lady Philberta staggered beside her, regained her balance, asked, "Goodness, dear, are you all right?"

"Yes, of course." Celeste took a deep breath. "I just hadn't thought—"

"Well, you must, and there's no telling me it was only one time. Everyone gets their start with one time."

"It was more than . . ." Celeste blushed again. "I assure you, if there should be issue, I will . . ."

"Will what?"

"I don't know, but I'll take care of the babe somehow."

"Marry Garrick," Lady Philberta advised. "I already have one chance granddaughter to manage a future for, and while I love her dearly, illegitimacy is a disadvantage for any child."

They had reached the house. Celeste stood staring at the diamond-paned window of Garrick's office, her fists clenching and unclenching. Lady Philberta leaned on her cane and watched, seeing the angry color rise and retreat in the girl's face, observing the distress and the rage implicit in every line.

With a grunt of fury, Celeste dropped to the ground. She grabbed a handful of gravel, and lobbed the largest rock at Garrick's window. The glass shattered.

Lady Philberta gasped.

Celeste hurled another, and another, some thumping against the brick, some taking a pane of glass. She stopped to smear tears off her cheeks, and threw one more. Then, as if she realized what she was doing, she dropped the remaining rocks and looked curiously at her own hands.

Impressed with all that raw emotion, Lady Philberta handed Celeste a handkerchief.

Celeste accepted it with the dignity of the queen, and wiped her eyes and blew her nose.

"If it makes you feel better," Lady Philberta said, "Garrick is probably now peering out of one of the windows, pistol at ready, expecting to see an ambush awaiting him. Shall we wave instead?"

"The cab drivers use a gesture in Paris. A rather vulgar gesture." Celeste turned her hot gaze on Lady

Philberta. "It is more suited to this situation than a mere wave."

Lady Philberta laughed. Damn, she liked this girl! She took Celeste's arm and urged her on. "If Garrick is autocratic in this instance, it is quite your fault. Give a man an inch, and he thinks he's a ruler."

Celeste smiled, but without grace.

"What would you do in Paris?" Lady Philberta asked.

"I haven't decided exactly how, but I will be independent. I will never rely on a man for my happiness again."

"I've found it's never wise to rely on anyone else for your own happiness."

"You're right, I'm sure. I can be a governess, of course, or I can set myself up as a teacher of languages. Or I can become a courtesan."

Lady Philberta thought of the conversation she would have with Garrick, and mentally rubbed her hands. "You certainly have the looks and the charm, but you said you would never rely on a man again."

"It would be nothing but a business exchange." Celeste glanced sideways at Lady Philberta. "In Paris, I've seen the game played."

Lady Philberta steered them toward the front door and the conversation where she wanted it to go. "But I suspect you would not enjoy the actual experience."

Celeste lifted one lovely shoulder. "How bad could it be? One man who will set me up in an apartment, buy me lovely clothes, show me off and pad my bankroll, but who would have no control over me. Surely if I chose him, I wouldn't mind so much the—" Celeste took a quick breath as she considered the actual act. "Or perhaps I would. *How* can I be so fussy about so basic a function?"

"Some women are. Most, I think, unless driven by desperation."

"I suppose." Celeste straightened her spine. "Very well. Instead, I will prepare young wives and new ambassadors to enter the world of diplomacy. You have to know who the players are, who you can trust, who will sell you for a brass coin . . . Diplomacy is not as easy as you might think, my lady."

Lady Philberta was ecstatic that Celeste had captured Garrick's heart. She was pleased that, even though the girl was common, she was eminently presentable. But to know she comprehended the complex maneuvering of politics . . . ah, that made her a valuable asset to the family business, both legitimate and clandestine.

But Garrick had thoroughly botched his love affair. He needed help, and Lady Philberta could provide it. "You may have noticed that Garrick is the master of manipulation."

"The worst kind of man." They had reached the front door. The footman opened it.

Lady Philberta waved him away and spoke to Celeste. "Garrick thinks things through, he always says the right things, he would never perform an action without knowing all possible consequences. But with you he acted impulsively, behaved in the worst manner, and said everything all wrong."

"He was insufferable."

"I know what I think that means. What do you think it means?"

Celeste turned her large-eyed, tragic gaze on Lady Philberta.

"Think about it."

"I'm going to Paris," Celeste whispered.

Lady Philberta nodded. "While you're there, think about it."

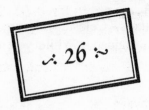

26

Milford stepped into his dark cottage, weary from the effort of helping Celeste pack and irate that she had to leave. As he trudged the stairs, he supposed he would leave, too. He wouldn't work for a man he didn't respect, and Garrick Throckmorton had lost Milford's respect with a single act.

In the loft, Milford shrugged out of his shirt, and tossed it on the laundry basket. Mr. Throckmorton had every right to take measure to assure Celeste did not marry Ellery. He had no right to seduce Milford's daughter, and so Milford would inform him.

He didn't light a candle; he'd lived here for so many years he knew exactly how many paces to the water basin, how many paces to the bed. He splashed water from the pitcher and washed his face and hands, then discarded his trousers. He hung them neatly over the chair, as he did every night, then walked to the bed and lifted the covers.

The bed was wide, meant for two people, and had sheltered only him since Aimee died. It was on nights like this that he missed her most, when he would have held his wife in his arms and listened to her rant about the harm done to their daughter and how someone would pay. Even *he* wanted to rant, and he had never ranted in his life.

As he slid between the sheets, he became aware of two things. The mattress sagged where it shouldn't. The familiar scent of woman was nearby.

He didn't know what to think.

Then he did. "What are ye doing here?" He didn't ask rough or mean, but he wanted an answer, so he asked firm.

Esther's voice came out of the darkness. "Ye don't take a hint well, so I thought I'd come right here and make matters clear." Her hand touched his shoulder. "I want to sleep with ye."

One thing at a time. "What hint?"

The bed shook as she chuckled. "I don't decorate everyone's tray with fancy-cut cheese and bread baked to look like a flower."

"Oh."

"And I don't flirt with other men, either."

"Have ye been flirting with me?"

Her hand stroked down his arm, and his skin rose in gooseflesh. "Everyone knows it but ye."

He caught her wrist and held it in the air. "All right. I believe ye."

"Did I read ye wrong? Are ye not interested in me?" She sounded shocked and embarrassed.

He was sorry for that, but matters needed to be settled. "I might be," he acknowledged. "But I have to know yer intentions."

"I intend that we should enjoy each other."

He didn't like that, and he made his opinion clear with his silence.

"I'm a widow. I miss the weight of a man in my bed. I'm old enough not to have to worry about havin' a babe, and I want some comfort on the cold nights."

" 'Tisn't right." He placed her hand back on her side of the bed. "Not without marriage."

"Marriage!" She sat up.

The covers fell away, and his eyes had adjusted to the darkness enough that he could see a lush, bare outline.

He closed his eyes. He had a stand to make, and he doubted his ability to resist such blatant temptation. " 'Tis the vows taken between a man and woman when they wish to couple."

"I've *been* married!" From her tone, it had obviously not been a success.

"If you wish to couple with me, you will be again."

She sat silent and still for so long, he opened his eyes. Her face was turned toward him. She was staring at him as if she couldn't believe her ears. "So ye want me."

"Aye."

"But ye'll not take me without the vows."

"Nay."

"Ye're a damned odd man."

He ran his fingertips, just his fingertips, down the curve of her spine.

She gasped and arched like a cat.

He took his hand away. "So I've been told."

Her breath sighed heavily in the darkness. "If I agree . . . do we have to wait until the churching?"

"To couple, ye mean." He pretended to think about it,

although under the covers a certain cockstand whispered the answer. "We could start the marriage sooner, as long as the wedding will be later."

He saw the flash of her smile bright in the night, and he loved her for it.

"Well, then." Slowly, she settled against him, and stretched her leg over his thighs. "We'd best get started."

"Aye." One hand settled on her buttock, the other caught her around the neck. "As long as we both know it's a promise." Before she could retort, he brought her lips down to his. A kiss was the only way to handle a woman like this.

Ellery held the pitiful excuse for a bottle of wine—pitiful because it hadn't gotten him anything more than slightly tipsy—close against his chest and scrupulously counted the doors in the North Tower. One, two, three doors from the right. Stopping, he swayed and counted again, wishing more candles lit the corridor so he could be absolutely sure . . . but it was the wee hours of the morning, and the best he could do was strain his eyes and count just one more time. Yes, three doors from the right in the . . . he stared blearily around . . . in the North Tower. That was where Celeste had said her bedchamber was. That was where he wanted to be.

Sweet little Celeste. Good little gardener's daughter. Someone needed to talk to her, to tell her she should marry dear brother Garrick and make his life miserable. Somebody needed to make Throckmorton miserable. God knew Ellery wished he could; that might relieve this sense of anguish that roiled in his belly. This sense that he'd blundered. That he'd ruined his life. That he'd driven Hyacinth away forever.

So he'd go to Celeste and just by being there, ruin her even more than she was already ruined . . . and Ellery would have failed to do the right thing one more time.

A bitter smile curved his lips. But so what? He was famous for failure.

Turning the knob, he opened the door as quietly as he could, stepped into the dim room, shut the door with barely a click. He was good at this, sneaking into women's bedchambers. Didn't even need to be sober. Could do it with his eyes closed.

So he closed them for a moment, and when he opened them he could see the outlines of the room. A sitting room. He frowned. A sitting room with a bedchamber beyond. Damned marvelous quarters for the gardener's daughter.

He wove his way across the plush carpet and stepped inside the bedchamber. It was huge, filled with a fireplace where embers burned low, a curvy dressing table, comfortable chairs, and a bed. A big bed, set on a dais, draped with velvet curtains closed against the drafts and with a cluster of fat candles burning on the far side.

Goal in sight, Ellery set the bottle on the dressing table—in situations that required possible immediate action, it was best to have both hands free—and tiptoed toward the high bed. Parting the curtains, he leaned forward toward the unmistakably female form reclining in the middle of the mattress . . . and a hand shot out, grabbing his shirt front and pulled him off-balance. He flailed his arms before landing face first in an ignominious disorder among the covers.

"What are you doing in my room?"

He blinked and spit out a mouthful of wool blanket.

It *sounded* like Hyacinth.

Cautiously he lifted his head.

Hyacinth's cold, furious features leaned over him like an avenging Juno.

It *was* Hyacinth.

"Vixen," he muttered, meaning Celeste, who had dared direct him to the wrong bedchamber.

Hyacinth misunderstood. "You call me a vixen? After what you've done?"

"Haven't done anything yet." Wasn't likely to, from the expression on Hyacinth's face. Although, by God, he'd like to. She wore a fine, white, ruffled linen gown, and through it he could see the glow of her golden flesh.

"You courted me. You made me love you. You foisted a child on me without telling me."

He groaned. "I told Throckmorton the kid was going to dish the deal."

"Don't blame that dear, sweet little Kiki!"

He hadn't known Hyacinth's gentle violet eyes could flash like that.

"It's not her fault her father is a philanderer and a libertine."

"Unfeeling."

"Yes, you are!"

"I meant you." But he mumbled into the covers for even in his inebriated state, he knew full well Hyacinth was right. "Didn't mean to make her." Hyacinth's breasts thrust forward, creating shadows that teased his imagination, and he didn't even have to imagine the color of her nipples, for the soft circles were clearly defined in delicate, glorious pink.

Hyacinth crossed her arms. "She is still your responsibility."

One nipple disappeared from his sight. He mourned it even as he answered, "I am a dog."

"Yes, and not anything noble like a great Dane or an English pointer either."

With other women, confessing guilt had always been good for a little sympathy. Hyacinth didn't know the script.

She continued, "You're more of sissified poodle or some little pug that piddles on the rug and runs away."

"Hey!" She was brutal.

"When were you going to tell me about your daughter? On our wedding night?"

"I didn't plan to tell you. I just sort of hoped you would . . . find out. And pretend not to notice. If you don't like her, we could probably leave her here with—" Immediately, by her indrawn breath, he knew he'd made a mistake.

"You would leave your own child with relatives?" Clearly, Hyacinth found him the worst sort of father. "Don't you love the girl?"

"Kiki?" He, Ellery Throckmorton, had never found himself in a beautiful woman's bedchamber at this hour of the morning discussing anything but pleasure, and if this was what marriage was like, he didn't need any part of it.

He peeked at Hyacinth. Except the view was magnificent and he did love the kid. When he thought of her. When she wasn't making him feel old and derelict. When he thought to play tag with her or show her how to make mudpies. "Yes, I love her," he said irritably. "I just don't know what to do with her."

"You need guidance," Hyacinth decided. "What did you like your father to do with you?"

He thought, which wasn't that easy, distracted as he was by her bosom and that wine. And the whisky earlier.

"I would have liked him to take me traveling as he did Garrick, but he died before he got around to it."

"Well, then. You should take Kiki traveling. It seems to me, with her gift of French and her charm which is so like yours, she would be an asset anywhere."

"Damme, but you're an innocent." Using his elbows, he crawled a little further onto the bed. No reason to dangle with his legs half-off when he could be comfortable. "No one's going to welcome my illegitimate daughter."

"I would."

She would. He believed her. Her black hair was in tousled disarray, her neck rose like pale velvet above her gown. He could love this woman with her sharp tongue, her knowledge of right and wrong . . . her father's wealth. He could really love her, and right now he couldn't remember why he had ever drawn back. Moving with careless guile, he slid his hand through the blankets and ran it up her thigh. "You're not only an innocent, but you're beautiful and kind, too."

Just when he would have reached the good parts, the female parts, she clamped her hand over his wrist. "How would you know? After I arrived here to celebrate our betrothal, you abandoned me in front of all the ton to chase after poor dear Celeste—when you knew better!"

He could have broken her hold. Of course he could, but a wrestling match would be tawdry. So instead he sulked. "Didn't do anything she didn't want."

"Of course she wanted you. All the women want you, but *you* gave *your* pledge to *me*. Is your word worth nothing?"

Hyacinth wasn't buying the *it's not my fault* excuse. He scrambled for another. "Frustrated."

"Frustrated? Why?"

"Couldn't have you."

"You didn't even try."

He lowered his head back into the blanket and tried to think. This sounded promising. It sounded as if she wanted him to try to get in her chemise. But he sensed a trick. If he could just figure it out . . .

"I'll try now," he suggested, and hoped the mattress would cushion any blow she aimed at his head.

Nothing happened, except that she released his arm. Tentatively, he raised his head.

She leaned against the snowy white pillows like Cleopatra waiting to be serviced. Lifting a brow, she indicated her full, luscious mouth. "I'm waiting."

This was too good to be true.

When he still didn't move, she eased the covers off her waist, down her thighs. Kicking her feet completely free, she smoothed her nightgown over her long, tall, generous curves. "Don't you want me?"

"I do. Oh, I do." He had to control his eagerness. Women loved a seducer, and Hyacinth deserved the best, because she was going to take pity on him and marry him. Slithering up the bed, he leaned over her as she reclined on the pillows. With a great deal more confidence than he'd had during the rest of this encounter, he said, "You're going to marry me."

She didn't answer.

"Aren't you?"

Taking his hand in hers, she looked at it, looked down at herself, then placed his hand right on the soft mound of her breast.

In all his years of tempting and cajoling and outright begging, he had never seen, felt, experienced anything so exciting. This girl, this virgin, had taken the lead and put his palm right on her . . . and her nipple was soft and supple, begging to be aroused. Without further thought, he groaned, "Hyacinth," and gently took her lips.

She didn't know how to kiss worth a damn.

So he taught her. With his fingertips and his lips, he showed her the pleasure points on her face, her neck, her ear lobes. He caressed her breasts until the nipple poked up, and she shivered and made soft moaning sounds. He was a virtuoso playing the sweet instrument of her body.

He unbuttoned the top buttons of her nightgown. He was a captain sailing her into the harbor of his arms. He bared the curve of her breast and leaned down to suckle.

And found himself flying through the air and onto the floor. He landed with a bone-jarring thud that knocked the air out of his lungs and left him gasping—in more ways than one. When he finally got his breath back, he croaked, "Wha . . . ?"

She looked over the mattress. "That was very nice. And that was enough."

Enough? She could spend ten minutes in his arms and decide that was enough? He must be losing his touch. Except . . . her nightgown still gaped over her chest, and every inch of flesh he could see was flushed with excitement. Her cheeks were cherry red, her lips were full, and she hid regret behind determination on her stubborn, beautiful face.

He tilted his head and tried to see her from a different angle. How had she suddenly become beautiful?

Because he loved her.

The revelation hit him so hard, the air was knocked from his lungs *again*.

At his gasp, Hyacinth leaned further off the high bed and tried to touch his chest. "Ellery, are you all right?"

He caught her fingers and, lifting his head, he kissed them. "Scrumptious."

"Did I hurt you when I kicked you off the bed?"

"Quite the opposite."

Her eyes narrowed on him. "I think the fall may have addled your brain."

"Permanently."

She freed her fingers and disappeared back onto the bed.

He shut his eyes and tried to adjust to the idea of being in love. With his wife.

"Ellery."

He opened his eyes. Hyacinth leaned over the bed, her hair hanging about in long, magnificent waves. "Yes, my darling?"

"Do you care about Celeste?"

He sensed the need to tread carefully. "She's very lovely and she's very sweet, but I don't care about her. Not like I care about you."

"That's good, because Throckmorton is in love with Celeste."

Was Hyacinth dotty? He sighed deeply. No, of course she wasn't. She had seen what he should have seen if he hadn't been so intent on running from his fate. He smiled up at Hyacinth. His very pleasant, palatable, toothsome fate. "Throckmorton is in love with Celeste. Yes, that serves him bloody right."

"Don't swear," Hyacinth admonished. Again, she disappeared onto the bed.

Yet he still found the evening unsatisfactory. Content to remain at her bedside like the dog she said he was, he lay back down. "Are you going to marry me?"

No answer.

"I need you, Hyacinth. I need your beauty, your wisdom, your kindness. I need you or I can never be the man I should be."

She appeared above him, sitting high on the mattress, one leg folded beneath her. Hiking up her nightgown, she extended a long, muscled calf. Pointing her toe, she pressed it to his chest like an accusing finger. "I'm not interested in a man who can't be the man he should be without me. I want the man I thought you were. The person I know you are. Strong, clever, determined, honorable. So the question is—Ellery Throckmorton, will you swear to be that person so I can marry you?"

The ruffles on her hem rode high on her thigh. If it was a little higher, if she moved over him a little more, he would be able to see paradise. Wetting his lips, he said, "If you would just . . ."

She glared down at him. "Did you hear anything I said?"

"Barely." He tried again. "I can be strong and clever and determined and honorable—was that the whole list?"

She nodded.

"You're sure? You don't want to add anything else?"

The pressure from her toe lessened and she began to withdraw.

Catching her foot, he placed it squarely on his chest again. Rapidly, he said, "Without you my life would have no meaning."

She appeared to be thinking. Or perhaps she was enjoying the stroke of his thumb on her arch.

"So if you force me to, I will go away and prove that

I am all those things, but it would be so much more fun if we went away together."

"Travel?"

He'd begun to know how her mind worked. "After the honeymoon, we could travel with Kiki."

"Hm . . ."

"What do you think of Central Asia?"

"Interesting!"

Desperation drove him. "I love you."

She considered him with far too much shrewdness. "I wager you say that to all the women."

"Well . . . yes. But I mean it with you."

"No more drinking," she said.

"Never to excess."

"No women other than me."

"I swear."

"Or you will never have another child."

Did she mean she would never have marital relations with him? Or did she mean she would take a knife . . . Looking at her resolute expression, he laid his hand on his chest. "I will never look at another woman."

She rolled her eyes. "Oh, Ellery . . ."

"I will scarcely glance at another woman."

Taking a breath, and with a great show of reluctance, she said, "All right. I'll marry you."

He realized, by the buzzing in his head, he'd been holding his breath. He took a gulp of air. "Thank you. I'm honored." He meant it, too. He'd always known this woman could tie him into knots. He hadn't known he would like it, or that the joy he felt in her presence could be more than mere desire. He admired her. He . . . he liked her!

Yet right now, something . . . more . . . held his attention. He massaged her ankle, her calf, the back of her knee. "If you would just adjust your position . . . a little . . ."

"Like this?" She slid her foot to the far side of his chest, kept her other knee on the bed, and in the shadows above him . . .

Bold. Hyacinth was bold. Absolutely brazen. Absolutely delightful.

But she was still perched on the bed. Running his hand up the inside of her leg, almost to the top, made him break out in a sweat of anticipation. "A little closer," he coaxed. "Just a little . . ."

"Can't you quite reach?" she asked.

"Not quite . . ." His fingers wiggled futilely in the air.

She leaped back onto the bed. "That's the way it's going to be until our wedding night."

A murmur of voices came from the breakfast room. No shouting, Throckmorton realized. Everyone was getting along.

He waited for relief to sweep him, but relief didn't materialize, probably because a scene between Ellery and Lord Longshaw, or Ellery and Hyacinth, or Mother and Lady Longshaw, or any combination of those people, would take the focus off of Throckmorton.

Instead, he knew, they would be talking about him and Celeste. They would be shocked by his cohabitation with an innocent girl. They might be speculating about his next move. They probably would pity him because she'd refused his suit, and Throckmorton could almost hear Lord Longshaw asking in biting tones if madness ran in the family.

"Good morning, Herne." Throckmorton greeted the footman in the doorway.

"Good morning, Mr. Throckmorton." Herne's tone left Throckmorton in no doubt as to his disdain.

Just as Throckmorton feared. The servants hated him.

"But I did propose marriage," he muttered.

He stepped into the breakfast chamber. There they were. Lord Longshaw, looking feral as always. Lady Longshaw, plump and fluttering. Mother, the sublime hostess. Ellery, eyes bloodshot. Hyacinth, seated at his side, smiling and at ease . . . what had she to smile about?

But no time to wonder. All eyes turned toward Throckmorton. Conversation died.

So he took the bull by the horns and initiated a conversation that would challenge them to combat. "I suggest," he said into the silence, "that we call off the merger between our families. An advertisement in the *Times* announcing the engagement is off between Ellery and Lady Hyacinth should do it. Then we'll watch the gossip fly."

Satisfied by their stunned reaction, he seated himself at the head of the small table made festive with dahlias of an inappropriately happy shade of yellow.

The cook herself served him, placing before him his usual breakfast of eggs and bacon, scones and coffee. Esther's presence should have warned him of trouble, but his mind was elsewhere, and he took a forkful of eggs without thinking.

His mouth puckered so tight he could scarcely get the fork out.

"I added a little alum to the eggs." Esther had rolled her hands into her apron as if to keep from smacking him. "I find it gives them a . . . flavor. Don't you think, Mr. Throckmorton?"

He stared at her with eyes bulging. The eggs were *awful*.

Oblivious, Lord Longshaw demanded, "What the devil are you blathering about, Throckmorton?"

Throckmorton grabbed the coffee and took a swig—and the taste hit him. Sweet! He never took sugar!

"And I sweetened the coffee." Esther smiled, a truly frightful baring of teeth. "A lot. Enjoy your breakfast," she said, and left.

The message was clear; as long as Celeste was in exile, he would starve before Esther allowed him another palpable mouthful of food—and he liked his food. "But I did propose marriage," he muttered. Then, to Lord Longshaw, "With all due respect, Ellery and Hyacinth don't want to be married."

Ellery gave a crack of laughter. Taking Hyacinth's hand, he kissed her fingers. "But we do, and as soon as possible."

Throckmorton gaped. When had that happened?

"Isn't that right, darling?" Ellery mooned over Hyacinth's hand like a love-sick bull.

Hyacinth accepted his homage as if it were her right. "As soon as possible for a proper wedding. I want my wedding to outshine even Her Majesty's and that, Ellery, will take time."

"You're not going to make me wait?" Ellery gave a good imitation of frustrated desire.

Hyacinth lowered her eyes in flirtatious demand. "But you said you'll wait for me forever. Won't you?"

"I will wait for you until the end of time," Ellery vowed.

Throckmorton sat in frozen amazement. The girl had managed to hook Ellery so thoroughly his brother hung

like a flounder on the line—and liked it! This couldn't
be the result of Celeste's talk with her . . . could it? That
nonsense about enticing a man didn't work . . . did it?

Lady Longshaw turned an artless face to Lady
Philberta. "Isn't that sweet?"

"The coffee is," Throckmorton muttered.

Lady Philberta smiled back, her smirk only a trifle
sardonic. "I would call it incredible."

Lord Longshaw leaned back in his chair, his mouth
so broad with humor he looked as if he could swallow
his own face. "So no more nonsense about a notice in
the *Times*. We've done well bringing these two together,
heh, Throckmorton?"

"Yes, I . . . yes, very well." Picking up the scone from
his plate, Throckmorton examined it. The golden crusty
triangle looked like the other scones, but was it really?
He broke off a corner of the scone. He sniffed it, then
held it away from his nose. *Garlic.* He dropped it on his
plate. "But Ellery, what about Celeste?"

Lady Longshaw's hands fluttered up, then down.
"Celeste? Who's Celeste?"

"You know who she is." Lord Longshaw's mustache drooped and quivered. "She's the girl that
Throckmorton—"

Hyacinth interrupted, "Papa! Not at the breakfast
table."

Lady Longshaw pressed her handkerchief to her
mouth.

And Throckmorton realized he had brought up the
one subject he had maneuvered to avoid. Standing, he
took his cup to the sidetable and exchanged it for an
empty one.

"I don't know what this Celeste has to do with Ellery

and Hyacinth," Lord Longshaw said crisply.

"Only that the girl tried to come between Ellery and me," Hyacinth informed him.

Lord Longshaw's eyebrows shot high. "But it was Throckmorton who had her."

"George!" Lady Longshaw choked.

"I apologize, m'dear, but everybody knows what happened."

"Actually, no, my lord." Throckmorton poured his coffee and tried hard not to give offense. "You have no idea what happened."

"Exactly right, Throckmorton," Ellery said. "It's best to give Lord and Lady Longshaw all the information. We would hate to have you discover our dirty little secret when we were unable to defend ourselves." He lounged in his chair. "Celeste is our gardener's daughter."

"Your gardener's daughter?" Lord Longshaw's brows bunched into black thunderheads above his eyes. "What was the gardener's daughter doing attending my daughter Hyacinth's betrothal party?"

Ellery smirked. "Celeste is pretty, she's young, she had just returned from Paris—and she was after *me*."

"I was suspicious of her right away," Hyacinth informed her parents in a righteous tone.

Throckmorton poured cream into his coffee—he never took cream, either, but pouring kept his hands busy—and stirred the liquid around and around until the swirl blended into a soft brown. Still he stirred, unable to cease lest he fling the spoon across the table at Ellery, or Hyacinth, or . . . any of them.

"Throckmorton thought it best to allow her to attend the party." Lady Philberta graced her eldest with an approving smile. "He gave her enough rope to hang herself. And of course look what happened! She did."

Throckmorton didn't know why Ellery and Lady Philberta were talking about Celeste in such a manner. He didn't know he could have been so mistaken about Hyacinth's character; her smug manner and easy betrayal of Celeste revealed a previously undetected corruption. And as he listened to Ellery, to his mother, to Hyacinth, wrath brewed in him. Celeste didn't deserve such shabby treatment. Only *he* was allowed to treat her so shabbily.

He put the spoon on the spoon rest so hard the porcelain chipped.

"Celeste disgraced herself as much as it is possible for a girl to do. But what did anyone expect?" Ellery tapped his nose and nodded wisely. "Blood will tell."

Control slipped a notch. Throckmorton stepped forward. "What do you mean by that?"

"Just what I said," Ellery answered, then turned to Lord and Lady Longshaw. "Celeste is a little nobody commoner gold-digger who wanted me and when I wouldn't be tempted, she went after Garrick—or rather, the Throckmorton fortune. Garrick handled her just as she deserved."

Throckmorton found himself moving on a tide of red rage.

Ellery didn't appear to notice. "So the gardener's daughter learned her lesson, and she's scampering back to Paris with her tail between—"

Jerking Ellery's chair out from underneath him, Throckmorton pulled him to his feet. With a single closed-fist blow, he sent him sliding across the table. Lady Longshaw screamed. Dishes flew, splattering oatmeal everywhere. The tablecloth bunched. The vase toppled, spilling water and flowers.

Dimly, Throckmorton realized he was making a scene. But he couldn't stop. The bastard had maligned Celeste! Just as he prepared to launch himself at Ellery . . . Hyacinth laughed.

The sound recalled Throckmorton to some semblance of sanity. He teetered at the edge of the table. He glared at Hyacinth.

She covered her mouth with her hand and watched him, wide-eyed and giggling.

Throckmorton glared at his brother, who sat up and calmly wiped egg yolk off his cheek. He glared at his mother, who tranquilly continued eating her toast.

Only Lord and Lady Longshaw had the grace to look shocked and bewildered.

"Ellery, what in the hell do you think you're saying?" Throckmorton roared.

"You're swearing, Garrick," Lady Philberta said.

"Damned right!"

"And yelling," Ellery said.

"What in the devil . . ." Throckmorton was repeating himself. He slammed his fist on the table, making the dishes jump, then pointed at Ellery. "Get over here and explain yourself!"

Ellery crossed his legs and grinned. "You love her."

The tie on Throckmorton's cravat must have slipped, for it suddenly tightened, and he choked, "What?"

"He said *you love her,*" Lady Philberta repeated helpfully.

"I do not!"

"It is so obvious, Garrick," Hyacinth said in a patronizing tone. "You love Celeste Milford."

"But . . . but she's the gardener's daughter." Lady Longshaw was caught in a scene whose every nuance baffled her.

In a fury, Throckmorton turned on the poor woman. "Who gives a damn if she's the gardener's daughter? We Throckmortons are common people—"

Lady Philberta snorted. "I beg your pardon, son!"

He waved wildly toward his mother. "Half common, then. But certainly in no position to make disparaging comments about a lovely, accomplished young lady like Miss Celeste Milford."

"I meant no harm," Lady Longshaw said faintly.

Throckmorton bent his glower on Lord Longshaw. "If you or Lady Longshaw find the concept of marriage between me and Celeste Milford repugnant, you should say so now before the ceremony between Ellery and Hyacinth takes place."

"They don't object," Hyacinth said. "And stop yelling at my parents."

"Actually—" Lord Longshaw began.

"We're getting married regardless of who objects." Ellery scooted across to Hyacinth, knocking more dishes askew, and took her hand. "We love each other. The question is, Throckmorton, have you got the courage to marry your lady?"

"I already proposed." Throckmorton looked at his fist, which didn't ache quite as it should. Was it possible Ellery had foreseen the blow and avoided most of its force? He certainly looked healthy enough. "She won't have me."

"Because you didn't tell her you love her," Hyacinth reminded him.

Why Throckmorton had ever thought Hyacinth a

meek, sweet girl, he couldn't comprehend. "That's because I don't . . . don't . . ." His cravat tightened again. Sliding his finger beneath it, he decided he would have to have a word with his valet.

Lady Philberta pushed back her chair. "Walk with me, Garrick."

Throckmorton was more than glad to leave the breakfast room with its mess of dishes, its scowling servants, and his brother's incomprehensible conviction that he knew more about the state of Throckmorton's heart than Throckmorton did. Garrick Throckmorton didn't fall in love. Garrick Throckmorton had a duty to his business, his family and his country that precluded such messy emotions. He had a daughter he adored. A mother and a brother.

A woman . . . a woman was more. Children grew up and went away. Mother and brother had their own lives. But a woman who was truly a mate . . . what a danger she presented. He'd seen other men with their mates. They shared more than love. They shared their lives.

They promised to share eternity.

No. He could not love Celeste Milford.

Lady Philberta opened the napkin she held and handed him a scone. "It's edible," she advised. "It came off my plate."

Grateful for any nourishment, Throckmorton broke it into pieces and ate as they strolled along the portrait gallery. The sun shone through the windows, the gallery was the epitome of stylish good taste, and Throckmorton could see nothing that brought him pleasure. If he had any nerve, he would ask his mother why she had been walking with Celeste the day before and why she'd allowed Celeste to break his windows.

He knew the answer. Lady Philberta had a lofty sense of justice. He had offended it with his treatment of Celeste. "But I did propose marriage," he muttered.

Lady Philberta ignored that. "Garrick, I've been worried about you in recent years."

"Why?" He thought of Stanhope's betrayal. "Have I not fulfilled your expectations?"

Hooking her cane over her arm, she leaned on him and led him to the portrait of his father. "All of them, and more. That's the problem."

Throckmorton found himself muttering again. "Women." His mother. Hyacinth. *Celeste.* Who understood them?

He looked up at the elder Garrick Throckmorton, framed in gilt and looking stern. Certainly his father hadn't. He had warned Throckmorton of that. "A man who asks a woman what she means gets what's coming to him."

Lady Philberta looked up at the portrait, too, but she dwelled on different memories. "You were such a bright boy, Garrick, so vivid, so interested in everything and everybody. In addition, you were our elder, and a son. Your father and I expected too much of you."

"You had the right."

"We might have spread our expectations around to our second son, I think."

She sounded so ironic, Throckmorton smiled. "Ellery would have always confounded you."

"He did. But you filled your own shoes, and his, too." In a shrewd maneuver, she seated herself beneath the portrait, allying herself with his father, making Throckmorton answer to both his parents. "You worked so hard to make us happy, you vanquished emotion, temper, all the parts of you that made you so alive."

The discipline which he so cherished apparently caused her anguish. "You take too much credit on yourself, Mother. You may have started the process, but it was in India, where a gesture or a smile could be misinterpreted and lead to trouble, where I learned to hide my feelings."

She shook her head. "In the last week, I've seen you come alive again."

"Mother, I don't love Celeste! If I loved . . ." Throckmorton had the potential for such passion. He knew himself well, and he knew that within him lurked a primitive man, one who demanded, possessed, lusted. He wouldn't allow himself to indulge that man, or he would burn and want and take and give until he was only half a soul, joined forever with *her*. With Celeste. "Let's not even contemplate love."

"If you loved . . . what?" Lady Philberta looked down as she stroked the smooth wood of the chair. "Celeste would be the center of your life? You would ache with desire?"

"Mama!" He didn't want to hear this from her.

"You would want always to be with Celeste and you'd worry about her when you were apart? You'd torment yourself with thoughts that she might need you and you're not there?"

"Yes. I suppose so," he said reluctantly.

"You were too young, you don't remember, but your father didn't want to love me. He thought he was so much older, which he was, and he thought he was smarter, which he wasn't. When he finally admitted his love, he said . . . all that. About how I was the center of his life and how he . . . ached for me. He never could quite say *I love you,* but that gruff, earthy, unsophisticated man was moved to poetry"—her voice wobbled— "for me." She blinked, drew a handkerchief from her sleeve, and dabbed at the tears.

Feeling like an intruder, Throckmorton looked out the window.

"I treasure the memory. I treasure all the memories I have of your father, even the ones when he behaved like an ignorant cad." She smiled mistily at Throckmorton. "You've already created *those* memories for Celeste. I think you should find her and create the others."

He nodded, moved by the emotional display from his usually prosaic mother.

"You're alive again, Garrick. You're living and suffering—and loving. Don't let that girl go."

Loving. Loving. How dare his mother accuse him of loving?

"Mother, I appreciate your concern, but I don't love Celeste Milford."

"She's going to Paris," Lady Philberta said.

His hands clenched. "She took the ticket and the bank draft and left me a promissory note."

"To be a courtesan," Lady Philberta added.

"What?"

Lady Philberta rubbed her head. "For someone who doesn't shout often, you do it very well."

That wild, capricious madness took possession of him again. He hurried toward the door that led to the gardens. He had to find Celeste. He had to convince her . . . a courtesan! She couldn't become a courtesan. She was too fastidious, too beautiful, too charming, too ... she'd be a wonderful courtesan, but he wouldn't permit ... but he didn't have the right to permit her anything. He had given up that right when he failed to give her what she deserved.

A courtesan ...

He didn't love. He didn't ... but his father's admission to his mother echoed in his brain. Throckmorton's thoughts *did* circle around Celeste. He *did* desire her so much he ached. He wanted to make love to her until she no longer suffered from this baffling sense of betrayal. How could she hate him so much she broke his windows? That she threatened to go to Paris and become a courtesan? How could she, after the way he'd pleasured her?

He knew he wasn't the right husband for her. She was everything he was not: vivacious, smiling, social. But he would always treat her with the care and the respect she deserved, and she didn't have the right to demand more. She would be happy. She would never know there was more to him than the physical joy he gave her.

But ... she would, because Celeste was intelligent, insightful, and ... his.

Stopping by the window, Throckmorton grasped the curtain in his fist and stared blindly across the gardens. Ellery was right. Blast him, he was right. In this last week while Throckmorton had been scheming and maneuvering and managing Celeste so she didn't get in the way of Ellery's betrothal ... she had crept into his heart. Sometime during his resourceful seduction, his artful banter, his adoring vows, his passionate kisses; at some point, they all became real.

Of course they had—for no other reason would he have so lost himself in her arms.

He would find her and convince her.

He loved her.

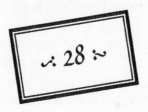

He loved her.

Resolve stiffened Throckmorton's spine. He strode toward the door. He would find Celeste, make her realize what they had, tell her—

Kinman rushed toward him with an expression of contrition on his bovine face and a shining bruise on his chin. "Sir, Stanhope has escaped!"

Throckmorton groaned. "Not now."

"Sir?" Kinman was supposed to be in London, following Stanhope, seeing who he contacted, arresting him. Now here he stood, announcing the worst news possible at the worst time possible.

In clipped tones, Throckmorton demanded, "How did that occur?"

"Stanhope was at the docks, boarding a ship bound for India. We'd been trailing him. Now we moved to detain him, but before we could reach him another group of men approached. We held back, wanting to identify them." Kinman barely contained a grin. "They began to beat him."

"Beat him?"

"If I understood them correctly, I believe they expressed their supreme dislike for being swindled out of their money for bogus information."

Throckmorton stepped close to Kinman and lowered his voice to a menacing whisper. "How did the Russians discover the information was bogus?"

Kinman shook his head. "I don't know, sir."

"His valet?"

"Certainly possible, sir, but we never caught sight of him. To tell you the truth, sir, I scarcely remember what he looks like."

"The best sort of spy. He fades into the background," Throckmorton said. "What happened with Stanhope?"

"We thought they were going to kill him. Since we wanted to question him, we jumped into the fray."

Throckmorton realized what had happened at once. "During the fight, Stanhope slipped away."

"I am so sorry, Mr. Throckmorton." Kinman looked sheepish as only a man of his size and disposition could look. "He disappeared. We believe he boarded the ship and sailed. They'll put in at Cape Town. We'll send a swift ship, and with God's help, we'll have men there to meet him."

Throckmorton didn't reprimand Kinman; Kinman hadn't reached his current position without comprehending how very badly he had mucked up. But Throckmorton said, "I would not be happy if Stanhope escaped again."

"No, sir."

Throckmorton considered. Right now, he could do nothing to bring Stanhope to justice. However, he *could* find Celeste and tell her the marvelous news. His love was the only piece missing from his marriage proposal. Celeste would be happy. She would accept him gladly. So he said, "I have urgent business, so—take care of everything. Keep me abreast of what's happening." He strode on without waiting to hear Kinman's agreement.

When Throckmorton stepped out into the gardens, he saw the undergardeners gathered around Milford, who towered above them. Everyone turned in unison to look at Throckmorton. Then Milford started toward him.

Throckmorton met him on the stairs. "Milford, I'm looking for your daughter."

In his slow, steady manner, Milford answered, "She's on her way to Paris, Mr. Throckmorton."

Shock held Throckmorton immobile. "To Paris. *Now?*"

"Yes, sir." Milford lifted his ham-sized fist. "And you're on your way to the stars."

Earlier in the week when Throckmorton had secured Celeste's travel itinerary, he had taken care when he'd picked the inn. She was a young, beautiful woman, thus the inn had to be clean, respectable, and located on the rural outskirts of London so she would not be bothered by the dandies and bullies who frequented London public houses.

Now Throckmorton squinted as his eyes adjusted from the bright sunshine of outside to the dim interior of the Ram's Horn Inn.

In the common room, the ceilings were low, the timbers heavy and dark. Rifles and shotguns of every kind hung on hooks over the doors. A great ram's head hung over the fireplace, and the walls were thick with mounted ducks and pheasants. A very manly sort of inn, was the Ram's Horn, but the floors were swept, the windows sparkling, and a delicious smell emanated from the kitchen.

The innkeeper, a gregarious fellow of elderly years, hurried forward to greet Throckmorton. "I'm Mr. Jackman, sir. An honor t' have ye, Mr. Throckmorton, sir." He checked at the sight of Throckmorton's face. "Been in a bit of a dust-up, then, sir?"

Throckmorton touched his bruised and swollen eye. "My gardener handed in his resignation."

Mr. Jackman laughed uncertainly.

"I'm seeking Miss Milford," Throckmorton said.

"She's back in th' private parlor, just as ye requested, sir. I've done everythin' ye requested, sir. Gave her th' best bedchamber in th' house, made sure th' parlor was free fer her, had me wife serve as her maid. Truth t' tell, I'm grateful fer th' business, sir. Summer is our slow time. Now, when 'tis fall an' th' ducks are flyin', ah, then we're stuffed wi' hunters all seeking a shot at them."

"If you could direct me to Miss Milford?"

Recalled to his duty, Mr. Jackman said, "I'll take ye, sir." He led the way down the short corridor to the back of the inn. "A comely lady, an' so pleasant-like. Settled right in. Came down an' ate a good lunch. Then she sat down by th' window t' read. Said she sails tomorrow. Anxious t' get back t' Paris, she says, an' go t' work."

Throckmorton's eyes narrowed as he considered the kind of work she would seek. "Is she?"

"Not many girls these days want t' work. Younger

generation, sir, all gone t' ruin. Here ye are, sir." Mr.
Jackman indicated the door, then waited with interest
for Throckmorton to knock.

His curiosity would, Throckmorton was sure, carry
him into the parlor to watch the reunion. So Throckmorton tipped him, thanked him, and watched until the
innkeeper had regretfully bowed and backed out of the
corridor altogether.

Satisfied he and Celeste would be alone, Throckmorton knocked decisively on the heavy wood timbers. For
a long time, there was no answer, and he worried she
had somehow found out who stood on the other side. He
knocked again and in his sternest command voice,
called, "Celeste, open this door at once."

The latch clicked. The door opened, but very slowly
and just a crack.

Celeste's reception of him was everything he feared.
She stood dressed in a serviceable brown traveling
gown, and she observed him with unwelcome dismay.
Some might even call it horror. She blocked the doorway. With peculiar emphasis, she said, "No, I thank
you, I don't want anything else to eat."

He had already decided on his strategy. He would be
firm, but honest, even if it hurt them both. So he answered, "I'm not offering you anything, I'm telling you
what you're going to get." Pushing the door back, he
settled his hands on her waist, lifted her out of the way,
and strode into the private parlor, a room of modest proportions, comfortable seats and a plethora of shotguns
and antlers. "Celeste, we're going to get married. Not
because I've compromised you, not because it's the
proper thing to do, but because . . . I love you."

She looked meaningfully toward the door. "No. Go away."

"No? What do you mean, no?" He'd been expecting . . . well, he'd been expecting her to throw herself into his arms, or at the very least pretend to consider before throwing herself into his arms.

This was harder than he expected. "You have to hear me out. I love you, adore you, will do anything for you. You must come back with me and become my wife and save me from a life of lonely duty."

"No, Throckmorton, listen to me—"

Going to her, he took her hands. "Why not? You said you loved me. Is that not still true?"

Seemingly of its own accord, the door creaked, then slammed shut.

Stanhope stood against the wall, a shotgun pointed at them.

Hatred, sharp and hot with betrayal of friendship, flared within Throckmorton.

In a mocking tone, Stanhope said, "She might still love you, although if she does I doubt her taste, but I believe she's trying to indicate that you're in danger."

Shock held Throckmorton still for a moment. Then he unhurriedly stepped in front of Celeste, careful not to alarm Stanhope whose battered face and trembling hands bespoke a violent agitation. "Stanhope. You didn't get on the ship."

"No, I didn't get on the ship." Stanhope mimicked him savagely. "I wasn't climbing a gangplank in full view of all your men and those damnable Russians, too." With the barrel of the rifle, he indicated the two of them. "A touching scene, Throckmorton. I'm grateful love has addled your senses. You forgot the very precepts of caution you taught me."

"So I did." The window that opened onto the pasture and woods stood wide, a breach large enough for a man to get through. Throckmorton hadn't noticed.

"He wants money, Garrick."

Celeste had eased herself out from behind him, Throckmorton realized. Blast the woman, she surely understood the danger she faced. He slowly but surely moved to stand in front of her again.

"He took the bank draft and the tickets from me. Give him your pocketbook and he can leave."

Stanhope laughed, a harsh activity that made his split lip open and bleed. "Isn't she a sweet dreamer, Throckmorton? You would never let me go, and I would never let go of you. You ruined me. You *ruined* me, you and Celeste, with your translations and your lies."

"My lies, not hers," Throckmorton said, glib enough to exonerate Celeste. "I used her."

"I knew!" Celeste protested. "I just didn't tell you, Garrick."

Throckmorton turned on her. "Would you be quiet?" She was sliding away from his protection again.

He glared and pointed to a spot behind him.

She flicked him a glance and kept moving.

Stanhope didn't seem to hear either of them. "You're not leaving here."

Celeste drew an audible breath.

"Either of you," Stanhope added. "You love each other so much, you can die together."

Perhaps that threat would make Celeste realize the danger they faced. Or perhaps she already knew, and suffered from an excess of courage. Another reason to

love her; a good reason to shout at her. Instead, Throckmorton focused on Stanhope. "What about you? You
won't escape."

"Probably not. The English are after me. The Russians are after me. The money is gone, vanished, damn
you." Stanhope fingered the shotgun's trigger.

Bitterly, Throckmorton knew he had no assurances to
offer Celeste. Stanhope was deadly because Stanhope
knew Throckmorton. They'd fought together. They'd
survived together. Stanhope knew every strategy. He
knew that, even now, Throckmorton was plotting to vanquish him. The only advantage Throckmorton had was
Stanhope's ongoing rage and the beating he'd already
suffered, and that advantage was balanced by Celeste.
When the fighting began, would she flee?

No, of course not. And he wanted her out of the range
of that shotgun. This close, buckshot would kill a
man—or a woman.

So with his most scornful edge, Throckmorton
smiled at Stanhope. "You've ruined yourself, Stanhope.
If you hadn't decided to sell your soul for a few pieces
of silver, you would still be at my side."

The bruises on Stanhope's forehead and around his
eyes darkened in a rush of rage. He stepped forward, the
swollen barrel of the gun quaking. "At your side? Nothing more than your secretary! Never given credit for my
brilliance, never—"

Throckmorton raised his voice. "Credit for your brilliance, indeed! What brilliance is that? The brilliance to
fail as barrister, to devastate my estate, to—" In mid-
spate, he leaped forward, slapped the shotgun sideways,
grabbed the stock.

Stanhope was prepared. He didn't release it, but

swung the barrel up into Throckmorton's face. The metal struck under his chin. Throckmorton's teeth snapped together. He staggered, losing his grip, falling backward, hitting the floor.

Off-balance, Stanhope staggered back, too.

With narrow-eyed intent, Celeste shoved a chair under him.

Stanhope stumbled, lurched and went over hard, landing on his back.

Driven by fury, Throckmorton leaped up and jumped on Stanhope with all his weight. Stanhope rolled. The shotgun slid away from them, but neither of them noticed. The shotgun no longer consumed their attention.

The desire for vengeance, hot and pure, burned between them.

Throckmorton smashed his fist into Stanhope's mouth. Blood spurted.

Howling, Stanhope caught Throckmorton's hair, holding him still for a forehead slam. Pain exploded in Throckmorton's nose. Rage exploded his gut.

Stanhope rolled on top of Throckmorton and pummeled him. Right and left, he punched Throckmorton while Throckmorton blocked and swayed, wanting nothing more but to win, to beat Stanhope within an inch of his life for daring to commit treason. For annihilating their friendship. Most of all, for daring to threaten Celeste.

He retaliated with a flat-handed slap to both of Stanhope's ears. For a moment, Stanhope's eyes rolled back in his head. Throckmorton kneed him, came up on top, and slammed his fist beneath Stanhope's chin.

Stanhope hit his head on the stone floor and with a gasp, went limp.

Livid, Throckmorton hit him again, and again.

Something caught his arm, and he swung around, enraged.

Celeste looked down at him, her eyes stern. "Stop. Garrick. Stop! That's enough."

She'd been saying that for a while, he realized. Saying that while they fought. She held the shotgun in one hand, and he thought that was a good thing. While she kept the rifle, he wouldn't be tempted to commit murder.

"He's unconscious."

He'd heard that tone before. His tutor had sounded as stern that last time Throckmorton had lost his temper.

"If you continue, you'll kill him," she said.

He allowed her to draw him to his feet. She was so beautiful, and Stanhope had wanted to kill her.

"I'll call the landlord. I'm sure he heard the fight."

Throckmorton swayed, all his concentration on her. She was alive. He had saved her.

Her voice softened, and she stroked his arm as if calming a maddened beast. "The landlord didn't know Stanhope came through the window. With the noise, the poor man is probably mad with curiosity."

The intensity of Throckmorton's rage became the intensity of passion. Tugging her into his arms, he held her. Just held her. She was alive. Breathing, talking. Holding him. All her intelligence, beauty, defiance, laughter, saved by him, for him. In his arms. *Alive.*

Through no fault of her own. He gritted his teeth so hard he could scarcely speak. "Blast you, Celeste, how dare you try to help me?"

"You needed help."

He had no interest in her commonplace tone and prosaic answer. "Why didn't you run when we started fighting? He could have killed you."

"He could have killed you, too."

She still didn't seem to realize her folly. "You could have *died.*"

In a voice muffled by his chest, she said, "It made sense to present two targets rather than one."

"Do you have no brains? Do not ever try to—"

A scraping sound. Behind him. Incredulous, he pushed Celeste away. Whirling, he saw Stanhope, beaten, violent, desperate—on his feet.

And Stanhope saw him. In a burst of speed and strength, Stanhope ran and jumped at the window. His body slammed into the frame. He broke through the crossbars, shattered the glass. He fell onto the grass behind the inn, got up, ran as if death itself was after him.

It was. Throckmorton dove after him. The copse of trees at the edge of the property offered sanctuary; Throckmorton leaped through the breach.

Still holding the rifle, Celeste ran to the shattered window. In the endless hour Stanhope had spent with her, he had threatened her. He had threatened Garrick. Most of all, he had confessed to being the wits behind Penelope's kidnapping.

Without a qualm, she lifted the shotgun to her shoulder.

But she couldn't shoot yet. Garrick ran after Stanhope, right in the line of fire. "Swerve," she urged as if he could hear her. "Swerve."

At thirty paces, Stanhope stumbled.

Garrick swerved to avoid him.

Celeste pulled the trigger.

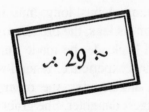

~ 29 ~

Celeste tossed the sheet back from Garrick's bare body, and smiled as she looked down at the expanse of Garrick's back and buttocks, marred by the half dozen small, round, red holes left by the wide spray of buckshot. Fondling the sharp point of the scalpel, she said, "Those certainly look painful."

Facedown on her bed at the inn, Garrick turned his head to glare at her. "I will wait for the doctor."

"The doctor is here, but he's taking dozens of pellets out of Stanhope's hide."

"Stanhope is a prisoner. He can wait."

"He doesn't have to." Garrick had been caught by the periphery of the blast. A few swollen wounds amounted to nothing more than minor discomfort for Garrick . . . and retribution for her. Sweet retribution. "You have *me*, and I wouldn't want you to suffer longer than necessary."

"It would be reassuring to have someone who had previous experience with gunshots."

He had quite a gorgeous, long, muscled back. Taken with the length of his legs, the breadth of his shoulders, and the muscled backside, he made quite a handsome package. "I do have experience. When I was a governess for the Russian ambassador, the older children were teasing the youngest daughter. She grabbed a pellet gun and shot little Laurentij in the cheek." Leaning over one of the wounds on his shoulder blade, she squinted. She could see the pellet, and with the point of the scalpel, she flicked it out.

"Ouch!"

"Very passionate people, the Russians. Given to bloody acts of revenge." Holding the pellet down by Throckmorton's face, she showed him the round, shiny, lead shot. "There's the first one."

He stared with the outraged gaze of a cantankerous patient. "That hurt!"

"That was easy. Wait until I start cutting." She swabbed the wound with whisky.

"Ow!" Lifting himself on one elbow, he turned toward her—although he took care not to display his lower body.

Idly she wondered what that meant. He couldn't be aroused in these circumstances . . . could he? Surely he couldn't be thinking about fornication when she stood over him holding a scalpel . . . could he?

And why should she care, anyway?

She knew the answer. Because although he was naked and furious, and suffered a swollen nose, a black eye and a split chin, he looked absolutely appealing.

The bruises on his face were rapidly turning darker.

His black hair fell around his face. "You're enjoying this far too much," he accused.

"Mmm . . ." She pretended to consider. "Yes."

"You're still angry at me."

"Very astute of you."

"I came for you, didn't I?"

"I was depending on it."

"I rescued you, didn't I?"

"Except for that part where I brought the villain down."

Garrick flopped flat on his stomach again. "And shot *me.*"

"You're welcome."

"I'm not ungrateful."

She placed her finger on another one of the wounds and pressed until the lead shot rose to the surface. She tossed it in a pan beside the bed. "You are. Dreadfully."

He turned his head and caught her hand. "Let me say now, I am grateful." He pressed her fingers to his lips. "I'm grateful for everything about you. For your beauty, and your intelligence, and everything that makes you *you.*"

"For my bravery in not leaving you to face Stanhope alone?"

He visibly wavered between pacification and exasperation. As she expected, exasperation won out. "You should have escaped." He sounded clipped, irritated. "If faced with such circumstances again, you are to save yourself."

The man never gave up. She sounded just as clipped and irritated when she said, "I doubt I shall face such dangerous circumstances in Paris."

His muscles clenched. "Celeste, I truly do love you."

As if she believed that. "I'm still going to take the shot out of you."

"No, I'm telling you the truth. I love you."

"You'd have to be a fool not to." She paused. "Oh, but I forgot, you are a fool."

"You sound like my brother," Throckmorton snapped.

He had caught her unwilling interest. "Your brother? What does Ellery have to do with this?"

"My brother, my mother, my daughter, my niece, and my future sister-in-law. Before I left to come after you, they all told me I was a fool."

"Good. It's unanimous. We all agree."

"Your father didn't tell me I was a fool. He just punched me in the face." Throckmorton indicated his swollen eye.

"Good for Papa. Did you know Esther put castor oil in your whisky?" The unmitigated horror on his face made her laugh. "I don't know that for sure. But if I were you, I'd check when I got back to Blythe Hall or you could make close friends with your chamber pot. Lie back down. I need to get these out."

He lowered himself, his body a lovely tan against the white of the sheets. "Don't you care?"

"About what?" She managed to push two more pieces of shot out of his back while he squirmed.

"That I love you?"

"Do you think declaring that you love me makes everything all better?"

"Doesn't it?"

She had to refrain from plunging the scalpel into his thick head. "Should I be so honored to be the recipient of your love that I will forgive everything? All your lies, all your betrayals, the way you used me?"

"You weren't angry about being used in connection with Stanhope."

"No, for in that instance I understand why you used me." With the point of the scalpel, she made a tiny cut over the swelling on his buttock. He gasped and held himself very still, and with the tweezers she removed the pellet. "I even agree that, when weighed in the balance, my pride is not as important as my country."

He sounded very serious when he said, "I never meant to strip you of your pride."

"But put together with your sneaking, underhanded seduction and that ticket to Paris and a bank draft, all in the pursuit of a suitable business alliance between the Throckmortons and Lord Longshaw . . . that doesn't carry the same weight as saving England, and taken altogether makes an ugly portrait of you and your mercenary soul. Your declaration of love can't clean the grime away."

"You're right."

"What?"

"I said you're right."

Her eyes narrowed on him. What does that mean?

"I did the wrong thing. I am always insufferably sure my way is best, and that is why I should marry, so I can be told, frequently and often, that I am wrong. Are you woman enough?"

He made her want to laugh, and she hated that. This was no time to remember the enjoyment she experienced with his conversation, no time to recall how well they fit, mind and body. "I'm woman enough to cut this last pellet out." She smoothed his buttock where the shot had punched a hole through the skin. This was the deep one, the only one that really required surgery. "You must remain very still."

He ignored her, stirring restlessly on the bed. "What about *your* declaration of love?"

"What about it? You didn't believe me." And right now, as she laid out the needle the doctor had left, she resented that, too.

"So I was right. You really don't know what love is. You never truly loved me."

How had this happened? How had she lost control of the conversation? She was no longer on the attack, he was, and that wasn't fair. For the first time in this affair, she held the knife, and in more ways than one. She wanted to keep it that way.

"I loved you enough to . . . to trust my body to you."

Slowly, he sat up, staring at her, revealing himself in all his glory. Despite his pain, despite her reprimand, he wanted her.

And from his expression of grim triumph, she realized she had been manipulated into an imprudent statement. She should have remembered with whom she sparred.

"You loved me that night."

If she had denied it, she would be nothing more than a wanton. If she agreed . . .

"One pellet left. Lie down and let me get it out."

To her surprise, he obeyed her.

Because, she realized, he'd used his body to distract her, then made his point. While entrusting himself to her hands, he was content to let her think about the state of her heart.

Cunning. The man was cunning.

With a light touch, she slid the scalpel along his skin, swabbed the blood that welled up, probed and found the

shot. She eased it free, took the single stitch necessary
to close the wound, pressed a pad on the site—and suddenly found it necessary to sit down.

She didn't care about his pain . . . did she? Taking
that pellet out had been just retribution for his
misdeeds . . . hadn't it?

Yes, this weakness was nothing more than her reaction to being held hostage, to putting herself in danger,
to shooting a man.

Sinking on the bed, she sat very still and waited for
her trembling to cease.

At once Garrick recognized his advantage. He sat up
again.

She tweaked the sheet over him.

"It's a little late for that." Removing the sharp scalpel
from her fingers, he gingerly placed it on the nightstand.
"You've seen it all. You've had it all." He took her face
between his palms and looked into her eyes. "You've
kissed it all."

She wrestled herself free. "All right! You've driven
your point home. We both understand we've had . . .
we've taken pleasure of each other."

"Are you sorry now for what we had?" Taking her
hand, he pressed it to his groin. "Did the light on my
sins make your love evaporate?"

It was hard to think when her fingers were wrapped
around his member, and the heat and the memories
pressed at her. He could give her such pleasure, yet she
had to resist. She wasn't going to marry him. At least
not out of gratitude. And certainly not out of lust. "You
are embarrassed because of me."

"Do I feel embarrassed?"

She used just a hint of her fingernails.

He let her hand go at once. "You don't embarrass me. I told you before. I'm not a snob."

"I believe you truly don't care that I'm the gardener's daughter. But with me, you lose all your heady superiority. You're no longer Garrick Throckmorton, lord of the spies, sovereign of business, in control of yourself and everything you do. You're Garrick Throckmorton, a man who gives into temptation. You blame me for what you consider a weakness. I do not accept the blame. I will not live with guilt, yours or mine, for all my life."

She had struck a rich vein, for he cleared his throat and looked abashed. "I might have thought that before," he admitted. "But when I'm with you, I'm not a man like any other. I'm better than all the others, better than I've ever been before, because I have you." He corrected himself. "Because I'm *with* you."

She didn't know whether to laugh or cry. He wanted possession of her. Even now, when he was trying to say the right thing, to convince her of his contrition, his true nature strutted through his conversation.

She should have anticipated his next move. She could only blame her own weakness for her lack of foresight.

Because he wrapped her in his arms and fell backward on the bed, taking her with him.

She struggled. "You're going to hurt yourself."

"Not if you stay still."

"You're going to bleed on the sheets."

He chuckled. "There's my practical girl." When she would have thumped him, he clutched her tighter. In his deepest, lushest, most dark velvet voice, he said, "I understand my mistake."

She hated that she fit into his embrace so snugly.

"I made our entire courtship a farce. You called me a liar. You wonder if you can trust anything I say. So what good does it do me to tell you I love you?"

She hated that she listened to the thump of his heart and heard in it the echo of her own.

"But I do love you."

She hated that she believed him, regardless of his confirmed record of being the biggest phony in England.

"Marry me. Let me prove my love to you. I'm not the richest man in England. Not yet. But I've got a great estate in Suffolk, a townhouse in London and a hunting lodge in Scotland. I've got servants who have a special reason to love you. A daughter who scolded me for letting you go. A mother who explained that I loved you."

"Good for her," Celeste muttered.

"I've got a huge garden that needs tending since my gardener and all the undergardeners have quit—"

"Oh, dear." She had put her father in a dreadful position.

"—But if you wed me, you could probably convince them to stay. I would give you everything I own. If you wished, I would even find you occupation as a Russian translator—"

"Don't forget French, Italian and a little Romanian."

He paused, and when he next spoke she detected a little more confidence in his voice. "Perhaps I'm not easy to live with—"

She snorted.

"—And perhaps you could find someone you could love more, but if you search the world over you'll never find a man to love you more than I do."

"And I'll wager you'll let me look," she said sarcastically.

"Well . . . no. I'm not a fool. I wouldn't take the chance."

She grinned. He was telling the truth with a vengeance now.

"I seduced you because I couldn't *not*. You are everything that is missing from my life, and I had to take you, drink of you, taste you just once." His hands moved in big circles on her back, massaging out the tension. "Only . . . once could never be enough."

His sentiments sounded heartfelt. His touch evoked the memory of his possession. More significantly, her own desire sabotaged her resistance. She wanted him to be sincere. She wanted him to love her.

In that low, vibrant, deep velvet voice he vowed, "For you, I would take up my family and abandon my home and my duty, and come to live in Paris to acquire your services."

"As . . . translator?"

"As courtesan! That is what my mother said you were going to do."

She hid her face in his chest, but not quickly enough.

"Are you laughing?" He tucked his finger under her chin and lifted her face, shining with humor. "You *are* laughing."

She tried to maintain her gravity. "Lady Philberta must have neglected to tell you she had talked me out of my decision to become a courtesan."

He stared down at her, intent on something he saw in her face.

She quieted, looking back at him.

"I have missed your laughter. You're always smiling—do you know that's what I first loved about you? That ever-present smile. When I wiped it off your lips, I felt as if I'd destroyed something more precious than gold." As though mesmerized by the sight, he caressed her lips with his thumb. "You never answered my question. Do you still love me?"

Insulted, she pushed at his chest until he let her sit up. "You are truly a dolt! True love doesn't disintegrate at the first touch of adversity. Of course I love you."

He sat up, too, so quickly that he flinched. "Then will you forgive me? Take a chance on me? Marry me?"

She thought about how he had callously planned her seduction, and cold anguish and hot fury curled up her spine.

Then she thought about dancing in the ballroom. Talking under the stars. Loving in the conservatory.

She knew the ruthless businessman and spy lived within him, and if Garrick was left to end his days alone, he would in truth become the bastard who used and discarded without conscience. But within also resided the man of great passion and resolute integrity. If she . . . if she accepted his proposal, she would have to live with everything that he was. He was excruciatingly sure of his brilliance. He would do what was right for her whether she wished it or no. He would cosset her, talk to her, love her until all other existence seemed dry and tedious.

Did she dare take a chance that he loved her?

He did. She'd known it even before he'd stumbled onto that truth.

Could she whole-heartedly forgive him for his perfidy?

She had to. She loved him. Putting her finger on his chest, she pushed him back on the bed and leaned close. "I choose you, Garrick Throckmorton. *I* choose *you*."

Throwing his head back, he laughed, a full, rich laughter that the old Garrick Throckmorton would never have permitted himself.

She kissed him while he laughed, reveling in his satisfaction. No matter that she made it clear she selected him; he was convinced he won her, and would be absolutely insufferable.

Still laughing, he kissed her back, holding her, running his hands over her. "Is the door locked?" he asked.

"Do you think I'm barmy? No, it's not locked!"

Rolling her onto her back, he kissed her with the light, delicate kisses of a seducer. "It should be," he insisted.

"No." Although she could be convinced, and soon.

Lifting his head, he stroked her hair. "I thought when I told you I loved you, you would run to my arms and stay there forever."

"You're conceited."

His thumbs glided in circles among the whorls of her ears. "After winning a woman like you, how could I not be?"

Sliding her hands around his neck, she brought him close and rewarded him for his brilliant reply. The heat between them flared; their mouths became more intimate.

Tearing himself away, he gasped, "The door."

"It's not locked," she assured him.

"I'll lock it."

She caught him when he would have risen. "Mr. and Mrs. Jackman are already shocked that I demanded to care for you myself."

"You are determined to make me pay for every little inconsequential hideous mistake I've made, aren't you?"

She adored hearing his frustration. "You've been wounded. You shouldn't indulge in rigorous activity."

"I'll stay very still."

"Then what good would you be to me?"

He glared at her, and when that made no dent in her determination, he submitted an offering. "Ellery is going to become a spy."

"I told you he'd be good at it." She trailed her fingers down his ribs, enjoying his nakedness. "What about Lady Hyacinth?"

He turned his attention to the buttons on the back of her gown, sliding them free with a light, quick touch. "She's going to marry him and become a spy, too."

"Lovely." She spoke of the plans *and* the buttons.

"If Mr. and Mrs. Jackman walked in on us now, they would be shocked anyway." For all his impatience, he kissed slowly, teasing with his tongue, gloating at her unqualified enthusiasm. "I think we should have a swing built in our bedroom."

"You are a very naughty man." She paused and considered, decided he might be right and decided not to notice as his fingers slipped her gown off her shoulders. "How will we explain it to the children?"

"Never mind them. How will I explain it to my mother?"

"Oh . . . I think Lady Philberta will understand."

"I will make you happy," he vowed. "And I will never stray."

"I know," she said smugly as she kissed him. "I know how to use a rifle."

"The door . . ."

"It's locked. It was all the time."